JUST ONE MORE

BOOK 1

LaQuarn Michaels

JUST ONE MORE

ISBN 978-0-980158533

Library of Congress Control Number: 2011939118

Printed and bound in the Unites States of America.

First paperback edition, January 2012.

Published by:

Transcending Works, LLC
P.O. Box 647
Lovejoy, Georgia 30250

For K.C.A II
Love You Always

Also by LaQuarn Michaels

The Last One

Just One More

Just One More 2

CHAPTER 1

S carsdale, New York. Home of the filthy stinking rich. A place where housewives squandered their husbands earnings on silk La Perla negligee, Louboutin red bottom pumps, and handsome chiseled chefs fresh out of culinary school to fuck on a whim. The small affluent town neighbored White Plains, New Rochelle, and was just a skip away from Manhattan. With Central Park, and Fifth Avenue in reach, all was perfect.

Hired help made a good living catering to the wealthy, especially in the section of Heathcote. Serving succulent roasted lamb, organic baby green salad, herbed whipped potatoes, and Crème Brûlée to sweeten the day was nothing out of the ordinary. Lou-Ann Dobbs adored her new digs. Having come from nothing to living the ultimate posh lifestyle was her highest achievement.

"Fucking your way to the top is easy Lou."

His response didn't deserve her breath, so she said nothing.

"Pussy is power. I'm glad you finally realized it."

She narrowed her eyes, "Excuse me?"

"Just say'n, I remember a time when you were giving it away for free. It's about time you've learned your worth."

Ha! My worth? Really? Clown!

"Aint shit free over here," she promised.

He often came out his face, said things to piss her off. She gave him a look of pity. His sorry ass couldn't accept that she was on top of her game. *Finally*. He slapped her ass so hard that it stung. A tear slipped and fell. She grumbled in pain, but that fiery tingle made her areolas stiffen. She wagged her finger and winked.

"You lucky I like that kind of shit."

His dark smoldering eyes bore into her bosom. He flashed a grin, licked his lips. She was a feisty bitch. Still, part of him wanted to extinguish her ambition, break her down, make her feel less than him. Stomping her dreams with the sole of his Timberland boot would make him feel like a man again. *Look at you. All high and mighty now that you've landed your pussy on Mount Rushmore. Fucking bitch!*

He was troubled by her success. Weakened by all that she'd obtained in so little time, he envied her power to make a man melt like butter and give up his wallet. In this case, Bradley, her new man had given up the *SL550 Roadster* Benz, the keys to the estate, and full access to the Black Card. Trips to Cabo just for the catch of the day.

Rendezvousing abroad just to stay ahead of the latest fashion trends. Favorite travel spot: Saint-Tropez in the summer where she could flaunt her *ItsyBitsyTinyWinyYellowPolkaDotBikini*.

His eyes roamed, taking in the exquisite décor as if it were his first time there. The furniture, rich and pristine. All original pieces dreamt up by her darling Bradley. The bed, the table, the rug, the paintings, all the fixtures down to the detailing on the door knobs; master minded. There was no denying the man had taste. *While I'm eating out of Styrofoam containers with plastic forks, begging for more damn soy sauce and duck sauce, this bitch is eating off authentic china and polished silver.*

"Must be nice," he sang.

"Drop it José," she warned.

"Just say'n, you be acting like you did something special to get all this. All you did was sleep with the right motherfucker. That ain't hard."

She tried her best to focus on her upcoming getaway to Fiji but his voice jolted her peace; made her backslide into a bad place.

"If it's so easy how come you haven't done it, *Brokey-Broke*?" Her rebuttal was soft, more settle, less threatening. She surprised herself. *Just breathe. Don't let him take you there. Think of Fiji.*

"Don't call me that."

"Oh, *Brokey-Broke* can't take the heat?" she taunted. Her voice controlled, leveled. He hated when she called him that. His nick name reflected his financial means to stay ahead.

"I said, don't call me that."

"Why not? The name suits you well."

"Really?"

"Really," she giggled.

"Don't act like I never had it. I used to have it. Not to this extent...," he waved his hand in the ether dramatically, "... but I had it."

"Key word, *used-to*. If you haven't realized yet, yesterday don't mean shit. Can't count yesterday's money as profit. It's all about today. New money. That's free game. I won't bill you."

She ridiculed him and poked fun; made him feel like shit on the bottom of a shoe. After every fuck, every intense level of orgasmic bliss, his insecurities took over causing him to kill the moment. It was routine, sort of like déjà vu in a sense.

"Oh so I'm a has-been?"

She shrugged. "Well."

He opened his mouth to retort, perhaps justify his situation, but instead of arguing the obvious, he stayed in his lane. *Same old conversation. You're only good for the dick. Accept it. Get over it. Aint no love here Brokey-Broke, Damn!*

"You've come a long way. I dig it. Just don't forget where you came from," he said in a tone laced with envy.

A condescending laughed escaped her, "That statement bugs me."

"Why?"

"Only haters offer advice such as that. How can I forget where I started from? It's niggas like you who constantly remind me of the block."

"Calm down baby."

"No, don't tell me to calm down. I know where I'm from, where I've been, what it took to get here, and where I'm headed next. So miss me with all that bull. Better yet, get the fuck out."

There it was. His dismissal. Suddenly and rapidly relieved of his duty to make her kitty scream in orgasmic fury. It was time for big dick José to get his things and hit the cold hard pavement. *Bounce!*

"Chill, I was just saying…," he stopped yapping long enough to take her in.

She stretched her stacked frame across the sofa that was wrapped in Ferrari leather. Purple satin throw covered very little, exposing more, if not all of her freshly waxed goods. Her scrawl was lethal. Her eyes were like fire tipped daggers. She was ready to spaz, act like her old self. The old Lou-Lou was emerging. Her feisty side turned him on.

"Damn, you all sensitive and shit."

"Shut up José."

"But…"

"I said shut the fuck up."

The rain outside beat against the window just as hard as José had beat her from an angle that made her scream moments ago. A ten in the face, good hair, chiseled frame, dick hung to great lengths. The man had potential, but when he opened his mouth, all fantasies went to shit.

"You'll mess up a wet dream." She sucked her teeth, now pissed that her cunt had dried from his pesky voice. Lou-Lou tried best to hold onto Fiji but José's little stunt had her ready to buck-fifty his ass with a straight razor.

"Let's not ruin the moment."

"Moment already ruined."

"Let me bring you back."

Seems as though that's all your good at, bringing me back. Holding me down. Not this time. Never again.

"Earth to Lou-Lou… anyone there?"

She looked on, passed him. Her eyes landed on a photo of Bradley. His strong features, piercing eyes, clean cut and handsome. Her arms wrapped around his broad shoulders. Happiness in their eyes. *You're risking a lot. The dick ain't worth the trouble.*

"Did you hear me?"

"Hear what?" she asked, annoyed.

"Let's fuck."

"No."

"You mad at me?"

She huffed, rolled her eyes. Again, she looked passed him, her eyes landing on Bradley's charming face. There was so much to love about that man, so much to fight for, so much to be thankful for. Lately he'd been under a lot of pressure. Work had him thinning around the hairline. He was stressed, but Fiji would change all of that. She was in her happy place, once again. Fiji in her view. Strutting her *ItsyBitsyTeenyWeenyYellow*

PolkaDotBikini with Bradley on her arm was more than enough reason to get happy.

"Come here."

"No."

Sand between her toes, sun roastisserizing her skin, making her golden. The winter months were known to be beautiful. November in Fiji was still deliciously tropical and warm. *Ooh, I can't wait.*

The rhythm of her breathing quickened as he touched her spot. His fingers worked her middle, bringing her chill factor back into alignment. Aftershocks from her orgasm came to reclaim the moment. Lovely toned legs tightened, squeezing a river of hot sweet nectar. Drenched cunt, slithered passion made way between her parted thighs. Fresh beads of sweat covered her body in a mist. The ceiling fan in full rotation to cool her wild fire. His offensive words were long forgotten. Bradley's face now a blur.

"Four finger magic," she moaned.

"I do what I can." He pulled his fingers away, sniffed.

"You so silly."

"I love the way you smell." He licked his fingers. "Love the way you taste."

Her eyes bore into him as shegulped the last of the Tequila. Hint of peppered agave, burnt citrus, and mint laced her tongue. A cig would have been a timely necessity, a tightly rolled *J* even better.

"Don't bother stopping in tomorrow."

He stopped licking his fingers. "Why's that?"

"I'm leaving the country on vacation."

His resentment bubbled. His face contorted. "Where to this time?"

"Fiji."

His jaw stiffened. *More stamps in your passport.* Deep in thought, he squeezed his forehead, brows knitted to a point. His feelings were hurt. José wore his emotions on his sleeve, always did.

"I'm just say'n; you living real good right now, just make sure you stuffing for a rainy day. You never know, *Naw Mean.*"

"There you go again."

"What?"

"Same old conversation. Just leave well enough alone. I got this." She grabbed his wrist, eyed his Rolex. A birthday gift from her to him. She replaced his knock-off with an official time piece.

"Seriously, you have to go. Bradley will be home from work soon."

José moved as if he ruled Father Time. He moved as if he had power to make the big hand stop at any given moment. He was a cocky son-of-a-bitch. His arrogance, border line offensive, but she loved it.

"Put some pep to your step would yah."

It didn't matter that Bradley was on his way home, and could be just minutes away. No, it wasn't like he gave regard to standing in another man's house shoes, rocking his fiancé to a tune only a thug knew how to. He wanted to be caught. He welcomed the day Bradley came home from work early, only to find him dick deep in his woman. The thought made him smile.

"Brad will be home any minute."

"So." Their unapologetic chemistry allowed him to say things like *so.*

"So, you should be going. *Hurry."*

His lustful eyes darted every square inch of her. Loving her thighs, loving her breasts, loving her sweet mouth and tender lips. Just moments ago, he'd found his way inside her. Pulsating bodies, trembling limbs, tequila shots heated their kisses to a scorching degree.

"How long will you be gone?"

"Don't know. We have an open ticket. There's no telling when I'll return."

"You want my opinion?"

"Nope."

"You should let me tap that just one more time. Word to my motha I'll make it quick."

Maybe just one more time. I mean, I will be gone for a good while and José does know how to hit my spot. She gave his request some thought, but then pulled herself together. Losing Bradley meant losing a lifestyle José could never afford to provide her. The choice was simple. *Brokey-Broke* had to kick rocks.

"Don't get me wrong José, I would love to hold you hostage for as long as possible but I have a life with Bradley."

"C'mon, I'll make it quick."

She giggled. "You don't know the meaning of quick."

"Don't make me beg."

Fifty percent Black, fifty percent Latino stared at her grinning. His eyes wandered her luscious body. His savage stare sent shivers down her spine. She wanted him to thrust his thickness inside her just one more time. *Just one more time for the road*, she thought. He stood bare chest, sockless, with his jeans unzipped. She grabbed him by the belt loop, kissed his rock hard abdomen. The fire of her lips and tongue worked his chiseled frame.

He moaned in ecstasy.

"Don't tease me."

She stood to face him. Their hot passionate tongues intertwined. The sound of a car whizzing pass in the rain broke their communion. The corners of her mouth wet with his lust. The yearning in his eyes caused her to weaken. He was working his number. Her index finger pressed against his juicy lips, halting the deployment of his tongue.

"I'll call you when I'm back in town."

"Be sure to do that."

She slid him more tongue, pushed him away, pulled him back into her grips, but only for a second. The sound of the mail truck caused her heart to pulsate.

"Hurry, get dress," she pleaded.

He obeyed her wishes, and in the matter of minutes was fully clothed, standing in the grand foyer. Sweeping staircase, mahogany floors, and big bay windows in all points of the home made him wonder just how much Bradley was worth. From what he knew, Bradley was some big shot broker and Wall Street was his playground. Obviously his chosen profession had proven to be lucrative in every aspect of the word. *The man is very skillful, full of technique and patience,* José thought with much admiration.

Bradley had shown great wizardry. He'd managed to transform little Miss Def Jam into a lady with class. Lou-Lou, a known rebel without a cause was un-trainable. Or maybe he just wasn't the man for the job.

He watched her peer out the side panels of the door, in search of her fiancé's arrival. He shoved his hands deep into the pit of his empty pockets. *I should I ask her for some cheese.* Open ended ticket meant there was no designated return date, which meant he would be without her helpful hand. *No, she just hit you last week. Be easy playboy.*

"Okay, the coast seems to be clear."

Watching José strut his sexy ass out the front door made her want to call him back. She pulled in her bottom lip and could only imagine the bag of tricks he had in store for her when she returned from Fiji. Unlike her fiancé, José kept it fresh, he kept it new. He knew which buttons to push. He knew how to rev her engine, control her throttle. Bradley fucked her to boredom, while José fucked her until she was unconscious. She watched him pull away in his old ass Suburban. Fresh oil stains bled the driveway. *Fuck, how the hell am I supposed to explain that to Brad?*

Caroline was out for a stroll. Her two shitzu's pulled her at a steady pace. Caroline gave the Miss America wave and winked knowingly. Lou-Lou reciprocated with a half hearted smile. She assumed that José's truck was spotted leaving the estate. The idea of Caroline knowing her dirty little secret made her uncomfortable.

"The rain finally let up."

Lou-Lou flashed a grin. "Thank goodness."

"Sun is shining. Birds are chirping. Beautiful day for a stroll isn't it?" Caroline said with glee.

Lou-Lou nodded respectfully. "Gorgeous day."

"Won't you join me?"

"Maybe another time. I'm pretty busy." She stared at the blood stains, then back towards Caroline.

They befriended each other quickly. Weekly shopping on 5th Ave, mani-pedis, hot stone massages and chocolate body wraps, developed a special bond between the two. The women of Scarsdale didn't exactly welcome her kind, but Caroline was different. Caroline gravitated towards the Hood, wanting to know, wanting to be, wanting to look and dress urban.

Lou-Ann Dobbs was Caroline's muse of fashion. She gave her the nerve to rock labels, add fire to her switch, and say what the hell was on her mind. In return, Caroline submerged Lou-Lou with esteem, etiquette, civility, and humility. With Bradley so busy with work, Caroline gave her access to the elite crowd.

"I would have called but I noticed you had company."

So she did notice. A look passed between the two. "Yeah, well... you know."

"Oh, yes. I do." Caroline winked.

A couple of months back Caroline barged in, carrying homemade biscuits, only to find José chewing Lou-Lou's pudding without the spoon. *Damn!* The chemistry between her and her boy toy was so magnetic that she forgot to lock the front door. Buttered biscuits went crashing to the floor, and Caroline hauled ass in horror.

It wasn't long before Lou-Lou was at Caroline's front door making her demands clear. She knew about Caroline's affair with the sixteen year old Mexican pool boy. She knew about the plumber, the UPS man, and the pizza boy who delivered at her home every Friday night around ten. Her husband was a man of the cloth, a pastor of a mega church. The kind of dirt she had on Caroline would not only ruin her marriage, but ruin her publicly. From that day forth, they had an understanding.

"Let me skedaddle. *Ciao Bella!*"

After a long hot shower, and slice of German chocolate cake, she turned on the tube. Maury Povich was on. *"You are not the father!"* she yelled at the flat screen that mounted the fireplace in her bedroom. Drapes were pulled tightly, giving the dark dungeon feel. The full body workout José dished out required some down time. She needed to mentally prepare for Bradley's complaining. Everyday there was a new issue, mostly with the fellahs he worked with. The world of Trading and Investing were as cutthroat as any other hustle. Brown-nosing, back-stabbing, black-balling, and whistle-blowing; a treacherous industry indeed.

With the crumble of AIG and the catastrophic plummet of Lehman Brothers, Bradley's executive position at Ridgemore Investments wasn't promised. With an already crippling American economy, New York was suffering. The world was suffering. Ordinary people had lost their livelihood. Pension funds erased, life savings spent, bonds liquidated to keep food on the table. Kid's college tuitions siphoned. America was tapped out.

"*Sit your old ass down somewhere.* Can't stand when these grown ass men bring their ghetto ass mommas on the show for support. *You sound stupid as hell.*"

The *Extenze* male enhancement commercial interrupted her fight with the television. She decided to do a once over in the room; had to make sure José's selfish ass didn't leave anything behind to arouse any suspicions. He couldn't just have his slice and be happy. He wanted the whole damn pie.

The room was tidy. The smell of *Budussy* cleared with a few pumps of *Oust*-odor-eater. She checked the bathroom, and noticed a third toothbrush in the holder. *Fucking home wrecker!* She removed the wet washcloth from the shower, tossed it into the hamper. Scooped his boxer shorts off the floor, and made sure there were no traces of pubic hairs on the soap. His DNA completely erased.

Everything seemed to be perfect, everything except the oil stained driveway. She hustled to the phone and called the expert. If anybody knew how to rid evidence from concrete, it was her neighbor Caroline. Her Mexican lover's car leaked more transmission fluid then a little bit.

"Caroline, I need your help."

She ran down her issue to Caroline, and within three minutes her neighbor provided step by step instructions on how to remove evidence of your lover's raggedy ass car. She was forever grateful.

After mixing the concoction, scrubbing and hosing the driveway, she hopped back into the sack and searched for the clicker. Maury was going off and Cheaters was coming on. She had nightmares about Joey and his crew setting up surveillance cameras in her home. At times she felt like she was being watched. Just yesterday she spotted a white utility van parked just a few houses away. The chiming of her cell phone broke into her thoughts. It was Bradley calling.

"Hey babe, what's up?"

"I've been calling you all day, that's what's up."

"Oh, been in the garden with Caroline. She's an expert when it comes to pruning. I didn't hear the phone."

"Gardening in the rain?"

"Yep, best time to extract weeds because the ground is soft. Besides, we didn't get much rain on this side of town."

"This morning there were flash flood warning signs. Eighty percent chance of rain in our county."

"We got a few sprinkles here and there."

Their moment of silence made her sit erect. She hated when he drilled her on details. Bradley was a financial guru. Numbers and money fueled him. When things didn't add up, he broke apart the dynamics and reconstructed it back together until it made sense. The sound of third party static infiltrated their conversation.

"Bradley... Hello, are you still there?"

"Shit. Goddamn," he sniffled.

"Are you crying?"

Something was definitely wrong. Bradley never cried. She reached for the remote, turned off the television, turned on the lights, and partially opened the drapes, all with one hand held device. She pressed the phone tightly against her lobe.

"Somebody die?" *Please say yes, please say yes.* She prayed he said yes. She awaited the day, the hour, the second she received the call that his rich, old decrepit grand pappy took his dirt nap.

"Nobody died."

Damn! "What's troubling you?"

"I got canned." Third party static sent razor sharp waves into her earpiece.

"You what?"

"I got canned."

"What do you mean?"

"I lost my job today. Those fucking blood suckers let me go."

"Oh, is that all?"

"This is a major setback."

"Oh please honey. Don't overreact."

He released a frustrated breath. "I'll be home shortly."

"I'll be waiting."

Her eyes rolled towards the top of the ceiling, and back. She reached for the remote, closing the drapes, turning up the volume on the tube, and set the home security system. She accessed the CCTV option on her remote, zooming in on the oil stains José left behind. His junk on wheels increased her chances of getting caught up. There was only so much cat litter, bleach and Comet she could use before the truth surfaced. Just as she was about to get back into her show, her cell phone chimed again. Kosha's face beamed brightly on the screen.

"How's my favorite cousin in the whole wide world?" Lou-Lou asked, cheerfully.

"Peachy."

"Well it took you long enough to return my call."

"Mom's gave me the message this morning. You know how she is when *One Life to Live* is on. Nothing else matters."

"Heard you got accepted into Spelman. Congratulations!"

"Mom's told you?"

"Kind of sort of, I had to pry it out of her."

Kosha sucked her teeth. "She's been on some real hating shit lately."

"Don't talk about my aunty like that, at least not to me," Lou-Lou said seriously.

"I'm not trying to be disrespectful but she's been riding me about going to Westbury."

"What's wrong with Westbury?"

"Long Island is too damn close to home."

"Didn't you get an acceptance letter from Rutgers?"

"A bridge and a couple of tows still connect us. Jersey isn't far enough. I need to spread my wings, experience life at my own pace."

"Stop fruntin, your ass try'na get loose. You try'na be grown. Don't act like I don't know the deal."

"Can I live?"

"No doubt, just don't get caught up. Atlanta is cool, but it's still a jungle."

"I still don't understand why you came back. Atlanta is where it's at. The culture, the vibe, the people, it's The Black Mecca."

"I have my reasons."

Lou-Lou's mind drifted off, thoughts of what she left back south tugged at her nerves. She made Atlanta her home. She'd become accustomed to the vibe, the people. It was truly The Black Mecca, but that was the past. *Can't dwell in the past Lou.*

"You still there?" Kosha asked.

"I'm here."

"I need a favor."

"How much?"

"How'd you..."

"Look. How much you need?" Lou-Lou didn't have time for the pleasantries.

"Four thousand, but five would set me straight though."

"What do you need with four or five thousand?"

"My scholarship will cover my tuition one hundred percent. My dorm fee is paid for. I need some wheels to get me around. Nothing fancy, just something reliable."

"Five thousand?" Lou-Lou asked again.

"Five thousand will allow me to purchase something free and clear, pay up the car insurance for at least six months, and keep that bad boy gassed until I find me a part time gig. Oh and there's student parking which will run a couple of extra dollars a month."

"You have to pay for parking?"

"Yes, if I want to be secure. Campus life can be rough."

Lou-Lou thought about her baby cousin walking to and from the Marta station at night in Atlanta. She recalled watching the news many of days feeling sorry for female victims who'd been robbed, raped and abducted just steps away from their dormitory. She would never forgive herself if something were to happen to Kosha. *Five thousand. That aint shit. I spent more on my Louis Vuitton luggage last week.*

"I got you. Just promise me you'll call me if you need help. Don't let me find out your ass is sliding down poles at *Magic City*, claiming your doing it to pay tuition."

Kosha laughed. "Trust me, I'm not that talented."

"I'm so serious."

"Okay, promise I'll call. *Dang.*"

"You better. Don't forget, I still got peoples in the *A*, which means if you're living foul, I'll be the first to smell it."

"I almost got my ass kicked today?" Kosha admitted.

"Where?"

"Harlem. St. Nick projects."

"What you doing in Harlem, and of all places *St. Nick*?"

"Went to see my man, well *ex*-man now. Caught this nigga all hugged up with some Dominican chic."

Lou-Lou released a frustrated breath. Her cousin was playing with fire. St. Nicholas Projects wasn't exactly an ideal location for a girl with so much promise. If Lou-Lou told her once, she told her a thousand times, there were too many risks associated with loving a dude who hugged the block.

"Why you still fucking with them hood niggas?"

"I need a thug in my life."

"No, what you need to do is find you a wholesome young man and stop selling yourself short."

"*Wholesome.* Where he at cause ain't no *wholesome* dudes where I'm from."

Kosha knew that her cousin spoke from the heart, and only wanted the best for her. Lou-Lou was experienced in the area of thug-loving. Having lost her first love to the streets, her second love to the penitentiary, and her third, to laced coke blunts on the project staircase.

"Did you keep it lady like or did you show your ass?"

"Oh, I showed my ass. I showed my entire ass. Knocked that nigga right in his mouth, was about to whup his bitch but thought about it. Here I am, in Harlem, on *her* turf, ready to jump on her over some dude. So, I ran."

Lou-Lou cracked up laughing. "You did what?"

"I ran"

"Where?"

"Subway. Got the hell outta Harlem."

"Better be glad you did. The Domo's stick together."

"True."

"Well, at least you've taken my advice about dating outside the hood. The last thing you need is for your name to start ringing bells where you rest your head at. Don't be like them bum bitches from around the way, fucking the same nigga. You're way too pretty to be taking somebody's sloppy left overs."

"Speaking of bum bitches, Sonia and her sister Daphne been talking mess about me."

"Let em' talk. Just keep doing you. As long as those bitches don't lay a hand on you, ignore them. They're not worth the time it takes to slap a hoe."

"What's that noise?"

Lou-Lou switched her channel, accessing the CCTV. The twenty second delay on the security alarm was at a constant blare. "Bradley's home." Her voice was dry.

"Don't sound so excited."

"Let me give you a call later."

She ended her call with Kosha preparing herself to deal with Bradley's latest drama. She craved a tightly twisted *J* but she was out of smoke. José claimed there was a drought in the hood but she knew better. His ass was broke and couldn't afford to buy her usual ounce. She put the thought on the backburner. Bradley was her main focus. With no Cannabis to choke on, she opted for the champagne.

CHAPTER 2

Downsizing was the way of the world. Economic times called for every red blooded American to shell back, reserve, and become thrifty. Even the exceedingly wealthy experienced some cutbacks.

Lou-Ann Dobbs had climbed the epitome of elegance and sophistication, being thrifty was just plain tacky. It was ludicrous to think someone of her stature would even consider lowering her standards. She didn't believe in living above her means. She believed in finding the resources and means to live wealthy.

When Bradley called with the devastating news of his recent layoff, she didn't panic. No, she popped the cork on a fifteen hundred dollar bottle of Cristal Rose, lit raspberry scented soy candles, and prepared a lush bath for her man.

Bradley had connections, he had outlets, and for God sakes the man had a damn trust fund. Gramps was loaded, had old money from a trade in Rubbermaid. Invested jars of pennies turned his family's portfolio from trash to treasure. And when the old man kicked the bucket, her brilliantly, handsome fiancé Bradley would stand to inherit millions.

She embraced him the moment he walked through the door. He'd been drinking that *Crown* again; she could smell it on his breath. He dropped his briefcase and allowed her to lead him into the family room. She led him to the sofa. The same sofa José had her bent over like a pretzel. Confusion found its way onto Bradley's face as he lifted a red lacy thong from the floor.

"Oops. Mari must have dropped those while folding laundry."

He eyed her suspiciously. "Thought Mari had the day off."

"Yesterday's mistake. I'll be sure to have a chat with her about this."

"Why would Mari fold clothes in the family room when there's a sizable laundry room designated for those sorts of task?"

She shrugged, and snatched evidence marked as exhibit **A**, stuffing the lacy fabric into the pocket of her Chanel bathrobe. The blazing fireplace released a cedar aroma. Mosaic tile reflected off his pain while she tried massaging the stress from his shoulders.

"Relax, you're so tense," she said, calm as a daisy. The news hadn't shaken or stirred her emotions the least bit. As far as she was concerned he was overreacting.

"Baby, I just lost my job. Those fucking bastards," Bradley exploded.

"Fuck em' baby."

"Can't believe this shit. After all I've done for the company, after all the sacrifices I've made to land the damn Deloma account. Brought the big boys in, holding the big guns and closed the fucking deal over lox and bagels. Who does it better than me?"

"Nobody baby. You're the best." She rolled her eyes towards the ceiling. Imported European crystal chandelier sparkled above. *So pretty.*

"We will have to downsize."

Her head jerked and rolled black girl style. She caught herself, scaled back into civility. Bradley required good manners, politeness, and class.

"Honey, let's not jump the gun."

"It is what it is at this point. My salary is gone. Finito."

"Don't talk negative."

"Baby, its reality."

"Who's reality?" Her voice elevated several notches. She closed her eyes, took a deep breath. "I'm sorry."

"Times are hard. I can't afford to keep this place on some weak-ass unemployment check. The severance package they gave me ain't worth a damn. Gosh."

Gosh. Gosh my ass. Lou-Ann Dobbs don't understand the words that are coming out of your mouth. Downsize...I don't think so.

"Baby cakes, listen. I need to put the house on the market, hopefully snag a buyer on a Short Sale. Need to call my realtor, make this happen as soon as possible. We can move into my Midtown condo for the mean time."

"What?"

Oh no! Oh hell to the no. Cathedral ceilings, imported floors, indoor heated pool, in-ground Jacuzzi, theater room, state of the art gym, a chefs kitchen to die for, tennis court, all nestled quaintly on several acres. The idea of moving into Bradley's midtown condo made her gag. It was too small, too stuffy and damn sure not her style. It lacked flare, lacked character, lacked all the extravagate amenities now offered to her. *Fuck that!*

He stood, and walked towards the breathing mouth of the fire place. She followed closely behind, wanting to push him in. She decided to keep her cool. She hadn't exactly earned the right as first beneficiary so she would profit nothing.

"I don't see the big fuss. You're a guru in the biz. As soon as the word gets out that you're available they'll be a bidding war."

The thought made him crack a smile, but beneath that manufactured cheese housed the truth. *I'm tainted. No one will touch me.* Wall Street was his playground, but with the new kids on the block, Bradley was forced to leave his turf. *Fucking cock suckers!*

She wrapped her arms around his waist, pulling him close. Their lips touched. As her Chanel robe loosened at the waist, he noticed the lacy see-through number for the first time. The frown on his face softened. Firmness pressed against his tailored slacks. She tugged at his ears, gently massaging his lopes. His eyes savagely ran up and down her well sculpted body.

"You like it?"

"Love it."

"And the earrings, how about the bracelet? I had Yosef customize it."

Yosef was his Jewish jeweler, also considered Bradley's third eye. Whatever Bradley envisioned, Yosef made it come into fruition. Her stones were big, clear, and set perfectly.

A lump formed in his throat. The knot in his pants relinquished its girth. He went limp, his shoulders fell in defeat. He struggled with what to say. How in the world was he to tell his woman that they could no longer afford to splurge. *Take it back. Return it all.*

"It arrived today. Yosef is amazing," she spoke into his ear, lucidly.

He dropped his head into an open hand. For a second, he experienced a moment of delirium. He ranted on about finances, cutting back, being frugal during these economic times. She hushed his tirade by slipping him some tongue. Sweet kisses against the mouth relaxed his nerves.

"Lou-Lou, sweetie, you know I love you right."

"I love you too."

"Would you hate me if I asked you to return the set?"

She looked up into his slushy eyes. His lanky frame began to fold in pain. She wanted to gouge his eyes, cut off his tongue and Lorena Bobbitt his penis. Coldness stiffened his bones. He preferred to face a Russian firing squad than to face her at the moment.

"Darling, you know better than that. All sales are final with customized pieces."

Dammit Yosef. I told you to clear all designs with me first. Bradley gritted his teeth. Despite his outrageous request, Lou-Lou felt compelled to make her man feel like a man. His job was his life. It defined him. She couldn't allow him to get lost, not yet.

They made their way up the staircase holding hands. French doors led to a steamy haven of candles and soft music. They undressed and slipping into an oasis of lushness. The jets burst bubbles against their nakedness. The built-in water fountain cascaded and swept the overflow of their issues.

"Champagne?"

"Yes, please."

It pained him to see the bottle of Rose flow smoothly into the flute. *$1500 bottle of champagne. For Pete's sake.* Although he would have preferred a shot of Crown, the champagne would have to do. They sipped in silence.

Her finger tips danced around his ankles, up towards his calf muscle, massaging his legs, softening her approach as she tugged at his shaft. He released a groan; his head fell back against the cushioned headrest. She slithered up against him, pressing her jugs against his face, rubbing them against his mouth. His tight pink lips gripped her nipple, and then swallowed more then he could chew. He loved her new breasts. For him, it was money well spent.

She straddled him, placing just his hard pink helmet inside her doorway to pleasure. She contracted her muscles, and pulsated slowly. Since her thug beau José had made some significant adjustments, she needed to make sure he fit like a glove. Bradley was packing, but José was horse hung.

His face turned flush, his mouth parted, gripping her waist, begging her to go low. As she locked her muscle around his eagerly twitching pistol, all she could think about was her zip code. It was all about location. The *haves* and the *have-nots* were separated by a measly five digits.

There was no way in hell she was moving into some tiny condo. She could care less if the place was gutted and renovated to her likings. Next he would be suggesting that they turned in her *SL550* Benz for a gently used *3.25*. Moving backwards was never an option. *Fuck that!*

He forced her hips low, pumping like a wild animal for a few seconds, then yelped. Seed pumped inside her as he growled like a beast on steroids. There was no way in hell she would give up all of this. Not without a fight.

"Fiji couldn't come at a better time. I'm packing light, promise. Just the necessities this time."

She watched her Wall Street Champion wither like bad lettuce. Right before her eyes, her man shrunk. He slipped into lushness. She waited a few seconds, wondering if he would emerge. Knowing Bradley's capabilities of holding his breath for long periods of time bored her. She grabbed the bottle of Rose, and took it to the head.

Bradley excelled at swimming. His long limps served as a tool to zip through ocean wide waters. As a kid, he'd been known to hold his breath under water for six minutes. Even now, as an adult he'd been determined to beat David Blaine's seventeen minute, four-point-four second record. Ten minutes and thirty two seconds later, Bradley shot up, gasping.

"Are you okay?" she asked, wiping his face dry with a hand cloth.

"Did I beat it?"

She wanted to lie, say he'd beat David Blains idiotic record, but she couldn't. Her face told it all. "No."

"I can't seem to do anything right."

"I don't see the big deal. Holding your breath only cuts off oxygen to the brain, therefore killing off brain cells." She knocked gently against his forehead. "As I was saying, Fiji awaits us baby. Charles is scheduled to pick us up at noon, and..."

"I fired Charles."

She looked surprised. "You fired the driver? When?"

"Today. I had to relieve Mari as well."

She didn't know what to say. Her bottle of champagne was empty. *I need weed.*

"We must cancel Fiji, at least until we get our ducks in a row."

Hurt plastered her face. "What?"

"Darling, we must reconsider the way we spend. Fiji, it's not a realistic move right now. I mean... it will be, in the future, but now we just can't afford it."

"But it's paid for." Her voice was hard, deep.

"Normally the resort requires a seventy two hour cancelation for full refund, but..."

"But it's paid for." Her voice was hoarse like.

"I was able to recoup some money back. Forty percent's not bad considering we canceled twenty four hours before the date of travel."

Did he just say he canceled Fiji? Without consulting me first? Did I hear you right? She choked back her tears. She'd been looking forward to Fiji for the last six weeks. They were to celebrate four years of togetherness. Seeing her watery eyes broke Bradley to pieces. "I'm so sorry," he whimpered.

Don't trip Lou. Don't scream. Don't cry. Shit happens. Bradley's a good dude. He means well. Don't spaz out. Just be calm. She inhaled, smiled. "No worries. Let's spend the week at the villa. We both could use a get-away. I'll call your travel agent; have her book us a first class flight." She stood to exit the bath. Sudsy water slipped from her backside. His eyes clung to her wall of art. Greens, pinks, blues, blacks sketched into her subtle skin.

"We need to talk." His face complicated with worry.

Damn. What now? She slid back into the bubbles, playfully splashing water his way. *I should drown your stupid ass. Put my foot against your throat and hold it there. Bet you'll beat David Blain then.*

He seemed tortured with uncertainty. He seemed destined to sabotage the mood. His knuckles turned white, face lost all color.

"I lost the villa."

Her eyes blinked in disbelief. "What are you saying?"

"The Costa Rican villa is gone. I lost it."

"How the fuck do you *lose* a villa?"

He looked away. Shame plastered his face. Tears dripped heavily from his lids. She stared at him viciously as he sobbed like a two year old. She waited for an answer, waited for an explanation. She tried hard not to snap, tried hard not to relapse. The hood in her was knocking; that bitch she kept under wraps was trying best to come out. *Just breathe Lou.*

"I lost it in a bet."

"You gambled the property, are you crazy?"

"I was up, had the pot, then... then Billy knocked down my King, with his..."

She waved her hand. "Fuck the specifics of how, the question is why?" Her voice now sharp like a million razors. He paused, swallowed hard. Allowing the news to set before speaking was his best bet. "First the plane, now the villa... are you kidding me?!"

Bradley's insatiable need to be amongst legalized prostitution and gambling had cost them their freedom to fly the friendly skies hassle free. Vegas called him in his sleep. They spent more time in Nevada than any place else. *The Four Seasons, Venetian, Sands, Mirage, MGM, Bellagio,* just to name a few, had him tossing major paper.

"I'm done gambling. I swear on a stack of Bibles. I'm done."

At first his need to be amongst oil tycoons, and Japanese billionaires was a good look. Bradley made a lot of connections, won the trust of new associates and drummed up new business for the firm. Bradley was Ridgemore's golden boy. He possessed a natural innocence that attracted clients. Word got out that Bradley was the man to see if you wanted to invest, flip old money into new.

"Say something."

"What you want me to say?" she snapped.

"Anything, just don't shut me out. I need you right now."

"You have a gambling addiction."

It wasn't until he lost their plane in a bet that she realized he had a serious problem. The plane was small, one that puttered with a loud engine, but reliable. Far from *G5* status but it served its purpose. Being subjected to long lines and fat women wearing ugly uniforms, waving a magic wand across her body was already a down grade.

"Admitting you have a problem is half the battle." She stood to leave.

"Wait, don't leave."

He followed the trail of water, down the steps, across the grand foyer and into the study. There he found her sipping something brown. Long lacy gown covered her tantalizing angles. He approached cautiously, wringing his hands, trying to find the right words.

"Honey, I just want you to know one thing."

"For-real Brad… you might want to keep your distance."

"Don't look at me like that."

She pointed an agitated finger at him. "*Ooh*… that's my word… if I didn't respect you… I would disrespect you."

"What does that mean?"

"It means stay the fuck back. Give a bitch a minute to digest."

"What I tell you about that street talk?"

She swallowed the brown liquid and slung the crystal glass across the open room. It missed him; hit a wall, and shattered to pieces. He stepped around the broken glass.

"First the plane, then the villa, and you don't think you have a problem?" Her brow arched. Curvaceous hip poked out so far that it looked as if a midget road shot gun.

He shrugged timidly. "Stroke of bad luck is all."

She grabbed another glass, slung it. *Damn, missed him by an inch.* "You fired the help, canceled Fiji, walked up in here talking about downsizing to a piece of shit condo, and you still don't think you have a problem?"

"Are you kidding? That's prime real-estate. The view of the Hudson is exceptional. Before the housing market took a nose dive a place like that would go for a hard fifteen million. That's on the low-end."

He thought of all his investments. Ground zero wasn't just a big black hole where the Towers once sat. Ground zero was his life. At the bottom, in the basement, fighting for a second chance. His credibility shot. *Maybe I do have a gambling problem?*

"I lost my job. We simply can't afford to live like this."

Another glass aimed at his head. This one clocked him, but didn't shatter until it hit the floor. "Dammit, would you stop throwing stuff."

"Admit you have a problem."

"What the hell is this, intervention?" She grabbed the crystal decanter that stored his favorite whiskey. *"No wait..."* He chose his next words carefully. "Darling, just listen to me. We can make this work. I'll sell the house, we'll move into the condo, I'll talk to my grandfather about letting me work for him, and when the economy picks back up, I'll buy you another villa, anywhere you want." She lowered the decanter.

Please don't drop it. That set cost me several grand. Might just be able to sell what's left of it on eBay. Lou-Lou placed the decanter back against the silver tray.

That a girl. Now step away from the bar.

She folded her arms and sulked. "Why can't you ask your grandfather to pay the difference on the house?"

He looked appalled. "I can't ask him to do that. I'm my own man."

"You're the only person I know whose grandfather is sitting on billions, who's worth Yankee Stadium, and is still paying a goddamn mortgage. Hell, he should have bought the damn house flat out."

"I'm a man. Men pave their own way. My father did it, his father did it, and I will do it. Just have a little faith babe."

She gripped her head. "This is some bullshit."

"It's a minor hiccup."

"This is more like a fucking catastrophe," she said completely devastated.

"Trust me."

"Trust you? How can I when you're always in Vegas gambling? I can't believe you lost the villa." She stomped her foot like a two year old.

On a small deserted Island, surrounded by jungle and white sands sat her little oasis, her slice of heaven, her private sanctuary. Beneath a silver moon, beachside candlelight dinner for two, Bradley proposed. Her bottom lip trembled. *I'm never going back.*

He couldn't tell whether she was more upset about the villa, or about him losing his job, their means of survival. Sure, his grandfather could bail him out. His gramps could make his life unbelievably easy, wealthy, but he was a man. *No hand outs for me.*

"Let's call the contractors in the morning, have them start the renovation on the condo. A nice face lift is all the place needs."

"Why so soon? I mean, there's no hurry right?"

He could barely look her in the face. His whole world was being snatched from beneath him. Things had taken a turn for the worst. With the crumbling economy, and recent layoff, all he'd worked for was going up in smoke. He now knew what it felt like to be black in America. *Damn!* He collapsed onto the leather chaise and cried a river. Life was so unfair.

"What else aren't you telling me?"

"The thing is... well, this is hard for me to say but... I'm in a jam, a serious jam. I'm damn near in foreclosure. I'm hoping to do a short sale, perhaps get from underneath this thirty year loan."

Her ears turned hot. *"Foreclosure?"* Instantly woozy, she stumbled towards the chaise, sat beside him. Hyper-ventilating from the word *Foreclosure* made her bust a sweat. *This is unreal.*

"I thought I could turn things around. I've burned some bridges babe. Did some dirty deals, deals that cost me my reputation. I lost my biggest account just recently. Billy and the guys, they won't return my calls, nobody wants to be seen with me. My own father has written me off. Gramps is going senile, when he dies, my father will be sure to keep me from my inheritance."

She sucked in a chest full of air. Eyes bulging from there to Timbuktu. "You're broke?"

"Piss poor, but don't let that worry you. I've got a plan."

"Don't worry? Really? Are you insane?"

"Darling..."

"Don't darling me."

He sat up, grabbed her face, and kissed her lips. "Trust me. We'll be back on top in a lickety split. Promise."

She couldn't believe it. When did all this happen? *My Black Card still works. Just bought that one-shoulder silk Robert Cavalli dress with matching pumps yesterday.*

He got down on both knees, prying her legs open, slipping between her. He looked up into her eyes. She looked away. *I can't do this. Came too far. Can't go back.*

Pleading eyes, runny nose, begging her not to leave him. As he professed his love for her, she could think of only one thing, how soon she would be able to fill up her Louis Vuitton luggage and bounce.

"Don't leave me."

"I don't do broke."

"What?"

"Check this here." She shoved him aside, stood.

"I'm not about to be ducking goddamn creditors because you failed to handle your business. I have needs."

"What about me? What about us?"

"I hate to say I told you so, but *I told you so*. When you lost the plane in Vegas, I warned you then that this relationship was threading on thin ice. You have a gambling problem. You need help."

"Lou-Lou, baby, we can make this work. The condo is almost paid for. I got about five more years on it. After that, I'll own it free and clear."

"Wait, you mean to tell me you're still carrying a mortgage on that as well?"

"Well, yes... who do you think I am, Donald Trump?"

She laughed inwardly. Bradley was just something to buy time. He was backed by a wealthy family and his executive position was a plus. After six months of dating, her lock-down finger was dripped with ice. Sure, she would marry him. Why not? It wasn't like she had any better prospects.

"Don't you love me?"

Love was never a part of the deal. He offered her more than she could offer herself. She loved the lifestyle he provided. She loved the V.I.P status that came along with being on his arm.

"You can't throw away four years just because I'm having a moment."

"Oh, is that what you call this, a moment?" she laughed. "Your so called moment has left us out in the cold, on our ass."

"But the condo..."

"Fuck that motherfucking condo. If you mention it one more time I swear I'ma lose it on your ass."

"What about our engagement, what about the plans we had to be together, forever?"

Forever, really, are you kidding me?

"The engagement is off, now move out my way."

She tried pushing pass him. He grabbed her wrist. His forceful grip demanded her stillness. She felt the muscles in her arm weakening.

"You're not leaving me after four years. You can't do this."

"Don't make me act like where I come from Brad. Now release me."

He swallowed hard, releasing her. "You... You... *black bitch*. You money thieving *black bitch*... Billy and the guys told me to leave your *black ass* in the hood."

Ouch! His words stung, but she didn't let him know it. She kept her game face, and came back just as strong on the rebuttal.

"First of all, we didn't meet in the hood. Secondly, Billy sucked the piss from my pussy. Bet yah didn't know that."

He preferred a knife through his chest then to hear those words.

"Yeah that's right. Billy ate this black pussy, ate it better then you." She whistled.

"Give me back my ring you ignorant ghetto bitch."

"Hell no. This is my ring."

His sudden speech impediment kicked in. "The *en*-engagement was a *con*-contractual agreement. That ring, *I* purchased for you, was a *s*-symbol of that contract. Since, *since* this nightmare is over with, the ring belongs to me. It's the law."

"Possession is nine-tenths of the law, so fuck you!"

"Don't *com*-complicate the *s*-situation. Give me the damn ring back."

"Over my dead body."

His brow arched. "*W*-we... *C*-can arrange that."

CHAPTER 3

He yanked her arm, forced her hand in a downward motion, and tried slipping the ring from her finger. With all her might she slung her elbow back, knocking him in the mouth. Bradley fell back against the kitchen counter. She pulled a knife from the butcher block, and held it like Becky did in the movies.

"Come on... do it so I can shred your ass."

He touched his lip. Blood stained his finger tips. His side tooth wiggled. He wondered if the damaged tooth was perm or partial.

"Damn girl, I had no idea you could fight. I mean, I know you're from the projects, but damn... you sure can handle yourself."

She narrowed her eyes, poked her hip to the left and slammed the knife against the table. Up the stairs she headed. He followed at a comfortable distance. Her slow sultry walk, suddenly turned stank and hoodrat like. She burst through the door of her walk-in and began yanking clothes from hangers. Designer shoes, purses, clothes, in all flavors and styles lined the walls, and compartments. *Don't forget the Cavalli dress,* she thought.

Lou-Lou looked over her shoulder, made sure Bradley wasn't standing behind her. He'd likely made a detour to his office. She fell to her knees, and proceeded to punch a four digit code into the safe deposit box. She grabbed her jewels first. Next she grabbed the cash. Her I.D, passport and credit cards followed. Her foundation was laid from the very beginning. Stuffing dough was the name of the game.

Lou-Lou heard Bradley enter the room, heard him cursing and swearing. She figured he took a coke break, his other habit besides drinking and gambling. She grabbed her secret cell phone from the stash box, pressed the power button. Relieved that he answered on the first ring. Loud music burst through the receiver.

"Where you at?" she yelled over the instrumentals.

"At the studio, why?"

She rolled her eyes toward the ceiling. José's underachieved; bootleg studio was in his mother's basement. He worked full time at FedEx, and spent his scrawny paycheck tinkering with beats and supplying weed and booze to his whack-ass rap group. He was New York's next *Swiss Beats*, at least in *his* head he was.

"Turn that shit down," she demanded.

Instrumentals lowered. His voice, pristine clear. "Why you sound tight?"

"Shit just jumped off between me and Bradley," she said trying to catch her breath.

"That nigga put his hand on you?"

"Somewhat, but I held my own."

"I'm on my way."

"José."

"What-up?"

"Bring that *thang-thang*... just in case."

"I'm on probation."

She sucked her teeth. "Man, bring the fucking heat."

Heavy footsteps were approaching. The door swung open.

"Who the hell is on the phone?"

She tossed the cell inside the purse with the rest of her valuables, and zipped it. After slipping the purse over her shoulders, she grabbed her luggage and began wheeling pass him. The suitcase knocked against each step as she made her way down the steps.

"You black bitch. I should have known you weren't equipped to handle being in my circle. You have no damn class."

She stopped at the threshold, face tight. "Call me a black bitch one more time and I promise I'll drag your ass up and down this motherfucker by the collar of your shirt. Scrape your white ass pink against the concrete."

He yanked his shirt over his head, slammed it against the floor. Feeling invincible, like the *Incredible Hulk* on steroids, minus the muscle. "I'd like to see you try it."

She shook her head and continued out the door. Bradley was out of control. She knew she made the right decision by calling José. It made no sense to break a nail over his stupidity.

"Get your black ass back here," he demanded.

She gave him the finger, and kept walking. "Fuck you Brad. You and your white lily friends can go to hell." She doubled back for her laptop and digital camera. She packed her trunk with all that would fit. She tossed her mink across the backseat of the Benz and slipped her traveling makeup kit in next. Going under with Bradley wasn't the deal. He promised to keep her laced in the finest. And now that he was reneging, it made no sense to stick around. Things were only bound to get worse.

He grabbed a fist full of her hair. She whirled around and slapped the taste from his mouth. He stood in disbelief, gripping the side of his face. She continued to pack her belongings, thinking of where the road would take her from there. Scarsdale had been good to her, but staying until the empire crumbled would only give Bradley false hope. It was best that they cut their ties now.

"You can't walk back to Queens."

"I don't intend to."

"The car stays."

She laughed. "Move out my way, got just one last bag at the door."

"You don't own shit here. This is my stuff. I bought every last stitch, down to your funky drawers, bitch!"

"I'm done with you," she yelled, just inches away from his face. Spit splashed his eyeball.

He blinked. "Keep your voice down. The neighbors..."

"Fuck the fucking neighbors."

***

They hooked up in Atlanta. Bradley was there on business, and Lou-Lou had just burned through a bag of cash she'd earn from a New York heist. The Southside hit set her straight, but since she wasn't used to that kind of money at one time, she blew it. The money came by way of blood, sweat and tears, but she'd spent it happily. Outside the Colony Square building, corner of 14th Street and Peachtree she stood. Shiny black Limo pulled up curbside. The back window fell.

"Hello sweet heart. You need a lift?"

At first she thought he was Justin Timberlake, but as she came closer she realized she'd been mistaken. White boy suited up, casket sharp beamed his big blue eyes at her.

"Which way you headed?" she asked.

He opened the door, slid aside, and patted the available space next to him.

"I'm headed *your* way."

The big wigs from Ridgmore sent their top gun in to close the deal with a wealthy, stubborn, tight wad heiress. One hundred million dollars was on the line, but the Ridgmore executives felt confident that Bradley was the guy for the job. And so they were correct. He closed the deal within the first hour, leaving him ample time to play.

Bradley and Lou-Lou *did* Atlanta. Being escorted in private limos to the *Fox*, weekend trips to *Chateau Elan*, candlelit dinners at the *Sun Dail* not only softened Lou-Lou's rough girl exterior, but gave her some insight on how to conduct in a professional environment. Her momentary ghetto relapses came and went, but for the most part she maintained a professional disposition. She was a hard-core chick trying to reinvent herself amongst the elite. Her vocabulary had to improve if she wanted to be more than just Bradley's bedside booty. She quickly dropped the slang, and became verbally sophisticated.

"Come to New York. I'll fly you in. Stay with me for the weekend."

Lou-Lou's answer was always no. New York was off limits. So much strife had occurred. Too much damage done. She'd burnt too many bridges, shitted on too many faces. That Southside heist was still fresh on people's brain. It just wasn't worth the risk. *He* wasn't worth the risk.

They saw each other once a month. He'd made it his business to check up on clients, as way of excuse to write-off his trip as a travel expense. Lou-Lou worked Bradley like a business. The longer she played her cards right, the more he spoiled her. Seeing Bradley whip out his plastic at the bat of her eyes made her wish she had met him sooner. For years she's been hustling backwards. Dope boys came and went. It was nothing to meet a bottle popping, party hopping, flashy car whipping dope boy today, and tomorrow see his ass on the news. Bagged and toe tagged.

***

"The ring stays, the car stays too. I'll call you a cab."

"Yeah, whatever my nigga. Don't hold yah breath on that."

He watched as she slipped behind the wheel and slammed the door. His face turned fire red at her obvious disrespect. Bradley chewed his bottom lip and spat his frustration onto the stone driveway. For the first time he noticed the oil stains.

"What the hell is that?"

He couldn't believe her readiness to quit, throw in the towel. He thought they had something special. He thought she was the one. Lou-Lou was ready to say good-bye to her old life. She was ready to burn rubber into her future. *So long sucker!*

Her heart skipped a beat when she noticed the keys weren't in the ignition. She watched him through the rearview mirror, dangling her way out of Scarsdale like a carrot. She gripped the steering wheel, took a few concentrated breaths. When the breathing technique didn't work, and that *woosah* crap hadn't calmed her nerves, she opted to violence. She exited the car, moving towards him like a raging bull.

"Give me the damn keys, Brad."

"Get off my property you black bitch. Go back to *da* hood. Go back to being broke, busted and disgusted." He shoved her.

She tried grabbing the keys, but he shook her like an NBA professional. They played tag for a few minutes before Bradley got tired of running. *Asthma.* "Give me my damn keys."

"Hellz no. Getz yo ghetto ass off my property before I call the po-po," he said, taunting her with the keys.

"What property? This is bank owned you broke bastard."

"I should have left your welfare, chicken eating, layaway, price tag switching, *you know what I'm saying*, illiterate ass in Atlanta where I found you."

Lou-Lou tackled Bradley to the ground, mauling him like a wild animal whose food had just been taken. She clawed his face, shredding his pink skin in different directions. Teeth sunk into the side of his face, leaving a circle the size of a gulf ball. Bradley regained control, tossing her up and over his shoulders. She fought tooth and nail, kicking, scratching and screaming. He struggled to subdue her rage. He was losing the battle. He needed to do something to override her wailing arms.

"Bitch."

An unknown strength resonated on the inside. His arms lifted her high above his head, tossing her into a sticky bush. Impelled by thorns, she released a screech that drew attention to those who hadn't already been eyeing the drama from their bedroom window. Her dress, rode up the back, revealing her bare bottom. Broken strap exposed one boob. She yelped like a wounded dog whose master had just run over its paw.

Bradley felt like acid had been thrown in his face. His flesh burned as O-negative oozed from gaping incisions. He touched his face, his neck, his chest, and could feel the grooves of her anger. His body leaked profusely.

"I'ma kill you."

Bradley gave her the finger. "Now, for the last time, get off my property you black-cunt-ignorant-*Nigga-bitch*."

The use of the *N* word was a thin line between life and death. She stared at him with daggers. The look in her eyes told him he was safer behind closed doors. Something told him to haul-ass back towards the house. His gut told him to call the police, and let the authorities deal with her madness. She limped painfully towards the driver's side door, popped the trunk, and headed towards the rear of the Benz.

"Whoa... *W*-wait... where'd you... *D*-don't point that thing at me." Panic rattled his every word.

"Black-cunt-ignorant-Nigga-bitch."

"I didn't *m*-mean it like that."

"Black-cunt-ignorant-Nigga-bitch."

"*B*-baby cakes... *P*-please... I *D*-didn't *M*-mean it. We can work this out. You can have the car. Take the car, the ring, and all the clothes."

He cried.

She cried.

Hand trembling, aiming her heat, heart thumping. His words brought her back 400 years, back to when Master used to whip on her ancestors. Back when Danny Glover beat on Whoopi in *The Color Purple*. His words released a poison so lethal, so uncontrollable not even God could reason. Her arm steadied, he flinched in horror.

José whipped into the driveway like a bat out of hell, adding a fraction of a second to Bradley's life. Only three rims spinning long after he ejected from the truck. He'd been riding the donut for well over three weeks now. José patted Lou-Lou on the bottom, lowering her arm. He stepped in front of her intended target.

"Who are you?" Bradley asked, sweating bullets.

José flashed a grin. Finally, he was face to face with the man who won over his women. He always wondered what this day would be like. Although, he preferred that Bradley caught him dick deep in walls that screamed his name, in his house, in his bed. But, now would have to do.

"Who am I?"

"Did I fucking stutter?"

"Oh, so you wanna act like a big shot?"

Bradley scoffed, "Excuse me."

"They call me the Maintenance Man," José said calmly.

Bradley looked passed José. Narrowed eyes landed on Lou-Lou, then the Suburban. His bionic ears picked up the noise from the drip. *The driveway.*

"You dirty slut bitch. You've been fucking this... this... thug in my house."

For the first time her face shown remorse. She opened her mouth to extend some sort of apology, but José bulldozed the moment. He bucked his chest, making Bradley flinch in absolute horror.

"Stay away from me," Bradley demanded, trying best to square his shoulders but it was no use. He was scared like never before.

José inched in close. Fist balled tightly, ready to pound his face in. Bradley backed away, tripping into the sticky bush. He yelped. José offered his hand, helped Bradley up, only to give him a stiff one to the jaw, knocking him back into the bush. José offered his hand a second time, pulling Bradley from the thorny hedge, only to shove him back down. He repeated this well deserved act several times before Lou-Lou spoke up.

"Give me my keys."

Screaming sirens quickly approached. Urgency in the air. The law was right around the corner. Lou-Lou figured one of the neighbors called the police. They lived in a prominent community. Attorneys, Physicians, and other leading business honchos squandered their fortunes to live in that zip code. There was no way in hell they would sit by and allow such a ruckus to transpire beneath their coke filled nose.

Bradley dug his trembling hand into his back pocket and pulled out the shiny set. Lou-Lou snatched the keys and moved towards the car. José talked mega smack to Bradley, walking backwards towards his truck, hoping, wishing, praying Bradley responded. He'd waited far too long for the moment where he could break his ass in two.

Lou-Lou yanked José by the arm, forcing him to gain control of himself. They didn't have time for a brawl. The law was closing in.

"Let's get the hell out of Westchester county before these crackers have our ass in a sling," said Lou-Lou.

They burned rubber down Hutchinson River Parkway, heading south. Lou-Lou led the way in her Benz, José followed in his raggedy ass Suburban. She prayed that he didn't break down in the midst of their getaway. She checked her rear-view every now and then to make sure they weren't being pursued. Bradley had the tag numbers. She figured an APB was out on the make and model.

"GPS, tracking device, *shit*," she said, flooring the pedal.

A million thoughts a second flooded her brain. Bradley had the power to pull the plug on her. She needed to ditch the car, and quick. They headed towards the Bronx, José's stomping ground. He sped up, cut in front of the Benz, and led the way towards the Bronx River Parkway. Their destination ended at Fordham road and St. Luke's. Ramiro's garage was a family owned business. José came from a long line of mechanics, which is why Lou-Lou couldn't understand the condition of his only means of transportation.

"Uncle Chino," José called out.

A short man with a jail house build turned and looked in their direction. José was a spitting image of his uncle. From the looks of his tatted neck and arms, she assumed Uncle Chino was a Latin King. As she got close, she noticed the gang related tattoos that inked his skin, confirming her suspicion. Both men shook up and hugged.

"Chino, this is Lou-Lou, my girl."

Hardly. "Hello, nice to meet you."

Chino took her hand and whispered in his native tongue. José laughed, wrapping his arm around Lou-Lou like she belonged to him exclusively. She elbowed his side, cleared her throat, signaling for him to get down to business. Time was ticking.

José's eyes darted, and landed on the Benz. "We need to get rid of the girl," he said. Chino leaned in, inspecting the merchandise. Custom rims, custom interior, top of the line system, new car smell enticed his eager pockets. He extended his index finger, caressing the vessel in a manner only the rightful owner should.

"When?" Chino asked.

"Yesterday," Lou-Lou said.

"Everything cool?" Chino asked José with a suspicious eye.

"Everything is everything, just need to get rid of it," José assured.

"Is it stolen?" Chino asked.

"I own it."

Chino measured Lou-Lou up, smiled. "Why not resale? Why chop such a beautifully legit girl?"

"Resale is not an option for me."

Bradley most likely reported the vehicle stolen. Since the ride was technically in his name, she figured she'd get something off the parts. She needed every penny she could get. *His ass probably behind in payments,* Lou-Lou thought.

"Why so many questions?" she barked.

Chino gave José a look as if to say *control your girl.* "I run a legit business," he stated plainly. She opened the car door, face twisted with frustration.

"With all due respect Chino, I don't have time to discuss the specifics of whom, what, where, and how. I just need this bitch chopped."

Chino rubbed his tattooed hands down his neatly trimmed mustache and smirked.

"You're sassy. I like that."

One hour later Lou-Lou road shot gun, José was behind the wheel. All of her belongings piled inside his funky truck. Her pockets were twenty thousand fatter. It was highway robbery for a ninety thousand dollar vehicle, but she did what she had to do.

They continued towards the Bronx River Parkway, heading further south. Signs for I-95 grabbed her attention. She'd left Atlanta for Bradley. Now that she and Bradley was no longer an item, she thought about returning to The Black Mecca. Life in the *A* was good. "What's that noise?"

"My gas indicator. I'm on *E*."

She leaned close to José. The needle kissed the red line, yellow light blinking.

"I need fuel."

"No shit Sherlock. Get off at the next exit."

They barely made it to the nearest gas station before the truck conked out. Lou-Lou couldn't believe it. There she was, dressed in Gucci, smelling like Gucci, and steering some broke down piece of junk while José pushed them the rest of the way. She sat behind the wheel, both arms folded in disgust. She thought of ditching his ass, but had no idea where the hell she was. *If I didn't have all that I owned in the back of this piece of crap truck, I would leave his broke ass gasless on the side of the road.* She was pissed and he knew it. After José caught his breath, he tapped his deflated pockets.

"Spot me a twenty."

She glared at him.

"I'll pay you back."

"Damn, you *stay* on some broke shit."

Before he could comment, and defend his financial situation, she hopped out. He watched her move quickly around the back of the truck, slipping plastic from her purse. Things between them were quickly changing. He grabbed his head, closed his eyes, knowing he'd better come up with a plan, real soon.

Bradley was a cushy situation. He provided a luxurious lifestyle, while José provided unbelievable sex. It was a perfect arrangement. Oh, and let's not forget the perks she kicked his way. Nice watches, clothes, sneakers, the works. José knew for sure he couldn't keep a girl like Lou-Lou strictly off his pretty boy looks, and big dick. The pressure was on.

"Son-of-a-bitch!"

His eyes shot open. "What's wrong?"

Her head rolled damn near off her neck. "Everything is wrong."

Bradley beat her to the punch. Her Black Card was denied. She tried another. *Denied.* She tried a third, and a fourth, and finally she heard the attendant's voice over the speaker requesting her to step inside to complete her transaction. She was embarrassed beyond words.

After gassing the guzzler they proceeded south, heading towards Queens. Lou-Lou demanded silence but for some reason José couldn't keep his jabbers shut. He rambled on about his multiple artists, and how much talent they possessed. He swore one in particular would be the next best thing since *Lil Wayne.* He pressed track 5, turned up the volume. He knocked his head, looking for her to do the same. She showed no expression, no enthusiasm for his work what so ever. Money was on her brain. She needed some wheels. She couldn't be seen in a broke down Suburban with a wannabe producer. José was fine, fine as hell with a package that filled the largest magnum made. He was good for one thing and one thing only.

"Have you bumped your head?"

"Am I asking for a lot?"

She sucked her teeth. "Man, drop me off at the Marriott."

"Why stay at the hotel when you can stay with me?"

"Check this here; I need to be fucked tonight."

His eyes lit up like a Christmas tree. His hand on her leg, sliding up her thigh, caressing her middle. "Mom's don't come down stairs for nothing. She's about sleep now."

"I need to be fucked by a nigga who can up-grade my situation." She flicked his hand away and adjusted her seat. "Million dollar pussy don't belong on a pissy-air mattress."

"I've got a pullout sofa."

"Same shit."

Her point was valid. Who the hell was he to ask her for anything? She called the shots. She was the Boss Bitch who took all the risk, who assessed all the damages, who shot her way to the top by spreading eagle and laying on her back. Who the hell was he?

"And cut that bullshit off. Your crew is whack. Keep your day job."

When they arrived at the Marriott, near LaGuardia Airport, thoughts of hopping on the next Boeing-747 entered her mind. She could return to Atlanta, and pick up where she left off. She could migrate to California, or maybe become a Florida transplant. Miami was always popping. She had options.

"Lou-Lou," he shouted out the window.

Chocolate mink covered her frame as she high stepped it towards the automatic sliding doors. Designer bags wheeled behind, leaving José begging for another taste of her kitty kat. *Take a picture because this is the last time you'll see this ass.*

A young Pakistani worker scooped her luggage and placed it on a brass luggage cart. His smile was bright and white. His skin, shaded dark and mysterious. Being treated like a person who possessed money was a feeling she couldn't live without. Bradley introduced her to a world of money, power, and respect. Anything less wasn't living.

She received optimum treatment the moment she reached guest services.

Ms. Dobbs your presence is appreciated, Ms. Dobbs thank you for choosing to spend the night with us. Blah, blah, blah. All she needed was the plastic keycard to where home would be for the next week or so.

"Smoking or non-smoking room?"

"Non-smoking," she said, knowing well she would light up a J the first chance she got. Smokers never wanted to stay in a room that smelled like smoke. She noticed José out her side peripheral, questioning the bellhop. "*Son, you playing me too close. I got it from here. Bounce.*"

"I'm just making sure my baby is safe."

Her face tight, lips curved, her posture defensive and ready to get on some rowdy shit. She drew breath.

"What's all that for?" he asked.

She huffed. "Hate repeating myself... hate explaining myself... hate being pressured."

Her fuse was short. A straight hood bitch was ready to jump out of a bag, fuck his ass up in the lobby. Bradley only received a portion of her. Beneath her certified stones, expensive mink, layers beneath the facade she put on for the sake of *Scarsdale*, was a real thoroughbred ready to scrap. Her fist balled tight, she stepped to him, her face inches away from his.

"Step off before I make a scene."

The smirk on his face made her heated. He leaned in, kissed her lips. A firm closed fist came across his chin. His state of shock caused him to stumble backwards. She read his body language, and could tell he was ready to react. She dropped her purse, threw her hands up boxer style. Her gully posture spoke volumes.

"What nigga-what!"

Her voice carried throughout the open space. All heads turned in their direction. His face turned red, his pride shattered. The young bellhop came to her aid, asked if she was okay, if she needed him to call security. She thought about having him escorted, thrown out on his ass. Besides, he wasn't a guest, and couldn't afford to be one. His broke down truck was occupying a perfectly good parking space that a paying customer could use. Just as she was about to answer, José turned on his heels and got the hell on.

After arriving to her suite, she tipped the bellhop a crisp twenty, kicked off her shoes, undressed down to her underwear, and collapsed onto the king size mattress.

"What a day."

First things first; she needed to obtain another whip. She sat up, grabbed her purse, and pulled her life savings from it. All she had, fit inside a medium size designer Hobo. That reality caused panic to set in. She measured several stacks between her index finger and her thumb. Stress overtook her as she counted the big faces. Kosha's five stacks were set aside from the gate. In fact, she laid away six, just because. The last thing she wanted was for her baby cousin to worry about money.

Atlanta was indeed the land of opportunity, The Black Mecca, the city of thriving, empowered, young ethnic ambitious professionals. It was the movement, the era from which a person of color could enjoy the fruits of their ancestor's labor. It was the modern day Harlem, a place to migrate families for a second chance. Black owned everything, human rights activist had a voice, relentless self promoting made profitable, black mayors like *Shirley Franklin* and *Kasim Reed* making a difference, but it was also the devils den, booty shaking central, a stripper's paradise, home of the *Trapper*, the belly of the beast. Good girls were known to go bad.

Next, she pulled the black velvet pouch, laid it across the bed. An assortment of glistening stones twinkled. Bradley had exquisite taste in jewelry. What she had in cash, plus her jewels still left her piss poor.

"I need that new Bentley Coup."

Going back to the Mercedes was a lateral move, a move she wasn't willing to make. It was all about image, and twirling a Bentley-Baby would definitely spark a few interests. With Bradley a thing of the past, and her money short, Lou-Lou was in search of her next set of deep pockets.

She made her way across the room, grabbed a bottled water from the mini fridge. Chino's business card lay against the coffee pot. He could snatch a Coup, for a fraction of the cost. Paying sticker price would leave her without a pot to piss in. *Dealer's price :: Chino's way*, she weighed her options. Either way she needed to twirl that vessel within a few hours.

Time was money, and in order for her to make more money, she needed to look like money. Looking like money required a makeover. Her once Scarsdale image needed edging. Wholesome and humble just wasn't going to cut it. A sudden knock at the door disrupted her thoughts. Aggravation painted her face.

"Who is it?" she asked abrasively.

"It's me."

She sucked her teeth, and stomped her way towards the door.

"José, that's word to everything I love…if you don't…."

She swung open the door. Bottled water slipped from her finger tips. Purified H2O splashed her manicured toes. Period blood stained her panties the moment she saw his face. Her eyes were deceiving her, they had to be. There was no way in hell he was standing before her, *alive*.

She blinked once, his image still there.

She blinked twice, his hand wrapped around her neck, silencing her scream.

CHAPTER 4

He moved cheek to cheek, whispered, "Who else is here?"
Her back slammed against the wall, thumbs pressed against her trachea. Erratic breathing had variation, inconsistency. Levels of struggle showed on her face. She was a fish out of water, windpipe ready to burst. With respiratory failure just moments away,

She could barely swallow, let alone speak. He released his grip, allowing her to suck back a chest full of oxygen. Tears formed a slippery road down her face.

He repeated his question. Deaf like noises projected from her agape mouth. Fear and confusion gripped her all at the same time. He lifted his shirt, pulled his glock. Cemented shoes had her bound. Death was on the horizon.

"You alone?"

"Yes."

They set in motion towards the bathroom. Razor sharp nails dug into the flesh of her shoulder, controlling her pace. "Slow." She obeyed. Sheen of perspiration covered her face. Untimely downpour of her monthly flow slid down her weakened knees.

"Move it." Inside the bathroom, she stood. A terrified version of herself beaming back from a wall length mirror. Her heart skipped three beats as he moved closer. He yanked the commercial grade shower curtain back.

"Get in."

He scanned her perfect body. Her toes manicured, trimmed in French. Diamond tennis bracelet hugged her ankle. Pear shape, flat stomach, he stopped at her breasts. They were much larger then he remembered. His lips set in a sinister grin. Brown face healthy, facial hair trimmed along his full cheeks. New York fitted cap lowered above his eyes. Cold, scared, and uncertain if she should take the next breath. His stature towered her, cornered her, and weakened her vitals.

She shivered. "What do you want from me?"

"Did I ask you to speak?"

Oh God, this is crazy. You're supposed to be dead, she thought.

"Turn around. Put both hands against the wall."

She tried to swallow, her throat dry as dust. She faced the ceramic tile, positioning her sweaty palms. Her fingers traced the grout, moving across each square block slowly. The intricate tattoo that stained her back was more than a tramp stamp. He admired it for a second, then said, "Shower, get dressed, we need to talk."

Steam followed her out the bathroom moments later. She appeared wrapped in a towel, damp hair slicked to the back, face red, eyes puffy, nerves scattered. He stood on the balcony, blowing trees. Fitted cap to the back, blunt in hand, smoke released from his nostrils. Old school stiff leg Levis, hoodie, classic steel-toe Timberlands was his attire. His pants, never sagging. His appearance, dark but always neat, always clean.

Her eyes searched the bed. Her diamonds were still in place. Her passport, I.D., and birth certificate untouched. *Where's my cell phone?* The wire from the room's phone was detached. *He's going to kill me.*

He stepped inside, sliding the glass shut behind him. "Relax. I'm not here to hurt you," he said, as if he'd read her mind. She looked fragile, weak, easily broken. He approached. She took a step back, flinched. Her breathing, still a bit ragged from being choked. He exhaled a cloud of smoke in her face, touched her damp hair, gathered her mane into a bunch, looped and tugged.

"This all you?"

"Yes."

He released her au natural, mopping it dry with his sleeve.

"Did you miss me?" he asked with a smile in his voice. Peace escaped her lungs. Anger inflated her chest. Resentment tightened her fist. She swung with all her might, knocking him in the ribs. He caved, coughed, laughed. She gave him another body shot. He fell against the bed, allowing her to release her fury *Mayweather* style.

"Okay, damn. Chill."

"You almost gave me a heart attack."

She gave up, collapsed next to him. Hot tears made a trail down her face. He passed her the haze and the lighter. She took one long exaggerated hit. Held the smoke back in her lungs long enough to feel the Cheeba travel her body. They laid in silence, beneath a cloud of smoke.

"You surprised to see me?"

"What you think?"

"From the looks of your period I would have to say yes."

"I'm just thankful I didn't crap myself."

He made a face, nudged her playfully. "Look at you. You look good. All grown up."

She smiled. "*Me*, look at you. You're *alive* and shit." She punched him again.

He stood up, pulled her into his chest. They hugged. She stepped away, wiped her eyes. Her emotions were getting the best of her. He gave her a minute to collect herself.

"We thought you were dead."

"We?"

"Yeah. *We*."

His face turned serious.

"It's been five years man," she whimpered.

"That night, after we took care of that business on the Southside, word got back that Chopper finished you."

He twisted his lips towards the sky. "Who you hear that from?"

"My brother told Tracy, Tracy told me, the hood was talking. People were saying you got hacked up. Head in one bag, legs and arms in another. I got spooked. Went to warn Jazzman, caught her pulling out. She was heading to Atlanta. Thought she'd heard but when I told her..." She shook her head. "It crushed her."

He looked away.

"I was so paranoid. Couldn't go back home. All sorts of things ran through my mind. Chopper killed you and he was probably looking for me. At the time, you couldn't tell me different. So, I headed O.T with Jazzman. That was the longest ride of our lives," she said meaning every word of it.

He imagined Jazzman behind the wheel, guilt tripping. Their last encounter wasn't a pleasant one. He envisioned Lou-Lou skittish ass talking a mile a minute making matters worse. She was just a kid when he met her. Eighteen, courageous, bold, with a bad attitude.

"Heard your baby mom's set you up."

He pulled his cap off, removed his hoodie, reached for the desire, pulled long and hard. Stocky and solid all over, his football *physique* was new to her.

"Well, say something. *Shit.* You show up now, after all this time. What part of the game is this?"

He stretched out across the bed, blowing smoke into air. He loved to listen to hood politics. Loved to hear who went out in a blazing glory. Loved to hear who was plotting, who was watching, who was snitching, and who was hawking what niggas jewels. Who bagged who's bitch, who got caught slipping. His favorite tale of them all, *what the hell happened to Roy?*

"Your brother still a NYPD pig?" he asked, changing the subject.

She opened the balcony door to let some fresh air in. "He made Detective. First Grade," she said proudly.

"It's funny how siblings could end up on the opposite side of the law."

"He keeps his nose out my business, and I keep mine out of his. As long as I don't do my dirt on his turf, it's all love."

"I feel you."

"Enough about me, what-up with you?" She desperately wanted to know.

There were moments in life that never left the brain. For him, the most tragic of events were embedded, woven deep into his soul like a pattern. Just like that, his lemonade turned back into lemons. Five years prior, Roy had a beautiful fiancé, new baby girl, newly constructed home, new whips in the driveway, and all together a new life. His world shifted suddenly. That night, at the pool hall, on the Southside of Queens, everything changed.

"That nigga Chopper was working for the Fed's."

"*No*. Shut up!"

"Word is bond."

"But he orchestrated the whole thing. The Southside hit was his idea." she protested.

"He was working for the Feds. His parole had conditions. I was the fine print. Jakes wanted me, but couldn't touch me. He set me up."

"But that was your man."

"Key word - *was*."

"Your baby mom's and Chopper family."

He looked at her sideways. That was privileged information.

"How'd you know?"

"Before my brother joined the force he worked Corrections at Rikers. He remembered Chopper when he first got shipped with the big boys. Judge charged him as an adult. Your baby mom's went to see him a couple times."

Roy rubbed his chin. He had no idea Chopper and Cookie where related. Not until the bitter end. And by that time it was too late to reason.

"I heard she's the one who put the bug in Chopper's ear to merk you."

He refused to believe such a thing. Yes, they had their issues. Yes, at the time he said and did some things that would drive any woman half crazy, but putting a hit on him was the last thing she was capable of.

"Negative."

"Oh, please. Don't act like you've never questioned it."

That scenario ran through him over and over, but at the end of the day, he shoved it aside, and told himself she would never partake in something so ruthless. She was no angel, but she was thousands of miles away from being gully. Cookie didn't have the heart.

"It wasn't in her. She wasn't the type."

"You threatened to take away her rights as a mother. You defamed her character. She had motive."

"True."

"Her cousin, her family, *that nigga Chopper* was her outlet. Sure, Jakes may have wanted you, but Chopper had a more personal reason for plugging you with that Southside hit. You caught two bodies that night, on his behalf."

"Kill two birds with one stone," he said, as he listened to her rationalize that night like a Private-I. He too replayed the events of that night. Even now there were many uncertainties.

"He dimed you out, fingered you, then came to body you, but something went wrong."

His presence was a complete and utter mystery. She speculated for years about what really happened that night. The fact that he was in her suite; breathing was more than she could handle. He stood, and headed towards the wet bar. Highball glass, four ice cubes, Vodka, with a splash of pineapple for her. He poured himself a shot straight-up.

"Thanks."

"Welcome."

He looked at her for a long moment before directing his attention outside. LaGuardia was in his full view. It was nice to be home. The concrete jungle, rotten-apple. A place where dreams are made, but often times crushed. She slapped his arm. Not hard, but hard enough to get his attention.

"You alright?" she asked.

"I'm good. Just thinking."

"About?"

"Jazzman."

Fragments of gun powder still on their hands. Bodies linked to the bullets in their chambers. They hopped onto the Van Wyck. Roy swerved in and out traffic, foot to the floor. His heart pumping, his hands tight around the wheel. He was two seconds away from slapping the taste from Jazzman's mouth. Their argument catapulted into something more. The tongue was lethal. Disrespectful words left both feeling hurt, betrayed, wounded. Jazzman was mouthing off, speaking to Roy as if he wouldn't put the heat to her dome.

"You put your hands on her," Lou-Lou said, reminding Roy of his faults from way back when.

"She provoked me," he said, defending his position.

49

Roy grabbed the back of Jazzman's neck, forcing her pretty face to the dashboard. He made her say his name, made her respect his gangsta. Conflict of interest existed between them. He was an animal. She was his weakness. His feelings were displaced. She had his heart, but her best friend Cookie was his baby momma. Jazzman refused to cross the line. Her loyalty was to her home girl. Roy admired her for it, hated her for it, and struggled to make her see things his way.

"That night was so hectic. I thought you were about to shoot her dead by the way you were acting," she said sipping her cocktail.

Lou-Lou sat in the back seat pleading for peace. They had blood on their hands. Bodies on the burners that sat in their laps, and now there was strife amongst them. They needed peace within their circle. One sided love caused division, caused their union to weaken.

"I would have given her the world," Roy professed.

"She didn't want it."

"You mean she didn't want me."

Roy was used to getting his way. Jazzman was supposed to accept the situation. She was supposed to say forget Cookie, and submit to him. Become his Queen; knock her BFF off the thrown.

"You overreacted. Jazz didn't deserve it."

"I know she didn't, but at the time, emotions were running high. She kept talking crazy. Kept talking like I wouldn't drop her ass on the side of the expressway with no pulse."

"You were out of control."

"I began to question her loyalty."

"Honestly, you were the selfish one. You wanted her to choose. They were good friends long before you came into the picture."

"I thought we had something."

"It's called business. You were the one who caught feelings. I swear you men always want what you can't have."

He took a pull of his desire, passed it to her, and then guzzled the shot of fluid.

"You don't understand. I needed her." She was his Eve, his Bonnie, his Jada, his Ride or Die chick. Together they could make power moves, rule the world.

"She was under a lot of pressure. We all were. Isis was on a damn machine, breathing her last breath. She died before we made it back to the hospital."

The mentioning of Isis name made him angry. He placed his hand at the top of his head, rubbed his waves. He regretted not being there with her. His partner, his sister, his family was gone. Their connection was unspoken. She knew him, understood him, respected him, and he for her. He slammed his fist into an open hand angrily.

"*Yo* for-real... Isis was the only, and I mean the *only* bitch that really had my back. Through all the ups and downs, she was the only person I could count on. She didn't give a fuck about busting off. She stepped up to the plate, made grown men shit their pants. That was my baby. I miss her. I loved her."

Tears slipped from Lou-Lou's eyes. "She loved you too."

Their moment of silence was broken by a blaring ringtone. Roy dipped into his pocket, tossed the BlackBerry to Lou-Lou. She sucked her teeth, sent her caller to voicemail. She took a seat next to him on the bed, crossed her legs.

"You don't trust me do you?" she asked, staring at him.

"Why you say that?"

She took the last pull of the roach and outted it. "Cause' you have yet to explain what really happened. Why the fuck am I sitting next to a dead man?"

He looked into her eyes; saw the spirit of her cousin, Isis beaming back at him. Roy remembered the day he took Lou-Lou underneath his wing. So naive, so eager to have hood acclaim, honor, respect. But what Lou-Lou quickly would learn was there was no respect and honor amongst thieves. She quickly learned she had to watch her own ass, protect her own neck.

"You're all grown up."

"Roy."

"You know, I promised Isis I would look after you. The first time I met you, you were so damn naive. I wanted to squeeze your neck because you just wouldn't stop yapping. Remember, your ultimate goal in life was to bag you a baller." He laughed.

She smirked. *Much hasn't changed about that.*

"Forget all that Roy. Tell me what happened."

His eyes bore into the carpet.

"*C'mon* Roy, you wouldn't have bothered coming out of hiding if you thought I was a trick. Obviously you know there's love, there's trust. Always has been."

She was right. Still, what he was about to unveil to her never left his lips before.

"When we parted ways at the hotel..." He placed a hand against his chest. "I felt her."

"Felt who?"

"Isis. It was like I knew she had passed. I got mad, wanted to kill the person who was responsible."

They looked at each other intensely. He grabbed her hand. Firm squeezes confirmed that he was about to drop some heavy knowledge on her. "If you repeat an ounce of what I tell you, I'll kill you." She nodded knowing he would make good on his promise. He let go of her hand, took in a few deep breaths and continued.

"I learned of Choppers real motives shortly after the heist. My man from Queens Bridge hit me on the cell, told me the lick. Word on street was me and two bitches stuck up the hall. Supposedly, I was the trigger finger behind the loaded guns."

She leaped off the bed, both hands planted at her hips. Worry etched her face. "My name came up?"

"Not even once."

"Jazzman?"

"Nope. Ya'll were free and clear. I was the talk of the town."

She sat back down, breathed a sigh of relief.

"See... the whole time Chopper was playing me. Yeah, I'm man enough to admit it. He played me like a fucking fiddle. Not only was the Feds looking to book my ass on murder charges, I had a price on my head."

"So your baby moms did call the hit."

"Yes and no. Chopper wanted to get at me for the shit that went down between me and Cookie. She didn't exactly order the hit, but she didn't exactly try to stop it either, *naw mean.*"

"Right."

"She figured with me out the way, whether that be jail or six feet deep, she would be able to retain full custody of our daughter."

The thought of his little girl weakened him. He pulled a cigar from his pocket. Thinking of her was too much to bear. He cracked his dutchy, filled it with cannabis, twisted and sparked up.

"With the pigs on my ass, and Chopper try'na put a few in me, I was on edge. If I got bagged, I'll never see day. If Chopper caught up with me, well that would have been the end. I'm fucking paranoid at that point. I'm hearing voices in my head, telling me to rob and kill everybody, straight cheese."

He inhaled his medicine.

"I was determined to find that nigga Chopper before he found me. I'm on the hunt, riding through *Rochdale, Baisley, 40 projects*, looking for this nigga when I spot Barry."

She gasped. "Barry?"

"Caught that punk at the corner of 107 and 160th street."

"Say-Word."

"Word is bond. Spotted that faggot coming out the corner bodega with that bitch Cocoa. Both of them looking flabby and sick."

"That monster ain't no joke."

"Life just wasn't fair. I mean, I couldn't comprehend how he was still breathing when Isis was toe tagged at the city morgue. He gave my girl AIDS and was still walking, talking, chilling, munching down on a beef patty with cocoa bread and cheese."

He hopped up off the bed, started pacing.

"Give it here before you let it burn out," she insisted.

He took a toke, passed her the blunt. "Barry fucked a fag in the joint, came home and slipped that virus up in Isis." His fist clinched, his voice coated in rage. Un-forgiveness written all over him.

"I followed him home."

Her eyes ballooned. She pulled strongly at the blunt, passed it back. "Say-Word."

Roy resumed puffing. "Word is Bond. Followed him out to Long Island."

***

Dead End street. Big house sat in seclusion. Death was in the air. Hazard lights blinked on Barry's Cadillac truck, keys still in the ignition. Roy could tell they were tripping off that white horse. He'd managed to slip from behind the wheel, and post up behind the big oak tree that centered Barry's front yard. From where he stood he could hear bits and pieces of their conversation. Their voices were choppy.

"... you gave it to me..." she said.

"...that was the plan..." he said.

"...son-of-a-bitch..." she cried.

"... before I go-*you*-go...bet that shit..." he taunted.

"...evil..." she spat.

"...taking more people with me too..." he confessed.

"...you ruined my life..." she shouted.

"... just die..." he demanded.

Barry's voice was layered in purpose, wrapped in intent, packaged in *somebody-gave-it-to-me-so-I'm giving it to you* venom. Hearing him say so made it easier for Roy to follow through with his plan. He waited patiently in the cut. Outside by the big oak tree. Black ski mask, gloves covered his murderous hands.

Hazard lights blinked, keys still in the ignition. Barry and Cocoa fought from the driveway, to the front door. She lashed out, clawed him. He pushed and shoved her. She grabbed him by the shirt, choked his boney neck. He clocked her in the eye, dazing her.

"*Whyyyyyy Meeeee?*"she cried.

"Why not you?"

Barry moved painfully inside the house, leaving Cocoa alone in the pitch of night.

She struggled from the cold pavement, headed towards the house. Roy's window of opportunity finally arrived. He tipped in behind Cocoa, knocking her scrawny body down a flight of steps. Barry turned boldly, pulling his *.9mm* from beneath his baggy *Coogi* sweater. Roy gave him a swift elbow to the chest, snatched the burner. His fragile body flew across the room.

"What-up *Dun-Dun*...what you need man... I got it. Anything you want," said Barry, panting like a stray dog.

"I should have killed your ass years ago."

Barry froze, he recognized the voice. He grabbed the nearest door-knob, struggled to stand, but his legs were too weak to hold him. The slits in the mask bore hatred, rage, un-forgiveness.

"Roy-*rizzle*... I know how you're feeling right now. I loved Isis too. Never intended for it to reach her. Just happened."

"Shut up!"

"Shit crept up in me... would have never penetrated her man... would have never hurt Isis knowingly."

"Shut. The. Fuck. Up."

"Killing me won't bring her back."

Roy yanked Barry by the collar, lifted him up off his feet.

"Where that shit at?"

A smile of hope emerged on Barry's face. "Let's talk business. I got them birds."

Roy jammed the heat into his mouth, knocking his two fronts back. Barry coughed and spit up blood. Roy turned his head just in the nick of time. Infectious fluids splattered against his shirt, missing the eye slits in his ski mask by inches. Barry tried to run. An outstretched leg interrupted his stride. He went face first into a steel door.

"Where that shit at?"

Blood dripped along the sides of Barry's mouth. Pain gripped his chest. He was in no condition to fight. He heard the hammer cock. Big gun nudged the back of his head. He knew Roy wouldn't hesitate to pull the trigger. Barry pointed towards the basement.

"Down there."

"Show me."

"C'mon man."

Roy kicked him in his bony ass. "Show me."

Both men moved at a steady pace. Cocoa was still unconscious, at the bottom of the staircase. Her scary skeletal make-up made Roy quiver. That disease did a wicked thing to the human body.

They stepped over what was left of her and made their way to-wards the back room. Barry gave up the four digit code to the safe with no problem. *Jack Pot!* Roy made off with twenty bricks, and a quarter of a million in cash. An hour later, Barry was still breathing. His position, hog tied in the trunk.

***

"What about Cocoa?" Lou-Lou asked, barely able to control herself.

"One to the head. Put her out her misery."

Lou-Lou swallowed the lump in her throat.

"It was my duty to put an end to him. Felt like I had to avenge Isis death." He took one last drag of the blunt, and passed it.

"I'm good."

He laughed. "Can't hang?"

"I'll smoke you into a coma boy."

"Yeah right," he said outing the flame against the bottom of his boot.

"Barry had to be stopped."

"But why take him with you? Why not leave him at the bottom of the stairs with Cocoa, one to the head?"

"I'll be right back," he said and headed towards the bathroom to take a leak. The door was cracked, giving her a view of his *crack*. His left hand leaned against the wall, tilting his athletic *physique* over the commode at a slight angle, allowing the yellow rain to drizzle.

Lou-Lou sat back and digested all that Roy just said. She did the math. Roy made off with the bag money from the Southside heist, plus Barry's bricks, plus an additional two hundred and fifty thousand. According to Isis, Roy was a miser. He hoarded his money, spending only when necessary. He wasn't the one to floss his achievements in the dope game. He flew below the radar, remained low-key. His everyday vehicle was one of a modest feel. Standard whip kept them jack boys at bay. At first glance, he looked like your average Jo-blow, but Lou-Lou knew better. *He had enough to fake his death, start over fresh.* Lou-Lou suddenly got happy. When Roy returned his eyes were red from the smoke that clogged his lungs.

"You want another drink?" he asked, moving towards the bar.

"I'm good."

"Thought you could hang?"

"I'll drink you under a table boy. Don't test the kid."

"Yeah right."

She watched him pour his own troubles. *Twenty keys, at twenty five a brick was a half a million dollars.* She wondered how much of that money he still had. Roy was smart, a true business man. There was no telling how many times he'd flipped that dough. In all actuality, twenty keys could have been thirty, thirty could have been forty. Barry was King Kilo. So there was no way in really knowing how much Roy made off with. He was unpredictable like that.

"Ironically, I needed him alive. Took that infested rat back to my crib."

She looked puzzled. She said nothing. She waited for him to continue. Her cell phone blared. Lines of frustration wrinkled her forehead. It was José calling, again. *Fuck!*

"You need to take that?"

"No."

Roy leaned against the bar, swiveling the fluid. He was tipsy. So was she. Weed mixed with liquor, wasn't exactly her idea of a good time. She did one or the other, never both. Roy ran his hand down the back of his head.

"I took him to the basement. He told me he preferred to leave at the hands of another. He said he couldn't live with that shit."

"Damn."

"He stood, facing me like a man. For the first time, Barry faced me like a man."

An unfamiliar emotion gripped Lou-Lou. She suddenly felt sorry for Barry. No one deserved that kind of punishment. The virus was a wicked disease that she wouldn't wish on her worst enemy.

"So I did it."

"How'd you do it?"

"The details of how is not important."

She backed off. Pushing him to give a play by play could cause unwanted suspicion. She was surprised he'd divulged that much.

"After I did it, Cookie showed up."

"Your baby moms?"

"Yeah."

"You two had words?"

He shook his head no. "I was officially a wanted man. Made no sense in complicating my situation."

***

He heard the front door open. Heard movement above. Heard heavy footsteps against the hardwood floors. He thought it was Chooper. Thought it was the law. Thought it was Barry's rescue team. He hid behind the custom made bar, gat in hand. Sweat pouring from the top of his head. Infected blood stained his shirt and pants. Roy had already made up his mind. *I'll fight to the death.* He wasn't going down willingly. Whether it be the Law, Chopper, or Barry's Goons coming to avenge his death, he planned to stand and fight.

The basement door swung open. Light switch illuminated the dark space. Size seven trainers descended slowly. *Cookie.* He wondered if she was alone, wondered if Chopper was lurking somewhere upstairs, waiting for the right opportunity to strike. She approached the bar, but stopped when she noticed the door to the sauna ajar. He heard her gasp and let out a small shrill.

A bloody massacre stained the walls and carpet. A picture perfect bloodbath shook her to the core. She trembled in absolute fear. She backed away, gripping her chest, stumbling into the bar, leaning against it for support. Her stomach churned. Her cheeks filled with air. Gag reflex war took place at the back of her throat. The scene before her very eyes told a story. Another soft shrill escaped her. She found her strength, and made zombie like movement towards the staircase. Cookie turned, took one last look at the bar. Devastation clouded her face. That look was permanently fixed, etched in his brain.

"Gasoline. Fire wood. Book of matches."

"You torched the place?"

He looked at her strangely. "You didn't know?"

"First time hearing it," she said sincerely.

"Needed to erase Barry's DNA. Needed to make the Feds believe I went up in flames."

"You're crazy."

"I know."

Her cell phone rang again. She sent José to voicemail. A few seconds later, it rang again, and again.

"Let me guess, that's your man from downstairs?"

She looked surprised.

"Oh, I witnessed it all baby girl."

"How, when, where were you?"

"I've always been here. Kept eyes on you. Kept eyes on you and Jazzman both."

Her cell phone chimed again. José was determined.

"Where you been all this time?" Lou-Lou asked.

"Below sea level."

She looked confused. "Where?"

"New Orleans."

She made a face. "The Big Easy?"

"Home of the displaced. Home of the refugee. It was easy for me to fly below the radar. Moved like a thief in the night. I reinvented myself. Obtained a new first and last name. Grew a scratchy beard and the whole nine."

"Your beard doesn't look scratchy. In fact, it's kind of cute."

"It's tamed now. But back then I was a grizzly bear. I almost didn't recognize myself."

He smoothed an open hand against his trimmed facial hair, smiled. "Believe it or not, I laid hands on The Big Easy, helped to rebuild after Katrina."

"You volunteered?" She laughed.

"Got down and dirty with it. Donated time and money. Had a chick in Baton Rouge who I was helping out. Young saucy I met while volunteering at the outreach center. She had one of them FEMA trailers, could cook a mean seafood gumbo, and had two kids. Twin boys, bad as fuck." He reflected, smiled.

"Baby daddy still unaccounted for. Most of her family swept away in the storm, so I looked out. Stayed below sea level for a good two years, and then moved towards the bottom of the map."

Her brows moved inward. "Where?"

"Miami."

"Oh."

"My chick from Baton Rouge wanted a commitment. Wanted me to change her last name, lock down that finger. Got missing before she put that period blood in my spaghetti sauce."

She laughed. "Boy you stupid."

"My cousin had things popping in Dade County. The money was sick. Stayed there for about a year. Bounced after a close call. Circled back to Atlanta."

"Atlanta?"

He nodded. "Got me a good thing going in the *A*," he said grinning.

"Wait; was that a twinkle in your eye?"

"Get outta here."

"My dude is in love," Lou-Lou teased.

"Whatever. So, now I'm here."

"Why?"

"Stevie Wonder can see that you need help."

She looked down at her hands, checked her perfectly manicured nails. "Me and my man broke up."

"I know."

"How you know?"

"I told you, I kept a close eye on you."

"Is that right?"

Her cell phone chimed again. She cringed.

"I still don't understand why you messed with José in the first place. He's broke."

"How'd you know his name?"

He looked at her sideways. "Need you ask that question again?"

She pulled the top of her rob closed, adjusted the belt around her waist. "I can't seem to shake this asshole. He won't take no for an answer. I mean, I've told him flat out that I was no longer interested."

He laughed. "You got him whipped."

She smiled knowingly.

"*Yo*-Son on the real, I need to get this bread. I'm fucked up right now," she said real husky like.

"How much you walk away with?"

"What you mean?"

"Come on, don't play a player. How much you get the white boy for?"

"Got some jewels. Some cash. Chopped the Mercedes. Didn't move fast enough on the cash advances. He canceled my credit cards before I had the chance," she said regretfully.

"Rule of thumb, hit the ATM first."

"I know this, but I was too busy worried about one-time." She sucked her teeth in disgust.

"All together I got a hundred stacks in cash, jewelry worth over two hundred-thou."

"That's pocket change. Weekend money."

She sulked. "I need upgraded wheels, need clothes, need jewels, need to shine. Gotta shine. Can't be seen in anything less than this year's model."

"That's your weakness. Your always try'na shine. You need to learn how to chill. Learn how to survive at the bottom of the barrel with them crabs, while sitting on cake."

"I don't fuck with crabs, and I don't do the bottom well. Been there, done that. Never going back."

"Listen. You spend way too much time keeping up appearances. Get more money. Stop spending frivolously."

"Gotta look like money to get money."

"True, but you have a history of barking up the wrong tree. Surviving at the bottom of the barrel allows you to sustain in this game. Gives you insight on who's-who. Learn how to spot a crab baby girl."

"Forget all that. I've got my eye on that Bentley Coupe. I need that in my life."

He chuckled. As much as she'd matured, he could still see where she had more growing to do. She was still blinded by the material, the price tags. Labels made her a slave. "So you ready to put in work?"

"Been ready," she said.

"Sutphin Boulevard. A couple of steps away from the Queens County Clerk's Office."

Her face scrunched. "Who's getting money over there?"

"That's not important."

"How much we talking?"

"Could potential be a cool hundred stacks in it for you"

"Potentially?"

"Give or take a stack or two... but for the most you'll clear nothing less than ninety."

Cha-Ching. Her eyes lit up with dollar signs. "Why we sitting here? Let's make moves, get that cheese."

"It's not that simple. We need a third wheel."

They stared at each other long and hard. She could read his mind. She knew exactly what he was going to say before he said. She quickly objected. "No. She hates me."

"I knew you two weren't speaking, but didn't exactly know why."

"Jazzman made it perfectly clear that I was to stay out of her life. I choose to honor her wishes."

"C'mon now, ya'll family. What could you have possibly done for her to write you off?"

She let his question linger, allowed it to fall by the wayside side. She preferred not to speak on the events that led up to her and Jazzman's fall out. *I'm embarrassed to say.* "Let's just say I abused our relationship. I took advantage in the worst way."

"She would want in on this," he said.

"How you know?"

He looked away. He knew something. She could tell. He knew something that she didn't know and that bothered her.

"Obviously you're in the *know*. Tell me."

"She needs a helping hand. If I were you, I would give her a call. Patch things up."

"I can't."

He threw up his hands. "Then we can't move on this opportunity. We need a third wheel to move this plan full speed ahead. She's the only person I trust."

"I can't call her. She'll hang up."

"Then we'll go to her house."

"Easily spoken, *dead man.* How the hell you think she's going to react to seeing you, alive?"

"Let me handle that. In the mean time, get dressed, pack your stuff, and meet me downstairs in the lobby."

"But I just checked in."
"José, he's thirsty for you. I don't trust that cat."
"Good point."

CHAPTER 5

J azzman shifted from the right side to the left. Egyptian sheets bundled three ways. Her top of the line mattress suddenly felt lumpy. Felt as if it had endured its share. Felt like the acts performed on such cushion needed to be burned.

She scratched at her scalp, and thought about her insurmountable debt. Her well had run dry. Her funds barely trickled in. She had an occasional drip, but never enough to sustain her lifestyle. Times were hard.

Now centered and feeling weighed down with worry. The ceiling fan provided a cool breeze against her naked body. She gripped a fist full of her braids. Her fingers became damp. *Sweat.* Most likely his, had to be. He perspired like a pig when they sexed.

The faucet turned on. An image of him standing over the sink, scrubbing his teeth, running her water freely made her cring. He gargled the last bit of her Listerine. Her eyes closed. Dollars and cents calculated in her brain.

She heard his cell phone chime, then quickly silence. She heard his muffled voice, and then heard him laugh. Water *still* running, *still* accumulating against her unpaid balance. Finally, the faucet silenced. One last chuckle, then his voice did the same. She heard the shower turn on.

The telephone lit up like a Christmas bulb. Red and white alternated slow, then fast. She used this feature after ten, or on nights when she had something long and hard lying beside her. She decided to let the caller go to voicemail. Holding a conversation was the last thing she wanted to do which was why Rick's presence was beginning to annoy her. All she wanted was a quickie and to be left alone. If she knew he would require a shit, shower and shave she would have opted for her battery operated boyfriend.

Red and white illuminated again, and again. The glowing object tugged her curiosity.

It's just a pesky bill collector I bet.

The caller was persistent. She jumped out of bed, and hustled across the large room. She answered, rolled her eyes towards the trey ceiling, and let out a frustrated breath. After a few clicks and beeps, his voice rang through the receiver smooth as cognac. She wasn't in the mood to entertain his mess. She provided access, and fitted the bill so that her son could have a chance to know his father, but he was beginning to go overboard with the calls.

"He's asleep."

"We need to talk."

She blew out the cherry scented candle. "This call cost money." Fifteen dollars bought him only twenty minutes per call, and he'd already used up his one-time courtesy for the week.

"I know, and I'm sorry, but this couldn't wait until next week."

"This better be important."

"You busy?" he asked.

She hated when he asked stupid questions. "I'm always busy."

"You know I'm coming home next week."

"*Hump*, still don't know how you getting out early."

"Good behavior."

"That's what you say. Sure you didn't cut another deal?"

"No deals. Just good behavior."

"I heard J-Rock got triple life. You get a dime but coming home in only Five. Sounds like another deal to me. What you think?"

"J-Rock popped a rookie cop. Shot him dead during a routine traffic stop. What the hell was I supposed to do?"

"Whatever."

"Baby, listen..."

"Who you calling *baby*?

"I need a place to stay. Just for a little while."

She laughed. "No."

"Three months tops. Promise I won't cramp your style."

"Don't worry about cramping my style because you won't have the opportunity."

The shower turned off. His wash lasted seven minutes, and thirty seven seconds. It took her only four minutes to lather, scrub, and one minute to rinse. She made a mental note to speak with him about being wasteful.

"You act like I'm asking you to go kill somebody. All I'm asking is for a spot on your floor."

"Kill for you?" She laughed.

"I wouldn't steal a bag of chips for you. I'm embarrassed to even claim you as my baby daddy."

A moment passed. Heavy breathing on both ends. He wanted a piece of her square footage. A home that she'd worked so hard to maintain and keep, he wanted.

"A spot on your floor, nothing more."

"Shut up, let me think."

Jazzman paced across her master suite. Thoughts rushing her like the speed of light. "This is a bad time. I can't," she said without much consideration.

"I'm begging. Three months. Hopefully not even that long. Just need an address."

"What happened with your aunt? Why can't she take you in?"

"She died."

She brought a single hand to her chest. "When?"

"Last week. Fucked me up. Yvette back to getting high. She lost the apartment while Aunty was in the hospital. Didn't know she was in the hospital. Been calling for weeks, been writing too. Parole Officer took a routine trip out there to survey the spot today, you know; make sure everything was on the up and up."

"And?"

"And there was no apartment. Yvette didn't pay the rent for months, plus she started a fire."

"A fire?"

"Don't know the details of how, but there was a fire." He took a long painstaking breath.

"You're all I've got."

She blew air. "There's got to be somebody else."

"There isn't."

She smelled his aftershave fighting its way between the cracks in the door. Aloe and Lavender infused with a bit of Almond captured her. *Damn!* She had her own issues.

"You and me under the same roof," she shook her head. "It won't work."

"I can't go back to Brooklyn."

Dead Silence.

The bathroom door opened. They made eye contact. He was dressed in jogging pants and tank top. Arms defined, chest hard, lips soft, eyes that made her want to have his baby. *Damn!* He mouthed that he was leaving. She held up a single finger. He tapped the face of his watch. She made a face which caused him to find some patience. He took a seat near the fire place, tossed another log in to buy time.

"It won't work," she said eyeing her lover from across the room. He was so damn fine, so damn sexy, so pleasing with his giving.

"Do it for Jacob," he said with desperation rattling every word.

"Don't do that."

"Don't do what?"

"You know what, this conversation is over."

"Okay, you're right. I'm sorry for trying to use him, but don't you think it would be good for us to bond?"

Bond. An adhesive love. That's all she ever wanted was for him and his son to bond. From the beginning, she tried her best to make sure Tony was a part of Jacobs's life. She compromised herself in more ways than she'd like to admit. Her son's happiness came first. It was Tony who jeopardized their livelihood. It was he who put their son in harm's way. But as usual, it was left up to the woman to hold things down.

"I can't do it."

"Why?"

"Because I've done enough, don't you think?"

"Jazzy just give me a chance."

Her chin touched her shoulder as she looked back at him. He loved it when she did that. It showed off her great cheekbones, and pouty lips. He sniffed her thong. She tossed the cherry scented candle at him. He blocked it with his heavy hand. She laughed, forgetting just that quickly about Tony.

"I'm not seeing the humor in all of this. A boy needs his father."

"Look, you can't live off me. My ends are barely meeting. Just got laid off, lost my job at the airlines. My mortgage due, I've got bills."

"I'll get a job. I've acquired some skills while in here," he said proudly.

"Forklift jobs don't pay that much."

"Thanks for your vote of confidence."

He came up behind her, rubbed the back of her neck, and kissed it. She didn't want him to leave. She now, all of a sudden, wanted him to stay. He mouthed, *call me later.* She held up an agitated finger. Her pleading eyes told him to sit. He obeyed.

"I'll have my parole officer contact you with the details."

"What part of *no* don't you understand?"

Rick rose midway.

"Sit down," she demanded.

He sat, checked his watch again, and exhaled frustration.

"Is that my son? Let me speak to him."

His cell phone buzzed again. His eyes went to his waist. Her eyes followed. Agitations painted her face. She wondered who was calling him. Whoever was blowing up his phone would just have to wait.

"I told you he was asleep, damn."

"Then who you talking to?"

"Don't question me."

"Is that your man or sumthin?" he asked with a slither of sarcasm.

"Maybe, maybe not, what's it to you?"

"Look, just think about it. Remember, I can't go back to Brooklyn. Streets don't forget."

She snickered. "Streets never forget, especially when snitching comes into play."

She hung up, made a frustrated noise, and snatched a fist full of her messy extensions. He watched as she walked in circles, mumbling, pouting, arms folded, face tight with anger. He gave her a couple of minutes, gave her time to fight an internal fight before speaking.

"Let me guess, Tony, right?"

He knew only what she told him. He knew just the basics, nothing more then a name and a charge. He was a number, a convict, a snitch. He was Jacob's father, her ex-man. A grimy nigga, always scrambling, always looking to come up, always looking to take down, cold hearted.

She nodded yes. "Sorry for throwing the candle."

"You messed up my new Air Jordan's but its all good."

He stood up, pulled her into his chest, kissed her lips. She rested for a quick second, felt his heart beat, felt his warmth. He rubbed her neck, releasing the tension, relaxing her nerves. "So what did he say that's got you all upset?"

She looked up, their eyes connected. He looked concerned, looked a bit nervous. She could tell that he was bracing himself for the worse. "Thought you were in a rush," she said giving way to a partial grin. Vibrations from his hip separated them. He looked down at his phone, so did she. It was an un-programmed number, prefixes began with 718. He mashed the *off* button.

"If you don't have time…"

He interrupted her with a kiss on the lips. It was nothing out of the ordinary for Rick to stop all that he was doing. He was attentive, he was kind, he was a real man who catered to her needs.

"You're more important."

"He's coming home next week."

"Home, home where, home here?"

"His aunt died, cousin back to smoking, and he has no other family. Brooklyn sure as hell doesn't want him."

He frowned. "What do you mean Brooklyn doesn't want him?"

She smiled. He wasn't from the streets, which was what she loved about him most. He was naive to the hustle, to the life she's always known. He was a good ole boy from Savanna, Georgia. He went to school, had a masters degree and a comfy cushion in his 401k. He owned a ritzy, upscale loft in Montauk, which was located in East

Hampton, dotting Long Island's South Shore. He grew up surrounded by water in the summer. His family owned a vacation property in Tampa. He had the privilege of seeing Paris as an intern, fulfilling his apprenticeship under the direct authority of one of the wealthiest men in the world. Rick was top pedigree.

"He's coming to live here; in this house, *your* house?"

She shrugged. "Haven't decided yet."

"So you're considering it?"

One hand on her waist, the other gripped her forehead. She couldn't let him go back to Brooklyn. He'd be dead in a week. She knew the game. She understood the consequences of his actions. Snitching on top dogs like Barry and J-Rock meant you were never to show your face again. It meant Brooklyn was off limits. She questioned his decision to go back there in the first place.

"God works in mysterious ways," she whispered.

"How so?"

"Huh?"

"You said God works in mysterious ways. How so?"

Who would have thought Tony's aunt would die, cousin would backslide, lose the apartment and force him in her direction. Who would have predicted he would need her. She looked at Rick. He waited patiently for an answer, a decision.

"Talk to me," he requested.

She liked him. She liked him a lot. They had fun together. Weekend trips to Tampa, just him, her and Jacob. Sandy beaches in the Caribbean during one of the worse recessions in history. He spoiled her.

"I'm waiting for some money to come in from an investment. Soon as I get the check, I'll break you off a little something."

She knew that translated into *my parents will be sending me a check.* He was a trust fund kid. College tuition paid for by Mommy and Daddy. Mortgage paid regardless if he stayed unemployed indefinitely. She hugged him.

"You're in the same boat I'm in. You keep your money. I'll be fine."

After seven solid years of working for Ridgemore Investments, Rick was laid off. He survived off his savings, severance package and unemployment benefits. Monthly extra's poured in from his parents, *just because.*

"You're saying my money ain't good here?"

"Last time I said that you stuck ten grand underneath my mattress."

He laughed. "You were going to lose your house. I couldn't let that happen."

She looked into his eyes. "Maybe I'm living above my means. Maybe this house was too big to begin with. It's just me and my son. What was I thinking when I bought this big house? Maybe I should downsize?"

He made a face, usually done so when the mood was too heavy. She laughed.

"In all honesty, this house isn't big enough. You deserve a castle, with a foyer paved in gold. Maids, Butlers, and a gang of lawn care folks to mow and keep your garden pretty. You deserve a personal driver, private jet, the clearest stones, and access to your own island." He took her hand, "You deserve more than this."

"You have champagne wishes and caviar dreams."

"I was born with exquisite taste. Besides that, I know royalty when I see it." He winked.

She blushed. "Thanks for bailing me out."

"Don't consider it a bailout."

"Thanks for the loan then. I'll pay you back, promise."

He grabbed her hands. "Don't consider it a loan. I'm doing my job as your man. I'm taking care of my lady."

His claim made her a bit uncomfortable. Even though they've been exclusive for quite a while, neither of them placed titles. Neither claimed ownership, but monogamy was definitely understood.

"I'll hit you off as soon as the money comes in. I know the water bill sky high, cable behind. I see the stack of bills on the kitchen counter. Don't think I'm oblivious to the struggle. I got you babe."

She exhaled. Her shoulders relaxed. It felt good to be recognized. It felt good to have a man who did, without asking. Rick was not only fine, but a stress reliever. He had the right words, right tools, and right moves to ease her cluttered mind.

"You sure know how to paint a perfect picture."

"In due time, with a little patience, that perfect picture can become reality."

"You don't have to feel obligated. Just because we have sexual relations doesn't mean you have to..."

"*Whoa.* Sexual relations? Is that all I am to you?"

He looked hurt. She didn't mean to sound insensitive, but she'd been promised the world before. There's been plenty before him, and just may be plenty after him. She liked him a lot, but couldn't let that wall down just yet. She had to protect her heart.

"Of course not. I'm just saying, don't feel obligated."

"What kind of man would I be to stand back and watch all your hard work and efforts go down the drain?"

He pulled her close. "You're young, talented, gifted, black, and you're a single mother raising a boy into a man. I can't let this recession take you under."

"You sound like you're apart of the Obama Administration."

They both laughed. Silence consumed them after the last giggle. Times were hard, harder than ever before. Depression was at her doorstep, knocking. He tipped her chin, and looked deep into her eyes. That far away look, he hated. It was a spirit of doubt, of failure that crept up on her like a bad cold. He needed for her to trust him more than anything now.

"So, where does this leave us?" he asked, getting back to the matter of discussion.

"Don't jump the gun. I'm still pondering."

"What's there to ponder? Either he paroles here or he goes to some halfway house."

"What you know about that?"

"That is the only other option right?"

"I don't know."

"My parents disowned my sister. After her third trip to the joint, they denied her an address. She wasn't welcomed. Not even to visit. She paroled to a halfway house."

"I didn't know you had a sister."

He looked down at the carpet again. Candle wax stiffened a spot beneath his feet.

"She's got me by five years. We were never close. Straight after high school she left Savannah and moved to Atlanta. She attended Georgia Tech, worked part time at a coffee house, and had her own crib."

His eyes landed on the space between her brows. He was someplace else, in another time, year, recalling something warm and fuzzy. "Moms flipped her wig when my sister asked for IKEA furniture."

"What's wrong with IKEA?"

"Nothing, but mom's hated furniture that came boxed with a million screws. She said it was cheap wood with cardboard durability. My sister begged her until my mother got sick and tired of being sick and tired."

"I'll never forget the bright fluffy pillows, retro style lamps, curvy mirrors, compartments, baskets, cubbies, and the sofa had a washable removable slip cover. It was practical, especially for a freshman college student."

She giggled. "Sounds like a good start. Where'd she go wrong?"

"She hooked up with some big time dope boy, started drinking, smoking weed, skipping class. Eventually she dropped out, most likely got kicked out. Either way, she fell off, turned to a higher high. Things just spiraled out of control from there."

"Where is she now?"

"She died."

"Oh my God, how?"

"Let's not talk about her."

"Okay, I'm sorry. Didn't mean to…"

"It's all good. It's just that my parents built a foundation for us both. They struggled so that we didn't have to. My mother didn't want her to have IKEA furniture because she felt she deserved better. All she had to do was follow the rules. My mother…" He swallowed the lump in his throat. "Her heart aches over the situation."

"I'm so sorry."

"She used to call me crying every day after my sister died. She wanted to know where she went wrong as a parent."

"It's not her fault."

"I know. But back then you couldn't tell her this. However, these days aren't as bad. Conversations about my sister have been reduced to birthdays, some holidays. Pops, well he handled things differently. He's got that *whatever* attitude, but I know deep down he hurt the same."

"When did she pass?"

"Five years ago."

"I can only imagine."

A familiar sadness consumed him. She knew the looked that clouded his world. She was all too familiar with the emptiness in his eyes. She had a father she never knew, a mother who was six feet under and an aunty who passed of Cancer. Life had thrown her several blows, but she managed to keep her sanity. Barely.

Rick took in a chest full of air. "Whatever you decide, whom ever you choose, I got your back."

"Rick..."

He held up his hand. "No need to explain."

"He needs an address. Ninety days tops."

"So, you've made up your mind?"

She looked away, "No. Yes. Not really." She took a deep breath. Confusion won the battle. "We got history," she blurted, then winced.

"He's Jacob's father. A boy needs his father, right?"

"You don't understand, babe. It's apart of the code."

"The code?"

"We have history, history I just want to forget. Just want to move on. But..."

"But he's Jacob's father. I understand completely."

"It goes deeper than that."

"You still love him?"

"Not even a little bit."

He stared at her. She held his gaze. Looking away was only an indication of guilt. She had nothing to feel guilty for. Had the shoe been on the other foot, and she needed a place to call home, Tony would have accommodated her, at least she hoped so. She pulled her micro braids back, wrapping them into a bun.

"I need a drink."

"Don't mean to stress you," he said, tugging at a single braid that fell short of the rest.

"It's not you."

"Then what?"

"Everything seems to be happening at once. Everything coming down on me, all at the same time. My back is up against a wall."

He tugged at her loose braid. "Momma said there'd be days like this," he quoted.

"My momma said nothing of the sort."

Jazzman barely knew her mother. She was just a kid when they had to scrape up money to bury her. Aunt Jenny went door to door and took up a collection. He tipped her chin, breaking her thoughts.

"Let's take a bath."

"But you just showered."

He gave her a naughty look.

"I'm feeling dirty all of a sudden."

CHAPTER 6

C olonial style, lakefront property sat at the core of the cul-de-sac. Four-sided brick. Double chimney reinforced the homes symmetry. Shingles, yellow like the sun. A line of naked bushes outlined the curves of the house. Not much grass, but enough to toss a ball to and fro. Modest size newly constructed porch sat two empty flower urns. Each knee high, sculpted in fine detail. Three steps away, a red door. No peephole.

"She's done well for herself," Roy admitted.

"*Focus* has always been her middle name," Lou-Lou added.

"Kids will do that for you," Roy said, having known from experience once upon a time.

"Do what?"

"Give you focus. Give you purpose. Make you think, and re-think prior to making a move. No hasty business, especially when you got shorties involved. *Naw Mean?*"

"I guess," she said, not knowing first hand.

Implanted ground solar lights dotted the driveway, stream lining the walkway with a soft glow. Lou-Lou couldn't help but admire the American dream. Deep down, somewhere in the pit of her stomach she yearned for a place to call home. Not just a house. Bradley had provided that and then some, but a home. A family, perhaps a husband with some *mini-me's* to call hers would be nice.

Easterly winds whipped and wailed vigorously. Wind chimes tinkered. The sky rumbled. A chorus of earthly sounds blended. There was a house on the right and the left, sandwiching the best looking digs in the middle. *She always made the right decisions.* Lou-Lou thought, feeling a tinge of envy pass through her.

"Shit," she blurted.

"What?"

"*Hum,* it's about to rain." A slight inconvenience for sure, but no real worry. Divulging her *Hater-rade* to Roy wasn't a good look. She'd rather drink that cup of green poison silently.

He laughed. "Scared of a little water?"

"No, I'm just saying."

Roy twisted his fitted slightly to the left, and reclined his seat. He had nothing but time. Lou-Lou wondered why Roy wasn't frantically looking over his shoulder. Why wasn't he on pins about being back in a city he'd set fire to? He'd caused despair, wreaked destitute on families, starving families who on many levels depended on the hustle of their fathers, brothers, uncles, many whom Roy had laid to sleep, permanently.

"I wonder who the Ranger Rover belongs to," he said giving reference to the vehicle parked in the driveway.

"It's probably hers."

"Could be, but I doubt it. She's not a truck kind of chic. She prefers to ride low." He grinned, staring off towards the house like he had X-Ray vision.

"Ah damn."

He glanced at her. "Ah damn, what?"

Roy had that look in his eye. *Entitlement. Right. Claim.* In his mind Jazzman was the one who got away.

"*Roy,*" she called his name, warning written all over her voice.

"What I do?"

He drummed his fingers against the steering wheel, winked. Seeing Jazzman face- to-face after years of being presumably dead, kept him alive. Her face, her grace, her smile, her body language was something he held onto. Even in the wake of his anger, his feelings of betrayal, he couldn't forget the way she laughed. Her giggle, so innocent, school girl like.

"I've got a bad feeling about this Roy."

"Relax."

"I can't."

The porch light came on bringing both of their faces close to the windshield. The front door opened, and out walked two individuals. Kissing and hugging, and rubbing their way towards the parked truck. It wasn't long before they noticed Jazzman's face. She was beaming. A set of eyes beamed back at her.

Roy's face turned cold. That spark in his eye, lost behind a menacing twitch, and uncontrollable quivering lip.

"That's Rick. Her man," Lou-Lou said, with certainty, "And I guess the Range belongs to him."

He glared at her. "Obviously."

Roy was sick. He wondered how long the public display of affection would last. Touching, grabbing, licking, sucking face as if their chance would never come again.

"Get it-Get it girl," Lou-Lou said, impressed with the show.

The sudden down pour of rain interrupted the couple's soft porn moment. Rick jumped into the passenger seat, blowing kisses at Jazzman as she stood on the porch in her robe waving bye.

"Oh, you ain't know?" Lou-Lou smirked. Finally she knew something he didn't know. For that, she felt compelled to fill him in.

"Shall I bring you up to speed?"

He glared at her. "What you think?"

"He's a *Trust Fund* kid. Pretty boy from Savannah, Georgia. His parents practice medicine. He loves her, adores Jacob. He used to work for Ridgemore Investments. He ran the Global Risk Management Division."

He looked stunned. "Bradley introduced them?"

"Sort of-kind of."

"What do you mean? It's either yes or no," he said aggressively.

"Bradley invited me to a company picnic, so in turn, I invited Jazzman and Jacob. I wasn't about to be amongst all those white folks without some back-up. It was a Central Park gathering for all the employees. You know, cook-out, Frisbee, kite flying, chit-chatting and what have you. Rick saw Jazzman sitting by her lonesome, reading. He dug her style. He approached, kicked the *Willy Bo-Bo* and the rest is history."

Roy laughed. "He probably don't know the meaning of kicking the *Willy Bo-Bo*. Did you see that guy? Give me a break."

"I'll be the first to admit, he's a cornball, but he's perfect for her."

"Perfect for her? Yeah, okay." His tone was troubling. She wanted to stop talking. Cease communication. Just forget she even mentioned Rick, but Roy insisted on knowing all there was to know about Jazzman's *so-called* love interest.

"Rick was let go from the company about a year ago. He got swept up in the first wave of lay-offs. With Lehman Brothers bankrupt, and AIG rowing down a river of bailouts, Ridgemore started to restructure, cut back. The Global Risk Management Division suddenly wasn't so global."

"How so?"

"You know how these companies do? Here today, gone tomorrow. Open one division, close another. Recruit one executive, ax the other. Corner office occupied with a *Yes-Man*, tomorrow it's empty. A race to who will fill that spot. It's all a game. Kiss and suck the tip of CFO, CIO, VP's dicks just to get ahead."

Roy chuckled. "Sounds worst then the streets."

She raised her brow. "You don't know the half. Corporate Thug'*N* is real. Globally, Ridgemore was losing money. *Millions.* There was no need for Rick, and eight hundred other employees for that matter. They let him go and closed the division. No gold watch, no farewell party. No, *He's a Jolly Good Fellow* sing-along. Just a personal escort from company grounds and a measly severance package to tie him over until his next gig."

Deep down in the pit of his pinky toe, Roy actually felt sorry for the man. That human emotion lasted for only a second. He listened to her speak. Lou-Lou had the inside scoop on Corporate America.

"So, Ridgemore lost money in one area, but gained a ton of business in another. Like the drug game. Weight not moving as fluid as projected, but individual sales are up, therefore keeping business at a steady pace," he said.

She smiled at him. He was always the brain of the crew. Roy was patient, always willing to learn. He took his time, researched a thing before buying into it. His steps, calculated, measured. Maybe that's why'd he survived thus far.

"Ridgemore Investments, a small boutique operation indeed, but they grew in the wake of a crisis. Investors started pulling their eggs from other outfits, all at once. Some transferred their business to Ridgemore; others transferred what was left of their portfolio to offshore banks."

"Hiding money?"

"No doubt. If you were smart you did. Those who hadn't lost the shirts off their backs buried what was left of their treasure in Swiss accounts, Cobblestone banks in France."

He rubbed his chin. "Interesting."

Roy was never a big spender. He lived off the essentials. Nice secluded crib, modest car, clothes average. His remedy to staying on top: *Hibernate.* Offshore accounts, stuffing cash in piggy banks the IRS couldn't touch. As old money slept, he worked on generating new dollars.

"Ridgemore played the middle, stayed where it was safe. Headlining the game were Lehman and AIG, both falling hard from grace."

"Guess the middle isn't a bad place to be."

"In this economy, the middle is a great place to be. Those who lead the pack get shot down first. Those lagging behind usually fold before they reach year seven. In some cases, if they're lucky, they sell off to the highest bidder. Merger."

She grinned, feeling proud that she'd learned something from Bradley besides how to sit and act proper at a dinner table. When Bradley and his comrades discussed business, she was all ears. Unlike the high maintenance, sadity hoes that huddled over dessert, chit-chatting about their next spa date; she was soaking up game. Besides, she hated being labeled. The color of her skin alone caused people in Bradley's circle to pass judgment. She came equipped with enough knowledge, just in case a snob tried to pull her card.

The Range crept by, easing out the subdivision slowly as if children were out playing. Roy kept his eyes glued to the license plate, memorizing every last digit and letter.

"He's clean. No priors. We already checked him out." She read his thoughts.

"We?"

"Come on now, Jazzman is *Miss Careful.* She's not about to let just any dude in a fancy suit come into her life, her son's life. He passed the Three-Check-Rule."

"Three-Check-Rule?"

"*Health Check. Criminal Check. Credit Check.* Jazzy's no fool. Rick's clean as a whistle. No STD's, no deadly disease, no criminal past, and his credit is A-1."

Roy nodded. "Good girl."

He watched the vehicle until he could no longer spot it out his rearview. *Still, I'll look a little deeper. Everyone has skeletons.* Lou-Lou pulled her cell from her purse, dialed Jazzman's number.

"It's disconnected. She must have changed it."

"Go knock on the door."

"Hell no. You crazy," she said, pouting. "She was very specific. I'm not to come near her, her house, and especially Jacob."

"What you do that bad?" he asked, now intrigued with curiosity.

Agitated fingers massaged her temples. "I'd rather not say."

"Can't be that bad."

"We don't rock like that no more. She's different. I'm different. We on two different levels. It's complicated."

He gripped the door handle, and slipped one leg out. Roy had no time to babysit guilty souls. *Females.*

"Where you going?" she whispered.

"Time is money. We need to hit this nigga before somebody else does."

Roy crossed the nose of the rental, moving swiftly across the street.

This is crazy. She jumped out and followed his lead. Rain poured on their heads until they reached the covered porch. The outdoor patio sconce was easily removable. Roy unscrewed the bulb, placing it inside the empty urn. He couldn't risk Jazzman hitting the switch, shining a light on his face.

Roy hit the ding-dong twice, tapped against the door once. Lou-Lou chewed her bottom lip, looked back over her shoulder, a complete nervous wreck. She knew this was a bad idea. They heard shuffling behind the door, heard two locks click, and heard her voice, full of love. "I know-I know, you left your wallet."

Jazzman swung open the door, waving a leather billfold. Cleavage peeking through the top of her terry cloth robe. Her smile faded. Her body trembled. Her stomach liquefied in fear. She turned, bolted towards the keypad. He grabbed her, but a second too late. She managed to trigger the silent alarm. Roy pulled his tool from the small of his waist, pointed it at her head.

"You shouldn't have done that."

The phone rang almost instantly. Roy snatched Jazzman by the hair, forced her towards the kitchen. She collapsed to the floor, breathing hard, and crying just the same. The cordless was mounted to the wall. He grabbed it.

"Make it believable or else."

At first she said nothing. He nudged the back of her head with the pistol.

"This is Jazzman Bridges. Yes, I'm fine. My password is...is... *Isis*."

"Close the fucking door," Roy barked.

Lou-Lou jumped from the sound of Roy's voice, realizing the door was still ajar. She closed it, but didn't alter her stance. She stood frozen, like a mime. Jazzman fought Roy tooth and nail. He had a time trying to restrain, partly because he didn't want to hurt her.

From the kitchen, to the living room, she put up a fight. He forced her to the sofa, leaned his solid frame against her body and whispered, "Calm down." Jazzman's watery eyes shifted across the room, landed on Lou-Lou. Screams muffled, *help me!* Restricted by pressure against her lips, tears communicated for her.

"Don't scream. I'm not here to hurt you."

Looking up at him in a horrified daze, she stilled her body, relaxed. Roy slowly removed his hand, and then the rest of his body drifted away from Jazzman's frame. She quickly sat up, scooted towards the far end of the sofa. Both legs pulled in like a scared little child. Bulging eyes darted from Roy to Lou-Lou, and back.

"What is this?"

Lou-Lou said nothing. Instead, she folded her arms. *This was Roy's idea. Not mine. He better get to explaining,* she thought. Roy slowly reached out to touch Jazzman's shoulder. She flinched in horror.

"Don't touch me. I'll scream."

"Baby, it's me. Roy."

She closed her eyes, shook her head. "No. Roy is dead. Right Lou-Lou?"

Lou-Lou knocked her hips across the room. She stopped in front of the big bay window, and froze. A picture of her, Jazzman and Jacob was framed in wood. The word *Family* etched in cursive. She swallowed hard. *She still loves me.*

"Not exactly," Lou-Lou said, softly.

Jazzman started to hyperventilate. "I don't understand. He's dead."

He reached out to hold her, pull her near his heart.

"Feel my chest rise and fall. I'm alive."

She screamed as promised. Again, Roy found himself pressed against her, big hand muffling her screech.

"Let her go Roy," Lou-Lou requested.

"No. Not until she stops screaming."

"She will, won't you Jazzman?"

Jazzman's eyes shifted towards Lou-Lou. She blinked yes. Roy released her slowly. Jazzman jumped up, ran towards the laundry room, Roy leaped off the sofa, tried to catch her, but knocked his knee against the coffee table. He fumbled and fell.

Sandwiched between a Spiderman fleece blanket and some fabric softener was the burner. Jazzman doubled back, gripping her toaster, pointing it from Roy to Lou-Lou. Tears and snot dripped, but her arm was steady. Her finger caressed the trigger.

"Somebody better get to talking." Her voice was ferocious. She meant business.

"Whoa Ma, chill. It's me," Roy said, struggling to stand. He rubbed his knee.

Jazzman narrowed her eyes in on Lou-Lou. "Tell me something or I promise I'll kill him. *Twice.*"

Lou-Lou opened her mouth to speak, but Roy cut her off.

"I'll explain, just put that down before you hurt somebody."

Jazzman became hysterical. Her arms got to moving, her voice elevating several notches. Both Roy and Lou-Lou ducked and dodged as to avoid any potentially discharged ammo. Jazzman was temporarily insane, which they understood, but getting shot while she experienced momentary delirium wasn't a part of the plan. He inched in close, tried to grab her but then stopped. The barrel was at the tip of his nose. His arms outstretched, surrendering.

"Baby, it's me."

It looked like him. It sounded like him. But it wasn't him. Roy was dead. "Nigga, back the fuck up," she demanded. Roy eased back on his tippy-toes, grinning. *The safety's on.* He thought of snatching the tool from her hands, but didn't. He needed her trust. "I see you still got the Nina I gave you for your birthday."

It was fresh out the box. She hadn't even busted it once. She lowered her tool, slid to a crouched position, cried. He knelt down, placed a firm hand against her shoulder. Her grip loosened, burner slipped to the floor, followed by a thud. He grabbed the Nina by the muzzle, slipped it into the small of his back.

"They said you were dead."

"The world needed to believe that. *You* needed to believe that. It was for your own good. Both of you." Roy looked up at Lou-Lou, only for a second, and returned his gaze.

Jazzman's heart lurched as Roy pulled her into his arms. *Oh God, he smells the same.* She held onto him. Face buried into his chest. His arms bore a familiar comfort.

Roy didn't waste time. He got down to the specifics. He explained everything. He spoke of things Lou-Lou hadn't known about until then. He exposed himself; put all his cards on the table. Lou-Lou realized their connection was deeper, stronger. He trusted her whole heartedly. He loved her. She loved him.

Jazzman was loyal. There was no need to threaten her into secrecy, unlike Lou-Lou. *"If you repeat an ounce of what I tell you, I'll kill you."* His voice rang in her head like a warning bell. *As if I would mention it.*

They were perfect for each other. Their styles, one in the same. Their chemistry layered in love, loyalty, undeniable respect. Their lust connection, massive, hard not to notice, even feel the fire burn between them. They had the makings of a beautiful partnership. However, their love could never be more than just a feeling. Because of Cookie.

"Things got ugly between us. I'm sorry for..."

Jazzman planted a finger against his lips. "No, it was my fault. I said things..."

"Shsssh." He wiped her tears. "Forget about it."

Her head pressed against his chest. She could feel his heart. Roy signaled for Lou-Lou to join them. She took two steps forward, and then took two back when she noticed Jazzman giving her the stank-eye. *She hates me.*

"I'll wait in the car."

Jazzman snapped her head away from Roy's warm body. "Do that."

Feisty, he loved that about her. He wanted to suck her face. Lip-lock her right then and there, but he fell back. He needed to be the voice of reason. Family fought, argued, but at the end of the day, Jazzman and Lou-Lou needed each other.

"Situations can be fixed if you allow it," Roy said to the both of them.

"Everything ain't meant to be fixed. Some things are meant to stay broke," Jazzman said.

"She's right. I'm out."

"Hold up Lou, we need to squash this now." Roy insisted as he stood.

Jazzman giggled. "Bitches kill me. Your victimized attitude don't mean shit."

Lou-Lou whirled around, shifted her weight from one leg to the next. "Excuse me?"

"Did I stutter?" Jazzman stood, took a step forward, but Roy gripped her arm, held her back. "Let me go," she demanded.

So he did. The last thing he wanted was to end up on her shit list, at least not this soon. Jazzman stomped her way towards Lou-Lou, stopping just inches away from her. Bottom lip pulled in, fist clenched. "You've got some nerve bringing your ass up in my house."

"Trust and believe, it wasn't my idea."

"*Ooh*, bitch... If my son wasn't upstairs..." Jazzman left the rest to the imagination.

Outside the rain poured, leaving no room for visibility. Emotions running high. Two seething cats looking to claw their way to battle, stood directly across from one another.

"We're family. Let's clear the air now, and be done with it," Roy suggested.

Jazzman cut her eyes in Roy's direction. "I came this close to losing my kid. On account of her, my son would have been snatched up. So, don't tell me about family. She almost ruined mine."

Roy looked at Lou-Lou, expecting her to take the floor, defend herself, but she didn't. She just stood there, like a mute. Succumbing to Jazzman's anger was only right. She owed her that much.

"Fuck her, and fuck anybody who thinks I'm overreacting. Walk in my shoes, then try speaking calmly about this bitch."

Jazzman's feelings were legitimate. Kids and money were the two things that shouldn't be tampered with. Lou-Lou had managed to run interference on both ends.

"I called you, to apologize for the ten thousandth time. You cursed me out, called me all kinds of bitches and hung up," said Lou-Lou, as tears fell from her lids. She wanted forgiveness. She needed it. With all the fine dining, splendid trips, and expensive tangibles Bradley offered, a void still remained. Jazzman and Jacob were her family.

"You gave a direct order. I went against you. You know I would never hurt Jacob."

"But you could have, you almost... Child services wanted to..." Jazzman got choked up. Instead of crying, she walked away.

Lou-Lou closed the door, locked it. *Guess I'm staying.*

"Jazzman, I'm sorry."

"Sorry? Really? That's funny."

"I swear, I never meant to hurt you."

"I warned you about José."

"I know. You did. I didn't listen."

"Wait, ya'll fighting over some broke ass wanna-be producer?" Roy laughed.

They both shot him a look which said their conflict ran deeper than that. José was a fraction of a man, a leech, a parasite who drank from Lou-Lou's cup of overflow.

"You let him use you, Lou."

"I know."

"He almost cost you your freedom. He almost cost me my son."

"I know. I know."

"He was pumping Crack out my backdoor, didn't you know?"

She wanted to lie, say that she was clueless, that she had no idea what José was up to. She wanted to plead her case, make it seem like she was in the dark about his dealings, seem like the innocent one. "He didn't do it all the time." *Ugh, did I just say that?*

It was the best she could come up with. Besides, part time hustlers deserved slack, right? José was a struggling producer. He needed to make ends-meet until somebody bought a track. His whole purpose of coming to Atlanta was to be a part of the Southern Explosion. New York had lost its edge. *Jay* was still at the top of his game, but he wasn't buying beats from the unknown. José left hundreds of messages for *Dupri*. He camped outside the *DTP* Headquarters, tried smooth talking the panties off the receptionist from *Grand Hustle*, but she was high maintenance and only dated rappers. Hustling was José's only other option, *right?*

"Once is one time too many."

"I didn't mean it like that, Jazzman. *For real*, I'm sorry."

José's skills were to eventually pay off. He was no drug dealer. He pushed poison just to stay in the light. Image was everything. The music industry was about faking it till you made it. And the silver lining was, when he made it, she made it. Flossing hard at the Source Awards, floor length mink to the BET Awards, air smooching *Nikki M*, winking and blowing kisses to *Drizzy*, bear hugging *Ross*, while sitting front row at the *Mayweather* fight in Vegas with her man José. *Dream deferred.*

"I almost lost my house, and my son."

"I know."

She didn't know. She couldn't possibly know how it felt to have a child snatched away. She wasn't a mother. She had no kids to call her own. Nobody depended on her, but *her*. People without kids made everything seem so damn unimportant.

"My son told his friends that he was sent to jail because his aunt's boyfriend sold drugs."

Lou-Lou gasped. She didn't know what to say. What could she say? What could she say to make it all better? She let a *part-time* drug dealer leave a footprint on Jacobs's life. "I know you hate me."

"You have no clue."

Jazzman moved across the room, flipped the light switch in the kitchen, and opened the ice box. She grabbed the *Absolute*, swung open the cabinet where she kept her collection of shot glasses. *Jamaica* led the pack, her favorite place of travel. Next was *Mexico, Bahamas, Atlanta, Vegas, both Carolinas, Florida, PR, DR, Virgin Islands, Hawaii, Amsterdam, Canada, St. Thomas, St. Maarten, Belize, and most recently Rio de Janeiro*. By definition, she was considered International. She settled on the Peach State, longing for a simplistic lifestyle, but her dreams came to a screeching halt. *All because of this bitch.* A slight growl escaped her.

Jazzman slammed the glass against the peninsula, poured. Courage spilled along the sides. Lou-Lou went out on a limb and followed Jazzman into the kitchen. They needed to get through this, put the madness to rest. She grabbed Jazzman's hands, pulled them to her heart. "I'm sorry." Her words were genuine. Jazzman felt her energy, her aurora, her vibes were all good, but yet and still she pulled away. Anger fueled her, covered her like a security blanket. The heat kept her warm. She wasn't ready to let go. Letting go was like saying *You Won!*

She pointed a finger inches away from Lou-Lou's face. A blatant act of disrespect. Lou-Lou sucked back a chest-full of air. Jazzman's obtrusive behavior was wearing thin. "You crossed me. I don't take shit like that lightly."

Lou-Lou was eighteen, new to Atlanta, with a duffle bag full of cash to blow. Meeting a guy like José was a dream-come-true. His car was flashy, his jewels were all official, and he was originally from New York.

To top things off he was part black, the rest Puerto Rican. A blend all young black girls wanted by their side. He had ambition when she met him. He talked a good talk, made her believe he was about to be put on. He was an aspiring producer, up and rising music mogul. His profile was perfect.

Jazzman slammed the shot glass against the peninsula, poured another round.

"They raided my damn house. We were new to the neighborhood." Embarrassment coated her face as if it happened just yesterday.

"I'm sorry."

Their last fallen out turned ugly, damn near physical. Red Dog squad kicked Jazzman's door in, raided her humble abode. Authorities found large amounts of substances that controlled and altered the mind and body. *"Put your hands where I can see them. Don't move."*

It was because of José that Jazzman had a 357 and double barrel shot gun pointed directly at her head. It was because of José that her front door was kicked in, *no-knock-warrant* style. It was because of him she almost lost her son to child services.

"I took you in."

"And I appreciate you doing what you did."

Lou-Lou was filthy broke; literally piss poor after only six months in Atlanta. The money from the Southside heist didn't last long. Irresponsible, careless, just plain stupid she was. Jazzman took her in, provided a roof, made sure she ate. She promised Isis that she would look out for Lou-Lou, and she did.

"You got evicted from your apartment. It was me who helped you move your things into storage. I twisted my damn ankle helping you carry your flatscreen, and what do you do? You repay me by allowing that nothing-ass-nigga in my house. He wasn't even man enough to help you move your things, let alone pay your rent."

José promised her the world, yet when her eviction notice came he was nowhere to be found. *M.I.A.*

"You said he would hold you down? Looks like he did exactly what I said he would do."

"You're right."

Her admittance to stupidity wasn't enough. Jazzman decided the drive that rusty needle a little further, a lot deeper. "You let that smooth nigga come in and make you lose everything. You burned through all your money in six months. You got evicted from your apartment. He wrapped your brand new Charger around a tree fleeing from the police. Then... *then* when I thought you couldn't be any more gullible, you let him sell drugs out *my* house... the police ran up in *my* crib." She pounded a closed fist into an open hand.

Lou-Lou was beginning to feel threatened. Jazzman's body language wasn't exactly communicating peacefully. Roy peeped the same awareness, so he moved in, slipping an arm around her waist. "Have a seat."

"No!" Jazzman barked.

Roy gave her a blank stare, easing back on his toes. She still had the floor.

Only Jazzman can get away with shit like that, Lou-Lou thought.

"My situation was good in Atlanta. My son and I were happy there. You fucked that up."

Jazzman closed her eyes and saw the horrid nightmare play out, felt her body being yanked from beneath the covers, and then her face forced to the floor. She heard Jacobs cries, heard him beg for his mommy. Heard Lou-Lou scream as José jumped out the second floor window. Felt the steel cuffs slapped against her wrist. *Dream deferred.*

"Because of you there were unmarked cars sitting outside my house for months. They followed me to work, to night school, and back home. They watched my son while he played with his friends. I couldn't shop peacefully for Tampons without feeling the heat on my neck. I had no choice but to come back to New York."

"I'm so sorry," Lou-Lou cried.

"Can't be too sorry, you're still fucking him."

Lou-Lou gasped, looked away. *How does she know?* Jazzman warned her about José. He was dirty, low down and not to be trusted. She knew his style, she read him from the second he opened his mouth. "He hollered at me first. Remember?"

"Oh, so you wanna take it there?" Lou-Lou felt her temper rising. Jazzman was going too far now.

"Say I'm lying."

"That's what you say, honestly I don't recall that."

"*Hump*, and there it is. See Roy, she's not completely sorry. If she were, she would be ready to admit, confess the truth and nothing but the truth."

"Alright Judge Judy," he joked, but there wasn't a damn thing funny.

José hollered at Jazzman first. He wanted her number that night at the club, wanted to dig deep into her honey walls that very same night, but she shut him down. *They* were new in Atlanta. It made no sense in jumping into bed with the first dude flashing a little cash. Jazzman had her sights set on bigger and better things, and José just didn't fit the bill. She wanted something different, which meant she had to do something different.

"No José, at no time, in my house, period. That was the rule."

"I know."

"Stop saying you know. You don't know shit," Jazzman yelled, pouring herself another shot.

Lou-Lou violated rule number one almost immediately. She waited for Jazzman to leave for work, made sure Jacob was fed, dressed and off to school before calling up her man. He was there every morning, like clockwork christening a home that didn't belong to him. They did it on the kitchen table, living room sofa, Jacob's bed, Jazzman's bed, squirming their sweaty bodies against her expensive duvet.

Roy grabbed the liquor bottle from Jazzman. "You've had enough."

"Hey, give it back." She tried for the bottle, but Roy placed it back inside the icebox.

"This bitch needs to know exactly how I feel," Jazzman said angrily.

"Then tell her."

"*I will*... but I need my *drink*," Jazzman said with a slur.

"No more liquor." Roy posted up in front of the freezer like a club bouncer on a Friday night.

Deep down in Jazzman's heart she knew it was time to move on. Let go. Her Aunt Jenny used to say, *Anger is only a trick of the devil*. It held you bondage to toxic emotions. "*All* is... *all* is... *all* is forgiven," Jazzman said, now hammered.

"You sure, I mean come tomorrow, next month or next year we won't have to revisit this issue? I'm tired of fighting."

"*Can't* promise that I won't *catch… catch* a feeling, can't promise I *won't… won't* be *rrrr*eminded and… *and* get mad all over again, but can promise I *won't* throw it up in your face, just because… know what I'm saying?"

Lou-Lou nodded. "I can live with that."

Jazzman pushed Roy out the way, opened the fridge, pulled out a cold bottle of Corona. She popped the top and placed the icy rim to her mouth. Before she could swallow, Roy snatched the drink from her hands. He searched the pantry, and found instant coffee. Moments later Jazzman had a hot cup sitting in front of her. Silence consumed them as she sipped.

"I think about her all the time," said Jazzman.

"Who?" Lou-Lou asked.

"Isis."

"Me too," Roy said.

"No seriously Roy. Lately, my thoughts have been with her, about her. If she was still alive, things would be different."

"Can't live in the past, Jazz," Roy said.

"I know. I'm just saying."

He grabbed her hand. "Don't do that."

Jazzman wiped a fallen tear, and sniffled. A second and third tear sprang forth. And just when she could no longer hold it together, her tears ran hot. He eased in next to her, pulled her close.

"It hurts," she confessed.

"I know it does."

Once again, they were having a moment. Lou-Lou didn't know whether to turn away or leave. *Oh God, get a room.* Roy kindly dabbed Jazzman's cheeks with the palm of his hand. She pressed her wet face, runny nose against his chest and stayed there for a few minutes.

Roy listened attentively as she complained about her issues, same issues half of America were dealing with. Same issues plaguing not only her country, but other countries as well. She shared the same burden as the white man, Chinese man, Native American man, Hispanic man, and all other hues in-between. Not having enough, just barely making it, was the same song sung every where she turned.

Everyone was looking for a bailout. Banks stopped lending, Mom and Pop businesses suffering, Auto industry folding. Fortune 500's cutting back their workforce, millions of folks without jobs, hundreds of thousands facing foreclosure. Repossession of cars, overdraft on bank cards, bad checks bouncing across the globe. Unemployment at an all time high. Government assistance checking and rechecking eligibility before dispersing food stamps and Medicaid. Gas prices yo-yoed, then stabilized. Retail revising, repacking merchandise into smaller quantities and selling for top dollar. More for less had quickly shifted to less for more.

Katrina came through once again, swallowing the nation whole. The nation's troubles now weighed the shoulders of one black man who promised *Change*. She wiped her nose with the sleeve of her robe and sniffled.

"My neighbor keeps his Porsche locked away inside the garage. Repo man has been coming through every other day looking for it."

"Things are bad," Roy said.

"Tell me about it. Jacob's tuition is kicking my ass."

"Have you considered public school?" Lou-Lou chimed in.

"Have you heard those kids read?"

"Good point."

Jazzman spoke through her nostrils. "It cost to live in South Merrick."

Merrick, New York, considered a Hamlet, was located along the south shore of Nassau County, Long Island. Its small town feel came embodied with a cosmo vibe. South Merrick was newer, trendier. Mansions with pools and docks faced the water, unlike North Merrick where the homes were more traditional styled with large wraparound porches.

"The economy has damaged families. Husband and wives don't see eye to eye. Kids can't understand why they can no longer receive piano lessons. Jacob asked me just yesterday 'what were food stamps?'" she snorted back her frustration, wiped her face dry.

"We come from food stamps, block cheese, powdered milk and church donations. Is it wrong for me to expect better for him?"

"Not at all Ma," Roy said.

"Jacob deserves better," Lou-Lou agreed.

"The media advises us to cut back, spend when necessary," Jazzman said.

"Fuck the media. Don't watch that shit. The news will have you popping pills and depressed, with anal bleeding from some medicine they prescribed you," Roy said.

"I've been with Delta five years. Five years, and they let me go. What happened to job security, seniority?" Jazzman blew her runny nose into a Kleenex.

"I worked my butt off in the freezing rain as a damn Baggage Handler, to Flight Attendant, to Sales, to District Sales, and finally when I'm promoted to my well deserved position as Regional Sales Manager, making some damn good money, they terminate my position."

Swine Flu outbreak, West Nile, Earthquake, Tsunami, Floods, Landslides, Domestic and International plane crashes, Terroristic threats, Bombings, and now Jazzman had to deal with lack. Her money was funny, downright hilarious. Each time she opened her purse in search of Mr. Benjamin she heard roaring pandemonium.

"You've done well for yourself. This is a beautiful home," he said.

"It's been a bitch trying to keep it. That South side jump-off set me straight. Took that paper and invested wisely. I was able to put a nice sizable down payment on this house, brought my Jaguar free and clear. Still got the house Aunty Jenny left me in Queens Village."

"Is it empty?" Lou-Lou asked.

"Occupied. Got this old retired gay couple renting. Still got my house in Atlanta. Rented that property to a section 8 tenant," she said remembering she had yet to receive the tenant's portion of the rent.

Roy nodded his head. "Section 8. That's *fo-sure* money."

"You mean a *fo-sure* headache," Jazzman said, recalling the drama that came along with dealing in that program.

"Anyway, what's the deal with you and Bradley?" Jazzman asked, shifting the topic away from her.

"The Bradley train is no longer leaving the station," Lou-Lou painfully admitted.

"I thought that was a done deal. You got the proposal, the ring, the fancy car, big house in Scarsdale; all you needed to do was say *I-Do*."

"Aint shit promised, nor is it written in stone."

"But you were so happy. Bradley kept you laced."

"He started something he couldn't finish. His gambling got out of hand. He lost most of what we had in Vegas. The plane, the villa, lord only knows what else. He lost his job, lost the respect of his father. His friends all turned their back on him."

"So you left him," Jazzman said flat out. Lou-Lou wasn't the kind of chick who was in it for the long haul. Her presence was strictly circumstantial.

"Had to. Made no sense in staying. I require too much."

"Wait, did you say he lost the villa? How the hell do you lose a villa?" Jazzman quizzed.

"He lost it in a bet."

"Damn. That's crazy. Rick told me Bradley was riding that white horse a bit more than usual," Jazzman said, and took a sip of her piping hot coffee.

Lou-Lou didn't verify nor deny, instead she shrugged. Roy was just about to question Jazzman about her new love interest *Rick*, but felt he'd be over stepping his boundaries. Prematurely interjecting back into her life could potentially set him back several steps. She rebelled under pressure.

"Bradley is old news. I'm here to discuss how I can get some paper in my pocket. My car, my house, my credit cards, my lavish lifestyle is gone. I'm working with a limited amount of funds, *pocket change*."

A look passed between Lou-Lou and Roy. He looked at both women intensely. "What I'm about to say, goes no further than us."

Both women nodded in agreement.

"Me and this chump name Flap can't see eye to eye. He used to work for me. Started off pumping packs out the Trap..."

Lou-Lou raised her hand as if she were a student inside a class of higher learning. "*Trap?* You mean the spot?" she asked.

"Trap... ATL... we heading south for this one ladies," he confirmed.

"Whoa, slow down. You said Sutphin Boulevard. A couple of steps away from the Queens County Clerk's Office," Lou-Lou reminded.

He smiled. "I've revised the itinerary."

"Somebody fill me in please," Jazzman insisted.

"We back in business. Your presence is required," Roy said.

Jazzman sucked her teeth. "Is that the only reason you came back?" Suddenly disgusted, she stood to leave. Roy grabbed her waist, pulled up to her bumper. "That's not the only reason I came back." Melting like butter, she tilted her head back. *Hmmm.*

Lou-Lou cleared her throat. "Hate to interrupt, but time is money. We need you on this one Jazzman."

She stepped away from the heat, sat back down. Eyes swept from the crown of his head, down to his feet, assessing all that *Good-Good.* She pulled in her bottom lip. *Damn!*

"Like I was saying, this dude Flap was one of my soldiers. Now he's the competition. I was cool with letting the little nigga get some money, cause we all gotta eat. Shorty became disrespectful. My clientele suddenly becoming his clientele. He letting birds fly for fifteen, five G's less than me. Tried talking to the nigga about it, but he got on some *I run this town*, shit."

"I see your dilemma," Lou-Lou said.

"We need to pay Flap a visit," he said, rubbing his hands.

"What kind of visit?" Jazzman asked.

"He got twenty bricks in the basement. I need all of it."

Jazzman chewed her nail, and then asked, "What happens to Flap?"

Lou-Lou sucked her teeth, rolled her eyes towards the ceiling. "What you think?"

"I could have sworn I was talking to Roy," Jazzman shot back.

Roy placed a firm hand on Jazzman's shoulder. "You know the rules. Nothing breathing, nothing moving."

Jazzman spit cracked nail from her mouth, nodded. Atlanta would work. She had undone business in the Peach State. Her tenant's rent was due, and since all certified mailings had gone unanswered, it was time to take it to the doorstep.

"How you know he got twenty bricks in the basement?" Jazzman asked.

"I just know," Roy said, staring at her in a way that made her middle twitch. Jazzman avoided eye contact, looked up towards the ceiling. He had her open, and with the liquor in her system, she found it hard to keep her legs closed.

"Roy, with all due respect, I'm different. I'm not the same chick from back in the day running spots with Isis. I've got a lot to lose," Jazzman said in her most serious voice.

He gave her that provocative look again. Just as she was about to lose eye contact, he gently grabbed her face, tipped her chin. "You won't lose. You can't lose. It's a for sure thing."

She politely moved his hand away. "Nothing's for sure. Just need to know you've done your homework on this dude Flap."

"Come on, have I ever let you run a spot blindly?" he asked.

"No."

"Just stick to the script and all will be well."

Roy was always reliable, always there to pick her up, but she couldn't help but question him. The information he dropped in her lap stuck to the four corners of her mind. She could tell Lou-Lou was on the fence as well, but greed tilted her into seeing it Roy's way.

Overtaken by second thoughts, and plagued with *what-if's*. Stepping back into the life came with consequences. Things weren't that bad, she wasn't on her last leg. She certainly had some time to weather the storm.

But she feared rock bottom.

Feared square one.

Feared having to start over from the beginning.

I have to do this. Jacob depends on me.

CHAPTER 7

"Would you stop complaining about the damn car," said Jazzman.

"You should have rented the Impala. It's roomier," Lou-Lou said for the umpteenth time.

"The Impala is notorious in the south for riding dirty. We don't need the extra attention. The Fusion works."

Lou-Lou gripped the steering wheel, and adjusted her bottom against the cloth seats. Having rode sixteen hours crammed into the tiny economy car made her agitated.

"This car is so wack," Lou-Lou retorted.

Both ladies peered out the black tinted glass, awaiting further instructions from Roy. They watched as cars pulled up, and pulled off. Quick hand to hand transactions took place.

"Did you peep that?" Lou-Lou asked, shaking her head.

"They moving work like its legal," said Jazzman.

For sure indictments surrounded the tiny home in South Atlanta. College Park. Burdette Road. Just two miles away from World Changers Church to be exact.

The night was still, all except the winds that chewed through thermals, and goose down bubble coats. Rain threatened the skies above. They could smell it coming. Crouched low in their seats, side mirrors adjusted perfectly, two sets of eyes darted from house to house.

"You scared?"

Jazzman inhaled. "A little. It's been a minute since I put in work."

"Me too. Bradley had a bitch spoiled," Lou-Lou snickered, trying to make light of the situation.

"We on some stake-out shit," said Lou-Lou with a second attempt in humor.

"We watching them. They could be watching us. The law probably watching *everything*."

Lou-Lou whipped her neck in all directions. "Don't say that."

"If this cat is getting dough like Roy says, best believe we not the only ones try'na get at him."

"Good point."

"You trust him?"

Lou-Lou paused. "Who?"

"You know who, Roy?"

Lou-Lou shrugged. "The verdict is still out. Can't call it yet."

"He seems eager to help us, but why?" Jazzman asked with a raised brow.

All the gushy warm feelings that flooded her the night before had turned cold. She had to be realistic. Roy was never an option. And the fact that he'd returned from the dead, forcing his way back into her life made her antennas stick up. Way up.

Lou-Lou allowed her question to marinate for a second.

"Maybe he feels obligated because of Isis. They were close. Like siblings. She always said he was her brother from another mother."

They eyed two dope boys outside the rundown single family house. They passed a blunt back and forth until it burnt down to a roach. They giggled, did a two step, and rolled up another. Lou-Lou wondered how they could sag in such extreme weather. It was colder than a hood bitch outside.

"Rain, sleet, snow, dope boys keep that work moving," Lou-Lou said, witnessing yet another sale. As the mighty wind whipped and howled, a lightning war took place above their heads. A shriek of thunder clapped.

"These kids have no clue," Jazzman said, wondered how high they would lift their legs and run if them boyz came surrounding the house. She wondered which, if not both would blow the whistle first.

"Bet the one with the braids would snitch first," Jazzman said with a slight head nod. She knew a snitch at first glance. Her baby daddy was a trick.

"Hell yeah, his scrawny ass would be the first to sing."

Lou-Lou's eyes elevated upward towards the satellite hook-up anchoring the top of the house. Shabby roof, fallen shingles, blue tarp flapping in the wind. Plywood boarded the attic. Filthy vinyl sidings and old tattered sheets were hung as window treatments. Exposed A/C units dripped of icicles. The clock ticked, and it was now thirty minutes past the hour.

Heat pumped to the max, music at a whisper, wireless piece caressing Lou-Lou's earlobe. Her cell phone vibrated. She answered. His voice was steady, firm, and felt to the fullest degree. She put him on speaker. They listened to Roy reiterate the plan.

"Money green Intrepid should be bending the corner any second," he said. Both Lou-Lou and Jazzman watched their side mirrors, saw headlights approaching. The Intrepid stopped midway.

"Lou, you go inside with Kema... Jazz, you pull the car around towards the side of the house..."

"Whoa... who the fuck is Kema," both ladies asked in unison.

"She's our way in. She's cool. Kema got the pull to get you inside. Without her, we don't have a chance," Roy explained.

"Forget that, I'm not dealing with nobody I don't know," Jazzman said, folding her arms angrily.

"I'm with Jazzman. You ain't mention nothing about Kia... or whatever her name is."

"Her name is Kema and she's my young pit-bull. Flap got a thing for her. He trusts her. Lou, follow Kema into the basement. Handle the bricks, Kema will cancel Flap. Once that business is done, exit the basement door; come up the side of the house. Jazz, keep the engine running."

"And where the hell will you be during all this?" Jazzman asked, now seething.

"It's my way or no way. Make a decision in the next three seconds."

They glanced at each other. The moment had arrived. Will they step back into the life, become what they used to be? Will they throw caution to the wind, put in work, just to stay on top? Drowning in a sea of debt, borrowing from Peter just to pay Paul, wasn't exactly how they pictured their lives.

Jazzman's internal struggle was written across her face. Lou-Lou stepped up, assuming the head position. She had nothing to lose but herself. Jazzman had Jacob. She had the world.

"What about the shorties standing out front? You know they holding, and looking to prove themselves," said Lou-Lou.

"Don't worry. I got them young niggas in my scope. They get outta line, I'm giving em' led."

They looked at each other, somewhat assured. "Roy," Jazzman called his name.

"Yeah."

"No hesitations. Have my back. My son needs me."

"Have I ever let you down?" he asked.

"Not once."

"Okay then. Let's get this money."

Lou-Lou prayed to God they weren't scoped pulling into the block. She prayed to God them young cats sitting outside the house, puffing on that blunt didn't grow a brain.

The slow moving Intrepid inched down the street. Dark tints made it impossible to see in. That feeling of danger crept into their spine. Lou-Lou reached for the hammer, so did Jazzman. Both slid to the floor board, getting as low as possible.

Safety *off*.

Finger on the trigger.

Pistols aimed towards the sky.

The Intrepid stopped, parallel parked next to the Fusion. The window came down just enough to release bellows of smoke.

"Who the hell is that?" Jazzman whispered.

"Shush."

Just then, the Intrepid continued at a deliberate crawl, stopping in front of the house. A young girl hopped out the passenger's side, all smiles, pulling strongly on a cigarette. The Intrepid sped through the four way stop sign, doing about eighty down a residential street.

They assumed she was Kema by the way she stared in their direction. Four foot eleven; hip poked out to the left gave her a hoodrat stance. A curly weave framed her jaw bone. Kema flicked ashes, discreetly motioned for Lou-Lou to step outside the car.

"I don't trust that girl. If you want out, we can be out, fuck that," Jazzman said, already looking to put the pedal to the metal.

Apprehension plagued Lou-Lou, made her think twice about going through with the plan. She could tell that the new girl would be trouble. "I'm good. If I ain't out in ten minutes..." She ejected from the driver side, looked in at Jazzman's worried face.

"... head north. Makes no sense in us both going down." She slammed the door shut, and broke into a light jog.

A drizzle of rain splashed her nose. Refusing to look towards the heavens, she wiped and kept it moving. As she neared, she quickly assessed. Kema had a nasty disposition. Her style, posture, facial expression made Lou-Lou instantly dislike the girl.

"You Kema?"

"The one and only," Kema said, flicking her cigarette butt into the street. She blew smoke in Lou-Lou's direction.

"Follow me."

They stepped into the dungeon of hell. The smell of canine feces wafted their senses. With each step taken, urine and loose dog waste squished beneath Lou-Lou's rubber boots. *I'm So Hood*, remix blared from a surround sound hook up. Bass from the music made the house shake.

Walls were covered in provocative posters of video vixens. Famous ATL rappers plastered another wall. *Ludacris*, *Young Jeezy*, *T.I.*, and those annoying *Ying Yang* twins stared back at Lou-Lou, grinning.

They passed what would be the formal dining room, but had been set-up like a prison gym. Weight-bench, pull-up bar, and rusty dumbbells added to the grungy décor. Makeshift liquor bar leaned against a corner wall, empty bottles of Grey Goose and Hennessy displayed like a work of art.

A *Terry Crews* look-a-like sat up from the weight-bench, sweat pouring off his head, drizzling down his chiseled chest. His face screwed up like something foul just entered the room.

Big & Brolic signaled for Kema. The music that beat in the background blurred their conversation. Lou-Lou kept her eyes on the new girl, kept looking over her shoulder, kept checking her watch for the time. Kema's smile didn't match her body language. The previous relaxed; hoodrat stance she possessed was gone. In place were stiffened limbs, manufactured smile. Something was wrong. Something was seriously wrong.

Big & Brolic signaled for Lou-Lou to approach. She moved at a snail's pace, heart thumping in her chest. He looked her over, tasted his lips. "You Five-O?"

Lou-Lou glared at Kema. "Hell no."

"Mind if I search you?"

"Kema what part of the game is this?"

"Kema don't run nothing up in here. Open your coat," he demanded.

She unbuckled her waist length Shearling, and assumed the position. His hands cupped her breasts, causing her to jerk away. "Put em' up, or get out." His breath smelled of shit. Or was it the sordid carpet beneath her feet? He gave her shoulders a firm squeeze before sliding his hands up and down her frame. A couple of minutes later, they kept it moving down the hall.

"*I'm Soooo Hooood,*" Kema sung.

"How much further?"

Kema looked back at Lou-Lou. "You made it through the worst of it. Trust me."

Trust you? Never.

They proceeded towards the kitchen. Lou-Lou thought she had stepped onto the set of a bootlegged *New Jack City* movie. The remake had two girls, both clearly under the legal age, bagging crack into tiny baggies. Some old naked broad with iron flat breasts stood at the stove, stirring and mixing, while puffing a cigarette. Thick smoke loomed her aged face. A girl with the worse weave in history stood at the microwave, ice grilling. From the looks of the cheese oozing from the Hot-Pocket, one would say that her meal was done.

"Kema. Who her is?"

Kema pretended she didn't hear the question. Instead she grabbed the roll of black plastic bags off the counter and pressed on. Down a steep flight of steps, they headed towards the basement. The air wasn't much better down there. A fog of smoke hovered the space like thick clouds in the sky. *Trap Living.*

"This doesn't feel right," Lou-Lou said, while coughing.

"It's cool. Big Flap wanted to meet you."

Lou-Lou blew out fear, and inhaled some courage, followed by lingering weed smoke. She had to keep her game face. Couldn't get caught shaking in her boots now, had to stay focused.

They entered the belly of the beast. Four juvenile delinquents surrounded a wall mounted flat screen, grabbing at the center of their jeans, cracking jokes as the homemade video played.

"Yes *Sir*, I's be'sa bout my bidness. Handles mine, fam. Handles mine real proper like." One guy said with a mouth full of cheap gold.

"Shawty juice box was slippery. Dat bitch knew how to ride it," another said tossing back a bottle of Henny.

"My nigga, we ought-a burn copies. Let em' go for a dub each. What you say?"

"Hell yeah!"

Kema stood watching the unsacred act take place. She *oohed* and *awed,* seemingly impressed with the double penetration inflicted upon the poor child.

"The one by the microwave, heating up the Hot Pocket, is that her?" Lou-Lou whispered. Kema gave her a sympathetic look. "Trap-Rules."

"Damn shame."

It wasn't long before Lou-Lou met the man. Flap was the General. Any product moved had to be approved through him. He was a fat greasy son-of-a-bitch with beady eyes, small lips and a nose that took up most of his face.

Flap laid his awkwardly proportioned body across an old beat-up sofa, eating *Hot Flaming Cheetos.* Lou-Lou couldn't help but think *He's the competition? Really?*

"It's against policy to disburse on consignment without checking to see for whom and why. Yah dig?" Flap said, crunching into a doodle.

"I dig," Lou-Lou said firmly.

"What's your name sweet heart?"

"Rule number one. No names."

He laughed haughtily, amused by her tough girl act. Fat and Greasy licked his lips. "Okay, where you from?"

"Why is that important?"

"Need to know who I'm in bed with."

Lou-Lou caught Kema giving Flap the seductive eye. Fat and Greasy ignored her advancement and stared down into the bottom of an empty bag. He knocked a few crumbs around, placing the corner to his mouth. *Crunch!*

"Kema tells me you're the man to see about some *X*."

He sucked the cheese from his dirty finger nails. "That amongst other things."

"Good. I need *X*...preferably blue dolphins, *Purple*, *Kush*, and *Yayo*."

Flap rested his hands on his gut as he twiddled his cheese stained thumbs. "You know your stuff."

"I know enough to turn a profit," said Lou-Lou.

"And where did you say you were from?"

"I didn't."

Flap was intrigued with curiosity. Her knowledge on pills made her come off as some sort of chemist. Her need to remain anonymous fascinated him. He was beginning to like this girl. "I got them skittles, you got dat paper?"

Lou-Lou looked towards Kema for assistance. "Flap we discussed consignment," Kema said.

"Check this here; I don't know this bitch. She could run off with my work," he roared. Mr. Nice guy was gone.

"Look. I'm a business woman. I gets it in, and I'm back to re-up with your cut plus interest," Lou-Lou assured.

He laughed. "So I've been told time and time again. It's nothing personal sweet heart but I too am a business man. Can't let you walk outta here with all that work. I've got a rep to maintain. Besides, I don't have a name. I don't know where you're from. You could be Five-O. Are you?"

"Big dude upstairs already gave me my cavity search."

As he laughed, his belly bounced. He slapped his leg, it jiggled. Flap was a Holy Hot Mess.

"Come on baby, I told you she's cool."

"Funny as hell. But cool? This remains to be proven."

"Forget it Kema, show me to the door." Lou-Lou was ready to leave the way she came, quick, fast and in a hurry. Things weren't going as smooth as Roy promised. He mentioned nothing about negotiating with the fat bastard.

Flap rolled his sloppy butt off the beat-up pleather sofa. Embedded food stains decorated his white-tee. His man boobs exposed at the sides. Tight curly hairs circled his dark ashy nipples. A bad case of Eczema attacked the folds of his neck. He scratched his rash, and then rubbed his belly. *This guy is the competition? He's making all the money? What has the world come to?*

"Where'd you say you were from again?"

The atmosphere in the room shifted. That uncomfortable feeling shot up the back of her spine, made her tremble. It felt as if the walls were closing in. Felt as if the room was getting smaller, and smaller. Flap was much taller then she had imagined. His frame towered over her, making her feel almost invisible. She was afraid to move.

"Texas. Houston."

"You don't sound like you from Texas. Sound like you from up north," he said playing with strands of her hair. She backed away, turned and looked for Kema to interject. The look in Kema's eyes told Lou-Lou that she was in a world of trouble if she didn't cooperate. *Fuck!*

All she had to rely on was herself, and that .22 latched neatly at her ankle, inside her rubber boot. Big & Brolic failed to cover that area. He was too busy groping and fondling tits and ass to notice.

"What, you don't like to be touched?" Flap asked.

"Can't stand it. Prefer people to keep their distance," Lou-Lou spat courageously.

Flap rubbed his double stacked chin, and then scratched his un-tamed pork chop sideburns. He stared at her, then at Kema who had her head hung low. Her loyalty was with Flap, not her. *Roy fucked up.* The layer of tension in the room was so thick, so dangerously felt.

"With all due respect Houston, shit is different here. Unless we fucking there's not much to discuss. I need the cash."

Game Over!

"I understand." Lou-Lou attempted to leave. He grabbed her arm, yanking her back into position. She could smell the heat coming from his breath.

"Hold on. I'm not through." She looked up into his beady eyes and gasped. Fear was all she felt. Hate was the next emotion. She hated Bradley for having her in this predicament. It was because of him she had to run the spot in the first place.

"Kema said your cool, and I believe her. So, this is what I'll do for you."

He released her arm, and took two steps backward, turned and headed towards the closet. Flap exposed himself, showed his hand. Once the last digit to the security code was punched in, and the access click was heard, Kema hopped over the desk and put the burner to his cheek. Lou-Lou swore she heard the girl growl.

Murder was in the air.

Flap slipped into a fetal position, begging for his life.

"Bag that shit up," Kema commanded.

Lou-Lou moved quickly around the beat up sofa, and started bagging bricks into black garbage bags. Never in her wildest dreams did she expect to see so many of them *thangz* at one time. Sweat poured profusely from her body as she emptied the closet. There was a knock at the door. Everyone froze.

"*Bra-Bra*, you gotta see this. Bitches swallowing *errthing*," A voice said from the other side. Kema snapped her fingers and mouthed *hurry the fuck up*. Lou-Lou kept bagging the work, trusting that she had everything under control.

"*Bra-Bra* yah heard me... come see this shit." The doorknob jiggled. Hard knocks followed. Lou-Lou dropped the product, leaned down to unlatch her *.22*.

Kema snapped her fingers. *"Chill. I got this."*

"Bitch, is you crazy?" *This bitch must be crazy if she think I'm not about to defend myself.* Lou-Lou held her tool pointed towards the door, cocked and ready to rock.

Kema leaned in, whispered something to Flap. He opened his mouth to speak but couldn't find his voice. She slapped him with the burner, and pointed it at his third eye.

"I'm busy," Flap said under distress.

"*Bra-Bra* you need to see these bitches."

He swallowed, and said, "Not now nigga. I'm busy."

After the last brick was tossed into the bag, Kema led the way toward the trap door. In the small confined space, scrap metal lined the wall. Trash littered the floor. In another corner there was a motorcycle helmet, boots and oversized leather riding jacket.

Above, a single florescent tube shone dimly. Flap was sniveling. His nose was a faucet. Snot drippings splashed his lips, slithered down his chin.

"Shut your bitch ass up," Kema snapped.

A deadbolt stood between them and the free world. The temperature in the room elevated several notches past scorching. Flap fumbled with the set of keys. His hands shook with each attempt to open the massive lock. Blunt force knocked the back of his head. He yelped.

"Hurry up." Kema's voice was low and menacing.

"Why you doing me like this?" His voice quivered.

"Shut up."

Time was ticking.

The difference between life and death was seconds.

Lou-Lou snatched the keys from his clammy hands, tried her luck. Before she could align the key with the keyhole a shot rang off, followed by a loud thud. Kema dropped Flap without warning. She shoved Lou-Lou aside, lifted her arm, and squeezed two shots off against the dead bolt. The trap door blew open. *"Go."*

They were welcomed with strong winds and relentless downpour. Their way out was parked at the corner. Black bags thrown across each shoulder as Lou-Lou moved towards the rental. Water from the skies made it almost impossible to maintain a firm grip on the plastic. The goods were slipping. There was no time for re-adjusting.

Heartless Kema on her right, two young thugs running full speed ahead on her left. The rental was just a few feet away. Thoughts of dumping the product entered her mind, but she kept trucking. Legs moving swiftly, Kema still at her side.

The heavens opened up, down came Gods tears. A bolt of lightning made them jolt. The sky lit up, crackled. Then, everything turned black.

Silent. The trunk to the Fusion popped opened, out jumped the grim reaper looking to collect souls.

"Drop," Kema screamed.

Lou-Lou hit the pavement. Face down, arms covered her head. The dominate sound of Roy's tool chopped several times. He bodied the two delinquents as promised. The velocity between each *boom* told her Roy wasn't about to let up. Lou-Lou looked to her left, saw bodies scattered. She looked towards her right, saw Kema running for the rental. With no warning, no heads up, Kema bailed, ditching her with the load. *Fucking Bitch!*

Stuck in the mud.

Face down.

Kissing the earth.

Dead grass pricked her lips. Her tears mixed with Gods tears. More gun fire erupted. Multiple shell casings dropped. It was war in College Park. A war she hadn't prepared for. Her little deuce-deuce wouldn't make a dent.

Chop, Chop, Chop!

Bullets whizzed through the air, thumping into the tattered house. Her ears rang. Everything suddenly at a distance, sounding muffled. His voice came in as a faint, pinch. He gripped her by the hood of her Shearling, hoisted her from the muddy earth.

"I got you."

The rental backed over the sidewalk, and roared its way towards them. The car stopped just inches away from where they stood. Her heart almost exploded as the bumper was an inch away from her knees. Jazzman jumped out, shoved her into the passenger's side door. Kema loaded the bags as Roy inflicted more pain.

CHAPTER 8

Buckhead restaurant, the lunch crowd was thick. Jazzman strutted in; shades covered her eyes, a light shimmer painted her lips. Her dark brown skin possessed a natural summer's glow. A glow most white woman desperately tried to achieve artificially. Winter white wide leg slacks, matching off the shoulder sweater, pearl white stiletto boots caused a wave of whispers. Two dirty old men sat at the far end of the bar, blowing kisses, winking, willing to pay for it. The older of the two placed his hand over the old ticker and mouthed *Marry Me.*

"In your dreams, Pops."

She noticed Roy, and Lou-Lou. They sat in the back booth, accompanied by a young girl with spiked hair, shaved sides, wearing the wrong shade of red on her pouty lips. As she neared she noticed it was Kema. Roy stood halfway, smiled, and motioned for her to join them.

"Hey beautiful," he said, pulling her in, wrapping his healthy arms around her frame. She inhaled him. His cologne, downright hypnotizing. He whispered, "Where have you been all my life?" She elbowed his side, stepping away from the awkward embrace. Lou-Lou snickered, loving how cute they looked together. Kema looked on, disturbed by the affectionate showcase.

Roy's eyes roamed Jazzman's backside discreetly then found its way back to her glossy lips. *You're beautiful.*

"I didn't mean to interrupt," Jazzman said, fanning her face with her beaded clutch purse. Her cheeks were on fire from blushing. Ladies Presidential Rolex caressed her wrist elegantly which caused Kema to gawk.

"Kema was just leaving."

"But Roy...," Kema whined.

He shot her a look. The table turned quiet. Roy was a man of very little words. He was a doer, a thinker, and an action taker. He said things once and only once. They all knew that look, especially Jazzman. In fact, she knew firsthand the definition of the evil glare. Having felt his wrath personally she knew that Kema was in a world of trouble if she didn't obey.

Girl, just go before this nut transform. Jazzman said to herself while scrutinizing Kema's choice in attire. High waist skinny jeans, midriff powder pink sweater, and wedge boots with tacky Eskimo hair poking out the sides wasn't exactly hitting.

"This table isn't big enough for the four of us," Lou-Lou said sarcastically.

As Kema eyeballed Lou-Lou's neckline and earlobes her top lip quivered. "This table is plenty big."

Lou-Lou snapped her fingers. "You heard the man. Beat it."

"Girl, you don't know me," Kema assured.

Lou-Lou leaned her bosom against the table, tilted her head *J-Lo* style. "And you damn sure don't know me. *Skedaddle Hoodrat.*"

Kema ran her tongue across her teeth. "The only *Hoodrat* at this table is you."

Lou-Lou giggled. "Roy, get this little girl before I act a fool."

"For the record, I'm grown. *Hood,* that I am. *Hoodrat,* that I'm not."

Roy's jaw began to twitch unnervingly. Jazzman linked her arm into his, giving him a slight tug in her directions. He was shedding skin, and the goon was about to rear its ugly head. She stroked his back once, relaxing his shoulders.

"I would advise you both to chill. If ya'll feeling something personal, pocket that shit for later. As of right now, this is business," Roy said point blank.

"Considered it pocketed for later then," Kema said in an almost threatening tone. Leaping across the table to choke Kema was Lou-Lou's first thought, but Jazzman intercepted, applying a strong hand against her shoulder.

"Cool. See me whenever, however," Lou-Lou said, having had the last word.

Kema stood, grabbed her purse and finger waved respectfully. Stooping to Lou-Lou's level would only prove to Roy that she was immature. She made her way towards the bar, and sat two stools away from the dirty old men.

After Roy sat, Jazzman slid in next, shaking her head. Lou-Lou could push anybody's button. She specialized in pissing people off. Her vulgar tongue spit words that caused riots. She was a thorn, a barbed wire, a callous cold-hearted bitch.

"You wrong Lou," Jazzman said.

Lou-Lou shrugged her shoulders, and glanced at Roy. She wondered why he didn't crack Kema's head to the white meat for not moving when he said move. The mere fact that she questioned him was enough to fatten her lip. *You slipping Roy,* she thought giving Kema the evil eye from across the room.

Roy leaned back, slung his arm across the rest and smiled. "I thought a celebrity entered the room the way necks were turning."

"For-real though... You looking good Ma," Lou-Lou added.

"Ya'll need to stop." Jazzman blushed.

The waitress approached with an extra menu and a glass of water for Jazzman.

"You hungry?" Roy asked.

Jazzman shook her head no, and then glanced down at her watch. Roy ordered a bottle of bubbly instead. "It's barely noon," said Jazzman.

"It's five o'clock somewhere in the world," said Roy.

"Noon is a perfect time to get tipsy," Lou-Lou added, wetting her lips.

They allowed the waitress to mosey a good three tables down before anyone spoke. Roy looked from Lou-Lou to Jazzman and said, "How ya'll sleep last night?"

"I didn't. I couldn't. I was too damn excited," Lou-Lou said rubbing her hands together.

"Me too, last night was crazy." Jazzman admitted. "Speaking of which, you got that dough?" She swiveled her fingertips.

"Damn, you can at least break bread with your peoples," Roy encouraged.

Jazzman checked her watch again. "I can stay for a second, but I must leave."

"*C'mon*, we haven't seen each other in years. Let's celebrate," he insisted.

"Wish I could, but I'm on a tight schedule." Jazzman checked her watch again.

"What's got you on the move?" he asked, grabbing her hands, kissing them.

Lou-Lou cleared her throat, looked away. They were obviously having a moment. She caught Kema glaring in her direction. "I need to catch up with my tenant, collect some rent, and then I'm on the next bird back home. Jacob has a football game," Jazzman said, pulling her hands away from his, placing them back into her lap.

Roy slipped a large package to Jazzman first, then to Lou-Lou. Both ladies grasped their fair share. A sigh of relief escaped Jazzman as she took a quick peek. Her mind turned into a human calculator. She crunched numbers, prioritizing her bills from largest to smallest. A good portion of her dough already spent.

Roy rubbed his chin, smiled. "I slipped a bit extra in there for Jacob. Make sure he gets what he needs."

Jazzman looked surprised. "You didn't have to do that Roy," she stammered.

"I know I didn't, but I care. I've always cared."

"Seriously it's not necessary. You didn't have to." Jazzman was grinning from ear to ear. He flashed a smile, her grin widened.

"If you need anything, for Jacob or for yourself, just let me know." There he was again saying things that made her shiver, and giving her that look. Jazzman tugged at her earlobe nervously. "That's nice of you. Thanks."

The waitress returned with their most expensive bottle of champagne and three glasses. Roy did the honors and before long they were sipping and toasting to brighter tomorrows. Kema watched from afar as she babysat a watered down Long Island. Furious because Roy hadn't broke her off her fair share yet. She couldn't understand why she had to wait for her cut. *These bitches get theirs first, but you make me wait?*

Back at the table, Lou-Lou asked, "What-up with your girl?" Kema was mean mugging from across the room. But she now had company, sandwiched between two old men, giggling like a school girl in heat. She looked back at them every now and then, winking at Roy, rolling her eyes at Lou-Lou.

"Up to no good," Roy said for certain.

"She's working the hell out of those two old men," Jazzman added.

"Kema can siphon cash through a straw. She's been known to get money from the tightest wallets," he said in an almost bragging tone.

Kema glanced in their direction again. She was eager to prove herself to Roy. She deserved a spot at the table. She was entitled to a glass of bubbly. Why couldn't she pop bottles with them? Why was she sitting several feet away with men old enough to be her grandfather? She was the one who bodied Flap. She was the one who risked it all. That bitch Lou-Lou was trying to take her place. Or was it Jazzman she needed to worry about? Roy had a look in his eyes she'd never seen before. The way he hugged her, smiled at her, didn't exactly spell Platonic. There was more between those two. She could feel it.

"I don't like the way that girl keep looking at me," Lou-Lou sat frustrated with both arms folded beneath her breasts. Her whining went unheard, for Roy and Jazzman's attention were on Kema. Somehow she'd managed to steal the show, *again*.

"Watch this-Watch this," Roy said in his best *Bishop Eddie Long* voice.

Kema's wandering hands roamed a pair of hairy backs, stroking their silver heads, whispering sweet notes in their ears, kissing their lobes. Her cocaine laced game gave them the speedy dick.

"What's her story?" Jazzman asked, seemingly intrigued.

"She's a treacherous southern belle. I found her running down Northside Drive. She just wrapped some dude Lexus off the exit ramp.

Buddy went through the windshield. She took off before the police came. Under aged, drinking, no license, on the way to the Sheraton to screw some old white dude. I saw the whole thing. Scooped shorty up, took her some place safe. She's been my bulldog ever since."

"Captain SaveAHo," Lou-Lou spat.

"Jealous?" Roy grinned devilishly.

"Of what? Of that? Stop it. She's a barstool hooker," Lou-Lou fired back.

"*Shush*. Watch this," he said.

Lou-Lou wasn't the least bit impressed. She yanked her BlackBerry from her purse and began a game of Brick-Breaker. Jazzman's foot knocked against Lou-Lou's leg. "She's a crafty one."

"Yeah, whatever."

Kema's finger tips traveled cautiously towards the center of their slacks, moving towards their pockets. She clipped both wallets, robbing the old geezers blind. Her motions were slimy, downright greasy. A true grimy chick she was. Both Lou-Lou and Jazzman gave each other a look. They made a mental note to keep Kema at arms distance.

"You seem thoroughly entertained," said Jazzman.

"Oh, I am. I like watching her work," said Roy.

"You bagged more than bricks, noticed a shit load of pills, and coke," Roy said, turning his attention back towards the table.

"Made no sense in leaving money on the table," Lou-Lou said refreshing her drink. She brought the glass to her lips, and smiled. "Since we're on the topic, how about you let me take them off your hands?"

He laughed. "There you go, always looking for a dollar more. Lou-Ann Dobbs, aka *wheeling* and *dealing*, aka *greedy*." He pointed his finger. "Greed will get you killed."

"No, aka *growth*, aka *a bitch try'na come up*. By any means deemed necessary."

Lou-Lou slapped fives with Jazzman as they both giggled.

"She does have a point Roy. She bagged it," said Jazzman.

"You're suddenly her spokesperson?"

"Hey, I'm just calling it like I see it. You mentioned bricks, and bricks is what she delivered, all twenty of them. You said nothing about overflow. She earned it."

Lou-Lou shot her girl a grin. Jazzman winked. They still had each other's back.

Lou-Lou took a sip of her Champagne, and placed the glass down. Still watching grimy ass Kema through her peripheral, she said, "I bagged it, might as well let me get that off."

"You got connects?" Roy asked.

"Of course," she lied.

He laughed. "Don't beat me upside the head."

She pursed her lips in order to keep her laughter at bay.

"Trust the kid. I got connects."

"In New York I'm sure, but Atlanta is different."

"Don't sleep on me. I know people." She assured him.

He rubbed his chin. "Let me think about it."

"Time is money. Gotta get this paper and bounce back to New York. I promised Kosha's I'll be there."

"How long will it take you?" Roy asked, now entertaining the thought of allowing her to take the extra work off his hands.

"Two days," Lou-Lou said with confidence.

He laughed hysterically. "I don't believe you can pull it off."

"Only one way to find out," she said with a pair of daring eyes.

He rubbed his chin again, looked towards Jazzman, then back towards Lou-Lou. "*Aight*... I'll give you a portion. If all goes well, maybe we can do future business."

Lou-Lou was all smiles. "Good looking. We about to get paid." Roy noticed Jazzman wavering; her thoughts were elsewhere.

"Jazz, you want in on this?" Roy asked.

"Who me... *naw*... I'm good."

"We could use an extra set of hands," Lou-Lou said beaming with prospects for more money. "We can be the dynamic duo. It'll be like old times."

"You two got it covered." Jazzman checked her watch.

"What about Kema?" Roy asked.

Lou-Lou rolled her neck. "What about her?"

"Take her along, she has connections. Just might be able to move that work tonight," Roy suggested.

"That girl goes nowhere with me," said Lou-Lou.

"Distribution is key. We need an insider. Kema know people. This is her city."

Lou-Lou gave Roy the stank-eye. *"Her City... oh please.* I know people too. Furthermore, I don't recall seeing that bitch name on the *Welcome to Atlanta* sign."

He released a mild frustrated growl. "You've been hugged up with pretty boy Bradley for the last couple of years."

"What you try'na say?"

"You're out the loop baby. Operations on the street have changed. She's affiliated. Night clubs, strip clubs, DJs, bouncers, and party goers. Let's not forget, she's the one who got us into Flaps front door. Without her, shit would have been a lot more difficult."

"With all due respect to you Roy, that bitch left me in the mud. I don't trust her. Besides, she may have street credibility, but I've got corporate connections in my back pocket."

"Is that so?"

"So it is." She winked.

"Both worlds one in the same, take her with you. School the young*N* on a thing or two."

"Did you see the way she was hawking Jazzman's Rolly? Did you see the way she eyeballed my neck? She's a snake."

"She reminds me of you when you were that age," he said.

"Whatever. You are so way off base. She's nothing like me."

"Walk then," Roy said firmly.

Her eyes enlarged. "Excuse me?"

"If you can't pocket your beef for some bread, then there's nothing else to talk about. You got your cut. You're free to leave."

"Roy, you don't understand."

"Oh, I understand. I understand that you can't see pass this katty bullshit in order to make some cheese." Roy clarified his position. He had to let her know who was in charge. He was the H.N.I.C calling the shots.

"I don't believe your putting that lil-girl before me," Lou-Lou said in total awe.

"That's not even it and you know it. We family, but I refuse to let you fuck up my cash flow because you on your period. It's time to grow up. Understand?"

Lou-Lou nodded. "Understood."

After a few seconds of silence, Roy decided to shift the topic.

"What-up with that chump Tony?" Lou-Lou excused herself for the bathroom. This was a conversation she wanted no part in. The topic of Tony always ended with a few un-Godly words. Jazzman dropped the menu. They stared long and hard at each other. Old hatred crept back into her veins. He hit a nerve. A muscle in her jaw spasmed. "Wow, just when I thought you've changed. Why you can't leave well enough alone, Roy?"

He shrugged, but instead of backing off, he insisted on digging deeper. "He's a trick."

"Unbelievable."

Her baby father was the last person she wanted to discuss. He was a trick, a turncoat, a snitch, DEA informant. She knew it, Roy knew it, and everyone knew it. He was all those things and more, but there was a line that she refused to cross.

"*C'mon* Roy, must we go there?"

"I'm just saying, he told on his crew. J-Rock got triple life. Crackers threw the book at him but he ain't start snitching."

"Rock and Tony cut from two different cloths."

"Don't make excuses for that dude."

"Please, never that. Can't stand him. Just calling it like I see it."

"He's a bitch-ass nigga."

She lifted the menu, shielded her face. "True. I won't argue you there."

"How often you speak to him?" She slammed the menu against the table. "Why?"

"I'm just curious."

"He calls once a week to speak to his son."

"Heard he's coming home soon."

"Yeah, heard that same news. Back to Brooklyn, back to the block."

He gave her a blank stare, and then focused his attention on Kema. She was making her exit. He watched as she scurried off towards the

Ladies Room. Pre-ejaculated thoughts had both geezers feeling like the "NEW" Twenty.

"What was that?"

Roy swiveled a tooth pick in his mouth. "What was what?"

"*That look*, you gave me a look. You know something that I don't know?" she quizzed.

"Do I?"

"Stop holding out and tell me," she demanded.

He chuckled. "I know nothing," he said with certainty.

"A big cheese such as you is always in the loop."

He laughed hard. "So, I'm the big cheese now? Where you get that line from?" She sucked her teeth, laughed. She had to admit, that line did sound a bit corny. He leaned in close. So did she.

"Now you and I both know Tony ain't allowed back in Brooklyn. To tell you the truth, he might not make it off Rikers Island alive."

Her heart thumped. Not because she cared for Tony, but because she cared for her son. He needed to make it off the Island. He had to. What would she tell Jacob?

"And your point is?"

"Don't bullshit a bullshiter. That's my point." He leaned back.

"Care to be more specific?"

"Things that are known shall not be explained," he said.

"Don't have time for riddle games. Just spill it."

"He's got a one way ticket to Merrick, *your* crib."

How the hell did he know? Who else knew? That information was confidential. She diverted her eyes down towards her wrist. She checked the time. Roy was a quarter past psychic and it was now time to rotate up out of there. He noticed how antsy she'd become and palmed her hands.

"Look, I've got pressing business. Are we through?"

His head tilted in astonishment. "Damn. So it's true? After all he's done to you, you letting that clown back in?"

She could barely look at him. Her eyes beamed across the room at Lou-Lou and Kema. Surprisingly they were talking, and not fighting. She watched as the two walked shoulder to shoulder out the main entrance.

"Why let him back in?"

"Because I can."

He released her hands, and eased his back against the leather cushion. "He's a snake. And the only way to kill a snake is to chop its head off."

From day one, Roy wanted to pump slugs into Tony. He hated his guts, and would have buried him long ago, but he loved Jazzman. As much as her baby daddy had it coming, he couldn't bring himself to deliver the pain.

"You showed up just when I needed you the most. I'm grateful for that, but don't you ever in your life question me about Tony."

He looked at her for a long moment. "You need more?

"More what?"

He swiveled his finger tips. She inhaled, refusing to break, refusing to let him know just how desperate she was for more of that green. Showing her entire hand meant exposing her vulnerability. She couldn't, she wouldn't let him know.

"You need more?" he asked a second time.

"Jacob depends on me. I've created a lifestyle for us that I must maintain. So, yes... I need more. Who the hell doesn't?" her voice cracked.

They locked eyes. He understood her pain. Bill collectors didn't give a damn about the economy. Their job was to collect. Her monthly obligations had a noose at her neck, squeezing the life from her.

"You ready to put in work?"

He heard the quick intake of her breath. Her eyes were now glassy.

"I'm ready."

***

A beautiful, snot nose, nappy head brown boy stood in the doorway smiling up at Jazzman. His olive shaped eyes, and pudgy nose reminded her of Jacob. His Spiderman pajamas flooded above his ankle. His tiny feet, bare and ashy. She noticed the huge red Kool Aid stain on the once creamy beige carpet and cringed.

"Hello, is Fantasia home?"

"How you know my mommy?"

She scratched the side of her temple. "*Hum*, we're old friends."

The boy looked Jazzman from head to toe. "You look fancy. I like your boots."

She smiled. "Thank you baby. Where's Mommy?"

"She upstairs with Mike-Mike. He not my daddy but momma told me to call him daddy... cause he buy me toys, and clothes, and he keep the lights on... and momma said he gone marry her one day and make us all a real family... cause we all have different last names... and momma hate explaining herself to people at school that she our momma."

"Can you go get her for me?"

"Yes ma'am. Please come in. It's cold outside. Mike-Mike, I mean *daddy* gets upset cause we keep the door open, cause he the one paying the heat bill, and he keep the lights on... Mike-Mike, *oops* I mean *daddy* be saying how all we do is suck up the heat, water, and eat up all the food in the kitchen... he said we cost money... that's why he took momma to the hospital the other day to get her tubes put into a knot."

"That's interesting."

"Daddy said we drive him to drink, cause us bad as heck. And the store don't sell enough liquor to stop the pain in his butt... and he said Momma cursed."

"What?"

"Momma cursed, cause Daddy said, and my Granny said too, that every time somebody breathe on Momma her belly get big. I try my best not to breathe around her. I hold my breath like this." The boy's cheeks expanded. Jazzman struggled not to laugh.

"That's nice baby, but can you go get your mother, please."

"Yes ma'am, just don't breathe around her cause Daddy and Granny will start yelling and telling Momma how all she gone be in life is knocked up. I don't want my momma knocked up... cause if the police come and knock my momma up, we'll have to live with Granny, and I don't wanna live with Granny cause she smells funny... and..."

"Okay, I promise not to breathe on your momma, now go get her, okay."

She watched the boy scamper off, hopping up each step, pretending to be a rabbit. Her momentary lapse in purpose ended, causing her temperature to rise. Jazzman's blood began to boil over. Her fears were no match for the reality she stood in. What she imagined in her head was only a mere fraction of the damages she saw.

"Unbelievable."

The carpet was just as nappy as the child's head. She questioned if her tenant owned a vacuum cleaner. She knelt down, examined the pink like substance and came to the conclusion that it was a glob of fruity bubbalicious. A trail of saturated juice stains pointed in all directions like a maze.

"Look at my house. It was fabulous, now look at it."

She stepped further into the living room and noticed the wall mounted plasma. *This girl can afford plasma televisions, but can't afford a thirty dollar vacuum cleaner.* Sponge Bob was living it up in Bikini Bottom while her long term investment was in piss poor conditions. *I better turn the plasma off before Mike-Mike get to screaming about the electric bill.* She grabbed the remote off the glass table and knew she had seen it all.

"What the..."

Stems, seeds, Marijuana flakes scattered about with left over blunt paper. A box cutter, beer bottle tops, and colorful baggies were dumped into a pile. Not having her rent money and damaging her house was one thing. Endangering the lives of children, in a house that she owned was something else. *I'm calling Child Services.*

The urge to climb the steps and put the burner to little Miss Ghetto Queen was growing by the second. Jazzman inhaled the stale air, taking control of her emotions. *This is just business, nothing personal.*

Hanging drapes, torn blinds, and a slightly shattered window were all violations of the Subdivision Covenant. The community had rules in which all residents had to abide by, and unfortunately Jazzman's house was the only one on the block that looked raggedy, inside and out.

An oversized hot pink leather sectional covered each wall, obstructing the walk way to the dining room. She slipped her leg through the tiny passage way, and stopped at a mural.

"What the..."

Crayons, markers, pencils, and pen markings decorated the dining room wall. Gum, clay and glitter added a special customized twist. Most people displayed their children's artistic side on the fridge. Most people framed their kid's drawings, and hung them around the house, swapping them out for updated ones every so often. But the monstrosity before her was unreal.

Her eyes shifted towards the back door. She needed some air before she went crazy. Sliding glass led to the patio. Outside Jazzman thought she would cry. She leaned over the wood ledge and couldn't believe her eyes. A mountain of big black garbage bags stunk to high heavens. Jazzman did what she knew best. She closed her eyes, and prayed.

"God please don't let me catch a case. Please Lord; don't let me hurt this girl. Please Lord, I feel like shooting this hoe, then calling Child Services on her ass. Please Lord, I need you right now."

She bit down on her lower lip, regretting that she'd only charged her tenant a five hundred dollar deposit. After connecting with God the only way she knew how, she headed back inside. Her eyes landed on the mural, and instantly her rage was back.

"This bitch is going to make me strangle her."

She heard heavy footsteps above. She heard a loud thunderous voice scolding the five year old. She heard a loud thud, and then a door slammed. She heard those same heavy footsteps moving down the steps. She could smell cigarette smoke. She could feel someone standing behind her. She heard the snapping and cracking of bubble gum. *God please don't let me punch this girl in the mouth. God please, please keep me.*

"Your kids are very creative," Jazzman managed to say professionally.

"My kids usually don't open the door for strangers."

Jazzman turned, wearing the most plastic smile she could regurgitate. She had to remain cool. She was running a business. It was a rental property, and every renter had their issues. She gave the girl a once over and laughed internally. Her cut offs squeezed her thunderous thighs. The young baby tee looked more like a scrunchy. Thick mascara clumped her false eyelashes. Jazzman had no words for the raggedy lace front wig.

"I'm not the one to beat around the bush." Jazzman started out.

"I'm not pleased with the conditions of this house. You've violated your lease, you've violated the community's covenant, and I would like you out in thirty days."

The girl poked her dented, cottage cheese hip out, flicked ashes from her cigarette onto the carpet, and rolled her neck.

Oh God this girl is going to make me hurt her.

"What you mean I need to be out in thirty days? My lease ain't up for five months, so I ain't *finna* leave till then."

"Your contract is void," Jazzman said, hand delivering the eviction notice.

"Expect your certified copy in the next day or so."

Fantasia took a drag, blew circles. She crumbled the notice in her hand, flicked ashes onto the carpet. "You can't put me out in thirty days. It takes at least sixty. We gotta go to court and let the judge make that ruling. I ain't *finna* pack up my family and move cause you have a problem with the way I live. You can't just put me out. I got rights too."

"Obviously this is not your first eviction."

"*Obviously* you think I'm stupid. I know my rights."

Jazzman pointed to herself, and then pointed to the girl.

"Landlord, Tenant, Land Lord, Tenant. I can do whatever the hell I want." Jazzman pulled out her trusty digital camera and began snapping away at the sordid conditions. The chandelier dangled from a single wire. *Hazard.* A hole the size of the five year old connected the dining room to the kitchen. Dirty cat litter boxes, dog feces, and mouse droppings congregated under the same roof.

"Low rent-section 8-ghetto-bitch," Jazzman mumbled as she recorded her findings.

"What you say?"

Jazzman ignored her, and continued to gather evidence for the judge. She headed towards the kitchen. Signs of a grease fire painted the once beautiful mosaic backsplash the color of tar. An ashtray with a gazillion butts stank to high heavens. She looked back at the girl who had the audacity to have an attitude.

"I heard what you said."

Jazzman dropped her camera back into her purse, removed the designer shades from the top of her head and approached. Fantasia took a few steps back. The look on Jazzman's face told her she had no problem scrapping in her fancy stiletto boots.

"You talk to all your tenants this way?"

"No, just broke ass, low budget bitches like you."

"What?"

Jazzman took a deep breath and thought maybe the girl didn't exactly have the best upbringing. Maybe her mother didn't show her how to be a lady. Maybe, just maybe her daddy was never around. Girls needed their daddy. Not that it was any excuse to not value self, but a daddy's presence was vital in a little girl's life. She gave her tenant the benefit of the doubt before laying hands in an unholy way.

"You know what?" Jazzman inhaled. Her hands came to a praying point.

"The people who need section 8 can't get it because of people like you. You give decent tenants with vouchers a bad name. I refuse to believe that all section 8 tenants are the same, but you're making it hard for me to ever consider using this program again."

"Now, I'm not here to preach, but these living conditions are hazardous to your babies. You got stems, seeds, box cutters and baggies on the living room table. You mounted a plasma to my wall without written consent. My window is shattered. My carpet is beyond repair. Do you know how much it will cost to snatch that pissy ass carpet up?"

The girl took a seat at the kitchen table and said nothing. The sound of the ringing telephone made her spring up.

"Sit down."

Big girl rolled her neck. "Who the hell do you think you talking too?"

"I'm telling you something for your own good. I'm doing what your momma should have done to you a long time ago."

"Don't talk about my momma."

Jazzman shot her a stern look. "I can't even imagine how much primer and paint it will take to cover that wall in there. I mean who the hell allows their children to mess up a wall like that? I'm all for being creative. I love the arts, but I'd be damn if I let my son scribble on a wall that I didn't own. *Who does that?*"

The wall mounted phone in the kitchen started ringing. Fantasia stood.

"Let *Mike-Mike* get the damn phone."

Jazzman pointed towards the sliding glass door. Embarrassment covered the girl's face, her eyes glued to the floor. Muddy paw prints from her Rottweiler dried against the linoleum.

"The backyard is not a dumpster. You can't just dispose of your garbage by throwing it over the damn railing. Trash service is just eleven dollars a month, thirty-three dollars quarterly. I can't even begin to imagine what upstairs looks like."

"Just keep my security deposit."

Jazzman brought her hands to her head before they ended up around the girl's neck. *Just keep my security deposit. Did she think she would get it back? Did she really have to say that?*

"Do you know how much it costs to maintain a house? No, you don't know. You don't know because all you care about is paying your funky twenty-five dollars a month. Speaking of which, you haven't paid it. You can afford a plasma TV, weed to smoke, beer to drink, but you can't put a measly twenty-five dollars in the mail."

"I can get you the money."

"It's much bigger than that now. It's going to cost me to get this house up to code. I have to hire contractors to come in and gut this place. Your funky ass deposit will barely buy paint and supplies."

Stripper music blared from the inside of a knock-off Gucci purse that sat on the kitchen table. She grabbed it, tugged at the zipper. *Jammed.* "Damn, it's stuck." She tugged, yanked, pulled but the zipper wouldn't budge. The lining was caught in the tracks.

"Look, I need to answer that. Are we done?"

"Bitch, no, we're not done. We're just getting started," Jazzman snapped.

Fantasia jumped from her seat, bucked her chest. "I ain't gone be too many more bitches. You can get the fuck out. Better yet, *get the fuck out.*"

Jazzman went to snatch Fantasia by the neck but froze when she saw the beautiful, snot nosed, nappy headed brown boy running towards them. He had fresh tears in his eyes. Her arms relaxed at her side. *Behave girl,* she told herself.

"Momma, Momma, Granny on the phone."

"Tell her I'll call her back."

"But Momma... Granny crying... something happened to Uncle Flap."

Jazzman burst into a cold sweat. Her body went numb. Her legs were about to give way. She leaned against the counter top for support. *Did he just say Uncle Flap?*

"Granny...said..." *Heeezzzz Cough.*

"...Uncle Flap..." *Heeezzzz Cough.*

"Dead." *Heeezzzz Cough.*

"What?" Fantasia grabbed the phone, shoving her son to floor.

"What you mean he dead... dead how... when... oh my God... no... my brother dead....Flap dead."

Jazzman heard children wailing, and screaming from above. Big heavy footsteps clonked and stomped down the steps. She turned, and saw the devil running towards her. He was black. He was so black that he looked blue. He had a slumped, stroke victim's face. The man was eerily unattractive, with Brillo pad nappy hair, dressed in boxer shorts, and torn tee-shirt. Tears slipped, softening the crust at the corners of his eyes. He bent down to console his woman. Fantasia had fallen to the floor, next to her son. She was in shock, hurt, mumbling with saliva dripping from the corners of her mouth.

"Mike-Mike somebody killed Flap."

"I know baby. Just got the word from Bra-Bra and em'. They say somebody set him up."

The moment was sensitive, vulnerable in every way. Jazzman couldn't breathe. She couldn't swallow; she couldn't stop herself from shaking. She needed to warn Lou-Lou and Roy, but first she needed to get the hell out of there. *Fast!*

"Calm down, take little man upstairs. Get the kids dressed. I'm taking you to your mother's."

"Nooooo... I can't take this... My brother.... My brother..." Earsplitting screams resonated from Fantasia's belly. The little brown boy sobbed hysterically with his head in his mommy's lap. A herd of footsteps came

clonking down the stairs. Mike-Mike halted the wild pack of kids with a glare that made Jazzman shiver. Without him saying a single word, the children made an about face.

"Look, pull yourself together. Get the kids dressed; go to your momma's house. She needs you right now." Mike-Mike looked back; saw Jazzman easing towards the door. "Who are you?" His voice boomed

Jazzman almost jumped out of her own skin. "*Hum*, I was just leaving."

His dark murderous eyes tore through her flesh. "I said, who are you?"

"The landlord... *hum*... I was just leaving..."

He swung open the pantry door, and grabbed a metal canister. "You here for money?"

"Hum... *no*... see... the thing is..."

He popped the top, grabbed a stack of bills and peeled back several wrinkled Benjamin's. "Will this cover the rent and damages?"

"*Y-Yes*. This will cover."

"As you can see, it's a bad time for our family. My brother was murdered last night."

Her head dropped, eyes searched the gritty floor. "Yes, of course. My condolences to the family." *Did I just say that? Ugh, just shoot me now.*

Jazzman couldn't get to her rental quick enough. She sped away from the house, hitting corners, swerving in and out of lanes. She hopped on Interstate 75N and headed for Hartsfield Jackson International Airport.

CHAPTER 9

B ack to back dreams caused paranoia to set in. Rick's firm hand pressed against Jazzman's stomach. Her eyes shot opened. She gasped. He held her close, kissing the back of her neck. Same recurring dream for the last two nights threatened her peace. Mike-Mike's cold eyes and mean slumped face was a vision she couldn't escape. The screeching sound of Fantasia was a sound imbedded in her brain. The look on those kids' faces tore her to pieces.

The cord around her neck was remorse. The pain in her heart was guilt. According to Roy, Mike-Mike wasn't a problem, but Jazzman knew better. His evil eyes told a story. A story not yet played out. Premeditated murder, get-back, retaliation was on the horizon.

"Don't know this cat personally, but he's nothing to worry about," Roy said when she finally tracked him down.

"Listen to me Roy. You and Lou-Lou need to get out of Atlanta for a while. I'm telling you, Mike-Mike means business."

Rick's arm slipped away, as she sat up. He'd been at her side since she returned from Atlanta two nights ago. His presence made a difference, especially now.

They'll be coming for me first. The getaway driver always catches it in the noodle. Look at the poor bastard from the movie Heat. Robert De Niro offered him a job right out the back door of a soup kitchen and bam... his ass is dead, Jazzman thought, fearfully gripping the sheets.

"You're losing sleep. Just call his parole officer back and tell him you've changed your mind," Rick said, interrupting the movie reel in her head. He rubbed tension from her shoulders. He kissed her neck again.

"Babe, you're entitled to change your mind." His voice was very convincing.

"I know."

Rick assumed her worries came from Tony, and his release. Why he assumed that clown made her lose sleep was beyond her understanding. Not to say his arrival didn't cause her nerves to go a little haywire, but he wasn't the source of everything.

Her thoughts shifted back to Roy and Lou-Lou. She wondered if they were okay. She hadn't heard from either of them. She hoped for the best, but was expecting the worst. Mike-Mike was looking to avenge Flap's death, while Roy and Lou-Lou were moving Flaps work. And Kema, she still couldn't put a finger on that girl. She knew things were bound to come full circle.

"You need to relax," Rick said, breaking her thoughts again.

"I'm cool."

"Call the damn parole officer, Jazzman."

"Can't."

His hands slid from her shoulders, wrapped around her waist. "You can. You don't want to."

She looked over her shoulder, kissed the tip of his nose. "I gave him my word."

He leaned back against the stacked pillows, brought both hands behind his head. He looked up at the ceiling for a while before saying, "I know what you need. You need a vacation."

"We just got back from the Bahamas."

"The Bahamas is nowhere. You can see Miami from the Bahamas."

"Well, I had a ball."

He quickly sat up, swung his muscular legs over the side of the bed, and stood. Family jewels swinging and dancing as he went to take a leak. He returned a couple of beats later still on the same topic.

"I'm thinking a cruise. Just you and me sailing the deep blue seas," he said, jumping back into his space.

"I don't do open bodies of water."

"Why not?"

"Can't swim. Never learned."

"Are you serious?"

"Grew up in the hood, didn't have vacation properties in Tampa to practice my backstroke."

"Stop it. You must have gone to the community pool as a kid."

"Dirty ass Liberty Pool wasn't the ideal place for swim practice. It was too crowded and too damn nasty. Floating tampons, dirty condoms, shitty diapers. A real Chlamydia pool."

He started to laugh, but noticed her look was serious. "You're kidding, right?"

"I'm dead ass serious."

"Come on; don't make me feel guilty for being privileged."

"Sorry for being less fortunate."

He scratched the side of his head, obviously in a state of bewilderment. "Why is this new revelation to me?"

She shrugged. "Beats me."

"I thought all this time you played the splashing game because of the black hair fear."

"The what?"

"You know, black girls and their hair... ya'll sistahs are afraid of getting your hair wet."

She laughed. "That's less of an issue for me. I'm just afraid of the water. I'm more than content with floating in nothing above my shoulder blades." She showed off her perfect set of whites. Behind her smile bore deep concern. Her melt down was coming fast and furious. She needed to hear Lou-Lou's voice. She needed an update from Roy. She needed somebody to say something to ease her anxieties.

When Jazzman called Lou-Lou at the hotel, she was informed that she'd checked out. Her cell phone was all of a sudden disconnected, and Roy wasn't returning her calls. Things weren't adding up. Something was definitely wrong.

"I don't buy that. Not learning how to swim is like never learning to ride a bike."

"Oh please, that's like saying never learning to drive is like never learning to swim. One thing has nothing to do with the other," she said knowingly.

"You should really consider joining the gym with me."

She pinched her stomach. The frictions she felt between her legs recently, whenever she walked was a clear indication of weight gain. Ten pounds found its way onto her curvy frame in less than two months.

Stress eating is what the media called it. She was a part of the millions of people who ate when problems arose. Chocolate layered cakes, strawberries topped with sugar, submerged in whip cream, drizzled in chocolate was a delight when her phone interviews hadn't turned into face-to-faces. Banana pudding with extra Nilla wafers, topped with vanilla ice cream held her prisoner when her face-to-faces hadn't offered her a solid position. Stress eating had half of America fighting obesity.

She dropped her head into a set of open hands. "Oh God, I'm fat."

"That's not what I meant."

"Yes it is. Admit it. I'm fat."

"You're not fat."

She straightened her spine. "Yes, I am. Look at me."

He exhaled. "You're thick. Not fat. There's a big difference."

"I haven't done a single crunch in three weeks."

"Three days, three weeks, three months, you're still fine as hell to me," he said, kissing her lips.

"You just suggested that I join the gym with you. That means I'm fat."

"No silly, I suggested you join so you can learn how to swim."

"Oh."

"There's a four lane Olympic size pool onsite. In just three months you'll be a pro."

Her thoughts shifted to Tony. Taking him in, under her roof, after all he's done was very big of her. She had every right to decline his stay, but she didn't.

"The Jacuzzi and sauna is unbelievable." Rick did his best to sell her on the idea, but she wasn't buying it.

"Sounds like a nice facility," she said half heartedly.

Rick was good to her, good to Jacob, but she didn't expect him to understand. Tony was going to be a problem, she could feel it. She wondered why she couldn't be like most females. Throw his ass out with the trash and leave him for the sanitation man to pick up. *Damn!*

Her cell vibrated against the end table. It was Roy calling. *Bad Timing!* She wanted to answer, wanted to excuse herself and get the lowdown, but couldn't. Rick was already going hard on Tony. The last person she needed to explain was Roy. She hit the *ignore* button.

His brow arched inwardly. He wanted to question her about the caller, drill her, but he backed off. "I'll call Sandy, my travel agent. She'll hook us up with a deck view. I'm thinking the Mediterranean Sea. Seven days."

"Burn or drown. That's the only two options."

He laughed. "You're paranoid. Nothing will happen."

"Pirates hijack ships. Don't you watch the news?"

"Stop it. Seriously, you sound a bit..." He circled his index finger near his temple.

"Planes crash, boats sink. Passengers can't even get from New York, to North Carolina without ending up in the Hudson River. It's the sign of the times."

"Wow... that sounds pretty strange coming from a once careered flight attendant."

"That was another life. Besides, they still can't find those NFL players lost a sea. Sorry, no cruises for me. I'll jump on a bird any day of the week, but no ships."

"I still don't understand what the hell they were doing fishing on that tiny ass boat. Oprah had the only survivor on her show and his story sounded a bit... fishy," Rick said rubbing his chin.

"Yeah well, I'm not trying to swim with the fish. They stay out mi casa, I'm staying out theirs."

She wasn't budging, so he changed the subject. "How was your trip to Atlanta?"

Jack hammering throb pained her temples. Images of Atlanta crowded her mind. She squinted, but the pain had risen.

"You alright, did I say something wrong?"

"I've got this sharp pain in my head."

He kissed between her perfectly tweezed brows. "You're stressing too much."

"I'm thirsty," she said, clearing her throat.

"Water or juice?"

"Ice water and two Advils please."

He jumped out of bed, and ran down the steps. She heard him yelp. Rick was notorious for banging his big toe on furniture.

"What am I going to do?" she asked herself. Mike-Mike was on her mind. Roy had surely underestimated this man's feelings. He was out for blood. She grabbed her phone and was just about to dial Roy when Rick came hobbling back into the room.

"That was fast," she said popping two blue pills into her mouth, and chased it with water. He sat, pulled his knee to his chest, and examined his foot. "*Ugh*. Hit my toe on the dining room table."

"Want me to rub it?"

He made a face. The last time he accepted her offer to massage his big toe she'd managed to do more harm than good. "No."

She shrugged. "Don't say I didn't ask."

"So, Atlanta was all business as usual?"

"Yes."

"Did you collect rent?"

"Yes, she paid some."

"What was the condition of the house?"

She sighed. "Terrible."

"You took pictures I hope?"

"Yes, took pictures."

"My parents had a condo in Orlando they used to rent out. It generated a nice income for many years up until about three years ago. The last tenant was hell to deal with. Once those keys get in their hands it's no telling what will happen. Pops convinced my mom's to sell, but Moms wanted to hold on to it. Location was prime. Just steps away from

Walt Disney World. She figured it would come in handy one day soon, with having grandkids and all."

She rubbed her temples. "Look, do you mind if we talk about something else?"

"No problem."

She stood, walked towards the bathroom. When she returned, Rick was seated at the edge of the bed, with his cell pressed against his lobe.

"Sandy, this is Rick. I need two tickets for that seven day cruise off the Mediterranean. Hit me back when you get this."

She grabbed her robe, pulled it over her shoulders slowly. *Roy, Lou-Lou, Tony, Rick, Flap, Mike – Mike, Fantasia, her son Jacob, bills, money.* Her thoughts held her hostage. He pulled her close, kissed her tummy, made soft kisses up and beneath her B-Cup breasts. She noticed him rising, felt his hand grip her waist firmly. His puckered lips and determined tongue danced across her stomach, and around her nipples. He had good range, good access to her treats. She grabbed his face, kissed his lips, putting a stop to his rhythm.

"Am I doing it wrong?"

"You can never do it wrong, baby."

"Then why'd you stop me?" he felt himself below, then felt her below. "You're not wet."

"I need a moment to think."

"You want me to leave?"

"I'll call you."

He chuckled nervously. "You'll call me?"

She gathered his shoes, pants, shirt, and placed them beside him. Hurt plastered his face. Anger tightened his once relaxed jaw. He grabbed her hand, pulling her into his lap. He tried to kiss her lips, but got nothing but cheek when she turned.

"Why you trippin?"

"I'm not. Just got a lot on my mind, yah know."

"So you want me to leave?" he asked as if her decision would change, as if the way he stared into her eyes would make her reconsider. Rick was playing her close, closer than usual. She needed a minute to *self*, minute to breathe, minute to think and re-think. She needed to call

Roy back, get the low down, and make sure everyone was still breathing.

"We need to talk about this."

"Please leave."

"Don't you think you're being a little extreme?"

"There are some things I need to handle, alone. I've got issues. I'm trying to come up with some extra ends. Can't take a vacation right now, can't do nothing at the moment." Her lips, pouty and cute. Perfectly arched eyebrow inched inward and froze.

"So you want me to leave?"

Was he deaf, did he not understand English? Jazzman articulated very clearly, annunciating every word and syllable. Both hands clasped together in a praying position.

"Give me a couple of days."

"What if I said I didn't want to leave?"

She removed herself from is lap and gave him a sharp look. She began to pace back and forth, chewing relentlessly at her nails. She liked Rick. She liked him a lot. He was good to her, good to her son. Well rounded, educated, had good genes. His parents were retired medical professionals. Father was blessed with surgical hands. Mother was a gynecologist, owned and operated a private practice for over thirty years. Family heirloom surpassed bronze baby shoes and playa-listic pinky rings with flawed diamond chips. His parents invested wisely. Rick's, kids, kids, whenever he decided to have any, would be financially set. He was perfect, sometimes too perfect.

"I love you."

She stopped pacing. *Did he just say he loved me?*

"Did you hear me?"

"I heard you, but why?"

"Why ask why?"

She folded her arms across her chest. "*Why* is relevant to what I might say next."

"We've been seeing each other for a few years."

"And?"

"Have you once been unhappy?"

"Can't say that I have."

"Why you staring me down like that?" he asked.

"Like what?"

"Like I said something wrong. Like I stole something."

"You pick a fine time to tell me."

"If not now, then when?"

"I just hope your decision to speak those very sensitive words have nothing to do with Tony."

"Of course not, I love you."

"Don't play with my emotions, Rick."

"I'm not."

"This is too much for me."

"Remember the first time we met?"

She smirked. "Yes. I remember."

***

It was the first day of summer. Ridgemore's annual company picnic was in full swing. The lawn at Central Park had blankets, coolers, and families spread out amongst the earth's greenery. The wind was strong enough to keep a kite, and gentle enough to kiss a newborn baby's head.

He spotted her, sitting beneath a tree with purple leaves. Book in hand, shades covering her eyes, grape soda sipped in-between each read paragraph. Both knees pulled up to her chest, rocking back and forth. He watched her turn each page, watched how her lips turned upward when she read something funny. Every now and then she would glance up, tilt her glasses, and yell something to a kid climbing a nearby tree.

"Good book?"

"Really good book," she responded while placing her bookmark between the printed sheets.

"What's it about?"

She smiled up at him. "Black love in Manhattan. A job proposal potentially threatening to steal the moment from two people who deserve to be together. The main character just proposed to the woman of his dreams, and within in hours he gets the call he's been waiting for all his life."

137

"So, he's stuck between love and having the career he's always dreamt of having?"

She nodded. "Right."

"There's a simple solution."

She giggled. "Oh really?"

"You see, all he has to do is relocate himself and his fiancé to where he can begin his successful career. Case closed."

"Oh, if life were only that simple," she said, staring down at the book.

"You're sporting the company tee-shirt, but I've never seen you around the office before. Does your husband work for Ridgemore?"

Smooth. She tugged at the one-size too big picnic shirt and said, "I'm a guest. And I'm not married."

He smiled. "What's your name?"

"Jazzman."

"Jazzman. That's pretty. Well, since I'm standing here, blocking your sun, would it be alright if I joined you?"

"I don't know you."

"The wonderful thing about not knowing me is now you have the opportunity to get to know me. I'm Rick."

"Nice to meet you Rick, but me and my son, and this *really* good book have sort of closed the circle to this party."

"Understandable. Can I call you some time, perhaps take you out? We can discuss the details of that *really* good book you're reading. Maybe we can read it together."

She handed over her phone without hesitation.

"Punch your number in."

***

As Rick spilled his soul, uncovering the intimate details of his heart, her mind was elsewhere. All she heard was *I love you because...* Every other word from that point sounded like gibberish. There was so much that needed to be done. In just two days Tony would be home. Two days to clean her house from top to bottom. She had to get groceries, and go to the salon. Just two days to renege if she wanted to.

"Have you heard anything I just said?"

"Yes. *No*. Not really. I need a moment Rick. Please, just give me a moment to get my head right."

"Why can't we just talk about this?"

"Because..."

"Because what? Talk to me," he said sharply.

Her mouth opened, and then closed.

"Say it."

"I can't do this right now."

He moved in close to her. "If not now, then when?"

She stepped away, turned, and headed towards her walk-in closet. He followed closely, grabbing her waist, begging her to stop. She swatted his hands, didn't feel like being touched. She dropped her robe, and reached for a pair of cut-offs.

"Give them back."

He held her shorts high above his head. "What do I need to do? Tell me and I'll do it."

"Rick, I just..."

"What?"

"I need space!" she screamed.

Space. That five letter word always meant trouble. *Space* provided opportunity for another to take the place of the other. *Space* divided and conquered. Rick blinked once and tears began to roll down his cheek. She turned away, couldn't stand to look at him.

"Did I do something, say something wrong?"

"I need to be alone."

"You don't mean that."

"You keep hitting me with questions, questions that I can't answer at this moment." Tears of her own sprung forth.

He squeegeed water away from her lids. "He's got you losing sleep."

"Just stop. Okay."

"I can't touch you now?"

"Give me a minute to process what I'm feeling."

"Look what he's doing to us. Look at your eyes. No offense, but you look like a raccoon." She folded her arms, shifted from one leg to the next. *No he didn't!*

"I can't express what I feel until I know what I feel. My life just became complicated."

"You know, women like you kill me."

"Women like me?"

"You talk all this crap about not settling, about how you can do bad by yourselves, how ain't no man about to bring you down because you better than that. Soon as some chump from your past come knocking, you let em' in. All of a sudden shit is complicated"

"I can't expect you to understand which is why I'm asking for space."

His head fell into his chest. Agitated chuckle, followed by deep breathing. His nostrils flared. The female species regulated on a *complicated system* was what his mother used to always say.

"I love you."

No response, no gesture, no suggestive movement that reciprocated mutual emotions. His shoulders dropped ten stories. Her cutoffs slipped from his grip. He backed away slowly. She watched as he dressed, as he slipped his size twelve's into his trainers, pulling tightly at his laces. Her hard-body-eye-candy drifted out the door. She followed behind him, down the steps, into the open foyer.

She called out to him.

He stopped.

They stood facing each other. There were more tears in his eyes than in hers. She reached out to him, wiped his pain away. It was hard watching him leave, but she had to let him go. Rick's truck hadn't made it completely out the driveway before she hit redial.

"*C'mon*, answer the damn phone, Roy." After a couple of rings, her call went to the generic voicemail. She hung up, called again. Hung up, called again. She did this for an hour straight, with no luck of speaking to Roy.

She kicked back, watched Chris Rock go hard on George Bush. *Kill the Messenger,* his standup comedy show had her in stitches. With all the issues surrounding her life, a little laughter was needed. She tipped the wine glass back, draining the last of the Moscato. *"You stupid Chris."* She held her side, cracking up in laughter.

The cell phone chimed, interrupting her first bit of happiness in many days. It was a *private* caller. She started not to answer, started to let the automated attendant get it. Started to just unplug the battery, and hide it beneath the dirty laundry for a while. Started to cut herself off from the outside world, pretend she was the last person on earth; pretend that civilization depended on her and her alone. Started to pull a *Lauren Hill* move, and fall off the face of the earth.

"What you doing?" Ricks voice brought on an instant migraine.

"Relaxing," she said turning Rock's voice to a mere whisper. She watched as he changed from Tuxedo, to business suite, to a shiny black jacket, still on queue, still in sync from his last joke.

"Can I come over?"

"You just left here three hours ago."

"Feels like three years ago. I miss you. I know that I agreed to give you some space, but I need to see you tonight."

She giggled.

"Television more important?"

"Don't start."

"Whatever. Can I stop by just for a second? I'm around the corner."

She jumped out of bed, turned off the television, and peaked through the drapes. Her neighbor Maria was throwing a baby shower for her daughter. Pink balloons and streamers decorated the brick face mailbox. Cars lined the cul-de-sac. She noticed Rick's Range Rover pulling into her driveway. Rims glistened; sparkling paint looked as if he just drove that baby off a show room floor.

"I'm in bed."

"I can see you," he said, then hung up.

She cursed beneath her breath, squeezing the receiver, trying best not to go off the deep end. She stepped away from the window, pulled on her cut-offs and tee-shirt. By the time she made it downstairs, Rick was standing outside her door. She heard three light taps against the steel frame.

She opened the door slowly, surveying him from head to toe. He sported a black button down, with white stitching around the cuff and collar. Black slacks, leather hard bottom shoes were fresh out the box. He moved past the threshold without permission. His fresh woodsy scent elevated her desire to touch him. Her once snobbish attitude took a backseat. *Damn,* was all she could say to herself as he took concentrated steps towards the dining room table.

He stopped at an open photo album. As he flipped through several plastic covered sheets, the ball in his throat bounced up and down. Pictures of Tony, of her, of when they *used* to be a couple. Cornbraids. Street gear. Tattoo across the neck. He scanned the next page. Tattoos covered his chest, back and arms. Glowing blunt between his lips, pistol in hand, one on his hip. She snatched the book, slipped the brown leather folder between the creases of her armpit.

"This is the kind of nigga you want raising your son?"

She was shocked. Rick never used the *N*-word before, at least not around her.

"Don't judge a book by its cover."

"I'm not judging, just calling it like I see it. He's a dope boy."

"*Was* a dope boy and please, watch your tone. *My son is asleep,*" she whispered.

"Think about all that you've worked for, all that you've earned and accomplished while he was away. Are you really willing to put all that on the line? Is he really worth it?"

"Rick, I told you. This is something I don't want to discuss right now," she said grabbing, her head. *I need a drink.*

He followed her into the kitchen. "I'm giving you a headache now?"

"Can we please discuss this another day, perhaps tomorrow?"

"Why put off tomorrow what we can accomplish tonight?"

She opened her mouth to speak.

He held up his hand. "Do you still love him?"

"No."

He rubbed his hands together. Shiny gold watch hugged his wide receiver wrist. He seemed partially satisfied with her answer. Partially satisfied to hear there was no love for Tony. A slight smirk found its way onto his lips, and then vanished just as quickly.

"Do you love me?"

She poured more Moscato into her glass. "Rick."

"Answer the damn question. Do you love me, Jazzman?"

"I care about you a lot. It's a good chance it could be love, in the future, *maybe*."

"Wow. Okay, I see."

A moment passed.

"Why you all dressed up?"

"I'm meeting a friend later for drinks."

"Just drinks?"

Just then, his cell chimed. "Aren't you going to answer that?"

"No."

"You should. It's not polite to keep your date waiting," she said with both arms folded angrily. He smirked, offering no comment to clarify her suspicions. *She's jealous!*

Rick eyed the brown leather photo album. She clutched it tight. Held onto those memories like they would fly away, leave her with nothing but her thoughts. The truth lined the inserts of those plastic sheets. The truth was hard for him to chew, even harder to swallow.

"I respect your wishes."

"Where does this leave us?"

"I'll wait. When you get tired of *what's-his-face*, you know where to find me."

CHAPTER 10

Downtown Atlanta was no Times Square, but it had its moments. Trendy shops, restaurants, high rise buildings, fancy hotels, a stretch of vendors dotted the sidewalks selling knock of accessories, and attire.

Atlanta had vintage charm, urban flare, an oasis of calm collectively poured into a melting pot of acceptance. The gay capital of the world, the land of opportunity, a place where you could reinvent, recharge, renew.

"Leaving us so soon?"

Lou-Lou slipped into the back of the meter cab after tipping the devilishly handsome bell hop a crisp twenty. *He's too young.* Her mind said, but her body was saying to *cougar* his ass. She wet her lips, smiled.

"I have business elsewhere."

Checking out of the Omni Hotel wasn't a part of the plan but she needed to be cautious. Flap's murder hit the streets and Jazzman's encounter with Mike-Mike had her a bit spooked to say the least.

"I'm say'n, can I get your number at least?" the younging asked, placing the last of her *LV* luggage into the trunk of the cab. She tilted her shades, looking up into a set of lazy brown eyes. *He's a baby, Lou.* "Sorry honey, I've got dignity, some of the time. *Stay cute.*" The driver pulled away, leaving her fantasy standing curbside.

Police directed traffic; students shuffled off to class. Georgia Tech owned that area. Kosha popped into her mind. She promised her five stacks. Five stacks would set her straight her first year at Spelman. Feeling proud of her baby cousin, who would be the first in their family to go off to college.

A group of conscience brothers huddled outside the Marta station, debating something heavy. Across the street, at the *Underground* stood a group of homo-thugs looking fruitylicious. As Lou-Lou let the window fall she inhaled awareness, culture, and southern goodness on many different levels.

Her ride came to a slow roll, and stopped in front of a small bakery. The air was filled with an abundance of sweetness that made her stomach growl. Regaining focus, Lou-Lou copied down the driver's name, and taxi number for safe keeping.

"Wait right here." She eased out the backseat. *LV* printed scarf shielded her neck from the cold. She clutched her purse, pressing her life savings against her bosom. Her pockets were on swole but she needed more dough to cop the ride of her dreams.

Pawnshop was stamped in metal letters against a woodened plaque. She tugged at the door. It was locked. There was a sign, *Ring Buzzer for Entry.* She mashed the buzzer, and within seconds the door clicked. Eager to hock her valuables, she moved through Fort Knox with purpose, with crystal vision. *Bitches gone hate when I get my new whip.*

The profit she made off Flap, and the return on her jewels would be enough to pull that new Bentley off the lot, *free and clear.* She quickly cased the joint, and to her surprise it was empty. *Okay, let's get down to business.*

The jeweler peered through the eyepiece, examining each stone with an acute eye.

"Look, its all official."

The jeweler looked up from one of the rarest pieces in her collection, nodded.

"These pieces are timeless, especially this one."

She picked up a gold locket smothered in baguettes. Bradley purchased that piece their first Christmas together. He rented a small bungalow in the Caymans, and surprised her with the locket, and breakfast in bed. Buttered croissants, fresh fruit, and a black velvet box decorated the silver tray. They were in a good place *emotionally* during that time. Life was perfect.

"You own?" His Middle Eastern accent thick.

"Of course I own."

"This is substantial amount of diamonds. We require thumb print. You agree to thumb print?"

She sucked her teeth. "Am I being arrested? You wanna do business or not?"

"Thumb print protects my business. Lately jewelry from home invasions ends up in my shop. I pay out big money to seller, only to find out the pieces were stolen. Much dead women jewelry passed through my hands without my knowledge," he said as if someone was listening in.

His index finger arched inward, directing her to inch closer. She leaned into the glass display and almost vomited. He smelled like pissed on cat litter. His dilated eyes were a clear indication he was high off something. *You off that Meth*, she thought holding her breath.

"Homicide detectives got me under surveillance. I don't know sellers personally. I run legit business. I buy gold and diamond from anyone looking to sell. But detectives making my business bad. Sellers scared to give thumb print."

"They take their jewelry to Decatur. No thumb print required there. I pay out good money if the value is good. That's why everybody comes to me first." He placed a sincere hand over his heart. Long stringy hairs popped out the top of his shirt. His nostrils and knuckles were just as hairy.

She inched away. *Surveillance. Detectives.* Lou-Lou slipped her dark shades over her eyes, and grabbed her stones. The eager Jeweler placed a gentle hand against her shoulder. "I buy from you."

"No thanks, I'm good. Sorry I bothered you." She shook his hand away, turning to leave. He made a cat like hissing sound.

"Beautiful lady, we do it, under the table. No paper work. No thumb print."

She looked around, over her shoulder and back. She was desperate. She needed to cash in, and fast. Riding around in the back of some meter cab wasn't cutting it. She needed wheels. *Bentley Wheels!*

"But how?"

"Two blocks up. Coffee house. One hour."

"Make it twenty minutes."

Twenty minutes later Lou-Lou spotted the Jeweler pulling up in an old shiny Lincoln Continental. His skittish behavior made her want to back out, perhaps find someone else to turn her stones into cash. His eyes darted from left to right as he headed towards the entrance. She gave him the nod, telling him it was okay to approach. His movements were erratic, causing her to feel a bit nervous. He scribbled the payout against a napkin, and slid it across the table. She looked up, face twisted. She flung the napkin back at him.

"Don't waste my time. My stuff is official. Certified. *I own*."

His shoulders touched his ears, his palms faced God. "But I come to this country to make money for my family. I make no money off this. I must turn profit."

"That's a crack head payout and you know it." She pounded a closed fist against the table. Heads turned. He ran his fingers against his greasy hair and nodded. He presented another offer, this one a lot more generous than the first. She could have gotten him for more, but time was money. The meter in her cab was adding up. She nodded in agreement. They transacted quickly, and parted ways.

Her next destination, *Bentley lot*. When Lou-Lou stepped out the taxi, all eyes were on her. Sales Associates, Mechanics, Managers, potential buyers, all watched as she moved through the lot with certainty. Her duffle bag, lined with her life savings, slung over her left shoulder. Lou-Lou eyed the yellow sticker price. "I want it." She wasted no time with sales pitches, pricing, or loan approvals. She pointed out the car of her dreams. Baby blue Bentley Coup with peanut butter interior shouted *Buy me*.

She slapped the cost of the price tag on the table. The finance manager looked up from his wire frame prescriptions and laughed a nervous laugh.

"You know this could cost me my job," he whispered.

"You owe me one, remember?"

"I owe Bradley a favor, not you. Besides, you need to go through proper channels, forms, identification, and IRS documents to show how you're able to pay the cost of the vehicle in full. Any purchases over $999,999 require strict documentation."

"So, make it happen Captain. Say that I won the lottery, inheritance, lawsuit or whatever sounds best. Just get me the keys to that beautiful bitch, *today*."

"It doesn't work like that Lou-Lou. You can't walk in off the streets and drop all this cash on the table. This ain't no damn rap video."

"Do what you do best and make me legit then."

"I'm required to uphold strict legal and ethical standards. This is not some Buy-Here-Pay-Here-Fly-By-Night. This is a well respected established dealership. My boss will have my nuts in a grinder if I did this."

"*C'mon*, man. You can do it. I know you can."

"If you want to pay cash money for a vehicle with no questions asked, then go to the hood. I'm sure one of those grease bums will be more than willing to take your cash offer."

"So you're saying you're not going to help me?"

"I'm saying I *can't* help you. Now if you don't mind..."

She grabbed the bag of money, knocking a steaming cup of dark roast over. Bank approval or not she was getting that car.

"Christ. Look what you've done."

She watched him pat dry the large desk with paper towels he'd saved from various fast food restaurants. "You still live in that cute little house in Fayetteville with the white picket fence?"

His skin turned blood shot red, his eyes ballooned alien size.

"You wouldn't."

"If memory serves me correctly the wife's name is Sarah. I'll just stop by and inform Sarah that you sucked piss from my pussy and kissed her babies with that same mouth, that very same night."

"Have a seat. That won't be necessary."

Bitches already hating! Lou-Lou snickered, noticing the audience she now had as she sauntered out of the finance office a proud owner of a Bentley Coup. It was nice having friends in high places.

She winked at some dude and his chick as they awaited the bank's approval on the same Mercedes she just had chopped up in the Bronx.

"Good choice. Rides good," she said on her way to the detailing department.

After paying her driver to unload her luggage into the trunk of her new car, she eased behind the wheel, adjusting her seat, and then her mirrors. Dirty mechanics tried desperately to get her attention. "You can't afford me *boo-boo*."

That new car smell, permeated throughout, making her feel like a million bucks. Her insides were screaming with joy. Her stomach fluttered in excitement. She inhaled, kept her cool, and stayed calm. Her fans were still watching. Haters were still clocking. It was important for them to know she was used to expensive toys. Bradley exposed her to the good life, so it was only natural that she worked hard at maintaining the image he'd helped her build. *What I look like riding in anything less. Bitches gone be sick!*

She applied a generous amount of gloss to her lips, checked her hair, and turned her radio dial to V103. The Noonday Mix was in full rotation. A northern flavor beat from her speakers. She felt right at home. She felt as if she was stunting on Jamaica Avenue back in the day with her cousin Isis, riding shot gun in her Mercedes. She slipped her designer shades over her eyes and peeled off the lot.

Car paid for bitches!

***

Lou-Lou secured a spacious suite at the Embassy Suites in downtown Atlanta. Her view of Centennial Olympic Park was perfect. *So pretty*, she thought while admiring the outdoor ice skating rink. There were thousands of twinkling lights, holiday cheer, festive tunes, and families loving one another.

Alone she stood, watching from afar like some spectator whose life was empty, void. She closed the drapes and grabbed the pre-paid cell phone she'd just purchased from Rite Aid. She read the instructions and before long, she had service. Lou-Lou immediately got up with Roy. His pockets were still on swole, this she was sure of.

"Who this?" His voice came through raspy.

"Lou-Lou."

"I called your room, was told you checked out. Your cell disconnected too."

"Had to make moves," she said.

He chuckled. "Never sleep in the same place twice."

She smirked. "Lightning never strikes in the same place twice. Why should I?"

"I taught you well."

"This is my new number."

She'd watched enough investigative shows to know detectives could pin-point every move with cell phone towers. Modern day devices could be tapped, providing a place, time and date to which a certain crime had taken place. So, she ditched her contractual agreement, and hooked up a pre-paid connection with a bogus credit card. She managed to lift a stack of loan documents off the finance manager's desk when he wasn't looking.

"You must have a bullshit pre-paid."

"Is it that obvious?"

"Your voice sound like shit. Where you staying now?" Roy asked, breaking through the static.

"In Atlanta."

"No shit. Where in Atlanta?" he asked firmly.

"We need to meet," she said, bypassing his question.

"When?"

"Now. I need that work."

"You got a buyer."

"Told you I got connects."

"Name the place."

"One hour. Atlantic Station. Underground parking lot."

One hour later Lou-Lou inched her new wheels into the handicap spot adjacent to Roy's truck. Roy looked as if he were asleep behind the wheel. Both eyes shut, head pressed against the headrest. She tooted her horn. His eyes bucked. Kema's head shot up. He smiled, held up one finger. She could tell he was thoroughly impressed with her new ride.

Kema wiped the corners of her mouth, finger waved respectfully. Lou-Lou's fingers drummed the steering wheel, teeth clinched. Half cocked smirked formed, froze. *Pocket your beef for that bread. Get money!*

It took Roy only a second to gather himself, which meant Kema's head game wasn't worth squat. He stepped out, walked around her whip, surveyed her new toy, inspecting from all angles. Kema held her composure. She fought back the urge to ride Lou-Lou's tip but she could no longer be phony. She had to give it up. The blue Bentley was wicked.

"Damn girl. That car is cleaner than the Board of Health," Kema complimented.

You mean cleaner than your drawers, bitch! "Thank You."

"The color is right. It suits you," Roy added meekly.

She smiled, knowingly. "Two seater, Push Start button, twenty inch rims, deployable spoiler, ethanol sipping, big body, eco friendly, baby blue Bentley. *Tell me a bitch ain't hurting them,*" she boasted.

"You killin' them, Ma," said Roy.

"Girl you gotta take me for a spin while you're in town."

Both Roy and Lou-Lou looked at each other. Kema was taking the chummy role too far. Nobody said they had to become best buds. Roy only required mutual respect, a clear understanding for the purpose of getting paid. Cruising down Peachtree with the top down, as if they were BFF's, was never a mandate.

"I'll see if I have the time," Lou-Lou said dryly.

"Okay. Let me know girl." Kema reclined in her seat. Window closed. The music beating from the truck insured their conversation wouldn't be heard. Roy jumped in. Bucket seats caressed his back. Peanut butter, and chrome interior flickered his senses. He checked out the features, mashing buttons, turning knobs. He was a kid in a candy store.

"She's a bit over the top at times, but she cool," Roy said, apologizing for Kema.

"Please, I'm so past that."

He gave her a look.

"Seriously. We spoke at the restaurant. She didn't tell you?"

"She mentioned something to the fact, but I need to hear it from you."

She lifted her designer shades upward. Their eyes connected.

"We good. Don't worry."

He narrowed his eyes in on her. "I hope so."

She let her frames fall, and she nodded. "Let's talk business."

"You've got a buyer?"

"Got several buyers."

He laughed. "What you do, put out an ad?"

"All it took was one call."

"You spoke to Jazzman?" he asked.

"Not recently, have you?"

"Tried calling last night, but she didn't answer. When she called me back I was in the middle of something."

She looked up at the truck; saw Kema bopping her head, jamming. "You mean someone?"

He chuckled. "Kema checked that nigga Mike-Mike resume."

"And?"

"He's a shooter. Did a dime up in El Doraldo. Kansas."

Her face turned serious. "So Jazzman was right?"

"Right about what?"

"Getting out of town."

"Relax. Kema's sources tell her nobody know shit. Homicide detectives have no leads."

"Jazz sounded petrified over the phone. Maybe we should cut our losses and push on."

"I said we good."

Jazzman called Lou-Lou first, than plugged Roy on a three way. Her breathing was choppy. Her usual eloquent flowing speech had broken up into seven final words.

Get the fuck out of Atlanta now!

"We need to move this work, but not locally, don't wanna raise any suspicions," Roy said.

"Out of all the Section 8 tenants looking to rent, what's the probability that Flap's sister would be the one to occupy the space?" Lou-Lou asked, eyeing her side mirrors.

"That is some eerie shit," Roy admitted.

"Jazz said Mike-Mike is out for blood, and I believe her."

"That's the word on the streets," Roy said nonchalantly.

"You don't sound bothered behind this."

"I'll find that nigga and body his ass before I let anything happen to us," Roy said, eyeing his cell phone. He silenced the ringtone, and got out. "Pop the trunk."

Lou-Lou popped the trunk, and slipped from behind the wheel. Roy slung the duffle bag in. From her side peripheral she saw Kema hawking. *Bitches wanna be me!* She moved in closed to him, hugged him. His lips, close to her lobe, but not touching.

"Be careful. Do the speed limit. If you get knocked, you're fucked. Don't call me." He released her.

"I know."

"I'm serious. Fly below the radar. Don't be speeding. Remember, I don't exist. To the world, I'm dead."

"I'll call you in a few hours."

"Do that."

He held the door open like a gentleman as she slipped behind the wheel.

"The bag looked a little light. Is that all of it?"

"A portion. Let me see how you move this and we'll talk," he said, closing her door shut.

"What about Kema?"

"What about her?"

"You gave me this big speech about letting her tag along, now you got amnesia. Is she rolling with me or what?"

Roy looked over his shoulder. Kema was in her zone, knocking her head to the music. After long consideration, Roy knew leaving Kema and Lou-Lou un-attended was a recipe for disaster. "She's on another assignment."

Lou-Lou wanted to ask for more details, but decided to leave well enough alone. After all, she was glad to be rolling by her lonesome.

***

Lou-Lou got on the horn, and immediately called Caroline. The surprise in Caroline's voice brought certain warmth to Lou-Lou's heart. She was missed. They hadn't spoken since the Bradley altercation. Caroline filled her in on all the happenings surrounding the Stepford wives in Scarsdale. Not much had changed since she left the old neighborhood. The stuck up, self centered and stinking rich still lived in a world of their own.

"So the rumors are true?" Caroline started out.

"What have you heard?"

"Girl, you and Bradley are the talk of the town. People are saying Bradley is broke, and that you took all his money. Even heard your Latin friend in the truck came to rescue you. Oh, and heard you almost shot him."

Lou-Lou laughed. "All is true, with the exception of me taking his money. He had none for me to take. He's broke."

"Shut up!"

"I'm serious. He lost his job, the house is in foreclosure, and he gambled the vacation villa."

"No way. Not the villa."

"Way."

"Damn. Who would have guessed?"

"His choice of drug was Vegas."

"Heard he takes the occasional sniff," Caroline said making hog snorts through the phone. Lou-Lou remained silent, didn't bother to confirm nor deny.

"I saw Bradley loading a U-Haul. And let me tell you, being discreet was the furthest thing from his mind. Bumping and thumping went on till about 6am. I barely got any rest, and the doctor says I need my rest."

"Doctor."

"Yes, doctor."

"Don't tell me you're pregnant."

"Three months," Caroline said with glee.

"Congratulations to you and the pastor."

"The pastor played no part in this."

Lou-Lou adjusted her earpiece. "Come again."

"The good pastor is sterile. Been since I met him twenty years back. Some freak accident when he was a kid left him with on testicle and unable to procreate."

"Caroline."

"Yes."

"Mexican Pool Boy, Plumber, UPS Guy, or Pizza Boy?"

"Sidney," she said, with a dreamy voice.

"Who the hell is Sidney?"

"My personal trainer."

Lou-Lou's lips spread into a grin. "So you finally gave him some rhythm."

"What was I thinking stringing that man along? Had I known what I know now, I would have been gave him some."

Lou-Lou laughed. "You silly."

"One night, I had a taste for something different. I called him. He came over. He bought the yoga mats, and a bottle of Tequila, the one with the worm."

"How old is he?"

"I'd rather not say."

"Caroline. How old?"

"Twenty-five, but he moves like a seasoned veteran."

"I can't do it. My conscious kicks in. Had this eighteen year old come at me today. I wanted to, but I held back."

"You have a conscious?"

"*Ha Ha*, funny. So you banged your trainer and got knocked up? Sounds like fun."

"Lots of fun. Never a dull moment when he's around. Things are serious. He's thinking of putting a bid in on Bradley's property. I mean... I didn't mean it like that... it's just that the house is being auctioned off .... Everybody knows... who would want to pass up a deal like that?...It's a beautiful home."

"Don't trip Caroline. No harm taken. Tell me about Sidney."

"Sid is Vietnamese, Black, with a dash of Caucasian. He has brown skin, slanted eyes, dark wavy hair, and can move like those brothers in the porno videos."

Lou-Lou couldn't help herself. She burst out laughing. Caroline had an image to maintain. A pastor's wife couldn't be seen sifting through porn flicks in some dark, seedy sex shop. She couldn't exactly order battery operated toys and other freaky paraphernalia via the .COM, so she entrusted Lou-Lou to fulfill her supplies.

"What did the pastor say about your immaculate conception?"

"I was called everything but the child of God."

"You don't say."

"He threatened me with a divorce."

"Damn. So it's finally over?"

"*Over*, over for who? Me and my baby ain't going anywhere. He tried to pull a Bradley move on me. Tried to put me out on the front lawn. I told that son-of-a-bitch if he placed one finger on my white ass, he'd better go into hiding."

"I heard that."

"I hold the key to his future, past and present."

"How so?"

"*Girrrrlllll*, if you only knew," Caroline said with much sistah-girl attitude.

"I wanna know. Shit, tell me."

"This is *me* and *you*, goes no further."

"Okay, you got my word."

"Promise me."

"*Me* and *you*, goes no further. I promise."

Caroline took a deep a breath. What she was about to reveal hadn't left her lips since she discovered the truth about her husband. The truth, she buried deep down in the pit of her stomach. "The good pastor got a boyfriend."

"Shut the hell up, Caroline."

"Real talk."

"Hold up, let me pull over."

Lou-Lou cut in front of an eighteen wheeler, swerving onto the shoulder. A forest of big oak trees, and a ditch forced her abrupt stop. A makeshift cross with the date of birth, and date of death was written in permanent marker, paying respect to the deceased. She sat behind the wheel, facing south on 75, shocked beyond words.

"Get the hell outta here."

"He's so queer it's not even funny."

"Whoa. That's deep. I would have never guessed."

"Oh, you wanna hear deep?"

Lou-Lou put the hazard blinkers on, and listened for the next bombshell.

156

"He came out the closet, told me he was into men fifteen years ago. I was devastated. Not only was he not able to give me a child, but his ass wasn't interested in giving me pleasure. Not for nothing but the man is huge. With a power tool like that a man should never be gay." She took a deep breath, collected her thoughts. Feeling the relief that came from revealing a secret so heavy made her a bit light headed.

"I would have left him then, but he begged me to stay."

"But why?"

"Status. You of all people should understand that."

"Touché."

"The first five years of our marriage was tough. We wanted children. We tried, but Pastor was shooting blanks. We believed that God would give us a child regardless of what some doctor said. It became frustrating. We began to argue. Things were so bad that we stopped sleeping in the same room. He had his, and I had mine. My house was cold for a long time. Still is."

"Damn."

"The church was becoming more popular. Our congregation was growing by leaps and bounds. Where most churches were struggling to keep members, ours numbers were multiplying. To denounce my husband during that time would have been social-suicide. I was first lady of a mega church, divorcing her husband because of his infidelities with a *man*, of all things was an abomination. So, I made a decision. *We* made a decision. I agreed to turn the other cheek, be his wife, and keep my mouth shut. He agreed to take care of me for the rest of my natural life."

"Did you get it in writing?"

"Damn straight. I'm no fool."

"I guess having this baby sort of changes the dynamics of the agreement."

"We've worked that out. Since my baby will most likely have Sid's features, I've decided to go into hiding for the next year."

"You sound crazy."

"Look, I'm protecting my investment. I'm a small town girl from Trumbull, Nebraska. Ever heard of it?"

She snickered. "No, never heard of it. Sounds country as hell though."

"I grew up in a double-wide sitting on thirty two acres of rural. My amusement park was a big oak tree with a tire tied to the strongest branch. We hunted deer, cooked rabbit, ate pig knuckles, hand washed clothes and hung them outside to dry. Agricultural, forestry, fishing, and hunting were the best jobs in town. With the exception of living on thirty two acres of land, my parents were dirt poor. I made it out, left right after high school."

She paused, and reflected back on her life. "Pastor and I met seconds after I stepped off the Greyhound. He was my meal ticket," she said with a smile in her voice.

"Didn't you love him, though?"

"Time allowed me to love him."

"How'd he find out you were pregnant?"

"Morning sickness. At first I couldn't keep a damn thing down. The wrong wind made me puke my guts. Then there was weight gain."

"I thought you put on a few pounds."

"A few? How about fifteen, all in my hips. Pastor confronted me about it. At first I lied, told him I was just gaining weight. But then he made me pee on a stick."

"No he didn't."

"Yes the heck he did. Held that stick until the thing turned pink with the little plus sign."

"Does he know about Sid?"

"He doesn't know by whom I bear a child, but he knows somebody got me knocked up."

"What's your plan?"

"Zimbabwe."

"What?"

"I'm leaving for Africa in the morning."

"What for?"

"I can't carry this baby in the states. People will talk."

"So what, you're going into hiding?"

"Yes. Just until after I have the baby. I'll be back by the time she's three months. I believe God for a little girl."

"But why Africa, why not Nebraska? Won't people miss you at the church?"

"My recent voyage was made public during last week's service. The congregation has been informed. Pastor has been collecting donations for the all girls academy he's building in Bulawayo. I'm there to head the project, make sure funds are allocated accordingly."

"What about health care, prenatal care, delivery? This doesn't sound safe. I'm concerned."

"Don't be. The good pastor has that all taken care of. I've got the best doctors the church can buy. Pastor flown in one of his gay friends from Europe to accompany me, so I'm covered."

"What if his gay European friend tells?"

"And risk his thriving practice in the U.K., I don't think so. I've got footage of him and my husband doing the Broke Back Mountain. If anything happens to me, my baby, or if that bastard whispers a drop of specifics, I'm leaking it. His wife would be thrilled." Caroline laughed. "Any ways, I've got the Global Phone. I'm still reachable."

"Caroline, this is crazy."

"Enough about me, what's up with you sistah?"

"I need a favor?"

"What, you need another recipe to rid transmission oil from the driveway," she giggled.

"No. It's a bit more serious than that."

"Talk to me. What can I do for you?"

"You can't mention this to anyone, especially none of those stuck up bitches in Scarsdale."

"I just told you my husband has a boyfriend and that I'm pregnant by my trainer. If you haven't noticed yet, I'm in no position to tell a damn thing. You've got my word, now spill it?"

"I need a huge favor. I'm in Atlanta."

"What you doing there?"

"On business. I've got this friend who's looking to get off some Blue Dolphins."

"You mean Ecstasy?"

"Yes."

Dead silence was the last thing Lou-Lou expected. Instead of Caroline dropping names from her exclusive *A-List* circle of friends, she heard nothing. Her bottom lip pulled in, suddenly nervous, awaiting a response. The corrupt side of her was unveiling. The truth about Lou-Ann Dobbs had come to light.

"Hello."

"I'm here."

"Well."

"I'm thinking."

Lou-Lou tapped her fingers against the steering wheel, now ready to take back her words. But it was too late. "My deepest apologies if I've overstepped my boundaries," she blundered.

"Girl, please. You said you're in Atlanta right?"

"Yes."

"Dr. Milton. He's the man to see."

"This doctor, he's cool?"

"Cool as a fan."

"Are you sure he'll be interested?"

"He'll be more than interested. If your stuff is good, he will be sure to introduce you to his circle of friends. And those sons-a-bitches got *Moola*. Just make sure you're not pushing no duds, make sure it's the real deal."

"Will you set it up?"

"Consider it done babe."

Things were looking up. After Caroline finished dishing the dirt on the good Pastor, and giving her Dr. Milton's information, she proceeded further south. Stockbridge, Georgia was the next destination.

***

As promised, Caroline put in a personal call to the doctor, and just like that, she was in there. Dr. Milton squeezed Lou-Lou into his already booked schedule.

"Scoot down just a little bit more."

"Like this?" Lou-Lou asked popping her gum, shifting her hips, tilting her pelvic bone.

"Come down just a little bit further."

"Is this good enough Dr. Milton?"

"Oh yes, that's perrrfect."

Dr. Milton almost forgot that his assistant was still in the room. The set of moist lips before him made the blood rush to the tip of his eager penis. As he examined the outer parts of her, he could barely keep a straight face. The assistant passed him the plastic speculum. He lubed it, and inserted slowly. Beads of sweat formed on his brow as he expanded the instrument, adjusting her muscles wide enough to see in.

"Any pain?"

"No pain."

"Good girl."

Dr. Milton swabbed her insides with a gigantic Q-tip, slapped her fluids onto a glass disc, pulled the speculum from her walls, and tossed the slippery utensil into the bio-hazard trash can. The doctor suddenly looked as if he had Parkinson's disease. His hands shook uncontrollably.

"You need help Dr. Milton?" the assistant asked.

"I got it."

He could smell her wetness. He licked his lips desperately wanting to lick hers. As he applied a glob of lubricating gel to his fingertips, he imagined how good she would taste. "Okay you may feel just a little pressure." He slid four fingers into her wetness, pressing his free hand against her abdomen. His eyes closed, as he felt the inside of her.

"Do you feel any discomfort or pressure?"

Lou-Lou placed both hands behind her head and said, "No."

He pulled out and quickly tossed his latex glove into the trash. Dr. Milton watched his assistant disappear behind the door carrying samples labeled *laboratory*. He scanned her chart. Beads of sweat burst, and slipped down the sides of his face. He mopped his face dry with a paper towel.

"Ms. Dobbs from what I can see you look to be pretty damn healthy. However, we will send your samples off for a culture check just to make sure".

She laughed, "Call me Lou-Lou."

The doctor smiled. "Well alright Lou-Lou, you're doing an excellent job at keeping yourself up."

"There's no need in letting my family jewels go bad," she jokingly said while hopping off the examining table. She let her paper gown fall to the floor, exposing all of herself. Dr. Milton leaped from his seat and said, "Let me give you a minute of privacy. I'll be right outside that door if you need me." He caught a glimpse of her perfect hips and her succulent breasts. He wiped the sweat from his forehead and turned on his heels to leave. She grabbed his arm. To her surprise, they were firm, toned and definitely strong. "Don't leave."

"Patient's privacy. It's the law," he said with his back turned.

"Oh please you've already massaged my breasts, finger popped me and inserted a pair of plastic tongs into my coochie-cat, what more privacy do I have at this point?"

Dr. Milton turned, looked her in the eyes, but not before scanning her from the neck down. "Are you sure you don't want me to leave?"

"Yes, I'm sure. Have a seat."

Dr. Milton sat back down on the swivel chair and watched her get dressed.

"So your good friends with Caroline?" he asked keeping his eyes on her lacey thong.

"Yes, she's a sweet heart isn't she?"

"Good woman indeed. I hear she's leaving for Africa soon."

"We've been good friends for many years," she said slipping into her jeans and tossing her shirt over her head. *My name is Bennet and I ain't in it.*

Dr. Milton swallowed hard. "If you don't mind, I would like to ask you a few questions."

"Sure, go right ahead." She took the seat next to him and felt his arm a second time.

"You work out?"

He blushed. "Three times a week. Keeps me centered."

Dr. Milton pushed his glasses up onto his nose and searched his paper for the right words. He was intimidated by her touch, her smell, her forwardness. He was a young handsome man with blue eyes, short spiked blond hair, and a well-defined body. *Caroline didn't mention he was fine,* she thought.

"When was the first date of your last period?"

"Didn't your assistant already ask these questions?"

He flipped through the folder and said, "I'm sorry, she sure did. Where's my head this morning?" She smiled and wanted to tell him exactly where his head was but chose not to. She loved it when a man fell weak in her presence.

"I see here that you've had two abortions, and no kids."

"Got pregnant when I was fourteen. Again when I was eighteen. Couldn't go through with either," she openly admitted.

"No need for an explanation." Dr. Milton assured her with compassionate eyes.

"How many partners do you currently have now?"

"Up until recently two, now I'm flying solo," she said with no hesitation.

He cleared his throat. "What forms of contraceptives are you using?"

"Condoms, what else is there to use?"

"Well condoms are the best form of protection especially if you have more than one partner. Have you thought about taking the pill or perhaps getting the shot as a backup precaution?"

"Nope. I'm good with all that."

Dr. Milton laughed at her facial expressions. "Have you ever had an HIV test done?"

"Fo' sure. Every six to eight months."

"Very good to hear."

"Can I suggest something?" she asked.

"Sure!"

She removed his wire framed specs, placed them on the counter. Dr. Milton squinted, smiled. She flipped the collar to his white coat, splashed some water onto his hair. Her fingers whipped his hair back and forth until his tress was punked and frizzed.

"Now take a look at yourself. You're so hot!"

He looked past his own reflection and zeroed in on her eyes.

"Caroline mentioned you had something for me." She slipped a sample package into his white coat.

"If you like it, call me."

Lou-Lou left Dr. Milton's office loaded with spermicidal samples, condoms, and packages of birth control pills. *Kosha could use these*, she thought. She hadn't made it to the expressway before Dr. Milton rang her cell.

"Hello...Lou-Lou. This is Dr. Milton."

A smile crept across her face. "Hey Dr. Milton, did I leave something back at the office?"

"No, I was just calling you because that pill..."

"Not over the phone," she said quickly.

"Yes, of course. Can you and I meet?" the doctor asked, now whispering into the phone.

"Sure, when's a good time?" Her fingers were crossed.

"Give me thirty minutes. I'll meet you across the street at the Mexican restaurant."

"Okay, see you then." She ended her call and busted an illegal U-Turn.

***

They barely made it through the first round of Margaritas before Dr. Milton requested the check. Shoving the salted rimmed drink aside, he stood, wrestled with his wallet.

"Allow me," she insisted.

"A lady never takes care of the check."

She slid from behind the booth, straightened out her attire. He scanned her frame, slapped a fresh twenty on the table and broke towards the exit.

"Where are we headed?" she asked once outside.

He looked at her, and then looked back at his thriving practice. He had obligations, but his phallus was throbbing for some attention. He'd only taken half a pill and was ready to bone. Working under those conditions was a sure fire way of catching a sexual assault case. He made a call, told the receptionist to cancel the rest of his appointments for the day.

She tailed his Maserati about a half mile up the road to the Hyatt. She waited patiently as he secured them a room. When she arrived, Dr. Milton was shirtless, and sprawled across the king size bed awaiting her touch. His pink nipples reminded her of Bradley. She shook the thought of the past, and focused on securing a well needed connect. If the doctor had the right kind of linkage as Caroline claimed, she would be able to expand her business.

"I'm so horny. Hurry up."

She removed her clothing, one layer at a time. It wasn't like he'd never seen her before, or as if he'd never fondled her breasts, inserted his fingers, or had his way with her. He'd seen and examined every square inch of her body. It wasn't like she was giving up her treasures to some broke ass dude like José for the pleasure of it. She was about to fuck the shit out of that white boy for a profit. It was all for the love of money.

"Come sit on my face," he commanded. She swayed her hips slowly towards the bed, placed one knee at the corner, inching towards him like a real tigress should. He licked and smacked his lips.

"You liked that Blue Dolphin?"

He grabbed the center of his khakis. "Can't you tell?" She straddled him. Dr. Milton shuddered. He felt her rump, spanked it, and shuddered again.

"When you left my office, I took half. It made me so hard. Couldn't stop thinking about you. I locked myself in my office, handled myself. When I released, it came back harder, stronger. I had to call. When I heard your voice..." He grinded against her middle and chewed his bottom lip.

"When I heard your sexy ass voice, I thought to myself... *I need to fuck her.*"

She giggled. "I'm glad."

"Oh baby. You are so damn sexy."

"You probably say that to all the girls."

"I love you."

That was all she needed to hear. The deal was sealed. After rolling on their protection she eased down against his erection. It was poetry in the making. He moaned, and so did she. Her first major account was closed. The doctor was roped in like a fish out of water. He needed her, and she needed him. It was about expanding territory. It was about capitalization, not procrastination. If sexing that young pretty boy doctor meant being introduced to the elite of pill poppers, then so be it.

CHAPTER 11

A crowd stood outside the Fox Theatre waiting to enter. Ticket scalpers played the sideline, hustling last minute nose bleed seats. *Jill Scott's* name was in big bold lights. Special guest *Kem*, and *Ne-yo* were also performing. The ladies were elegant. The men were suave and debonair. Celebrities had the red carpet treatment. Big names stopped to flick it up with fans, and sign autographs.

Lou-Lou took her time, cruising by in her new whip. As far as she was concerned all eyes should have been on her. She pumped her breaks when she noticed the casting crew from *The Real Housewives*.

"I should rob these bitches."

Roy laughed. "You'll be wasting your time."

"They got dough, especially that white girl. She got adulterated cash. The kind I love."

"Thought that was your favorite reality show," he said, humoring her.

"It is. I'm just saying... they posted up like it can't happen. I should pull over, put the burner to all those bitches, and make them up their jewels."

She looked over at Roy, who was cracking up. "Why you laughing?"

"Why you hating?"

"Please, never that."

"When white boy Bradley had you living like a housewife you weren't looking to put the heat to them, why now?"

He made a good point. She did nothing, all day long, but look fabulous. Hair done, nails done, outfits fresh out of SoHo. The best of the best was at her finger tips, compliments of Bradley.

"Leave the Housewives alone before you catch a case."

"You're no fun."

"Slow it down." He focused in on someone in particular, smiled.

"What, you see somebody you know?"

He licked his lips. "I think so."

"You want me to pull over?"

He hesitated for a second. "Naw, keep it moving."

Lou-Lou looked out her rear view, spotted several big face watches in the crowd, waving. "You sure, cause all I need is a second. Promise, I won't be long."

"Drive."

They pulled up to The Cheesecake Factory in Buckhead. Roy advised her to Self Park. He refused to valet because of the marijuana smoke. The last thing he needed was for some hating parking attendant, making minimum wage to report him to the law. He was cautious like that.

"You're paranoid."

"I'm on point. My cousin got bagged all because some young punk wanted a larger tip," Roy said spraying cherry-vanilla spray. She coughed, and gagged. "That's enough."

While inside the restaurant, Roy ordered them both a shot of Goose. They chit-chatted about a little bit of this and that, while trying to make a decision on what to order. After going over the menu, Roy settled on the salmon, while Lou-Lou went with the chicken parm.

"Take the shades off."

"Can't be seen alive."

"Right, I forgot."

"Drink up." Roy insisted.

Lou-Lou eyeballed the shot, squinted. Her stomach had endured enough abuse. She shoved it aside, grabbed the sliced lime, and licked it.

"I knew it. You can't keep up."

"Boy, you don't even know the half. I got this." she grabbed four ounces of Goose, tossed it back. Fire oozed down her throat, face metamorphosed.

Skkkeeeuuuttt

A loud screech came from the adjacent table. Lou-Lou clinched her teeth in pure annoyance.

Skkkeeeuuuttt

College aged girls laughed it up, slapped fives, throwing up sorority hand signs. Academic gang banging was acceptable, especially in Atlanta. More laughter exploded from the table as one girl, the *high yellah* one, spoke in a tone that demanded undivided attention.

Skkkeeeuuuttt

A thunderous roar had everyone in the restaurant turning their heads, annoyed.

When their food finally arrived, neither said two words. They just dug in. They were both famished to say the least. "I've gotta get back to New York by Friday," said Lou-Lou, with a mouthful of spaghetti noodles.

"You can't leave yet. We're just getting started."

She dabbed the corners of her mouth with a cloth napkin. "I promised Kosha I would be there. I can't disappoint her." Her cousin was on her way to something positive. Within just a couple of days, she would be opening another chapter to her life. Jump starting a new journey was always exciting.

"So, tell me," he said.

"Tell you what?"

He leaned in.

So did she.

"How'd you get them *thangz* off so quickly?"

She winked. "That's top secret."

"Oh, so I can't know who your connect is?"

"He's private. Doesn't want his face or name disclosed."

"Must be somebody important."

Dr. Milton was important indeed. He was the link to helping their whole operation get off without a hitch. "I would say so."

"I still can't believe you got rid of all of it."

"*O* ye of little faith."

He shrugged. "Can't blame a man for protecting his investment."

"How'd Kema do with her share?" she asked.

"She did well. Not as well as you though. But then again she's responsible for getting off keys, not pills. Different crowd," Roy justified.

Lou-Lou held back her arsenal of questions, held back her need to feel offended, and just said, "Well, like you said, this is her city."

Roy's eyes darted across the room and back. A crowd of loud talking men were at the bar, posted up like they owned the joint.

"Have you spoken to Jazzman?" she asked.

"No. Have you?"

"We playing phone tag," he said, looking around, scanning each face from behind his thick, dark shades. It was a habit of his. Checking his surroundings was a must.

"I need to call her."

"Yeah me too," said Roy, seemingly half there.

"Any more info on that dude Mike-Mike?"

"He's talking big shit on the street, but according to Kema he has no clue which street to turn down, or whose door to knock on first. Feel me?"

Roy fumbled with the salt and pepper shakers. His attention was definitely elsewhere.

"What you looking at?" she asked.

"Black leather, blue jeans, you know him?"

"Where?"

"By the bar. *Ol'* boy standing next to the chubby dude with the red skull cap. He's been hawking."

She looked over her shoulder. "I dunno, I might. He looks familiar."

Lou-Lou dropped her fork and leaned back to unbuckle her jeans. She felt the *Itis* coming on. Now feeling lethargic, she waved for the check.

"Dessert," the waitress asked.

"No room. How about you?" she asked Roy, who's attention was still on *Ol'* boy at the bar. Lou-Lou snapped her fingers. "You want some cheesecake?"

"I'm good. What's the total?"

After paying the bill they proceeded towards the door.

Skkkeeeuuuttt

Lou-Lou stopped dead in her tracks, cringed.

"You forget something?" Roy asked.

"Yeah, sort of."

She handed him the keys.

"Get the car. I'll meet you out front."

She headed back to where the college girls were, still making that horrible screech. Their sweat shirts represented their schools to the fullest. *High Yellah* stopped talking when she noticed Lou-Lou approaching.

"Can we help you?" *High Yellah* asked, rolling her neck.

"First, stop making that fucking noise. People trying to enjoy their meal. And two, dinner is on me."

Lou-Lou slapped two bills on the table. "I'm paying the tab."

"Wow, thanks," said the college girls, stunned at the two crispy Benjamin's that lay next to the spinach dip.

"Thank me by seeing it to the end. Finish school."

Lou-Lou left the restaurant feeling like she'd given back to a good cause. If only she'd listened to her brother and gone to school. Those girls had a real shot at life. Her cousin Kosha had an opportunity to leave the hood, and make something of herself. She was determined to do whatever it took to ensure Kosha's transition was a smooth one.

Lou-Lou became a bit misty eyed as she thought about all the opportunities she'd given up to run the streets. And for what? Authentic labels, fine cars, bling... oh and yes, hood validation.

"What's up beautiful?"

She peeked over the rim of her designer frames, and smiled at the gorgeous specimen that stood before her. It was *Ol'* boy from the bar. She gave him the once over. Hard body, amazing teeth, low fade. *Damn he looks even better up close.*

"I've been watching you."

"So I've noticed."

"You remember me?"

"Can't say that I do."

He leaned in, whispered something that made her dimples deepen. "You remember me now?" She removed her shades. Bottom lip pulled in, teeth pressed down, *pressure marks*. She nodded. "Oh, yes."

"Damn. Guess I didn't leave a lasting impression."

"Why you say that?"

"You never called me."

"My phone got damaged. Had to replace it. Lost all my contacts." She blurted out as if rehearsed.

He laughed. "Cute. I've heard that line before."

"You mean you've used that line before?"

"Both."

She sized him up.

He licked his lips.

Definite chemistry between them.

"You know, that contribution you made back there will stay with them forever."

She looked surprised. "You peeped that?"

"I did. That's a good look on you. Young girls need encouragement. They need role models."

She blushed. "Thanks. I do what I can to encourage our future leaders, but I'm far from a role model."

"You have a good heart. That should count for something, right?"

"I guess so."

An awkward silence passed through them.

"What's my name?"

She looked around, as if the answer would appear in the form of smoke signals. Embarrassment covered her face. She searched her mental database, but was unable to retrieve a name. Not even a first initial came to mind.

"You don't remember the god's name. Damn, that's messed up *Lou-Lou.*"

Their one night stand didn't exactly turn into breakfast. They met at a party some years ago. They did the *bang-bang, skeet-skeet* in the bathroom of some club which no longer existed. Patron shots lined the bar, and before long her dress was hiked up her back, with her undies dangling ankle length. Their sexual encounter left her torn, literally.

"Don't hurt your brain. Allow me to re-introduce myself. Government name is Ameir... It's Arabic... Means Prince... but my peoples call me Ace."

She extended her hand. "Government name is Lou-Ann... Was told it means famous warrior.... Not sure how true that is... but my peoples call me Lou-Lou."

He grabbed her hand, pulled her in for a hug. Immediate goose bumps. Feeling a tad bit awkward, she wiggled her way from the embrace.

"Speaking of your peoples, what's up with your man José?"

Her brows arched inward. She sucked her teeth. "That's not my man."

"Don't bite my head off. I'm just asking. Haven't seen the brother in a few years. Did the music industry open its doors for the god?"

"Nope. He's still at home with his momma."

A condescending laugh escaped him. "And you chose him over me."

"Excuse me?"

"José. You chose that dude over me."

She looked away. He was right. Telling him so would hurt his feelings. All recollection of Ace went out the window the moment she laid eyes on her half breed beau. Ace kisses were still wet against her neck; his sweat had yet to dry between her legs before she was playing one friend for the next.

"*Ooh*, that was trifling of me."

"*Yes*, it was, but hey, that was a long time ago," he said shrugging the past.

"Yo Ace, your friend got a friend?"

Ace looked over his shoulder, told his crew to hold up. Hoots and hollers continued more rambunctiously.

"Friends of yours?" she asked.

"Sort of, I mean, not really. I'm out with a buddy, taking part in one last hurrah."

"Oh, I see." She glanced down at his finger.

He held his hands up in a surrendering fashion. "Not me. Him." He pointed.

"The one in the leather coat, red skull cap, *wasted*. He's getting married tomorrow. I'm single." He stated firmly.

"He's blown. You sure he'll make it to the altar?"

"Not my business."

She kept a close eye on Roy. He stood outside the car, obviously having a heated discussion with someone over the phone. *It's probably that bitch Kema.*

"That's your man?"

"He's my cousin."

"You married yet?"

"Not even close."

"Good. Let's say I ditch my peoples, you ditch your cousin, and we go somewhere a bit more private."

"Private? Like in drinks and dinner?"

"Damn girl, I just saw you swallow a whole chicken with some noodles. You still hungry?"

Her mouth fell open in shock. He burst out laughing. She slapped his arm.

"I'm messing with you. We can do drinks, dinner, or we can meet up at my place."

"Tempting, but I've got some business with my cousin right now."

He pulled his cell out. "What's your number, I'll call you later." Seven digits rolled off her tongue lucidly. Seconds later, she felt her phone vibrating on the inside of her purse.

"That's me. Plug me in."

Roy pulled up. The window fell. Bellows of smoke escaped. Music bumped at a mellow degree. *Chrisette Michele's* soulful voice layered in richness. Ace gave Roy the head nod, Roy threw it back. There was weird tension in the air. She couldn't put her finger on it. Ace leaned in, hugged Lou-Lou from the back, kissed the side of her cheek.

"Be on the lookout for my call beautiful."

She slid into the passenger's seat, thinking of ways to ditch Roy. Ace was playing his cards, and his deck, she wanted to shuffle. She immediately saved his digits. *Damn, should have taken a picture. I'll get him next time. Might just snap a picture of his dick; upload it as my screen saver.*

Aggravation rested heavily on Roy's face.

"You alright?"

"I'm cool."

"You seem bothered."

"Who was money?"

"An old friend, why?"

He made a grunt noise.

"Many years ago we met, talked, fucked. Traded him in for a better look. *At least I thought,*" she mumbled.

"Got a bad vibe off dude."

She dropped the cell back into her purse. "What you mean?"

"He looks a bit off to me."

"Off as in crazy?"

"Yep, crazy off."

"He's cool."

She popped a stick of mint gum into her mouth, chewed, cracked, and blew a huge aromatic bubble. When it burst tiny spurts of saliva sprayed like a can of aerosol. She looked at Roy, winced. "Sorry."

Her phone chimed.

It was Ace.

Damn it feels good to see people up on it.

CHAPTER 12

Crazy. *Deranged. Loon. Unbalanced.* Roy spotted a cuckoo bird at first glance. Lou-Lou had to admit, Ace did have a slight demented look in his eyes, but she liked her men a little *loco*. She didn't mind that he was a bit touched. As far as she was concerned everybody had a little crazy in them.

She grabbed him between his legs, stroked him. "You don't need it," she said, still holding him, still stroking, increasing his hard on.

"Seriously, you can tell me the truth. Do I need it?" he asked again.

She laughed and kissed his lips. "You're perfect."

The Extenze commercial came on ten times, and every time Ace asked the same question. He hung generously, but still wondered if he was enough. Lou-Lou figured it was a guy thing. Inner complex caused him to question if his size was sizable for pleasing.

"A male enhancement drug is something you don't need. *Trust me.*"

"I've broken a few headboards in my day, but you know, you can never be too sure."

"You're so humble."

They laughed.

"You looked real good tonight," Ace said.

"Thanks. You did too."

"I was surprised you answered your phone."

"Why?"

"You know that girl rule. Never answer on the first ring, first knock, first glance type stuff. I had rehearsed this long corny message to leave you, but then you answered."

"I'm not for the games. If I wasn't interested, I wouldn't have given you my number, would have lied and said my cousin was my man."

"True."

"But I'm glad you called."

"Glad you answered."

They smiled at each other.

"So what was the message?"

He chuckled. "Ah *C'mon*, don't do me like that."

"You might as well tell me. You've obviously thought long and hard about what to say."

"I've already got you here."

"Oh. I see. Why work for it when you've already hit it."

He scratched his head. "Don't put words in my mouth."

She held back her laughter. "Well, tell me the message."

"No."

"You'll get an instant response. That way you'll know whether to use that line again or not?"

"That makes sense, but no."

"Pleeeeaaassseee?" she begged.

He wet his lips, leaned into her ear, whispered. She started to laugh. "See. I knew I shouldn't have said it."

"It's cute, but could use some work."

"I'm a bit rusty. I'll be the first to admit. My boys made me go out. They said I was all work and no play."

"You should learn to live a little."

"I think I'ma need a little help." He smiled.

"No problem. You've got the right chick." She grabbed her bottled water, took a sip. "You got any kids?"

"No wife, no kids, just me, myself and I."

"Good. Real good."

"What about you?"

"None yet. Need to find me a husband first."

She laid against his chest, fingered the small hairs around his nipple. Her hands moved towards his twitching pistol, and back up to his chest. *He's got José faded. What the hell was I thinking? Oh, yeah, it was the hair. Guess I needed that mixed Puerto rock thug in my life.* She snickered.

"What's funny?"

"Oh, nothing." She yanked a single hair from his nipple, causing him to yelp. He grabbed her hands, held them as the sting subsided. "You're into causing pain?"

"I like it rough." He smacked her rump, causing her to jump.

"You mentioned that it's been years since you've seen José."

"Haven't seen that brother in about five years. Shit, haven't seen most of my old crew in a long minute. Most of the guys I used to run with either locked up or dead."

"Five years is a long time. Life happens," she said almost sadly.

He ran his fingers through her hair. "Sounds as if you know firsthand."

"Let's just say I'm compiling notes for my memoir."

"Sounds interesting. I'd love to read it."

"I'll be sure to sign an exclusive copy, just for you."

He kissed her forehead, then her lips. "I've been traveling from the moment I enlisted. It feels good to finally relax." She looked up at him, noticed he had a booger. She dug her acrylic nail into his nostril and scooped it.

"*Oookay*, that was gross."

She plucked it across the room. "I'm just taking care of my man." *Did I just call him my man? Damn, must be the dick. Slow down girl.*

"Oh, so I'm your man now?"

She cleared her throat. "I noticed a bunch of military magazines in the bathroom. I assumed you were in some sort of service, but forgot to ask."

He glared at her. "You're going through my shit already?"

"Boy no, I noticed it... you had them on the counter... they were out... so I took a peek... and..."

He kissed her lips, slid her some tongue. "Chill. I'm joking," he murmured against her mouth.

"Oh, cause I was about to say... I'm not the snooping type."

He gave her the *yeah right* face. All women were snoops. "Just came home, been in the desert for the last year."

"That explains your hard body. *Damn* you're fit." She bit his nipple.

"Ouch."

"Where were you deployed?"

"Most recently Afghanistan, before that I was in Kuwait" He pointed towards his military issued tags, badges, fatigue satchel and Army boots, which were hung neatly inside a partially opened closet.

"What position you play?"

"Sharp-shooter amongst other specialties."

"So, you like to shoot and blow shit up."

He smiled. "Love to shoot and blow shit up." She loved a man who handled his tool well. Her brother was a cop. He taught her how to shoot. Her aim perfected many weekends at the range.

"Well, alright Mr. Certified Sharp-Shooter. Go ahead with your bad self."

His chest inflated proudly. "Protecting and serving my country is an honor."

"*Bullshit.* I'll be damn if I'm going to fight somebody's war."

"If it weren't for us, there wouldn't be a land of the free. America is the greatest place in the world. Why you think folks are fighting to get here?" His voice elevated a few notches.

"Don't get me wrong, I appreciate all the soldiers. Without you, the land of the free wouldn't be so free. I get it."

"Forgive me. I get pissed off when I hear people speak about the war as if it's senseless. We do what we do so that our people can walk down the street without worrying if a nuclear missile will land and end all of humanity. We protect and serve this goddamn country so that people like *you* could receive mail free of Anthrax, travel by plane without worrying if another 9/11 will occur. We sacrifice our lives so that Americans can buy American goods, keeping Americans gainfully employed in this fucked up economy."

Just leave it alone Lou-Lou. She told herself, but she couldn't hold her tongue. "I dig what you're saying, and I completely appreciate your contributions to my well being. However, it's messed up that a kid can enlist at eighteen, shoot and kill or be killed, but can't legally drink until twenty-one."

"It's fucked up that our fellow men and women can protect and serve, only to be discharged to a world that expects a resume packed with civilian experience. It's fucked up that our soldiers, the ones who fought on the battle field to *protect and serve* can't get a damn job outside of being a goddamn correction officer, or security guard, or a damn school bus driver."

"Did you know a great percentage of our Veterans are homeless? They gain all these skills, to be skillfully unemployed. I mean, tell me, where's the true benefits?"

"That's not always the case. Joining the service has done wonders for many. It's all about what one does with his or her time while enlisted. The possibilities are endless."

"Really?"

His jaw clinched. "Our president..."

"Blows dick real hard," she spat.

"Don't talk about Obama."

"Why the hell not?" she challenged.

He shook his head. "Look. Just don't talk about Obama."

"His skin color doesn't change the fact that this country is fucked up. Don't get me wrong, I'm glad he's helped change the course of things, but he's sending this country into the shitter just like the first forty three ass wipes before him."

He gave her a sharp look. "*J*-just don't talk about Obama, okay."

"Fuck Obama. Fuck Bush. Fuck Bush old ass daddy. Fuck Clinton and his wife. Fuck the whole sticking rotten political system. Our soldiers deserve red carpet treatment but instead they get fucked with no lube."

She searched his face, decided to press further. "You sign your John Hancock on that dotted line, promising to protect and serve, only to realize it's a joke, but you're bounded by blood. The only way out that fucked up contract is dead, jail, or disability. Wanna get out the Army before your time, lose a leg, an arm, get exposed to some shit they don't have a cure for. Or better yet, just die."

He opened his mouth to speak, she cut him off. "I'm sorry. Don't know where all that aggression came from." *Shit, this is the reason I don't discuss politics, or religion. Damn!*

She wiped the beads of sweat from her forehead. He forced a smile to his face, chuckled. "It's cool. You're entitled to your own opinion. Freedom of speech, right?"

The moment was destroyed. Their romantic high now plummeted into a sea of discomfort.

"I don't mean to go hard, be the pessimist and what not. I'm just calling it like I see it."

He sat there, staring at the wall. "Over in Afghanistan, I almost died.

"How?"

"Towel Head crept up behind me, put one in my noggin." His voice was razor sharp, unforgiving.

"You got shot in the head?"

He grabbed her hand, and placed it at the back of his dome. She pulled away, made a face. "It's still there?"

"No doctor will touch it. Too dangerous of a procedure. I'm stuck with the slug. But hey, I've seen worst."

"You caught one in the dome and you still repping hard for the Army."

He shrugged. "No big deal. I'm fine. My sergeant ordered me to therapy."

"Mental or physical?"

"Both."

Okay, it's time to bounce. This dude got issues.

"Been to specialist after specialist and all diagnosed me with PTSD."

"Wait a fucking minute. Are you telling me you got some STD?"

He laughed. "No. *PTSD*. Post Traumatic Stress Disorder."

She relaxed. "Oh. What's that?"

"It's a sever anxiety disorder that develops after trauma."

"Oh, I've heard about that. War heads come back home twitching, crazy as fuck."

He chuckled. "You can develop this disorder from anything traumatic, not just the war."

"So you're paranoid all the time?"

"Not all the time."

"Why are you telling me all of this?"

He shrugged. "I'm usually not this open. I guess I feel comfortable with you."

"So, does it hurt?"

"Does what hurt?"

"Your head goddammit."

"I have my days."

"If you don't mind me asking, what are you doing for work?"

"That's a sensitive matter."

"Oh, top secret. I get it."

"No, nothing like that. Because of my injury, and my disorder I'm tied to a damn desk. I work as a dispatcher, mostly third shift. I would rather be at war blowing up shit, protecting my fellow man." He smirked.

"A dispatcher?"

"The pay stinks, but my medical is paid. That's always a plus, especially with the cost of healthcare."

Okay, you're crazy and your broke... whoa, would yah look at the time. She sat up, stretched her arms high above her head, and yarned. *Time to push on; find me a deeper set of pockets.*

"My brain works perfectly fine, but my doctors won't okay me back into the field. So, at the moment, I'm stuck talking to truckers all night about their routes, their kids, and the damn weather. It's boring."

She got down on both knees in search of her bra and panties. Once she located them, the hunt was on for her top, her skinny jeans and socks. Her coat and boots were most likely in the foyer.

"It pays the bills right?"

"Barely, I've been kicking out a lot of over time to supplement."

Over time. Supplement. Oh no, this will not work!

"Would I be too forward in asking you to stay the night?"

"I like forward, but I can't."

"Why?"

Because your ass is crazy. Roy said he caught a bad vibe off you. Damn, when will I ever listen? "I've got prior commitments."

"More business with your cousin?" His tone was a bit abrasive.

She nodded. "Something like that."

"I understand. Maybe we can get together tomorrow. I've got my friend's wedding at three, reception at four; I'm looking to dip out the back door before six."

"Your peoples were bent back off that Goose. You think the groom will make it to the altar?"

"He better make it. I rented a damn suit. Besides, he owes me detail money."

She stopped, made a face. "Don't tell me he hurled in your ride."

"All over the back seat of my brand new Tahoe."

"Damn. That's messed up."

Wait a minute, did he just say brand new?

"Just pulled that bitch off the lot a few days ago," he said.

"How new is new?"

"Zero-miles-new. Haven't even taken a road trip to open the engine up yet. Had he not been scheduled to get married, I would have blacked his eye. Straight-up."

"Must be an expensive note," she quizzed.

"It's paid for."

Okay, am I missing something here? I wonder if he got bank and just pulling my chain. Niggas always try'na test the kid. He pulled her close, slipping the strap to her bra off her shoulder. He kissed her chin, her neck, her lips. She stopped him.

"What are you doing?"

"You know what I'm doing."

"Can't, gotta leave…"

"Please stay."

"I don't have any clothes."

"I've got extra toothbrushes, clean towels, you can borrow a T-shirt if you'd like." He kissed her lips, unhooked her bra, and ran his eager finger tips down her skin.

"Besides, it's late. You really shouldn't be on the road this time of night."

"I know, but…"

His fingers tugged at the elastic on her panties. She threw her arms helplessly around his neck, pulled him in, nibbled on his ear. Crazy or not Ace was an incredible lover. "Your soldier is at attention."

"He's looking to bust a few rounds."

"Just make sure his aim is right."

"Oh, his aim is impeccable. My soldier is a decorated veteran."

They fell against the mattress. Fitted sheet was half off, pillows bunched into a corner. He pulled her aboard. She pushed away. "Whoa. I don't *raw-dog* for nobody."

He sat up quickly. His bugged eyes darted from every square inch of the room and back to her. There she was with her hip poked out, hands at her waist, looking disturbed.

"*W*-what's wrong?"

"You try'na get up in me. I don't fuck around without the plastic cap."

"*Ah* baby, just wanted to feel you, grind against it a little. Wasn't going to put it in, I'm not stupid."

"Yeah well, I don't grind without protection."

She rolled back the hat, and pounced upon him like a hungry tigress. Grinding him fast, then slow, then fast, then slow, then pausing to catch her breath. She tensed, spasmed, and yelped. *Leg cramp!* They've gone round after round, and now her body was bailing on her.

"No breaks." He slammed against her middle without regard to her flesh.

"Wait."

"No breaks."

"Ace, wait... I'm going dry. Got lube?"

"No breaks."

The burn against her vaginal lips caused her to buck at his speed. She figured her body would be kind enough to produce some lubrication. Perhaps secrete in her favor, but it didn't. Friction stretched and pulled the rubber.

"Fire. Burn. Stop."

"You like that don't yah...You like that don't yah.... You like that don't yah... Say you like it... Say it... Fucking say it."

"Fire. Burn. Stop."

His arms wrapped her waist, clamped and locked, pushing against the resistance, inflicting more pain. Beast like sounds escaped him.

"Ace, stop, the rubber..."

He growled, pinning her arms behind her back, pressing up and in, up and in. His pace quickening with each plea, each cry, each tear drop of agony. The more she begged, the harder he plunged. The more she cried, the faster he bucked.

"Ace. Stop. Fire. Burn. Please."

"Who the fuck is Ace?"

His eyes were dark, and lacked sympathy. His once gentle touch was now cold and menacing. He pumped fear into her veins with the chill of his tone. Just when she thought she couldn't take it anymore, he released. Animalistic roar echoed throughout. The chains around her waist broke; she hopped off the saddle of hell.

"Motherfucker," she shouted, bringing a stiff open hand across his face. He lay there, still as a board, looking up at her like she was lunch meat. She grabbed a T-shirt that was flung across the arm of the nearby elliptical.

"Where the hell is my purse?" She tripped, cursing him in every which way.

"You fucking bastard. I should have your ass killed."

His cell phone rang, and it was at that moment everything changed. He was another person, different. He snapped out of one trance, and went into the next. He was now locked inside another time period, another zone. "My phone, where's my phone?"

"How the hell should I know?!" she screamed.

He yanked the sheets off the bed, tossed the mattress, and tipped the dresser over like some crazed maniac. "You see my phone?" His eyes, glowing with evil. He shoved her out the way, moving quickly towards the kitchen. Pots and pans fell. Silverware was thrown from drawers, and the sound of glass shattering against the floor made her haul ass towards the door. She was barefoot, bare bottomed, wearing a T-shirt that reeked of his cologne.

Just inches away from escaping the madness, she stopped. The ringing cell phone was on the floor, right next to her leather coat, and boots. Her purse was just a few inches away, with her car keys dangling from the shoulder strap. With her way to freedom staring her in the face, she chose to pick up his phone. She gasped. "Impossible."

"You found it." He snatched the phone from her python grip, knocking her into the closet door. Dazed a bit from the unsuspected blow, she crawled towards safety.

"Hey little Sis... what you been up to?"

Lou-Lou stopped, curiosity getting the best of her. *No! Keep going! Run! Now!*

He chuckled. "Are you still coming to the wedding... *good*...Well, I've got company." He stared at Lou-Lou, arching his finger, asking her to come here. Everything in her body told her to run, leave, head towards the parking lot and never look back. She reached for the doorknob, lifted herself, found her balance.

He placed the receiver to his chest. "Come here baby."

No Lou-Lou, here's your only chance. Just go! Against her better judgment, she took two baby steps forward, and stopped. *I need to know the connection.*

"No little Sis, she's no hoodrat. This one's a keeper." He wet his lips, smiled. He grabbed her into his arms, plunging his eager tongue down her throat. She reciprocated the affection, holding on to his rock solid soldier. She leaned her ear against his chest. She heard her voice. Her insides heated up.

"Damn girl, hold on for a second," he said, swatting Lou-Lou on the ass.

"Not you Lil Sis... calm it down. I heard everything you said... no I'm not getting head while you on the phone."

Lou-Lou smiled. *Now there's a thought.* He pointed to the receiver. His fingers quacked open and shut, poking fun as his sister rambled on and on.

"*Okay, okay,* alright already damn Kema I said I got company. I'll see you at the wedding. Love you, bye." He placed his cell on the glass wall unit. "My sister Kema forgets who's actually older at times."

"Your sister... her name is Kema," she asked cheesing like a Cheshire cat.

"Moms had her at forty. She came unexpectedly as you could imagine," he said handing her a picture off the wall.

The girl in the photo wore a basic China doll cut, with a bit of shimmer on the lips, dressed in a white button down shirt, small crucifix dangled her neck, cheesing like she just won the Monopoly game at Mc Donald's. The girl she knew ran up in traps, stole life savings from old geezers, and would lay a bitch down on *GP*. The two were one in the same.

She took a seat on the sofa that reeked of Febreze and some other undisclosed odor. More military magazines scattered about against the coffee table. She leaned across the armrest to pull the string on the lamp.

"No."

She froze. "No what?"

"No light."

"You some kind of vampire or something?"

He chuckled. "No, just trying to keep my light bill down."

She yanked at the string anyway.

"You're hard headed."

She sat back, crossed her legs. Winced in pain.

"Tell me about your sister."

"I was in my first year of high school when I got the news."

She looked down, realizing she still had the photo in her hands. They resembled each other around the eyes, but that was it. "Wow, you have a sister. That's great."

Ace reached for the photo, placing the frame neatly against the wall. He stood still, looking up at his beloved angel like a work of art.

"You two don't look much alike," she said, hoping to dig further into their DNA, bark up their family tree, perhaps hang from a couple of branches. Learning how one moves, allows you to calculate, measure, and become equipped with dealing with them effectively.

Bradley never walked into a business meeting without first researching his intended client. Background, footnotes, reference guides was a fool proof formula to maneuvering through sticky situations. Sure, Lou-Lou promised Roy peace but there was so long she could pretend. Having seen Kema in action, she knew they're time would come. *Soon.*

"We got different dads. Mine wasn't into paying bills, so he ran off. Her dad was a good man, took care of home, but died from a bad liver. We both fatherless."

"That's too bad."

He shrugged carelessly. "Not really. She's the best thing that's happened to us, my mother and me. When I was over in Afghanistan, blowing people up..." He cracked a grin, still staring up at his beautiful *Motif*. "...all I saw was her face. Without her I would have died." He lowered his chin to his chest. "She saved me."

"Wow, that's... that's just amazing. You two see each other often?"

"My job doesn't allow me much free time, but we make it a priority to meet for dinner every other week."

"A priority huh?"

He moved towards the kitchen, grabbed two glasses, filled them with ice, and snatched two grape drinks from the pantry. He wiped the rim with the tail end of his shirt, popped the top and poured.

"My car broke down two days ago. Damn transmission went suddenly. So, here I am stranded on 285, two in the morning on the way home from work, and my cell rings. It's my sister calling, but before I can say two words she starts in on me. *Where are you? What happened? You alright? What's wrong?*" He chuckled.

"So."

"So, it's like she knew that I was in trouble. She always seems to know. Don't ask me how, but she can feel when I'm in a jam."

"How special," Lou-Lou said uninterested.

"The next day she took me to the lot and bought me a new truck."

"Wow, your sister must be rich."

"Not even close, but she works a good job. She makes good money."

"Doing what?" Her tone of voice shifted, causing him to look at her strange.

"I mean, what does she do for a living?"

"She's in IT. Handles computers. I think." He laughed. "Don't get me to lying. All I know is she's paying top dollar for mom's living expenses."

"Living expenses?"

"Mom's is fighting the big C. Baby Sis got her set up real nice down in Griffin. Lakefront community and the whole nine. Momma like to feed the ducks on the lake. Kema's been the backbone of the family. I mean, there's times when I'm not exactly feeling myself and..."

"You mean like tonight?"

He looked clueless. "Did I say something... do something that may have offended you?"

She leaned forward off the sofa. "Are you fucking serious?"

"Very serious."

"You practically raped me." She sat back forcefully, crossed her legs. The springs in the sofa made a noise. He doubled over, held his midsection. Laughter came from the pit of his stomach, and he couldn't control the tears. Those came relentlessly.

"You play too much."

Wow, are you kidding me? You dry fucked me, burning away my pubic hairs. She thought, clinching her legs tightly. Just as she'd found the nerve to get up and leave, he knelt before her. Her medium size hands covered with his huge catcher mitts. He brought them to his mouth, kissing each finger tip. She had to admit, it was nice, quite lovely in fact.

But still, she was disturbed. She liked it rough. Loved it when a man took charge, beat the pussy up until she couldn't walk, but what happened tonight was against her will.

But still, her pussy was probably the best pussy he'd had in forever. She was sure of it. He went deep, thrusting his hips into honey, only made him deaf to the word STOP!

She cracked a grin. His actions were justifiable.

"Stay the night with me." Before she could decline, he pressed his hot mouth against her lips. *No* wasn't an option. "Stay the night with me, please?" he mumbled, delving his tongue into her mouth. Fingers intertwining, gripping, their hands closely linked.

CHAPTER 13

"I love you."

Confessions of Rick's heart had her losing sleep. The impact of his declaration had her in need of some serious console. The head and the heart were in two different spaces. Speaking with Lou-Lou was a must. Not to say Lou-Lou was the *Love Doctor, Relationship Guru, Expert on Matters of the Heart.* But to say she knew a thing or two about maneuvering through hairy moments such as this.

Lou-Lou shopped in *Loserville*, and maintained a track record of almost nuptials, just barely jumping the broom, extensive engagements which never ended at the altar. As far as Jazzman was concerned there was a lot to learn from a woman like that.

"I'll wait. When you get tired of what's-his-face, you know where to find me."

She sat in the same position clinging to his words, his voice, his broken smile, and broken heart. He, in so many words had given her an ultimatum. "Bastard." She battled with herself, battled with the idea of losing a good man. Rick was damn near perfect by her standards. "Don't lose the best thing that's happened to you," she told herself.

Internal fight weakened her, made her vulnerable. As much as she hated to admit, her baby father still had a hold on her. Even from behind a prison wall he still managed to pull her strings like a Puppet Master. She lifted the glass of wine from the table, sipped it. "Not this time."

She told herself it was over. Time and time again, she told herself he no longer had a place in her heart, but the thought of seeing Tony made Jazzman consider his love.

She couldn't ignore the butterflies that fluttered her stomach. They were real.

Lou-Lou was the only person that would understand. She was the only person who would keep it real, give it to her straight. She picked up her cell phone, and hit *send*.

"Oh my God. You had me worried sick."

"Jazzman… is …. that … you?" Static crept through the line, broke up Lou-Lou's words. *"Jazzman?"*

"Yes, can you hear me?" The phone went dead. She redialed Lou-Lou's number. Busy signals shrieked. She waited a couple of seconds and tried the number again.

"Can you hear me now?" Jazzman asked, now completely annoyed.

"Yes, what's good?"

"You and Roy are selfish. I give ya'll the heads up on Mike-Mike and suddenly Roy stops answering his phone, your phone is disconnected and you check out the hotel, without so much as a postcard."

"I know. Sorry about that. I needed to make moves."

"I spoke to Roy today. He *finally* returned my call. He gave me your new number." More static waves shrieked through the receiver.

"Had to dead the other line. Got this cheap ass pre-paid."

"You moved that product yet?"

"And you know it. Got this white boy doctor, he's my cash cow."

"Doctor?"

"Gynecologist. He's cute too."

"Stay focused."

"I'm just saying, he reminds me of a younger Bradley."

Jazzman sucked her teeth. "When you coming home?"

Home? She had no home, not really any way. Her home was gone, auctioned off on the courthouse steps. Her home would be where she was, and at the moment she frequented the best of the best hotels.

"Did you hear me?" Jazzman broke into her thoughts.

"In a couple of days. Me and Roy try'na make one more move, and we blowing town."

"Ya'll being greedy. Bring your ass home Lou, I'm telling you that dude Mike-Mike means business."

"Relax. We got this."

Jazzman heard a man's voice in the background. Heard Lou-Lou press the phone to her chest, and muffle their conversation.

"Is that Roy? Put him on the phone."

"No."

"Who is it?" Jazzman really wanted to know.

"Hold on."

Jazzman heard muffled laughter, some shuffling and scuffling for the phone, then a long loud smooch to follow.

"Sorry about that. What was I saying?"

"Girl, where are you?"

"In Decatur, at my friend's apartment."

"This friend got a name?"

"Ace," she whispered.

"You just met him?"

"Yes and no. He's an old friend of José's. You might not remember, but we met him a few years ago. At that club in Stone Mountain... the same night we met José... he was the dude..."

"... you boned in the bathroom... oh I remember Ace just fine."

"Oh my God, you remember that?"

"How could I forget, you could barely walk straight."

"Well, I ran into him tonight, outside the Cheese Cake Factory in Buckhead. Was waiting on Roy to pull the car around and he noticed me, or I noticed him... we noticed each other."

"Yeah whatever, you got a second to talk?"

"I got a few minutes. Ace went to get more condoms. We fucked through a six pack already."

"*Whoop-De-Doo.* He left you alone, in his apartment?"

"You sound surprised."

"He must not know you."

Lou-Lou chuckled. "Whatever."

Jazzman fumbled with her rumpled sheets. There was a lump beneath the comforter. She reached in, and pulled out Ricks black boxer shorts. She brought them to her nose. His scent brought her back to just hours ago. They made love pelvic to pelvic, grinding harder than ever before. Make up sex was the best, but they hadn't really made up. So, maybe it was more like break up sex, or sex to be continued after you *make-up-your-mind* sex. Jazzman was confused.

"Are you alright?"

"Yes." She exhaled, tossing the boxers onto the side of the bed. She pulled the sheets back a little further, found a lonely sock, next to his sock a saturated rubber. She lifted, and examined it.

"How's Jacob?"

"Driving me crazy."

"He's just doing his job."

"Tony will be home tomorrow."

"I heard."

"Roy told you?"

"He mentioned it."

"What would you say if I told you, he's coming to live with me?"

"*What*, are you serious?"

She now had Lou-Lou's undivided attention. This was information Roy failed to provide, which made her lip curve slightly. Roy was a man's man. Unlike some dudes who gossiped like females. Roy was not one for divulging details or facts.

"Tony's aunt died."

Lou-Lou gasped. "His aunt died? Roy didn't mention this much."

"Yes, and Yvette started a fire in the apartment, she back to smoking that shit. He needs a place to stay." Before Lou-Lou could ask the million dollar question, Jazzman cut her off. "Three months at the most. Three months for him to find a job, save up some cash; find a studio apartment or whatever he can afford. I just can't see him back there. Streets don't forget, Lou. We both know that from experience." Sadness covered her words.

"Damn girl, you told Rick about this?"

"Things are so crazy between us. He feels betrayed."

"His feelings are valid."

"I know. Trust me. I know. After telling him I needed some space, he leaves, comes back, tells me he loves me, loves Jacob, and wants me to marry him. He said that he would have patience. That he will wait on me. Then..."

"Then what?"

"I let him inside me. Couldn't resist him... he was looking so damn good. After we had sex I asked him to leave."

"Why'd you do that?"

"I don't know."

"Damn girl," was all Lou-Lou could offer.

"I told you about the money he's been dishing my way to pay my bills."

"You mentioned it."

"Tonight, I offered him the money back, but he wouldn't take it. He went on about loving me, taking care of me, me being his better half, his partner for life."

"How much you offer him?"

"Ten thousand."

Lou-Lou whistled. "That's a nice hunk of cheese."

"He caught up my mortgage, Jacob's tuition, and other stuff. I was considering downsizing, but Rick wasn't having it."

There was that godforsaken word again, *Downsizing*. Downsizing was the root of Lou-Lou's problems. "How would you feel if you just dropped ten thousand on some dudes bills to find out his baby momma is coming to live with him? Rick just paid for another man's roof, meals, and opportunity."

"There's no opportunity."

"Where there's air, there's opportunity."

"*There is no damn opportunity.*" Jazzman said, now pissed. She guzzled a good portion of her wine.

"Don't get snippy with me."

"Sorry."

Jazzman stood, and headed down the steps. "Shit."

"What happened?"

"I almost twisted my damn ankle on Jacob's skates."

She made her way into the dining room, flipped the switch to the chandelier and stopped. The photo album that housed her memories of Tony rested next to the open bottle of wine. That album was laced with good times, with promise; with what she thought was love. She turned her back on the book, squeezed her eyes shut.

"If you know like I know, you better send Tony ass somewhere else."

"It's too late. The paper work has already been processed. He's scheduled to parole here."

"Okay, let him parole there but don't let him live there. Pay up three months on one of those all inclusive kitchenettes. The rooms are matchbox small, but he'll have a bed, outlets for a crock pot, mini fridge, and a bathroom the size of those on an airplane. He won't have to worry about paying utilities or nothing."

"That's not a bad idea, but what about Jacob?"

"What about him?"

"This would actually be a good time for them to bond."

"Whoa."

"Whoa what?"

"You still love this dude."

"Girl, please." Jazzman exhaled. "What if I do run with your idea, his parole officer can pop up at any time. He might violate his terms, get sent back."

"You got a whole lot of *what-ifs* for a nigga who did you dirty."

"Shit, I'm confused."

"Rick is a good man. You better hold on to him."

Jazzman pulled both cheeks in. "He's a definite catch."

"Prime pickings, which is why I don't understand you're dilemma. I know Tony's your baby daddy but life goes on. Let's not forget that mess he pulled when you came up pregnant."

Tony slapped five crisp one hundred dollar bills into the palm of her hand and told her to abort their son's future. He insisted that she terminated. He was adamant about not being a father. He moved out, left her with morning sickness, swollen feet, enlarged belly and a mountain of bills to pay.

"He bailed. He left you bare foot and pregnant," Lou-Lou spat.

"You don't think I know that?"

"He left you in a bad predicament. You had that baby by yourself. Alone."

Jazzman slapped an open hand across her forehead, squeezing that horrible memory from her brain. "Don't take me back to that place. That was another life."

All Jazzman wanted to do was put the past behind her. But as of recently, the past had trudged its way back from the dead, *literary*.

Lou-Lou was right. Life went on. The wheels kept spinning, the seasons kept changing. People changed. She changed. She grabbed the bottle off the table, poured another glass of wine. She stared down at the album. Her fingers traced the edges of her memories. There were pictures of him, of her, hugged up. *Kissing. Happy. Loving.*

"I tell you one thing; I ain't never hustled this hard in my life. I've got my hands in a little bit of everything. Need to streamline my efforts, trim some unnecessary fat, get to the meat of things," Lou-Lou said, talking in riddles.

Jazzman wasn't sure if she wanted to respond. She wasn't sure if she wanted to entertain the forthcoming conversation. That was territory she didn't want to visit with Lou-Lou, especially with her love life in the trench.

"Ace got a military background. He got access to..."

"Please don't."

"Just hear me out."

Heavy breathing occurred on both ends. "Listen. We both know what it is to struggle. Hell, we've both been through the ringer. We made some decisions, had to lay a few fuckers down. The bottom line is..."

"The bottom line is we made it out, in one piece. Let's not go back." Jazzman tipped her glass, took a gulp full. Her cheeks expanded. She swallowed hard.

"We need to up the ante, go harder, go stronger this time. Ace got..."

"Just leave me out of this one."

"He's our ticket to military issued burners," Lou-Lou whispered.

Jazzman's hand went into the air, fell and landed on her hip.

"Yep, the girl has gone crazy. *Have you lost your mind?*" she whispered.

"Have I?"

"Count me out."

"*C'mon*, you can't possibly be satisfied. After catching up your mortgage, paying the IRS, and the rest of your bad debts, you're left with nothing. You're probably hoping a job comes through to keep you above water, aren't you?"

"In fact, I am. I'm hoping to be gainfully employed very soon."

"Very soon ain't soon enough. Let's get this paper."

"I've got Jacob to think about."

"You've got bills to think about too, which comes like clockwork on the first of every month. Rick is a *great* catch, but how long do you expect him to deal with your shit?" Jazzman felt that brutal reality in her gut. "You're about to move your son's father in, some buster ass coward who once left you for broke while he did his thing."

Jazzman giggled. "You're calling me a bag lady?"

"Honey, Erika Badu had you in mind."

She sighed, "Things will work out. Right?"

"It's up to you Home-Skillet. You call the shots."

"Sometimes I hate being the one to make all the decisions. Right now, I wish I could journey back in time, be twelve for just a day. No eleven, eleven years old playing dress-up, sipping tea, with my best friend Cookie."

A deep sense of loneliness overcame her. It seemed like forever since she'd laid eyes on Cookie. Lies, deceit, broken vows of loyalty changed them. Her best bud Cookie was somewhere in the world working off bad emotions.

"Wow, haven't heard you mention her in a while," Lou-Lou said with a tinge of irritation in her voice. "Tony is trouble. But, you know best. All I'm saying is Jacob is used to a certain lifestyle. By helping Tony, you run a risk of losing the only support you got. And let's be honest, it's not like Rick is your husband. He can move on tomorrow, and you will still have those obligations. Why disrupt all that you've worked for?"

As much as Jazzman hated to admit, Lou-Lou was making sense. If Rick had a change of heart, if he turned flip-mode and decided not to have her back, she would be screwed. Even though Rick was aboard the same ship as she was, he still had bank, and his parents, even larger bank. It was nothing for him to get ten, twenty stacks. All it took was one simple phone call. No questions asked.

"And let's be real. Tony is fresh home. He's in no position to help you grow."

Jazzman gave much thought to changing Jacobs's school, and perhaps moving into a smaller place. The public school system made her shiver. Failing test scores, lost of accreditation, lack of funding for the next generation. Her head ached at the thought of moving into some apartment, God forbid a tenement building.

"And let's be real. You can't trust Tony. He's a snitch." Jazzman envisioned nosey neighbors, loud drunk talk, blaring music, smelly ethnic foods, and the infamous plastic tumble-weave blowing in the wind each time she opened her front door. She visualized hoodrats, and their hoodrat babies, hopping in and out of their baby daddys' car all times of the night. Fussing, fighting, police being called out to squash domestic disturbance. She pictured having Mexican neighbors who housed half of Mexico under one roof. She could foresee *INS* kicking their front door in, hauling everybody back across the border.

"And let's keep it real. The economy is in the toilet. Job market reeks of shit."

Jazzman was grooming her son to join the elite crowd. Jacob was to be amongst future scholars and professionals. She came from the wrong side of the tracks. It made no sense on dragging her son backwards.

"This dude Ace, can you trust him?"

"He's a work in progress," Lou-Lou said with a smile in her voice.

"Work out the kinks. Contact me when you have a for sure plan in place."

"Will do," Lou-Lou said having won half the battle.

***

The next morning, Jazzman called Rick and invited him down to the Spa for a mani and pedi. Rick was a true mans-man, who took pleasure in keeping himself shitty-sharp. Dirty hands, crusty toes, unshaved, untamed beard was unrefined to him. Most women would probably question his attentive detailing to stay immaculate. His blemish free outer appearance would surely intimidate the average chick who couldn't keep herself together. Not Jazzman, she loved that he took pride in how he looked and smelled.

"I've got a few things on my calendar this morning," he said with a trace of bitterness in his voice.

"Can you make some adjustments for me?"

"You didn't have much to say last night, why the change?"

"I've had some time to think."

He hesitated before asking, "What time?"

"I'll pick you up in an hour."

They sat in high-back, pink leathered massage chairs. Their feet submerged in milk, honey and lavender oil. Hydro-therapeutic jets massaged their toes, caressing their ankles, bringing life to their very being. Her eyes closed, her inner voice turned down low, barely audible. Pessimistic thoughts captured by each bubble that burst against her skin. The Asian woman scrubbed the soles of her feet, looking up every few seconds, showing off her coffee stained teeth.

"You pretty," the Asian woman said, grinning. Jazzman wished she had a box of whitening strips, some floss, and a nice firm electric tooth brush to give the woman as a gift.

"Thanks."

"French Tip – Fi-dollah-more."

"Sure."

Jazzman glanced over at Rick. They hadn't said but two words to each other. When she picked him up at his condo, he bypassed the usual smooch, and tossed her the head nod, as to say *what's up*. His silence was a concern, but she drove without forcing him to engage conversation.

"You look nice today," she said.

"Thanks."

His cell rang. He quickly silenced it.

"That's a nice sweater you have on."

"You bought it," he said curtly.

His cell rang. He quickly silenced it.

"This feels good doesn't it?"

"It does," he said, exhaling loudly.

"Am I annoying you?"

"No."

"Wish I could do this once a week."

"That would be nice," he said.

"You smell good."

His cell phone rang *again*. He silenced it *again*. She watched as his finger tips moved quickly across the keypad. *Who the hell is he texting?*

"I'm sorry, what did you just say?"

"Forget it."

The constant ringing of his cell deepened her curiosity. The tension between them was as thick as a block of Government cheese. He sat up like a King, while two Asian chicks flocked to his every need. One at his feet, bathing his pretty toes and the other massaged his temples and shoulders, melting away his stress.

"This is a black man's dream," he said.

"French Tip, fi-dollah-more," Jazzman said, then laughed.

His eyes shifted to the left. "Oh, you got jokes?"

"Just kidding baby."

He nestled his head into the seat, and sunk deeper into the vibrating chair. His cell interrupted his peace.

"Someone needs your attention."

"She can wait."

Who the hell is she? A wistful pause captured her. Their eyes met. He could tell she wanted to say something. It was evident she wanted to question *who* was blowing up his cell phone. Her lips parted, and then closed. It wasn't the place, damn sure wasn't the time.

"It could be important."

"Like I said, she can wait."

Ooh, this motherfucker wants to play games. Be cool, chill. Don't stress Jazz.

Last night's talk with Lou-Lou shed light. Her words made Jazzman wake up and realize Rick was not to be toyed with. He was a good man, who deserved a good woman.

"You haven't had much to say since I picked you up."

He glanced at her. "I'm trying to relax."

"You're right, enjoy your foot rub."

A set of legs strolled through the door. Shapley, short curly hair tapered at the neck, simple rose tattooed the back of the ear. Rick's eyes followed the woman until she disappeared behind the door marked *Wax*. She felt the softness of her midsection. *Damn!* She needed to feel that burn. The last couple of days, all she did was eat, down wine, and think about ways to renege on her promise to Tony. *I need to work out.*

The lady at Rick's feet stood, and scurried across the room to fetch two hot towels. He flipped through the latest Forbes Magazine. It was business as usual for him. He spent most of his time tracking the rise and fall of Fortune 5's, researching new tech companies, making educated guesses on stock movements. He kept his pencil sharpened.

"We should drive up to Tampa this weekend."

She gave him a sideways glance. "Can't."

"Why?"

"You know why. Let's not discuss this right now." Her voice was sweet.

A moment passed. "You're the one who wanted to talk. Let's talk," he said.

"I know, but not about that. Not here."

"Just because Tony is coming to stay, doesn't mean you have to babysit does it?"

"No, but I'm not about to leave that fool in my house unattended, at least not yet. There are rules I need to lay down." She flashed a fake grin. He closed the magazine, rolled it tightly, and swatted an opened hand. "Need to have the old family meeting, huh?" She whipped her neck in his direction. "What's your problem?" Heads turned, customers started to whisper. He shrugged and reopened the magazine. "Forget it."

"Forgotten," she spat.

He closed the magazine again. "For what it's worth, I respect your decision. You're a good person, Jazzman. Most women, or men for that matter wouldn't give two shits about what happened to their ex. But you, you're different. You have a heart. That's one of the things I love about you."

"Is this some poor attempt to make me feel bad? If so..."

"Sweet heart, I can't make you feel any way about you, then what you *already* feel about you." Tension thick, emotions running high, acceptance was key. It was a hard pill to swallow, but Rick wouldn't give her up. It was the first time in many moons he'd felt a connection like the one they had.

He shooed the two Asian women away, and slipped his socks on. He angrily yanked at his shoelaces, choking them tightly. He reached for his wallet, pulled out his card and waved for the bill.

"Rick."

"What."

"I invited you. It's my treat, remember?"

"You have another mouth to feed. Keep your money."

The Asian woman at Jazzman's feet carried a tune, and then spoke something in her native tongue. Those who understood snickered. Jazzman snatched her foot away, causing nail polish to splatter against the woman's clothes. She glared, ready to smash her exfoliated foot against a pie shaped face. "Now fix it," she demanded.

Rick scribbled his name forcefully onto the computer generated receipt. His jaw was tight and flinched in disappointment.

"I'm going next door for a drink."

Twenty minutes later, she found him at the Mexican restaurant. He sat at the bar, tossing back shots of Patrone, spilling his troubles to the short man wearing the sombrero. Tortilla chips and extra spicy salsa sat before him. She tapped him on the shoulder.

"I'm ready."

"Señor Santos, she is the one," Rick slurred, pointing over his shoulder.

"You're drunk."

"I'm tipsy."

"Same thing."

"Sit down, have a drink with me."

She checked her watch. "We really should be going."

"*Damn*, you can't enjoy just one drink with me?" he snapped. Heads turned. She slid into the seat next to him. Not because he asked her to, but because she didn't want to cause a scene. She rubbed his back, kissed his neck. He smelled so good. *What have I done to you?* Rick never raised his voice. They never argued. He was always pleasant, even when they disagreed. "Bring her a shot." She waved off the bartender. "I'm good. Thanks." He motioned for the bartender to hit him again.

"You really should slow down," she whispered.

"I can hold mine just fine, besides your driving."

She checked her watch again. "We should really get going."

"Why, what's the rush?"

She grabbed his hand, interlocking their fingers. She slipped of the stool. "Can we discuss this in the car?" He tossed the drink back, slammed the glass down.

***

They drove twenty minutes in silence. Rick watched the passing cars, deep within his own thoughts. The sky rumbled, with threatening clouds congregating above. Drops of God's tears fell against the earth. He tried remaining in a constant state of maturity. He attempted forms of empathy, struggled with understanding her position, but at the end of the day, he was mad as hell. He was pissed off, beyond words, ready to push her up against a wall and shake her.

They stopped at a light. Jazzman shook her head. Watching the young push the young in strollers angered her. Funky peacock hair style, fire red tips. Smoking a cigarette, cell phone pressed to the ear, pushing her baby with the flats of her forearm. The light turned green. She stepped on the gas, and then slammed the breaks. Just inches away from a young boy draped in cheap silver, pants sagged below his ass.

"The young are so creative," he said.

"Creatively stupid," she added.

Rick held his peace for the most part. Raising his voice at her wasn't the key. Although he had very little answers, he knew challenging her at that moment would ruin what they had. He reclined his seat, placing both hands behind his head, and chilled. After several more minutes of listening to Jamie blame it on the alcohol, Rick spoke up.

"Can you let the CD play through?" She mashed the *repeat* button again. "I love this song. *Blame it on the juice, got me feeling loose...*" He lowered Jamie's voice a notch. "This whole code thing you mentioned the other day. Does it come with benefits?"

"Excuse me."

"You mentioned this "code" thing back at your place, the other day. Something about you doing for him, him doing for you, you both looking out for each other because of this code. I'm oblivious to it. Explain."

She took a sharp breath, lowered Jamie a couple more notches. "It's complicated."

"I'm an educated black man. I'm sure if you explained the complexity of this..." He held up two fingers on each hand, arching them inwardly. "...Quote un Quote "code" I'm sure I will understand."

"You're funny."

"I'm serious."

She pulled up in front of his condo. He repositioned the seat in an upright position. She struggled with what to say to ease his concerns. Truth was, seeing Tony after so many years excited her. He was her first love. Her thuggish beau from Brooklyn who stole her heart from the moment she laid eyes on him.

They met at Madison Square Garden. She accidentally spilled Hawaiian Punch on his outfit. They were Ride of Die back in the day, but things turned for the worse when she became pregnant. She shook the thought. "Three months is all he's asking for. Allow me to provide that much for him."

"Provide." He laughed. "Seems as though I'm the only one *providing* around here... Just paid your fucking mortgage... just paid for that convict to live happy."

"I offered you the money back."

"Speaking of which, how the hell are you able to pay me back ten thousand dollars? You don't work."

"Don't worry about how."

"Just yesterday you were worried about the water bill; today you're able to dole out ten grand. It doesn't make sense to me. What the hell are you into?"

"You're missing the point."

"*No*, you're missing the point," he snapped.

"My son will have an opportunity to be with his father."

"*Whatever*, this is about you and him, not about Jacob. It's never about the kid."

"Think what you want."

"I'm fighting against those thoughts. By allowing me to think what I want... by allowing my brain to wrap around this fucked up reality..." He closed both lids tightly. A single tear fell from both sides. He was getting emotional. Liquor and emotions were a bad combination.

"What do you want me to do?" That famous question resounded from her lips once again.

"*What do you want me to do?*" He mocked her. "Do what the fuck you have to do... to... to maintain your happiness," he said.

"You're drunk."

"I want you to tell me that it's nothing. Tell me that he means nothing to you, and mean that shit."

"I did. I have. *Damn.*"

He grabbed her, held her by the arms, gripping her tightly. Her eyes grew to the size of dinner plates. Her heart pounded rapidly. Rage rippled through his body in waves. Patrone lingered his breath. "I love you."

"Rick, let me go."

"Tell me you love me. Say it."

"Rick...Stop... You're hurting me."

"I just wish you could see... I wish you could feel what I feel..." He leaned in, mashing his lips against hers. She squirmed and wiggled, until she was able to break free.

"Get your drunken ass out my car."

"I'm sorry." He held his head. "I'm so fucking sorry."

"Get out."

"Come up for a minute. We should talk about this."

"Get out my car."

"I kept this bitch running. If it wasn't for me you would be on four flats, driving on fumes. I paid for oil changes, tires, tune ups, checkups, hiccups, fuckups, detailing inside and out. Paid for the side mirror you knocked off backing out the driveway. Paid your goddamn insurance so that your ass would be covered in case of an emergency... *paid for...*

paid for..." He pounded his fist against the dashboard. "Even your breaks need changing. Can't you hear the squeak each time you stop? Who's going to fix that, Tony?"

"I'll do it," she answered child like.

"You used me."

"No. That's not true." She pleaded with him to get out, but he refused to budge. His erratic talk had her jumping every few seconds. "You need to calm down."

"You need to calm down," He mocked her. "I see how some brothers say fuck black women. I see how some brothers end up catching a domestic charge. Ya'll ain't got no damn respect for us. Always taking us through the wringer. And for what? Huh? For what?"

She didn't answer, instead she just listened. She rolled the window down, let in some fresh air. Dog walkers approached, and he silenced his rage. Rick protected his image at all cost. He inhaled a few gulps of air, sobering a bit.

"I admit, I'm a little drunk, took one too many shots back at the bar. Please accept my apologies."

"Apology accepted."

"You mad at me?"

"Yes."

"What can I do to make it up?"

"Get out my car, Rick."

"Wait. I'm sorry. Let me make it up to you."

CHAPTER 14

I t was a quarter past three, which meant Jazzman was late. It was all Rick's fault. Had he just let her leave when scheduled, she would have been home in time to meet Jacob at the bus. Her son was too young to be a latchkey kid, so it was important for her to be there.

"Come on, answer the phone."

Maria Rodriguez, her neighbor wasn't answering her mobile or her house phone. She worked from home and almost never left the house, accept to buy groceries, and sneak an occasional puff of the cig. Maria was her eyes and ears. With her being just steps away, Jazzman knew she could always count on her. But today of all days, Maria had not picked up, and that left Jazzman stricken with anxiety.

"Maria, answer the damn phone."

Worry wrapped her into a stray jacket, causing her to experience a mild case of palpitations. The thumping in her chest was a backdrop serenade to her ill thoughts. The recent increase of registered pedophiles that moved into her county didn't ease her. The thought of some sick bastard touching or even looking in Jacob's direction made her see red.

Traffic was at a standstill. The Hempstead Turnpike was backed up for miles. She tuned into Hot97 and heard about a multiple car wreck at the Jones Beach Exit.

"Damn."

A five lane highway, turned into one. Cars crept pass the scene, inching by debris, rubber necking in the process. When it was her turn, she blew pass the wreckage, and sped the rest of the way home.

A sudden calm came over her when she spotted her son. Jacob dribbled the basketball, and then attempted to take a shot at the basket. It bounced off the rim, and shot across the yard. He ran fast to retrieve it. When he returned to the concrete, he bounced, dribbled, and jacked the ball high into the air, missing the basket by miles.

"Good job Jacob."

That voice made her heart gallop. He stood leaned against the garage door like he was *Tyson Beckford*. "Good job son. You the best!"

She inched into the driveway, parked. She sat behind the wheel for a second, watching father and son play a long overdue game. He coached, directed, and got excited whenever Jacob attempted to shoot. Even when the ball was way off base he still applauded and slapped fives with his little man. It was amazing how much Jacob looked like Tony.

"Mommy, look who's here."

She held her tears at bay, slipping from behind the wheel. Jacob grabbed his daddy's hand, and pulled him to meet his mommy. They met half way, at the center of the concrete. Harden feelings began to soften.

He considered her lips first. Glazed, and glistening in the right amount of shimmer. They made eye contact. She held his gaze long enough to steal his breath. Her once shoulder length hair was cut short, right above the ear. She wore a conservative blue tailored blazer, white peasant top, and jeans. Her jeans hugged and held all of what he left behind.

He considered hugging her, but waited, allowing her to take the lead. He was screaming on the inside, wanting desperately to grab her into his arms. Wanted to feel her softness, embrace her like only a man with feelings should embrace a woman.

"I wasn't expecting you until late this evening."

"I hope that's not a problem."

She looked down at her son. Her son looked up at her. He was all smiles. *Damn he looks like his father.* "No problem at all. How was your ride in?" she asked, fumbling with her keys.

"Rough, but who's complaining. Just happy to be off that bus, even happier that I'm a free man."

She looked at her son. "Sorry I'm late baby, got caught in traffic."

"That's okay mommy. Daddy was waiting out front for me."

Beep Beep!

Jazzman twisted back, saw Maria climbing out the front seat of her F150. A mini Latin Diva who drove big trucks, big boy style. "Carla had the baby this afternoon."

"Congratulations Grandma!"

Maria straightened her blouse, poked her bosom high. "Okay, knock that Grandma stuff out, but thanks!"

Jazzman giggled. "I was running late, tried calling you."

"Girl, I went loco when Carla's water broke. Left my cell, my purse, my head, all on the kitchen counter. I was a complete mess." Maria stopped her chatter when she noticed that fine piece of ass standing next to Jazzman.

"Where's my manners, I'm Maria. And you are?"

Before Tony could introduce himself, Jacob chimed in boisterously. "He's my daddy."

"Oh. Well, nice to meet you daddy." Maria popped her chewing gum, giving Jazzman a salacious grin. "Girl, when you get a moment, *call* me." They watched as Maria disappeared into the house. Seconds later her blinds adjusted. Jazzman shook her head, laughed. *She's my eyes and ears.*

"Were you surprised to see your daddy?"

"Super duper surprised. I thought I was dreaming." Jacob gained a visual connection through jail house photos. To see his daddy up close and personal was like a dream come true.

"I would have picked you up from the station but..."

"It's no problem. My legs work just fine," he said kicking out his legs one at a time.

"Mommy, can we bake Daddy a cake?"

"Hum, well let me think about it."

She moved passed Tony quickly, careful not to brush against him in any way. As they walked behind her, she heard Jacob telling his daddy about his Lego collection, his Battleship game, and his new Wii station. He rambled on about all the cool toys he had, and how he couldn't wait for them to play with each other.

"I've been meaning to get this lock fixed," Jazzman said, struggling with the key. Her jittery hands made it impossible to align the key with the hole. He stepped up behind her, reached over her shoulder. "Mind if I give it a try?" His closeness caused her shoulders to fall helplessly, and then stiffened. "Sure."

While inside, they kept their distance. She watched attentively from the kitchen's pass through as Tony and Jacob played video games. Soda cans and bowls of popcorn covered her glass table. Every now and then he'll look over his shoulder, steal a peek at her.

"How does baked chicken, macaroni and cheese with cabbage sound?" Jacob became excited. "I love macaroni and cheese!" Tony smiled at his son, and then looked up at her. "Sounds good to me, haven't had a home cooked meal in years."

She leaned into the freezer, pulling out a five pound bag of wingettes because they thawed easy. She stood there for a second, cooling herself off. *Okay girl, get it together. Stay strong. You have a man. A good man. You can do this.* Tony had her thinking salacious thoughts. Her body began to tingle in all the right places. *Rick loves you and you love him.*

A gentle hand pressed against her shoulder. Goose bumps invaded her body. The frozen bag of meat hit the floor. Both hands flew to her chest. "Shit, you scared me." They both leaned over at the same time, headbutting one another. *Ouch!*

He held his head, laughed. "I'll go down. You stay up."

Going down was always his favorite. Stop it Jazzman. Just stop it! The artic feel the freezer presented did nothing for the fire between them. She moved towards the sink, grabbed the stopper, and proceeded to run hot water.

"This arrangement can't be easy for you, but you don't have to avoid me like the plague."

She snatched the bag, tore the plastic across the top, opened the zip lock feature, and tossed the wingettes beneath the running water. "Who's avoiding you?" He leaned against the granite counter top, smiled. "Did you design the kitchen?"

"Yes, I did. Got most of my inspiration from some silly magazine, but I love it."

She looked around at her pride and joy. The kitchen was the heart of the home. The color grey splashed the majority of the kitchen, while red fired back from an accent wall. Top of the line stainless steel appliances, hanging pots, and rooster printed dish towel summed up the décor.

"Been here for almost an hour and you have yet to give yah boy a hug."

She looked at him quickly, then over his shoulder. He was right. She was being rude. The least she could do was give the man a stinking hug. There was no harm in that right? A hug between two old buds was just a hug. Nothing more, nothing less, right? Her eyes darted from one end of the room to the other as she dried her hands with a paper towel.

He studied her face. "He's upstairs looking for his Battleship game."

"I need a drink... want a drink... got beer... got wine... got Patron... which do you prefer?" She held the fridge open, looked in. He removed her hand from the handle, pulled her close to his chest. She pushed him away.

"You're over stepping yourself. Let's not confuse what this really is." He tipped her chin, looked into her eyes, saw that she still cared. "I missed you a lot," he said sincerely. She shook him off when she saw her son standing there, holding his Battleship game.

"I'm ready daddy."

"Okay son, let's do this." Tony looked back over his shoulder and winked.

Jazzman stirred cake mix until all the lumps had disappeared. She cut, chopped and simmered cabbage. She baked chicken, macaroni and cheese, and sipped wine. When dinner was done, she fixed them both a plate.

"You're not eating?" Tony asked.

"I'm not hungry," she said.

"But mommy, we didn't pray. We always pray before we eat."

She stopped at the edge of the steps. Wine glass filled to the rim, thoughts of a bubble bath on her mind. She turned, forcing a smile to her face. "Daddy will pray with you." She looked at Tony for support, he looked away.

"All good things come in *threes,*" Tony said; his smirk evident.

Jacob rubbed his chin like a little man. "Mommy you make three."

As they held hands and bowed, Jacob led them in prayer. He was the glue which connected them. Joined together for the first time in years brought unwanted tears to Jazzman's eyes. Tony squeezed her hand gently, assuring her that what she felt, he also felt.

Finally, flickering candles surrounded her tub; oil burner gave off a lavender scent. Bubbles covered every inch of her chocolate skin. A damp rag covered her face. She prayed a silent prayer, asking God for clarity.

How was it possible to feel the way she felt after so many years? He did her wrong on so many different levels and yet she still cared. He was never good for her, not even a little bit. She lifted her wine glass, sipped the red liquid. The taste of orange and berries sweetened her tongue.

There was a knock at the door. A slight jiggle to the doorknob caused her to panic. Her back curved like a mad cat. "Who is it?" she asked hoarsely.

"Mommy, it's me."

She relaxed. "Yes baby?"

"Can I stay up for a little while longer?"

She reached over the side of the tub, grabbed her phone to check the time. There were five back to back calls from Rick. "It's going on nine o'clock. You have school in the morning."

"Yes, but tomorrow is Friday... and I already bathed... and I put my jams on... and... I brushed my teeth and washed my face... and... me and Daddy wanted to play another round of Battleship."

"No, go to bed."

There was silence. She could hear him conferring with his daddy. Tony was teaching him how to run game already. She sat up in the tub, saw two sets of shadows standing outside her bathroom door. Her eyes beamed across the large room. Jacob had a bad habit of busting through doors. To her relief the door was locked.

"I want you in the bed at 9:30 on the nose. Not a minute after. Understand?"

"Okay," Jacob said excitedly.

After tucking Jacob into bed, Jazzman headed downstairs. She checked the stove, windows, and doors, making sure everything was locked and in the *off* position. To her surprise all the dishes were washed, the living room was cleaned and the floor had been swept. Tony found several blankets and made himself a neat pallet on the floor. He took up just enough space, allowing him to stretch both arms and legs at the same time.

"There's a guest bedroom upstairs." She pointed.

"The floor works just fine."

"Don't say I didn't offer."

"Thanks for dinner."

"Don't mention it."

"Didn't know you could throw down like that."

She set the alarm system, and pulled the drapes closed. "You can't help but learn your way around a kitchen with a kid."

"Oh, and that *Sock-It-To-Me* Cake was off the chain. You put your foot in that."

She blushed. "Thanks." She tugged at her belt, fastening her robe tighter around her waist. He watched as she re-wiped the counters surface, and re-swept the floors. She was a neat freak, always had been.

"Why do I still smell cabbage?" she asked.

"Oh, I dipped back into the Tupperware, took a couple of spoonfuls." She sprayed a few pumps of Vanilla Lavender to rid the lingering cabbage odor.

"He's gotten big."

"Growing every day it seems."

A moment of silence passed. They both attempt to speak at the same time.

"You go."

He shook his head. "No, you go first."

She scanned the room and decided to take a seat on the sofa. He leaned back comfortably against his pallet. He was shirtless. Stomach so flat, a quarter could bounce off it and ricochet off the wall. She couldn't allow her eyes to fall below the waist line, but they did. *Damn!*

"So, tell me about Rick."

She looked surprised, then upset. "Jacob down here telling my business?"

"No, not at all. Dude called the house while you were taking a bath. I guess he couldn't reach you on the cell."

"You answered my phone?"

"Of course not, Jacob did."

Her lips formed into a small *O*-shape.

"Over heard dude asking Jacob a bunch of questions," Tony said tight faced.

"What kind of questions?"

He sat up. Did a single crunch, and fell back onto his pallet.

"Where's your mommy... is she alone... did she have company... where was the company sleeping?"

"The company? Wow." She looked furious.

"Had the nerve to ask my son if you were bathing alone."

She closed her eyes, took a deep breath. He came up, crunched and fell back again. A flow so flawless made her stop, and watch him work. He was just twenty crunches in before she felt herself twitch below. One hundred and fifty crunches later, he sat up. A light sheen covered his face, arms and neck. *Damn! Damn! Damn!*

"You know I'm not trying to stop whatever you got going on, but I thought maybe dude was out of line."

"Let me be the judge of who's out of line and who isn't."

"You're the boss."

He stood, and perused the collection of books tucked neatly away in built-ins. Titles such as *The Audacity of Hope*; *Think Like A Lady, Act Like A Man*; *The Art of Persuasion*; and *The 48 Laws of Power*, in no specific order lined the first shelf. *"Best Mom of the Year"* Trophy and other glass trinkets decorated and hung precisely from ledges.

"Since when you become an avid reader?" he asked.

"Since when you start using words like avid?"

He looked over his shoulder, and laughed. "I'll have you know I wasn't just sitting on my ass while in the joint. Got my GED, and I'm just a few credits shy of my Associates. Learned a few things to help me out during my search of employment."

"Good to hear you made use of your time." Her smile was genuine.

"It was that or catch another charge. More time on top of what I already had would have broken me. I saw too many come through the gate with simple bids."

"Simple?" She questioned his choice of words as if jail was some vacation, retreat, a place to go and just be "simple". As far as she was concerned one day in jail was too long.

"Six months turned into one year. One year turned into two. Two turned into four. Shit. One cat came in on parole violation and ended up catching him a body. Crackers gave that man life."

"So it's the white man's fault?"

"You know what I mean."

She sat seemingly interested in what he had to say. Truth was, her mind was on Rick. The audacity of him to engage in conversation regarding her, with her child was unacceptable. She played it cool, kept her anger in check.

His eyes scanned the remaining titles, and stopped. It was a picture of him and his son when Jacob was just a year old. He remembered that moment like it was yesterday. It was the first time he'd laid eyes on his brown face. He turned back; saw that her mind was elsewhere.

"What you thinking about?"

"Nothing important."

"I did a lot of reading, and worked out every day."

"What else is there to do?" she said blandly.

"You have a beautiful home. Your man must have some major paper."

She stared at him for a second before responding. Tony was the type to count money by what he saw on the surface. Material possessions equated success in his eyes. He was a typical non-business minded individual with half a brain. Extremely showy, only impressed with the tangibles. To him the more you bought and had, the better off you were. So cliché.

"What makes you assume that?"

"This big ass-house for one... red and brown leather sofas... fancy artwork... flat screen televisions... granite counter tops. All that's left to roll out is the red carpet. What he do for a living?"

Her head fell into her hands. She giggled with much agitation. *And to think I was just about to give you some. Ugh!* "You really don't get it do you."

"Get what?" he asked, completely oblivious to how she was feeling. How his words had affected her, how downright disrespected she felt at his accusation. She was never the type of woman who laid on her back and expected a man to take care of her. She was a go-getter, determined, strong willed, strong minded, and earned her way like the rest of the boys.

"I bust my ass to make all of this happen. I vowed to do whatever possible to ensure a good life, a *better* life for my baby. Went to school, got my bachelors degree, got a job, and bought this big-ass house, all on my own. So, don't come at me on some gold-digging mess because that's not how I'm cut."

"Let's not forget my truck... I did leave you the Lac... I'm sure the resale got you back a nice little penny."

She laughed.

"Say it didn't."

She folded her arms across her chest. *Why even bother?*

He hesitated before saying, "And on top of you busting your ass, making a life for you and my son, Rick helps out. I mean I would hope that he does, especially if you lying on your back. Ain't shit free in this world."

"Yeah he helps out, only because he wants to, not because I need him too. Besides, it comes a time in every woman's life when you stop fucking with broke niggas." She crossed her leg, leaned back, showing some skin. *Now take that to the bank.*

"Thought you knew what real money was, guess I was wrong," she said sarcastically.

"I know real money, and I aint talking about that chump change Barry was tossing me back in the day to do his dirt. I'm talking that kind of money you find in pool halls, close to midnight, on the Southside of Queens."

Her eyes went south, she shifted in her seat. She spotted a kernel of popcorn on the floor, saw a piece to Jacobs Battleship game imbedded into the area rug, radar picked up a fragment of crumbled leaf at the back door. Her eyes zoomed in on microscopic material like a Martian from out of space.

"Heard about that job you, Lou-Lou, and that nigga Roy pulled off. Shit hit the fan, joint started buzzing, names where dropped... heard your name in particular."

Liar. She stood to leave.

"Am I hot, or am I just getting warm?"

"You're out of line."

"That's why you skipped town, moved south. You needed to get away, right?"

"I don't know what you're talking about."

"You came back, but why?"

"I came back because I wanted to come back. Why the fuck is you all in my business?"

He looked through her. "Something brought you back. Something happened in Atlanta that caused you to book up and leave." Jazzman headed towards the staircase. He knew her well. That she hated. "How much you walk away with?"

She stopped, and turned. "I don't know what you're talking about."

"South side hit. How much you walk away with?"

"You got three months to find yourself a place. Ninety days!"

He smirked. "Understood."

"You are not to answer my phone, collect my mail, receive mail, or have anyone in my house. Be sure to get yourself a P.O. Box in the morning."

"No problem."

She climbed two more steps and stopped. "If anyone asks, you're a cousin from down south, and you're here only for a few months."

"Well call me cuzzin Pete," Tony said in the deepest southern drawl he could muster.

She popped him the finger. "You're an asshole."

"Can't help it."

CHAPTER 15

Newspaper in one hand, ceramic mug with the pink ribbon in the other. Tony glanced up at her, took a sip, and said, "Good Morning."

"Morning," her response was groggy. She opened the fridge, looked in, and closed it. "You're into pink now?"

He glanced down at the mug. "Not my color, but I do like the cup. Fills up nice. You know my mother had breast cancer?"

"Thought your mother died in a car accident."

The heat from the coffee singed his lip. Toffee colored liquid dripped along the sides. "She did, but she had cancer too. Thanks for allowing me to walk my son to the bus this morning."

"Don't mention it. I needed the extra Zzzz." The kitchen drawer was slightly ajar with junk mail poking out the sides.

"You've been sifting through my things?"

"I needed a pen. Jacob's crayons were all broken, could barely write with them." He took another sip. "I'll get him a new box today." Tony caught a glimpse of cleavage as she leaned over to grab a skillet.

"What are you looking at?" she asked with much too much attitude.

He shook his head and laughed. He could never understand why women asked stupid questions. She was dressed in black spandex, matching halter top, and track shoes. It was clearly obvious to why a man would look.

"You hungry?"

He adjusted his paper. "Starving."

Jazzman whipped up scrambled eggs, turkey bacon, waffles, hot maple syrup and a fresh cup of coffee. He looked over his spread and got happy, real happy.

"Dang, you make a brother feel like he at IHOP straight after the club."

"Remember when we use to break day?" She wasn't sure why she asked. It was one of those questions that slipped away before she had enough time to consider its validity.

He nodded. "Broke day sitting in IHOP, in the back booth, eating, talking, and..."

She rubbed the back of her neck. The nostalgic look on his face made her spot tingle. The way he bit down on his syrupy lip, made her get up from the table and find something to do, something to clean, something to busy herself with. She attacked the dishes.

He took a sip of his coffee. "You know, I didn't mean to get in your business last night."

"Yes you did."

"Well, maybe a little but you know I didn't mean to offend."

"I'm not offended. Who said I was offended?"

"C'mon, I know you. You were offended."

"No I wasn't. You got a smart mouth, and should probably watch what you say, and how you say certain things, but I wasn't offended. Not by a long shot," she said, scrubbing the skillet with a piece of Brillo.

He stood, placed his dish in the sink. They held hands beneath the running faucet water. Warm, flowing, liquid spilled onto their shaded skin. She gave him a playful elbow towards the chest. He backed away, looking at her from behind. She felt his lustful eyes cruise her body. She started to think, maybe just maybe the spandex were a little far-fetched. A nice pair of sweats and Tee-shirt would have been more appropriate. But Jazzman, like most women, felt the need to show off her complete package, especially to an ex-lover who became her ex for one reason or another.

"You're getting ready to work out?"

"I'm talking myself into taking a jog. Since I've been out of work, all I've done is eat."

"We should work out together."

"*W*-well, I was considering joining a gym."

"Don't waste your money. I'll train you. For free."

She scanned his body. He was fit. No fat. All muscle. "Huh, well, see the thing is..."

"Rick wouldn't appreciate me whipping his girl into shape, not that you're out of shape."

"Good save." She scrubbed the last of the dishes, rinsed and placed them in the rack. "I've put on a good fifteen pounds." He opened his mouth, but she cut him off.

"Don't lie to me. Tell me I've gained weight. Just say it."

"You're beautiful. However you can stand to tone up around the waist and..."

Her shoulders fell. Her self esteem plummeted a notch. "Are you ready for me to evaluate?"

She took a deep breath. The truth was going to hurt, but she needed to hear it. Rick told her what she wanted to hear. Tony on the other hand obviously didn't mind being frank.

"Evaluate."

"Easy version or the real deal Holyfield version?"

She pressed her back against the fridge. "Give me that Holyfield."

He snatched the measuring tape from the top drawer. "You can stand to lose a few inches off the waist. Your thighs are rubbing."

"How the hell do you know that?"

"Your black spandex pants are fading in that one area. It's called friction."

Damn, I've got friction at the thighs. This is some bullshit, she thought. He grabbed the back of her arm. "Your back arm is good, but could be tighter. As we get older, we lose elasticity. What that means is your flab will still jiggle long after you've waved bye."

"Ooh, that's not sexy."

He laughed. "Not sexy at all."

She turned around. "Please tell me my butt is okay. This is my personality... can't lose that."

"Your personality is firm, perfectly round, sits up high and...*damn*... it's... it's nice."

She smiled. "Thank God I haven't lost my personality."

They both fell out laughing. "I'll have you fifteen pounds lighter and completely toned. I'll have you looking better than you've ever looked in just six weeks."

She twisted her lip. "Six weeks. Isn't there a magic pill I can take?"

"No."

"Will it hurt?"

"It will be intense, you will hate me, but I will get you results."

"I... don't... know... Rick kind of mentioned something about me joining his gym, and taking up some swim lessons."

He stared at her. She looked away. "Swimming is good. You should try it out. If you don't get the results you're looking for, the offer still remains."

"Okay, bet."

He eyeballed the clock over the pantry.

"What are your plans for today?" she asked.

"I've got a nine o'clock appointment with my parole office in the city." He sipped the last of his coffee, and placed the mug into the sink. "Afterwards, I've got to head over to 26 Federal Plaza to get a new social security card. From there, I'm off to 125 Worth Street for a copy of my birth certificate. If I have enough time to spare, I'll shoot pass the motor vehicle to get my driver's license re-newed. I'm hoping to be back to meet Jacob at the bus stop by three."

She loved how focused he was. Maybe he was a changed man.

"I can drive you around. I mean, if you want me to. It's not like I have anything else going on today." The idea of jogging quickly faded. Before he could accept her offer, the telephone rang.

"Jazzman speaking," she answered in her professional, *I need a job* voice.

She fanned her hand before her face. "Yes. Of course I can meet this morning. Okay. No, Thank You. Thank you very much!" She sat the phone down and brought her hands to her chest.

"Good news?" Tony asked.

"Don't know yet. I've got a third interview. First two had gone really well. This usually means an offer is about to be extended."

"When?"

"Today. This morning. Can I drop you off at the Long Island Railroad?"

"Only if you have the time. Your gig is more important."

"Can you be ready in the next twenty minutes?" she asked, already leaping up the steps to her room.

Hearing from Sheila, down at Human Resources was the call Jazzman been waiting for. Her business suit was already dry cleaned and ready to be slipped into. It hung by itself at the far end of her walk-in. Respectable high heel pump, stockings and conservative pieces of jewelry tied in her professional finish.

Tony was blown away by her transformation. Her sexy business persona made him feel like an oil lube man, looking forward to his fifteen minute lunch break. She was dressed in a Democrat navy blue skirt, matching jacket, starched white button down and flight attendant scarf around the neck. She looked fresh, bright and conservative.

"You clean up good."

Her head jerked in his direction. "I clean up good?"

He stuttered. "You know what I mean. You're looking good in your get-up. I've never seen you in a suit before."

"Fitted jeans, tight waist tops and heels are not the only wardrobe I own. Every professional woman should own two if not three good sharp suits. You never know when that call may come," she said, and then looked him up and down. He was dressed in blue jeans, white button down shirt and those God awful state issued jail house boots.

"Shit, where I'm from suits are worn to funerals. So forgive me if I'm not up to speed on what's required to look so..."

Her eyeliner pencil glided back and forth against the rim of her lid, and stopped. She blinked twice, and then used her index finger to wipe away any smudges. "So what?"

"You look beautiful." He left the conversation at that.

She dropped him off at the Long Island Railroad as promised. She turned on her navigational system and sped away from the curb, leaving Tony to discover freedom on his own.

Her meeting lasted all of twenty minutes. Sheila from Human Resource slid the offer letter across the desk, and said, "The job is yours if you'll accept it." The blond-haired, blue-eyed lady was all smiles. Her perfect teeth, perfect layered bob, and big ass diamond on her lock-down finger was impressive.

"When do you need me to start?"

"In two weeks."

"I'll take it."

***

Jazzman did the pee-pee dance from the car, all the way to the house. Just as she made it onto the porch she realized that her keys were still in the ignition. Too far of a walk to head back, she left them there. She rung the bell seven times, and then pounded against the door. *"Open up."* Tony swung open the door, looking like he was ready to curse somebody out. "Oh, it's you."

"Get out the way," she said, dropping everything in her hands, and running towards the bathroom. She slammed the door shut. *"You would not believe the traffic out there,"* She yelled through the door. *"Traffic was so damn ugly, so damn thick. It took me..."* She wiped, flushed and washed her hands all in that order.

"It took me close to two hours to get home. They had some damn construction going on. I had to detour, come back around, ended up on..." She stopped talking.

"Why you looking at me like that?"

"Congratulations," Tony said.

She removed her wrist watch, then her diamond studded earrings, and placed it on the table in the foyer. She looked at him, grinning from ear to ear.

"Is it that obvious that I got the job?"

"Yep."

"I got the job," she said just above a whisper, while clasping both hands together.

She walked in circles, both eyes closed, summing up the moment that led to her accepting the position.

"I walked into Sheila's office today and owned it." She jumped up and down like a two year old. "I mean it's only a six week gig, but it's a start. If all goes well they might want me to join the crew permanently." She paused. "All will go well, right?"

He nodded. "All is well now."

"I tell you, getting laid off from the airlines has been a blessing in disguised. Never in my wildest dreams would I have considered becoming a Corporate Flight Attendant."

"Corporate meaning private?"

"Yes, private jets baby. Top shelf bubbly, expensive cigs, marble, Italian leathers, mink floors, the works. The pay is great, the benefits are lovely and I'll be able to rub shoulders with the wealthy."

"So you'll be catering to the rich instead of the working class?"

"What's wrong with that?" she asked, studying his face.

His lip was slightly curved. Not seductively, but in a way that spoke volumes of frustration. His concentrated eyes shifted across the room and back. He stared at her and said, "*That*, just arrived for you."

Jazzman cupped her chest, and gasped. *That*, which he referred to caused her to stop breathing. She covered her mouth and ran towards the arrangement. A field of pink tulips covered the kitchen island. Strong arched stems supported each elegant flower.

"Oh my God, these are beautiful."

She glanced over her shoulder for a second to see Tony leave the room. She didn't get a chance to ask how his day went, had he received all his necessary documents, did he make it to the DMV to renew his driver's license? That moment of guilt only lasted a second, and then quickly vanished.

As she was sure he had made it up stairs, she grabbed the card. It was already open. Instead of getting angry, she brought the sweet smelling card up to her nose, and smiled.

The message read so simple:

I'm so lucky to have you.

Congratulations!

Rick

She took a seat on the bar stool, and dialed Rick's number. His voice spilled into her ear like a soothing melody. "Well hello Houdini."

"It's not magic," he said.

"To me it is."

She looked over her shoulder, noticed a stack of mail. She figured it was nothing but bills. She heard Tony coming down the steps. He didn't bother looking her way, didn't bother taking in her happiness. She watched him roll up his pallet, and tuck away his life belongings into a raggedy duffle bag. Tension was thick. She ignored his vibrations, ignored his obvious attitude, and continued her conversation. Tony moved passed her and the beautiful arrangement, and headed out the front door.

Bong!

"What was that?" Rick sounded concerned.

"Oh, um, a wind must have caused the bathroom door to slam shut."

He wasn't buying it. "That was a strong wind."

She pressed her mouth against the receiver, loving the fragrance of the tulips.

"How'd you manage to have a lovely arrangement, such as this beat me home?"

"It was nothing. I called in a favor."

She called him first. As soon as she exited Sheila's office, and made it to her car, she called him. Before she could say that the job was hers, Rick was already online scheduling a rush delivery from a local Merrick florist.

"I'm sorry for everything. I was in a bad place yesterday. Grabbing you, yelling at you, calling and questioning Jacob was wrong."

"Rick, you already apologized. We're cool."

"Really?"

"Yes. Really."

A second passed. "Thank you for the flowers, they're beautiful."

"You're worth it. When do you start?"

"Two weeks."

"Cool. We can kick it a little before you get all serious on a brother," he joked.

"You say it as if I'm this bitch when I'm working. I'm not that bad, right?"

"Let's just say, a brother loved you more on your off days."

"Why didn't you say something?"

"I love a woman who goes head first into what she loves to do."

"I do love it. Corporate flying would definitely boost my resume. I can eventually contract myself out, become my own boss. Maybe open my own agency, get a crew under me. Offer the Premier, Exclusive Package."

"Premier-Exclusive-Package. Damn, that sounds sexual. How much will that cost?"

"For you, no charge."

"I don't mind paying."

"Don't I know it," she said, fanning her face with the card.

"You sound happy," he said.

She envisioned herself on private yachts, planes, catering to the rich. "You have no idea."

"That's what I love about you."

She blushed. "What you love about me?"

"Your desire to reach further. Let's go out tonight and celebrate."

"Okay, sounds like a plan," she squealed. Jacob's small feet came trotting through the door.

Bong!

"Another wind?" Rick asked.

Jacob slammed his book bag against the floor. Disappointment owned his face. Both arms folded against his chest, tears in his eyes, lips stuck out from there to Africa.

"No. Can't," she said quickly.

"No, you can't what?" Rick asked.

She told him to hold on. Her attention now with her baby boy. "What's wrong?" she asked her son. "Those stupid third graders bothering me again. They keep teasing me about my widow's peak. They said I look like Frankenstein."

Rick snickered. Jazzman wanted to laugh but kept her face serious. Kids were so damn cruel. "Can I call you back?"

"Wait. Please, say that we're on tonight. I need to see you."

"I can't," she whispered.

"Yes you can," Rick said in a whiny voice.

Tony stepped in seconds later. She heard plastic shifting behind his back, charming smile on his face. He walked up and kissed the center of her forehead. Surprised by his altered emotions, she sat frozen.

"These are for you," Tony whispered in her free ear. His lips touched her lobe, she quivered. *Damn, Damn, Damn.*

"Are you still there?" Ricks voice interrupted their moment.

"Yes, I'm here. Sorry about that."

"We're on tonight or what?"

Jazzman looked down at the flowers. Colorful carnations, mixed with seasonal daisies. He mistakenly left the price tag on the wrapper. $7.99 special. They were nice. Not as nice as Rick's arrangement, but it was the thought that counted. She looked at him, mouthed the words *Thank you!*

Tony dangled her keys, "Found these in the ignition."

She covered the receiver with her hand. "Oh crap, was the damn thing running."

"No, but you left the door open. I took it for a spin to the store. Hope you don't mind." She did mind, but now wasn't the time to give him the third degree. "It's cool. Thanks."

"Jazzman, are you there?"

She pressed the phone against her ear. "Yes. I'm here."

He released an aggravated breath, and repeated himself for the third time.

She hesitated, and then said, "Let me get things situated with my son first."

"Cool. I'll be by to scoop you at ten."

"*Wait.* It's probably best if I met you at your place."

CHAPTER 16

Later that evening, Jazzman pulled into the parking garage. Rick stood near the elevator dressed in gray sweats, and matching thermal top. His bowlegged stance made her bite down on the inside of her cheek. He directed her to park. Confusion rested on her flawless face.

"It's reserved," she said, pointing at the big red sign which said so.

"It's reserved for you."

"For me?"

"I took care of it this morning. No more driving in circles for my baby. Whenever you see fit to use it, do so."

She backed her Jag in slowly, feeling stunned beyond words. Rick expressed how expensive designated parking cost in his building. The mere thought of him dropping thirty thousand on a parking space, just for her, got her excited.

"Conveniently next to the elevator, right beneath the security camera," he said pointing towards the eye in the sky. He helped her from behind the wheel. She gave him a hug. His breath, warm against her neck. She quivered, and stepped away.

"You sure, I mean this space set you back thirty grand."

"Got it for twenty-five, but who's counting dollars and cents?"

"That's a huge discount. How?"

"The office manager kinda sweet on me."

"I thought she was gay. You mean she like men?"

"Baby, I can make the hardest dike see it my way."

She gave him a once over. "*Hum*...You ain't lying."

He grabbed her by the hand, kissed her lips and led her towards the elevator. "I thought we were going out tonight?" He leaned in, pushed the button. "Change of plans."

Jazzman stepped through the threshold first. Scented candles, dimly lit room, full course spread with all the trimmings placed carefully against a rectangular shaped table. She was blown away by the set up. Completely taken back by the chilled champagne, chocolate covered strawberries, and soft music.

"Hope I didn't go overboard with the food."

"I don't know what to say," she blushed.

He took her by the hand, and led her towards the kitchen. A variety of cheesecakes lined the counter. Not just any cheese cake, but some of New York's best wafted her senses. She covered her mouth. "Junior's Cheesecake. How'd you know?"

"You talk about it all the time. I took a trip out to Brooklyn after we spoke."

"Strawberry; Brownie Marble Swirl; Apple Crumb; my favorites." She moved in close, forcing him against the sink. Their lips met. A soft lingering kiss they shared. Their tongues danced a slow, free style number. Her hands traveled down his chest, towards the center of his happy place.

"Damn girl, sure you don't want to bypass dinner?"

She stepped away, gave them both some well needed space and air. "Let's eat."

He fed her small amounts at a time. Lobster and steak, dipped in garlic butter sauce, intrigued her palate. A small amount of butter dripped from the side of her mouth. He leaned in, licked.

She laughed. "Never had anybody lick my face before."

"Was that too weird for you?" he asked, wiping her face with a white cloth napkin.

"It was kind of sexy."

"You want me to do it again? I can do it again, can lick you where ever you want me to." She pushed him away. He came back for more, snaking his tongue in her direction. "Let me drip butter down your crack."

"Noooo," she squealed.

"Let me lick it from your crack baby." Her face told him she was considering it, but she shied away. "You're so silly."

After dinner, they made love on the kitchen floor, right next to the humming dishwasher. Afterwards, they sipped cold beer. Tall neck Corona's with a twist of lime. He was bare chest, barefoot, wearing nothing but his boxers. Jazzman lay comfortably with her head in his lap, looking up into his eyes. Her body wrapped in cotton.

"Why Atlanta," he asked.

"I wanted a change."

"Change is good," he said sipping his beer.

"But why Atlanta, why the dirty?"

"What do you mean?"

He tipped his beer bottle again, guzzled. "Nobody's really from Atlanta. People migrate there for one reason or another." She looked across the room at the red and white box from *Juniors*. She had a taste for something sweet.

"Lived in New York all my life and never been to the Statue of liberty. Never once visited Ellis Island... Still have yet to see Ground Zero. I remember the twin towers vaguely. Most of the time I remained Queens bound. Traveled from South Side, Jamaica Queens, to Queens Village, to Lefrak City, to Laurelton every now and again... seen most, if not all of Long Island," she said and shrugged.

"It's weird. Imagine living in a place all your life and never, ever seeing historical landmarks. Been up and through Brooklyn, took the E-Train into Manhattan many times before but never once did the tourist thing. Millions of people come to New York as tourists and have seen more then me."

"Why is that?"

"Stuck, stagnated, a product of my environment I guess."

"That's sad."

"The excitement never dwelled on the inside of me. Sure, I've seen New York in its rawest and most purest form. I've been to the BX, traveled uptown to Harlem, and kicked it on 125th Street with my homegirls. I can say I've seen some of the most prominent, memorable locations that told a story."

"I've seen stuff that's not accessible with just a click of a mouse. The kind of things and places I've seen, a tourist would dare not travel. The New York I know is different from those who relocate here with a hope and a dream. Those straight off the boat could probably relate."

"What you mean?"

"Immigrants. Mexicans. Jamaicans. Haitians. Indians. Asians. New York is combined of so many different nationalities and backgrounds it's not even funny. Most of which have no other choice but to reside in the hood."

"You're not an illegal immigrant are you?"

She covered her mouth and snickered. "No. Born and raised here. U.S. Citizen."

"Hey, thought I'd ask. You do have high cheekbones, and your ass is like one of a... what do you call it, *Big Body Gal.*"

"My mother and father both were born here."

"Okay. Don't bite my head off."

"Anyway, as I was saying. I know the side streets, back blocks, hoods, and ghettos. Where I'm from, we associate with potential terrorist everyday." She laughed, he didn't.

"Everyday?"

"Hassan and Habib run the corner bodegas. We spend money with them everyday, sometimes three, four times in a day. They run twenty four hour operations. They got what you need. Loosey's, condoms, aspirin, candy, food, pampers, envelopes, stamps, nail polish remover, even peroxide. You name it, they got it."

"*Jesus*, you fund their business, they support our demise. Their shipping money home, and in return sending us bombs in the mail."

"*Naw*, not the ones in the hood. The Habib's are cool. Shit, they like us, just trying to make a living. They make deli fresh sandwiches. Roast beef, sliced cheese on a toasted sesame seed bun. Shit be good too."

He looked at her, shook his head. Did she really underestimate the Arabs, with their American sandwich making, convenience store owning, *we down for the people* bull? Was she that blind, naïve to the fact that "these" people whose skin looked like ours were probably slipping small dosages of chemical into their roast beef, sliced cheese, on a toasted sesame seed bun. Was it ignorance, or just plain stupidity that made people trust, *no* turn a blind eye to what was really happening beneath their nose?

"There's no way in hell I could spend my money with them," Rick said in complete bewilderment.

"Habib and em' like family. They get down."

"What do you mean?"

She sat up, pulled the cold rim to her lips and laughed.

"C'mon, stop it." She took a swig and swallowed.

He looked dumbfounded. "I don't understand."

"They get down. They *wit* shit."

"A much different world then what I'm accustomed to, I guess."

"I guess so."

"I'm just a good old boy from the sticks. I've never met Hassan, Habib and em'. Where I'm from we don't associate with terrorist. Hell, closest thing I've seen to a terrorist in my neighborhood is when my Aunty Binky threatened to blow up the post office. They arrested her for making terroristic threats, but that's about it."

Jazzman imagined his Aunty Binky being hauled off to jail for talking out the side of her neck. Wig half cocked, mouth twisted, smelling of Seagram's 7. Small town folks made her laugh.

"Oh, and my Uncle Earl once spent ten days in the county for stealing out the Dollar General store. Would you believe that mess hit the newspaper?" Jazzman laughed so hard her side hurt.

"Guess what he got caught stealing?" Both hands covered her mouth in suspense. "I don't wanna guess... Tell me."

"Polident."

"Shut up. The denture stuff?"

"Uncle Earl was a dollar short, and he'd left his wallet home and didn't have his debit card. He didn't feel like going out to his pick-up for change and the rest is history."

"So he cuffed the box of Polident and got caught," she said, shaking her head.

"Not only did he get busted stealing, but his son, my poor cousin was the arresting officer."

"Okay, I'm through talking. Shut up," she burst out laughing.

"I'm serious."

All of Rick's family lived within a five mile radius. Aunts, uncles, cousins, grandparents, alive and dead, all resided and rested in one little town.

"*Oh, oh, oh* God my side hurt," Jazzman said, laughing until tears rolled down her face. Rick stood up, went to pull two more cold ones from the fridge, and sat back down.

"Can I ask you a question?" he asked.

"Sure."

"What's a *loosey*?"

Beer shot from her mouth and nose, spraying him in the face. He sponged beer away with the tail end of the sheet. "*Okay*, that was unexpected."

"Oh God, forgive me," she helped to clean him up.

"You're joking right?"

"I'm serious."

Oh my God, the man is clueless. "Hum, it's a single cigarette usually purchased for like seventy-five cents. Depending on the cost of a pack, determines the cost of a loosey. From what I hear a pack is running close to ten dollars. Habib and em' will sell one's and two's, or whatever the customer needs at the time. You understand?"

"Yes, but isn't that illegal?"

She held her laughter, didn't want him to feel bad for not knowing about the hood. Of course there was no resale on packaged goods, but who cared? Habib and em' weren't the only one's hustling loosey's. If you had a pack, and someone wanted to bum a smoke, you charged. Simple as that.

"Resale on a pack of smokes is very illegal, but that's how most people survive. Everybody got a hustle. Whether it's selling dinners, loosey's, or doing hair out your kitchen, they got a hustle."

Her last statement left him judgmental, critical of the way people in urban development's lived, or conducted business. "I know you've at least been to a couple of plays. The theatre is where it's at in the Big Apple. The theatrics, the stage, the spot light," Rick said with much enthusiasm.

"Never seen the Phantom of the Opera, never seen Cats, never had the privilege of seeing an Alvin Ailey number. Hell, never been to a Broadway show."

"Stop it."

"Straight up, no bullshit. I've *never* had the opportunity to see New York as a tourist. I've never had a chance to experience the Apple. I've seen its pain, its rage, its police brutality, its domestic violence, its many Central Park rapist, but never as a tourist. Guess I was brought up to survive New York, not explore it."

"That's sad."

"Sad but true."

"Enough said, we must go."

Her brows rose. "Go where?"

"Into the city, explore Manhattan as a tourist. We'll get matching *I Love New York* T-shirts, buy a map, take the gypsy cab up and down Fifth Avenue, and buy hot dogs and hot peanuts off the corner. We can even visit one of the many sex shops. Buy sex toys and XXX videos. Oh, better yet, we should book us a room at some five star hotel, stay the night, have a limo pick us up in the morning, shoot to Dean & Deluca for a shot of espresso and then ditch the limo. We could then head out to Rockefeller Center and..."

"Dean & who?"

"You're kidding me right?"

She inhaled strongly, and looked away. "Can't do it."

"Why not?"

"It's a long story."

He tapped his bare wrist. "I've got time."

"Your ears won't appreciate this story."

"*Ah* come on, can't be that bad."

A single tear slipped, and fell into her lap.

"Are you crying?"

"No. *Yes.* Man, I don't know where that came from. Sneaky tears," she said attempting to lighten the mood.

"You can talk to me about anything."

"I know."

"Well, lay it on me."

"What's done is done, Rick. Makes no sense to visit my past."

The sheet fell, exposing her breasts. He reached out to grab her perfectness, she covered quickly.

"We can get a room for a week at whatever hotel. Something real nice with butler services. I'm talking *Five Fucking Star* baby. I'm talking being celebrities for the moment. Let's make the help *Google* our fucking names."

She smiled at the thought, but leaving her safe haven was risky. She fit well in her new life. Deep out in the middle of nowhere was where she wanted to stay. Folks she knew from her previous life had no business on her side.

"We can see Broadway plays, travel to Brooklyn for a slice of cheese cake at Junior's... see the Statue of Liberty, visit Ellis Island, ride the Manhattan Ferry, take crazy pictures. We can even ride the metal horse to Spanish Harlem, buy jewelry from the vendors, and get shish kabobs drenched in BBQ sauce, sop up flavors with that hard ass block of Italian bread they give you."

"How do you know so much about New York?"

"I visited twice before I made it my home, *officially*. Straight after high school me and a couple of my partners bought greyhound tickets. Miami was the original plan, but then we said, Miami could wait."

"You took the bus? *Jesus.* That must have been a miserable ride. Stop and go. Stop and go. Confined to a small space, with strangers, and a compartmentalized bathroom, *ugh*."

"Actually, it wasn't that bad. We had music, food, stories to tell, five year plan to discuss. It was memorable." He went into a far off place.

"And the second time?"

"The second time," he paused, "love brought me there."

"Sounds romantic, tell me."

"You want another slice of cheesecake?"

"Oh no, let's not change the topic now. You all up in my *bidness*, let me get all up in yours."

"That's not fair, you haven't told me anything."

"*What*, boy please. You learned what a loosey is, found out about Hassan-Habib and em', discovered how us folks keep our head above water."

He hated how she used the word *us* as if she was still living amongst those circumstances. Even though she had *transcended* above her environment she still referred herself as *us, we, togetherness*. She was loyal.

"Right after college, I moved here."

Her eyes grew larger than life. "You lived in New York, when, how come you never mentioned this before?"

"I didn't think you'd be interested."

She sat Indian style. Focused. "See, that's where you're wrong. I'm very interested. What happened, why ya'll not together?"

"You sure you don't want another slice of that cheesecake?"

She gave him a look. "Spill it."

"We viewed the world differently. I wanted a family, kids, wanted to move back South and have the American dream. She wanted to pursue modeling, work the runway, and see Paris, Rome, Egypt."

"Egypt?"

He waved his hand. "You don't want to hear this."

"I do. Tell me."

"Small town boy meets big city aspiring actress. Her name was Bola, an Egyptian beauty whose family migrated to the states in the late fifties. Tall, slender, with a cute figure. Born and raised in Manhattan. Her folks owned several apartment buildings, Dry Cleaners, Laundromat, and a small ethnic restaurant on the upper Eastside. We met in Atlanta at a *Bronner Brothers* hair show."

She looked at him suspiciously. "You try'na tell me something?"

"Get your mind right. Don't even play yah self. This girl at Kinkos, where I used to work begged me to buy a couple of tickets. She convinced me that there would be honeys there, so I bought four."

Jazzman laughed. "Typical."

"Me and three of my boys rolled up in a rented Navigator, dressed real dapper."

Jazzman couldn't control herself. "Were you ridin' *Spinnaz* too?"

"See, I knew I shouldn't have started this story."

"No baby, go ahead. I'm sorry." She instantly muted her laughter.

"We met at the hair show. At that time Bola's modeling gigs trickled in. So to supplement, she modeled her hair. Her hair was long, black, and beautiful. That was what caught my attention. Thick stands fell past her shoulders, down the center of her back."

Jazzman pulled at her short messy tress and suddenly felt self conscious. "So," she said, wanting him to continue.

"So, my friend from work introduced us."

"And..."

"And right after I graduated from college, I resigned from Kinkos, packed what I owned into my Chevy Camaro and moved to New York. We got a small apartment in the Village. I mean real small. Bola and I were happy for about two years, maybe three. We both were doing well in our careers. Her agent booked her for small acting roles; modeling gigs, hair shows, etc... she was on the go most of the time."

"As for me, I landed a job with an up and coming brokerage firm making sixty-five a year. It was good money back then. Twenty-two, making over sixty G's, model girlfriend, my own apartment. I was on top of the world. I traded in my old Camaro for an Audi 5000. We were doing well, but then... then Bola missed her period."

"Pregnant?"

He stood, walked towards the kitchen, opened the fridge, pulled two more cold beers and returned. "I begged her not to get rid of my baby. Her mother begged her to keep the baby. Bola had other plans for her life. Being a mother wasn't one of them. So, she aborted, and moved out."

Jazzman touched his shoulder. "I'm sorry. Where did she go?"

He shrugged. "She discontinued all contact. Changed her number, email address, she practically dropped off the face of the earth."

"What about her parents, her mother?"

"Her mother was a sweet woman, but her obligation was with her daughter. There wasn't much information her mother could provide, other than that she was okay. That was about five years ago."

He guzzled his beer, and belched. "Last time I heard she made it big overseas as a model. Paris, Rome, Egypt, her dreams came true. She set out to do something and she did it. That was Bola. *Determined*."

He summed up his ex-in one word *Determined*. She summed up her ex-in one word *Convict*. She quickly shook the thought of Tony and refocused.

"Instead of breaking our lease, I stayed an additional three months."

"What was that like?"

"Some days good, some days bad. There was no telling how I would wake up, or go to sleep. Tried becoming the single bachelor, but the women I did take back to my place couldn't overlook the picture on my nightstand, of *her*."

"So you never got laid?"

"Nothing meaningful," he said, shaking his head.

"I was hopeful for her return. A week before our lease was due to expire; I got a postcard in the mail, from *her*. She said some crap about always loving me, how I was a good man, and how she prayed that I found the right one, and when that day came, I would know....*blah, blah, blah*."

His eyes stretched across the room, landed on the kitchen wall. He focused in on the imaginary hieroglyphics of his life.

"Postcard came from Atlanta."

"Wait a minute, this chick moved to Atlanta anyway and left you in New York?"

"Apparently, she landed a gig there and failed to mention it."

"So, what did you do?"

"What did I do?" He looked up towards the ceiling. He was still angry, still hurt. She could tell a part of him still missed her, even loved her. "I moved out. Headed to Long Island. I've been here ever since."

"You don't miss Georgia?"

He grabbed her hand. "Terribly, but my life is here, with you."

CHAPTER 17

C uriosity rode the back of her thoughts.

    Bola+ British+ Model+ London+ American jump started her Google search. That search string produced 4,860,000 results. She had more coverage then British model Naomi Campbell. Articles, photos, interviews, live footage. Her regal face plastered everywhere. She was tall, lean, beef jerky brown skin, with Rapunzel hair. The fashion world abroad loved her. *Black American Model Captures the Essence British Style. America & British Meet. Red Blooded American, British Soul,* Were just a few of the headlining titles.

    Part black, part Egyptian, tall, slender, cute figure. Born and raised in Manhattan. The way his eyes lit up when he described her made Jazzman feel a certain way. She shoved the laptop aside, and sat quietly, while obsessing over one photo in particular. Even though Bola was his past, she couldn't help but feel green. It wasn't every day the man she was dating had an ex-girlfriend, who happened to be a supermodel. *High Fashion Supermodel* with killer legs.

    Rick wanted to know her past. He wanted to know her choices, decisions, good or bad. He wanted to know what made her move south, to Atlanta, and back all within a year's time. He wanted to know about her mother, her father, her close and distant relatives. He wanted to know what schools she attended, public or private, university or community. Who was her child hood besty? Were they still tight? Who was her first love, first hurt, first kiss, first *everything*. The complexity within those questions alone sent her running.

There was a knock at her bedroom door. "Come in."

Tony peeked his head inside, and smiled. "I didn't hear you come in this morning."

Jazzman tiptoed into the house shortly after 3am. Rick wanted her to stay, she wanted to leave. Their conversation had gotten so heavy, so intense. They started to argue. Words were said. She stormed out, leaving things undone.

On her way home, he called her cellular. Seemed like a hundred rings between them. She refused to answer, refused to be burdened with that same old question of *Why Atlanta?* She didn't want to think about Atlanta. Thoughts of Bola crept back into her mind. Her face, her success, her life intrigued Jazzman.

"Did anything happen while I was gone?"

"No. We kicked it a little bit, ate some food, he went to sleep. Can I come in?" She motioned him with her hands. He stepped in, and closed the door. Squeaking sounds came from the doors hinge.

"I can take care of that with a little oil, if you want."

She nodded. "That would be great."

Tony took a quick tour of her room, taking in its décor. Her custom walk-in closet was packed with clothes and shoes. *Prada, Louis, Fendi*, all in that order lined shelves and compartments. Her dresser, covered in expensive perfumes and make-up.

"How many shoes does one woman need?"

He checked the door to the closet. It too needed some lubrication. Both hands stuck inside his sweats as he perused her private quarters. He stopped at the window, pulled the sheer panel aside, then the darkener slightly to the left.

"That lady Sheila called. You're needed in Houston. She said that she would call back with the details."

She scrunched her nose. "Houston? When?"

He shrugged. "She mentioned corporate headquarters, orientation, new hire packet. She left her number." He stuck the blue sticky note to her forehead. She peeled it away, looked at it. His hand writing was pretty.

"I wanted to thank you again for the flowers."

"It was nothing."

"It was something to me."

They looked at each other for a moment, then away. He noticed her laptop. "Doing some work?"

"Just a little research, nothing work related."

His eyes fell upon her. Stayed pressed against her face, and then quickly traveled her frame. There she was, dressed in a long cotton shirt, a stack of decorative pillows behind her. The rim of her eyes, red and puffy. "Got a lot on your mind?" he asked.

"I guess you can say that."

He stood at the end of the bed. His fingers traced the rail of the footboard. "How was your evening?"

"Nice," she said, pulling her legs in, suddenly feeling indecent.

He didn't expect her to talk about dude, about their evening, but thought he'd ask anyway. The house phone rang twice, back to back. Ricks name popped up on the caller ID. He didn't see any point in mentioning it. As far as he was concerned, that dude wasn't important.

"I watched *Training Day*, saw *American Gangster* for the first time. Those movies were the coldest."

"Loved Denzel in both movies. I hope you watched these movies alone. Jacob is not allowed..."

"Don't worry. He was sound asleep before Denzel got to extorting fools for the cash."

She pulled both lips in, looked down, and began to pluck invisible lent from her cover. She adjusted her top again, realizing she had nothing on underneath. She folded her arms against her well awakened bosom, scooted further back against the mountain of pillows. She hunched her shoulders in a way that told him she was uncomfortable.

"Am I making you nervous?"

"No. Why would you say that?"

"You can't stop moving."

"Can't get comfortable, this damn mattress is... I just can't get comfortable."

He made his way towards her side of the bed. He touched her cheek. Her body was betraying her. Her body was giving up the fight. Her body was screaming, *Fuck me!*

His hand moved from her cheek to her hair. His fingers, pressed against her scalp, gently. She wondered if Rick played in Bola's long flowing hair. Did he strum her strands from root to tip? Did he pull her mane while they made love? Did her luscious locks of love smell of sweet berries? *Oh God, I'm obsessed.*

She closed her eyes, enjoying the scalp massage. Magical fingers combed her tress seductively. Each hair follicle awakened, stimulating her roots, breathing life into her scalp. His knee pressed against the mattress. Her eyes shot opened.

"Wait."

Knee retracted. His wandering hand pressed the center of his sweats. The attempt to cover his erection was useless.

"We can't do this."

He grabbed her face, attempted to kiss her lips. He got nothing but cheek.

"No, we can't."

He exhaled. "Why not?"

"Forgive me if I'm sending mixed signals. It's just that..."

He waited for her to say something, anything, but she just sat there and cried. He tried to console her but she pushed him away, asked him to leave. Tony backed away, and left with led pants. Jazzman placed a pillow against her face and screamed.

The next morning, at breakfast no one said a word. Not even Jacob had much to say. The sound of silverware clanking against plates, and sips taken in-between bites was about to drive Jazzman crazy.

"Pass the syrup please," she said looking down at her plate.

Tony shoved Aunt Jemima across the table in one smooth push. He stood up with his half eaten plate and headed towards the kitchen.

"I'm done too mommy. May I be excused?"

"But you haven't finished your eggs baby," she said.

"Neither did daddy."

He was right. Jacob followed in his father's footsteps, and just like that she was left alone. Chilled coffee, cold eggs and two pancakes drowning in syrup sat before her. Tony helped Jacob with his coat, backpack, and they both headed out the door.

She dropped her head into her hands. Feelings of abandonment flooded her insides. And just like the men in her life, she too scooted back from the table and abandoned breakfast.

Upstairs, she stood in her bedroom window, waving good bye to her son as he boarded the cheese bus. His usual vigorous wave replaced with a simple toss of the hand. She made a mental note to have a talk with the bus driver about those stupid third graders.

Unable to sleep, she showered and slipped into some comfortable sweats.

Once the sun was up, she was up. No power nap to resurrect her tired body. There was a knock at the door. "Just a minute." She quickly pulled the tee-shirt over her head. *Save the Ta-Ta's* was stamped across the front.

"I need to make a few runs this morning. I'll be back in time to get Jacob off the bus."

"*O*-Okay."

He stood on the other side of her door, staring at her. She wanted to talk about last night, but couldn't bring herself to face him. After a minute or so she heard him leave. She collapsed onto her messy bed, relieved.

She immediately called Sheila. Jazzman was surprised to hear orientation was bumped up earlier than scheduled. She mentioned something about the CEO leaving for Europe at the end of the week, and wanted to meet all the new recruits pronto. Sheila booked Jazzman's last minute flight to Houston, and emailed the itinerary.

Leaving a messy house was against the rules of travel, so she decided to clean. A fresh cup of coffee, and a bucket full of cleaning supplies helped jumpstart her morning. She tuned into Hot97 and got to work. She swept the floor, mopped, vacuumed, and replaced her plug-ins throughout the house. Loads of laundry washed, folded, and put away. Lavender scented fabric softener gave off a delightful smell. She did anything to keep her mind off of Bola, off of Rick, and off Tony's big hard erection.

Houston in the morning!

She danced from the kitchen, to the living room, to the laundry room, back out towards the foyer. Shaking, and dipping, bending and gyrating her hips. *Gotta get my hair done. Need to pull the Louis luggage out. No, that's too showy. I'll take the all black leather Doonie & Burk duffle on wheels. That screams business.*

He *To Do* list mounted as she realized how much she needed to get done. Tony was new to her camp, and he needed a crash course on how to run her household. She grabbed a pen, pad, bottled water, and plopped onto the sofa. The house was clean, laundry done, fridge fully stocked, she'd paid her bills online, and the Jaguar was gassed up. She tapped the pen against the pad, took a sip of water. Paper blank, mind running, nerves shot.

Houston in the morning!

The doorbell broke her concentration. Jazzman guzzled her water on the way towards the door. She pulled the curtain back, peeked out and stepped away from the window quickly. Rick stood outside, holding a package wrapped in silver decorative paper. White crush velvet bow looped perfectly at the top. She snatched the rag off her head, took a whiff of her pits, and checked her teeth in the hall mirror before opening the door. He stepped in without an invitation.

"Hey baby, been trying to call you." His voice amplified. His eyes scoped out the parameters. There was no sign of Tony. Not even an indication a man lived under that roof. His eyes scanned the shoe rack, positioned on the far left side of the door. Size eleven dirty work boots gripped his chest.

She closed the door and folded her arms. She wanted to hold onto her anger, wanted to keep the drama going but it was hard to stay mad at him. Especially when he came bearing gifts.

"I was in the area and decided to stop in," he said, leaning in to kiss her lips.

She halted his passion. Open hand made him pause. She walked away, leaving his puckered lips to kiss the air. He knew that game all too well. Rick decided to play along.

He followed her into the dining room cautiously. His thuggish limp magnified to the fifth power. He could be so lame at times, but that was part of the reason why she loved him. He was no thug, far from a gansta, and he damn sure wasn't made for jail. Rick kept his nose and fingers clean.

"Where's your baby daddy?"

She snarled at him. "Not here. Out being productive I hope."

He loosened a few buttons on his shirt, and relaxed. "Why you jet on me like that?"

"We were beginning to argue below the neck. You said things, I said things, we said things that hurt. Before we said something that would damage us permanently, I left."

"I've shared all of me, and you... you've shared nothing."

"Rick, please..."

"Please what, Jazzman... I'm digging you... feeling you... but I can't seem to get through this thick ass exterior wall you got up. Each time I feel I'm about to get one leg over the wall, you raise it."

Her eyes drifted across the room, and landed on the plasma.

"Look at me." He blocked her view.

"My past is very complicated."

"So, who doesn't have a story? I tell you all about Bola, about our could-of, should-of, would-of been baby... and... and when I ask about your life, you run out the damn door."

"I needed to get home. Jacob expects to see me when he awakes."

"Let his father pick up some of the slack now. Isn't that why you opened your doors to him?"

Rick took a deep breath. Tony was another topic, another argument, for another day. He'd showed up expecting to see her baby's father sprawled across the sofa, drinking a forty ounce, puffing a blunt and watching television. At least that's the way it happened in the movie *Baby Boy*.

"I want to know you." His voice, more relaxed, more calm.

"You do know me."

"I want to know all of you."

"My past isn't important."

"To me, it is."

"My past might change the way you feel for me. Might change our future."

"Nothing can change the way I feel for you."

"Nothing?"

He hesitated. "If you were originally born a man named Tyrone, and had a sex change... that will most definitely change the way I feel. I'd most likely catch me a case behind some shit like that."

She sucked her teeth and laughed.

"Let's go out tonight," he said, loving the smile on her face.

She hesitated. He hated when she did that. Hesitation meant she had something better to do with her time. The toe of the size eleven, dirty work boots turned up, smiling at him.

"That won't be a good idea."

"Is it because of him?"

"No, it's not because of him. It just won't be a good idea, that's all."

"Damn, this dude moves in now you acting different."

"I'm not acting different. How am I acting different? I'm the same today, as yesterday, as tomorrow. I'm not different."

He moved close, stood in her way. "Am I asking for a lot?"

"Look, I'm leaving for Houston in the morning. Sheila called, said that the CEO is leaving the country for a month, and all new recruits needed to fly in early for orientation."

He had the stupid look. "Okay, I apologize for jumping to conclusions, but you gotta understand how I'm feeling."

"Apology accepted."

He snapped his fingers. "Since you can't leave the house, I'll come to you. We can rent *The Book of Eli*, eat popcorn and drink wine."

"Hum...well..."

"Ah, c'mon, you're leaving for Houston in the morning. I need some quality time with my baby. I'll even drive you to the airport."

"I'll be gone just two days."

"So."

"Rick."

"Yes."

She said nothing, but instead moved towards the kitchen for a cold one. Having Rick upstairs in his boxers, drinking wine, eating popcorn, with Tony under the same roof hardly qualified as *quality time*.

"You want a beer?" she asked.

"It's not even noon."

"It's five o'clock somewhere in the world."

He followed her, tipped her chin, and kissed her lips, tasting the beer on her tongue. "I just offered to come back, later tonight, after Jacob is asleep and you ignore me."

"The thing is..."

He waited for her bullshit explanation.

"The thing is..."

"Save it Jazzman. Just save it."

He slammed the package on the floor and headed back the way he came in.

"Rick... wait..."

"Fuck You."

Hours after Rick stormed out all Jazzman could do was cry. She shed more tears than a little as she felt caught in the middle of a love triangle. Her baby daddy had her heart, always did. Rick, he had her mind. They both had a piece of her soul. She loved them both for different reasons. A knock at her bedroom door interrupted her thoughts. Before she could say anything the door opened.

"Jacob is fed, bathed, and is fast asleep dreaming of how he can help SpongeBob take over Bikini Bottom. You need anything?"

She lifted her sleep mask, and squinted from the hallway light. A familiar funk escaped his armpits. "You smell."

"Just finished working out. I'm about to shower." His eyes shifted towards the cable box. He eyeballed the time.

"Going somewhere?" she asked.

"Yeah... need to clear my head."

"Oh."

"You alright?" he asked.

She buried herself beneath the thick comforter. "I'm fine."

He moved in and closed the door behind him. "You don't look all that hot. Are you coming down with something?" He touched her forehead with the back of his hand.

She shooed him away. "Nothing a bottle of Tequila can't fix."

"You sound borderline suicidal."

She made a face. "Things could never be that bad, and you stink. *Move* funk boy"

"You want some company?"

"No. Tonight, all I want to do is be miserable."

"You sure? I mean, after I shower, I can run to Redbox and get two flicks. We can take a few shots of Tequila together."

Tempting. "No, no thank you."

"Well, alright. You really should take it easy on the booze. You have business in the morning."

Houston in the morning. Damn!

"I know."

He turned to leave.

"About last night..."

He stopped; hand on the doorknob, heavy breathing.

"I'm not a tease, it's just that..."

He looked back only to find her standing. Her see-through number made his heart gallop. She staggered towards him. "You should get back into bed before you hurt yourself."

"You do something to me... to my body... that no other man has ever been able to do."

He smiled, and rubbed his chin as if he were contemplating his next move. "So why you playing a nigga shady?"

"I dunno."

He stepped to her. Back rounded, head tilted, bottom lip pulled in. *Sexy!* He leaned in for a kiss. Her head thrust away. *Shut down!*

"*C'mon* on girl, stop playing and give me some of that."

"I'm in a bad place right now. I want to but... Rick, he's a safer choice."

"So, I'm the bad choice?"

More like reckless. "Well...yeah."

"That's cold."

"What I meant is you're not the best choice for *me*. That doesn't mean that you're a bad person. Rick, he's...what I'm trying to say is..."

"Yo, it's all good. I dig it." Tony rubbed the top of his head.

"You mad?"

He glanced at the cable box again. "Need to shower."

"Wait. Don't go."

CHAPTER 18

Forbidden fruit, *off* limits. Living under the same roof with familiar legs had him ready to poke a hole in something. She came with a big *Look but Don't Touch* sticker stamped across her ass. He wanted to sink his teeth into her nectar, suck her sweetness, experience heaven on earth, but she was in a bad place.

"What the fuck does that mean, a bad place. *I'm* in a bad place," he said, looking down at what she started.

Warm water cascaded down his tense spine. His hand wrapped around a brick. Smooth motions released some of the tension caused by her indecisiveness. He washed his funk, thinking of ways to switch gears, perhaps go from the concerned ex, to not giving a fuck. *The nice guy never gets the girl.*

Five years in the joint had him looking to head back to the hood, and find him a chick with no expectations. Chicks from around his old way fucked for free. They gave it up, just to say they've given it up to a nigga fresh home.

"I should see what's up with Rita grimy ass. Bet she's still on a nigga dick."

He turned the water off, grabbed a towel and stepped from the shower. Just then the door flew open. "Did I come at a bad time?" She stepped in, still in her see-through number, slizzard off Patron. He could have capitalized on the moment, took advantage of her, and fucked her until she passed out into a drunken stupor. But there was no fun in that. He required her full mind. What he planned to inflict upon her beautiful frame would have her saying *Rick Who?*

"Listen, don't take what I'm about to say personally but..."

He held his hand up. "You don't owe me anything, I owe you."

She swallowed hard. Pecs stared back at her, screaming *touch me, tease me, lick me.* He picked up a bottle of baby oil and splashed himself. She placed her back against the frame of the door and stared closely at his scars. Markings of a rough life covered his frame. Markings of a night of passion covered her neck. Rick pissed on his property. When she wasn't looking, he narrowed his eyes in on her.

"Sheila booked me on a seven o'clock flight out to Houston."

"When?"

"Tomorrow."

He grabbed his electric toothbrush added a line of minty fresh. The buzzing sound reminded her that she needed batteries for her clit-tickler.

"It's just two days. Can you watch him?"

Buzzing stopped. Foaming bubbles filled his mouth. His neck tightened. He spat, rinsed, stared at her with daggers. "Did you really ask me that?"

"Well, it is short notice. I'm just being considerate of your time."

He slammed the toothbrush against the sink. "Do what you need to do. My son is good with me. I know the routine."

"Mind recapping for me?"

His nostrils flared, teeth clinched. "Up by 6, teeth brushed, face washed and dressed by 6:20. He's to be fed by 6:30 and out the door no later than 6:57. Bus pulls in at 3:09; he gets a snack, juice box, and completes his homework no later than 5:30pm. Dinner is served at 6:00pm; he shit's-showers-plays until 9pm, afterwards lights out."

"I didn't intend to question whether you were capable or not, I'm just asking. Need to be sure Jacob keeps his routine."

"I got this," he spat.

"Damn, don't be so sensitive."

He glared at her.

She sucked her teeth. "I'll leave a copy of my itinerary taped to the fridge."

"Cool."

"What are your plans for tonight?" she asked, looking up from her fingernails. He imagined those same fingernails digging deep into another man's flesh.

"I'm making a few runs. Need to see about some money."

"What kind of money?"

"The kind you spend."

She twisted her drunken lips. "Don't be smart." He dropped his towel, on purpose. She stared without shame. "Oh boy."

Houston in the morning!

Houston in the morning!

Stay focused girl!

He covered his package with state issued boxers.

"You really should throw those dingy things away."

"I will, soon as I get this paper."

"Any luck with the interviews?"

"Not really, I'm filling out applications, but I got some fo' sure dough I need to see about." She knew he was headed to the same place that got him five years in the penitentiary. *Brooklyn* was on his mind.

"Brooklyn don't love you no more." That comment made his jaw twitch. He stared at her reflection in the mirror. "Brooklyn will always have love for me."

"Don't do anything stupid. You're on parole, remember?"

He hissed. "How could I forget?"

"Who are you seeing about some money?" she asked.

"Don't worry about that."

"Let me guess, Wayne?"

"He owes me a favor or two."

"Wayne is hot. You should probably steer clear of him. I know that's your people and all, but I've been hearing things."

He looked straight through her. She wanted to say more, wanted to fabricate a story to which he would believe, but chose to leave well enough alone. Her lips held lies, her eyes disclosed the truth.

He yanked a T-shirt over his head, frustrated, flustered, seconds away from saying what was exactly on his mind. He stared at her neck, shook his head and walked out the room. She followed closely, damn near on his heels. She tripped, and fell. *Man down!*

He kept moving without looking back. Damsel in distress had to fend for self.

"Damn, you can't help me up?"

"I'm in a hurry."

She helped herself up, yanking at the sheets on his bed. Tony had finally taken her up on the offer to move into the spare bedroom. The floor was overrated, plus he figured this was the best way to get between her knees.

"Wait a minute," she demanded.

He stopped at Jacobs room, looked in. A genuine smile crept across his face. He hated to leave but if he stayed another minute, he was definitely going to snap. He closed the door, and turned to find Jazzman with both arms folded. He looked down at her tapping foot, up towards her bruised neck and laughed. *She has the audacity to have an attitude. Typical Black Woman Shit!*

He attempted to walk pass her. She held up both hands, he paused. Only out of respect, only to keep the peace, truthfully he paused only because he needed her. She had the power to put him out, take his son away. He couldn't let that happen.

"If you're not ready to commit to being a full time daddy, leave now."

"What the hell are you talking about?"

"All this running around, all times of the night, has got to end."

He put a tight fist to his mouth, muzzling his rebuttal. *This girl has lost her mind. She must be drunk.* As much as he wanted to show emotion, and express how he really felt, he couldn't.

"You're right," he said.

He was very much displeased with her behavior, but who was he to comment? Jazzman was living the life she had designed for herself. Who was he to come and alter her way of living? Bruised neck and all, *who the hell was he?*

"Can you please be in my house no later than midnight?"

"So I've got a curfew now?"

"According to the rules set forth by your parole officer, I guess you do." The way she said *rules, parole officer*, got him heated. He kept his cool, didn't say or do anything to offend her.

"There's some things I need to take care of which could probably run past midnight. I can't promise that I'll make it back before then, but I can promise that I'll make it back before you're scheduled to leave for the airport."

"I guess that's good enough."

***

Tony wrapped his hand around a cold one and guzzled. He picked up the plastic covered menu, scanning the items. Three dollar beer, five dollar shots, one dollar soft drinks all night long. Fifty cent wings, six dollar personal pan-oven baked pizza, and sub-sandwiches drew in a crowd. Tony looked up, only to see his partner from back in the day approaching.

"Oh shit... Is that my nigga *Trigger*?"

Tony stood, and slapped fives with his old crony. They gave each other a brotherly hug. "Wayne, it's been too long."

"Five years son, but you looking like you held your own." Wayne shadow boxed his face. "You still nice with the hands?"

"*Son*, you don't want it," Tony said, jabbing back. They laughed, and then took a seat in the booth. Tony looked around, took in the ambiance. "Your place is nice."

Wayne shrugged. "It's a work in progress. It's been open about two years now."

"Business seems good though. Look at all the people."

Wayne scanned his establishment. A half cocked grin appeared. "Yeah, we get some big spenders up in here on the weekend. Finally got approved for my liquor license. I'm killing them at the bar, but between me and you they try'na shut a nigga down."

"Who?"

"The police commissioner. In the last year, four people got shot. Two up the street, the other two just steps away from the front door. None inside though, my security air tight."

"Damn."

"They say my business does nothing but encourage the young black youth to act in violence. Damn news reporters have been buzzing around my restaurant like flies to shit waiting for something to kick off."

"That's crazy."

"*Yo'* these young niggas *been* wildn' out, long before I opened my doors. You mean to tell me I'm the reason for the violence?"

"You selling pizza puffs my nigga. How they figure you the cause for a motherfucker getting merked?"

Wayne blew air from his lips. "Fuck if I know. I'm just a black man try'na make an honest living." Wayne tossed the head nod to a couple of big guys with the word *SECURITY* stamped across their chest and back.

"I'm a business man, but these hood niggas keep thinking I'm still that dude from back in the day."

"So you don't get down no more?"

Wayne wiped his mouth with his hand, held it there. "I ain't said all that. I'm just saying a brother like me moving different these days."

"How different?"

He shrugged diplomatically. "Real different."

"I feel you. Gotta fly below the radar," Tony said, and then chuckled.

"Enough about me, what-up with you?"

"Maintaining."

"Trigga mutherfucking Tony, *damn son*, I thought I'd never see your face again. Thought you were a fo-sure gonner, a *lifer*."

"Things turned in my favor."

Wayne gave him that look. Same look Jazzman gave him. Same look he expected to receive from people who knew him from the beginning. Tony and Wayne hustled packs together. Small time change back in the day had them joined at the hip. They had each other's back. As kids they spent most of their re-up money at Dr. Jay's, and McDonald's. Splurging at Kings Center Mall was a Friday night tradition.

"I couldn't handle being boxed in for life, so I told a few things. Just enough to keep my black ass off the *row*."

"Hey man, I'm not judging."

"Yes you are. You're judging as if you wouldn't have done the same."

"First of all, you couldn't have paid me to flip weight for Barry grimy ass. Second, you know damn well I do my dirty by my lonesome. When shit hit the fan, nobody can roll over on me. And third, I'm not judging. Word life, you did what you thought was best. Besides, Barry had a death sentence. Why the fuck would you throw your life away for a nigga who was already dead. And four, your ass never could handle pressure."

"What you mean by that?"

"Remember that time we got caught jumping the turnstile at 71st and Continental? Your ass started crying, begging the police not to take you to jail."

"Whatever, I was nine."

"Remember the time we went to the Bronx to buy some work from Papi and em'? We were literarily steps away from the spot when Jakes swooped in and bagged everybody. Your ass peed your pants."

"I was twelve."

Wayne sucked his teeth and twisted his full lips towards the sky. "Okay, remember that time you left Chauncey holding the bag?"

"You got me mistaken."

"Oh no son, my facts are straight. Chauncey called me from Central Bookings right after he got bagged. He needed bond money and you, you skipped town, went to Queens to lay up for a few days."

"What the fuck is this, roast Tony day?"

"It's your make-up home boy. You're not good under pressure. You my peoples, and will see a task through to the end, but if the *boyz* come gunning, you telling shit from the first grade and that's word to my motha."

"So what you try'na say?" Tony asked, chest bucked in the air, ready to squabble. Years of pinned up aggression needed to be released. Wayne could be the one.

"Take the battery out your back son. All I'm saying is you couldn't pay me to do a crime with you. Shit, better yet, if you make moves, don't even involve me."

Wayne pointed at one of the waitresses and ordered a couple more beers. "How's that sweet piece of ass you were dealing with?" he snapped his fingers. "Jazzman, right?"

"Don't act like you don't remember her name now."

Wayne laughed. He got a kick out of seeing Tony get heated.

"Damn, chill out, son. I'm joking." Wayne looked across the room, spotted a commotion brewing. Two dudes by the pool table weren't seeing eye to eye. Security moved in, calmed the situation.

"She told me you tried getting at her."

Wayne snapped his neck back in Tony's direction. "She's a fucking a liar," he barked.

"Hey, it's nothing. If I were you, I would have tried. In fact, been try'na get in them panties since I been home."

Wayne laughed, pounding his heavy fist against the wood table. A true over dramatic New Yorker he was. "You ain't hit that yet son?"

Tony guzzled the rest of his beer. "I think I need something stronger."

Wayne called the same waitress over. She knocked her hips back their way with a *stank* look on her face. "What now?"

Wayne glared at the girl. "Come again?"

"*Sorry.* Is there anything else I may get you?"

"Bring us a bottle of Patrone. Two shot glasses. Order of wings..."

"How many wings?" she asked in one agitated breath.

"Fifty-fucking-wings. Half hot, the other half lemon peppered," he snarled.

"Is that all?"

"No that ain't all," Wayne snapped, looked at Tony who was laughing his ass off.

"Add an order of cheddar cheese fries, two bottled waters... side salad... am I missing anything?" Wayne looked over at Tony. His smile was huge. Cheddar cheese fries were a nostalgic dish. Brought him back to the park bench they broke day on. Cheddar cheese fries drenched in hot sauce had him feeling at home.

"Side-salad. What up with that?" Tony asked.

"Wifey got me on this new diet. She said I'm getting the muffin top."

The wide hipped waitress, with the stank attitude mumbled something beneath her breath before scampering off to place the order. Tony fell out laughing.

"What that bum bitch say?" Wayne asked, missing the insult.

Tony shrugged. "Man, where you get her from?"

"Don't even ask. I gives these hoe's a paycheck and they think cause we fucking they can talk greasy."

Tony patted his rock hard stomach. "Side salad, that is kinda funny."

"*Yeah-yeah*, whatever kid. So, you ain't hit that yet?"

Tony stared into the crowd of blue collared workers. Plumbers, truckers, sanitation workers and your occasional drug dealer mingled freely. *Jada Kiss* raspy voice blared through the speakers, giving a down home, authentic New York feel.

"Don't tell me you still beating off."

"That girl is a trip," Tony said rubbing both hands together. He flashed a waitress a smile. She smiled back.

"That dude she with got her mind all..." He did a circle motion with his hand.

"You think she in love with this dude?" Wayne asked for his own knowledge of knowing.

"Let's put it this way, he's that romantic type she's been looking for all her life. He's that dude she's read about as a child. The one she's been dreaming about since she could understand male and female relations."

"Prince Charming?"

"Yeah, that nigga."

"Dude got his shit together?"

"And then some."

Wayne rubbed his chin. "Romantic huh?"

Tony told his friend about the garden of Tulips, and the card that accompanied it. He even told him about the photos he found of Rick and Jacob at Chuckie Cheese. The thought of some other man holding his son, in their lap, for an *Etch-a-Sketch* photograph burned him up.

Tony told Wayne about their obvious break-up to make-up, soap opera bull crap that had her stepping up in the crib fifteen minutes past the five o'clock hour.

"She came in at what time?" Wayne asked completely astonished.

"Her house, her rules."

"*Fuuuccckkk* that, you should have checked that situation."

"What was I supposed to say?"

"*Bitch don't bring yo' ass up in this house again at that hour.* That's what you should have said. Man, you can't let these broads run over you like some punk."

Tony couldn't help but agree, however checking Jazzman for her wrong doings meant being homeless. Working-off-emotions was a sure fire recipe to losing his son. He needed her. "You don't understand."

"No, you don't understand. She's a woman, you're a man. You call the shots. Bottom fucking line," Wayne said angrily.

"It's about picking and choosing battles. That's a no win situation right now. Dude got his shit together, I don't."

"You control *all* situations. Regardless of what you're pockets look like now, you run shit. That's *your* pussy."

He swallowed the chump-pill and sunk a little further in his seat. Tony listened to Wayne go on about respect, being the King of that Castle, demanding this, demanding that. Who was he to demand anything, especially when he wasn't bringing anything to the table? He had a growing boy at the house. Bills needed to be paid. Jazzman was used to a certain lifestyle. Who the hell was he to re-arrange stuff? In order to get respect as a man, you had to do grown man things.

Jazzman was a single black woman, who up until that point was raising a young black boy into becoming a man. Besides, he had way too much respect for the mother of his child to start talking crazy. As Wayne yapped on and on he couldn't help but feel himself shrinking under the scrutiny. He was glad he hadn't divulged the passion marks that decorated her neck. He kept that fine little detail to himself.

"Home boy try'na show you up."

Tony cut his eyes across the table. "*C'mon* man, you don't think I know this? That dude throwing cash at her, trips at her, Tulips and shit."

"Trips… what kind of trips?"

"I overheard her talking about going to Tampa for a quick getaway. Jacob says he owns a beach house. This dude obviously makes her happy," Tony said, then hissed.

"She landed a job with some agency. She leaves for Houston tomorrow for orientation."

"That's good, right?"

"Of course it's good. I'm happy for her."

"So what's the problem?"

"She asked me to watch my son while she goes out of town for a two day orientation."

"I don't see your problem."

"Man, she said it like I was a paid babysitter and not his father."

Wayne laughed. "You sensitive *Poo-Butt* ass nigga. You mad at the wrong shit. What you need to be worried about is that nigga try'na steal your woman."

"Yeah, whatever, man. I know how she meant it, and that's the way I took it. To top things off, I think scramz is try'na pop that question."

A look of hurt plastered Wayne's face. "Word, how you know?"

Tony made note of that look and continued. "I can feel it coming. They going through it right now, but in the midst of all their confusion, I hear church bells."

Wayne laughed. "You don't hear shit."

"I'm telling you. He's about to pop that question."

"Don't let him. That lock down finger is yours. She obviously still feels for you or she wouldn't have let you live there."

"It's temporary."

"*Nigga* is you crazy? She still want you, can't you see that?"

Tony nodded, tipping the shot glass back, slamming it against the table. Wayne was right. Jazzman was his girl. Jacob was his son. They were his family. Rick was messing with his heart.

"When's the last time you saw her?" Tony asked staring his friend dead on.

"Saw who?"

"Jazzman."

Wayne suddenly busied himself with his cell phone. "Shit. Been bout a year or so, I guess. I speak with her from time to time, though. I check in on her and the Lil-man as I promised you."

Tony knew he was lying, but chose not to call him on it. He wondered what it was that had both Jazzman and Wayne on the hush-hush. He accepted that either of them would speak the truth, but he also knew time revealed all things.

"I need to hold a lil sumthin' until I get on my feet."

"You know I got you covered," Wayne said.

"Also, I need some wheels. This train is for the birds."

"Man, I told you; when you touched down to look me up. That offer is not extended to many, if any, naw mean?"

Tony cocked his head left. "You heard my aunty died?"

"My bad man, didn't know if I should mention it. My deepest condolences."

Tony rubbed his face with an open hand. It was hard receiving death news behind the Iron Gate. Death news on the inside made inmates thread lightly. There was no way of telling how a prisoner would process such information.

"Your cousin Yvette didn't make things any better. With your aunt in the hospital, her place became the spot real fast."

"Heard there was a fire," said Tony.

They eyeballed each other.

"Between me and you, that wasn't no accident. Yvette was working for that nigga Piru. From what I hear she came up short. *Real short.*"

"Who the fuck is Piru?"

"Piru *da man* in the Fort. He runs shit over there now. From what I hear, Yvette was supposed to have been home, but stepped into the stairwell to get high right when Piru's goons came and torched the place. Heard they ran through your aunt's crib with lighter fluid and blow torches."

"Where can I find this Piru?"

Wayne shook his head. "You don't. He usually finds you. A bit of advice, leave that shit alone. Yvette came up short one too many times. Business is business. Besides, my man rolls with an army. You're better off letting that one ride homeboy."

"Let me be the judge of that."

Tony's eyes shifted towards the main entrance. He looked passed a couple of big girls, passed the greasy, sleazy; wanna-be thugs that held their attention. He looked passed the waitress who flashed a smile his way earlier and set his eyes on a red bone with dual colored micro extensions. Wet-wavy-black, with a four inch streak of gold laced the center of her head. Her hairstyle reminded Tony of a black mustang accentuated with a gold racing stripe down the center of the hood. She was built like a stallion, one thousand percent thoroughbred.

He watched as she moved through the crowd, stepping high in her stilettos boots. As he zeroed in on *All-That-Woman*, Tony couldn't help but imagine himself with her, naked.

Wayne caught him staring. "You wanna get at that?"

Tony nodded trance like. "Hell yeah."

"Her name is Champagne. Let me introduce you two."

Wayne sent word by one of the waitresses that Champagne's presence was needed. Twelve easy steps she took before stopping at their table. She flashed a smile. Tony grinned, twirled the ice inside his glass.

"Champagne, this my man *Trigger Tony*."

"Nice to meet you," Champagne said.

Wayne licked his lips. "Champagne is a working girl."

"Oh, what kind of work do you do?" Tony asked.

A look passed between Wayne and Champagne. "I do whatever needs to be done."

Tony glanced over at his friend who clearly hadn't filled him in.

"Hook my man up. Give him that platinum package you offer."

"Who's paying?"

"I'm paying, and as you know, my money is good," Wayne said arrogantly.

Champagne slid in next to Tony, rubbed his chest. Wayne stood and left the two to get more acquainted. "How old are you?" was the first thing Tony asked. Grown in the hips, didn't exactly mean she was legal to do grown people things.

"Old enough."

"What's your age?"

"Age ain't nothing but a number."

"Shorty, don't waste my time. You legal or what?"

"You into paying tuition?"

"College?"

"No doubt. I'm in my fourth year. Guess that makes me legal."

He nodded. "I support the academics of tomorrow's future. Just as long as the future is looking to give special-head. I mean, *stay ahead*."

"My head is on straight. My GPA exceeds standard."

"GPA, that's a new one," he confessed.

"GPA, good pussy all the time."

"I like it. You seem to be pretty smart."

"I'm the best."

"*Aiight*, where you wanna do this?"

Champagne whispered something in his ear that made them both laugh.

"Don't keep me waiting too long," she said, sliding her hips out the booth. He watched her sway her ghetto booty out the same door she came in. Tony felt himself getting excited. His day started out lousy but his night was about to end with much more then he'd bargained for.

Outside, as promised, Wayne slid Tony a set of Keys. The first Key belonging to a Charc-Grey Beamer parked outside the restaurant. Tony couldn't help but noticed the way that baby glistened in the moon light. Chrome rims poked out just enough to be considered dangerous. Equipped with all the bells and whistles, he knew he was about to hurt'em.

"That's me?"

"All day long," Wayne said, feeling like Santa Clause.

Tony circled the whip, stopped at the trunk. Yellow New Jersey plates caught his attention. "Is it dirty?"

"It's all legit, papers in the armrest." Wayne popped the trunk, lifted the spare, unzipped a duffle, and introduced Tony to the second *Key*.

"A little welcome home present from me to you. No charge."

Instant paranoia set in. Pressure built on the inside of his chest. He stepped away from the trunk. His hand covered his mouth. Tony looked around, took in his surroundings, noticed Ms. Champagne pulling up in her shiny red two-seater. She parked at the corner, waited.

"You still know how to move one?"

Tony scratched his head. "Don't want no parts of that."

"*Nigga* is you crazy?"

He thought about Jacob, and the promises he'd made him. That key of cocaine was tempting, but being there for his son meant more. Street life equated to life in prison, and another second behind bars would surely ruin his chances at raising his son. After long consideration Tony said, "I'm flying straight. I appreciate the wheels though."

"Respect."

Wayne noticed one of his wide hipped waitresses standing outside the restaurant sucking back nicotine. He whistled for her to come. She did. He whispered instructions, and just like that the second Key disappeared.

***

Sun rays poked through the clouds, as Tony sat parked outside. His entry into Jazzman's home was blocked with a link chain. He figured she'd done that on purpose. Their conversation before he left home wasn't all that pleasant. In fact the ultimatum she hit him with had him reevaluating his living situation. That Key of cocaine had the wheels in his head spinning. He was suddenly second guessing his decision to let that bird fly solo. That Key provided flexibility. It provided say-so. At that moment he had none.

The porch light flickered. Seconds later he noticed Jazzman standing in the doorway, both hands placed on her hips. A for sure argument rested on her tight lips. He tugged at the keys in the ignition and made his way towards the house. The image of his night with Champagne slowly started to dissipate. The closer he got to the door, the more uncomfortable he became.

Jazzman was dressed for success. She stood in all black. Two piece suit, classic straight leg, crisp white high-neck button down. Her once drunken state now sobered in anger. Her finger pointed, just inches away from his face. He took a step back, just in case she decided to swing.

"Why you backing up?" she asked, moving towards him.

"Stop playing."

"Come here, let me talk to you."

"Don't wrinkle your suit Ms. Lady." He took another step backwards, giving himself some space to duck any blows. "*Aiight*, cause a scene for the neighbors. Go ahead, I don't care." His point was a valid one. She stepped aside, allowing him entry.

"Whose car is that?"

"Mine for now."

"Where you get it from?"

"A friend loaned it to me," Tony said, heading up the steps. All he wanted to do was rest, and of course savor the thoughts of Champagne. It felt like his first time. Well, not exactly, but it was an experience he'd never forget.

"Jacob's alarm goes off in an hour. Please don't let him see you lying around. He doesn't need that sort of image in his thoughts."

"Sort of like seeing his mother cry over some cornball ass dude?"

She loosened the buttons on her jacket, pointed her finger.

"Fuck you."

"I'm sorry. I didn't mean that."

"I've been doing just fine raising him, alone. So don't go judging me. You think cause' he's never seen your flaws up close that you're perfect? You ain't perfect."

"I never said I was perfect."

"My son is smart. So don't think for a second you can contaminate his mind."

He turned back, took a seat on the sofa and listened to her complain. She pointed towards the front door. "That attention seeker out front will get your ass thrown back in jail. Have you checked the papers on it? Is it insured? Who is the car registered to? You better pray to God that car isn't stolen."

"Relax. It's not stolen, and the papers are good."

She peeled away her suit jacket, placed it on the back of the chair in the dining room. "These cops will lock you're black ass up. Trust and believe their looking to catch a fresh home, ex convict slipping. You're coming in my house, smelling like smoke, liquor, and cheap ass perfume."

Silence engulfed them.

"D.U.I is what they call it. *Driving under the influence* will get your ass thrown right back in."

"What is this really about?" he asked, causally-cool with both arms positioned behind his head.

"It's about you and that... that thing out front. It's about my son."

"*Our* son."

"Whatever, *our* son."

"I feel like I'm being chewed out because your little date with your man didn't go so well. Direct your steam towards that nigga cause I'm not for it."

She folded her arms across her chest, wrinkling her blouse.

"You don't know what you're talking about."

"You all stressed out, drinking hard liquor, by yourself. You're walking around here in the same funky ass sweats for the last two days. You barely combed your hair, all because of this cornball. You throwing pussy at me, then taking it back, and then throwing it again. I mean come on, what's this really about?"

"*Oh*. I see. Must've gotten you some last night."

"You asking or telling?"

Strangled noises came from the back of her throat. She looked so cute and sexy, all charged up. He watched her closely, thought he'd saw a bit of steam shoot from her ears. He wanted her, but on his terms.

Jazzman pulled herself together, checked her emotions. Who he gave his loving to shouldn't be a concern of hers. "The itinerary is on the fridge. Next to the spice rack, there's an extra cell. Use it for emergencies only."

"I'm good, got a phone of my own."

She wanted to explode. "I'll be gone just two days."

"Two days is a long time to be gone away from your man."

She grabbed her suit jacket, slipped it back on.

"Don't worry about me and *my* man. We spend more than enough time together. And if you must know, he's flying into Houston to keep me company."

Energy shifted back into her court. She now had control. He stared at her with daggers. "That shit on your neck is tacky, *real* tacky. That's some sick vampire shit." He laughed. "What kind of man sucks his woman black and blue right before she starts a new job? Appearance is everything. Your words, not mine."

She gasped, tugging at the high-neck top. It took her over two hours to find the right look to disguise Rick's passion marks. "Is it visible, I mean... can you see it?"

"Why you let that clown do that to your neck?" His question hung in the air like a funky odor.

"He didn't mean it. I mean he meant it, but I wasn't due to start for another two weeks and..." She stopped explaining herself when she noticed he wasn't paying attention.

"When's the last time you saw Wayne?" he asked, changing the subject again.

She held her face steady. He watched as she shifted from one leg to the next. *When's the last time you saw Wayne?* That question took her for a loop. He was supposed to be in the hot seat, not her. He was the one being interrogated. He had no right to question her while she was questioning him. Who the hell did he think he was?

"When?"

She fumbled over her words. "It's been a minute."

"What's a minute?"

A couple of months, why?"

"According to him it's been a little over a year."

"Couple of months... closer to a year... who's counting. Why are you asking?"

"You're name came up earlier, that's all."

"In what manner?" She rolled her neck.

He stood, and rubbed the top of his head. "Wayne is my man."

"You telling me something I already know."

Tony removed his shirt, and stared at her coldly. "I could have bagged all your slut bucket friends back in the day, but I didn't."

"There's nothing happening between me and Wayne if that's what you're implying," she said, snapping her neck in three different directions.

"Better not be. Fucking with my people is serious violation."

CHAPTER 19

"**W**hat up, where you been at?" Roy asked.

"Been working on some new money," Lou-Lou whispered as she inched out the front door of Ace's apartment. Twenty-four hour fuck fest had her body screaming *Calgon take me away*.

"Care to be more specific?"

She glanced over her shoulder, tipping quietly away from the love nest. When she made it to the bottom landing, she froze. The ground was wet from a storm that had blown through. There were fallen trees, damaged wires. The parking lot was black. She moved through darkness with the glow from her mobile leading the way.

"Damn," she spat.

"What?"

"Can't see shit. We lost power hours ago. Looking for my damn car."

"Where you at?"

"Leaving Ace's apartment."

"Who?"

"The guy from the restaurant."

"I hope he's worth the time. Had you answered your phone you could have bitten a piece of this cheese."

A noise beyond the bushes made her stop. She unzipped her purse, reached in, and grabbed the first thing her hands connected with. *Rat tooth comb*. The pointy metal tip would serve well as her shank.

"How much cheese?" she asked, ready to stab and jab on contact.

"Does it matter now?"

Just when she thought the coast was clear, a fat black cat appeared from within, prowling its way toward her.

"*Shoo.*"

"Who are you talking to?"

"*Shoo, shoo. Get outta here.*"

Stomping and shooing at the feline did nothing but encourage the fat fur ball to move in her direction. She stomped and kicked until the cat froze. Its tail became erect, stuck straight into the air like a lightning bolt.

"It's pointing its paw at me. Man, this is bad. This is real bad."

"Who's pointing its paw?"

The cat hissed, and crossed her path. She swallowed the lump in her throat. Bad omen was upon her, she could feel it. Maybe it was a sign for her to leave well enough alone, perhaps never return to Ace's apartment. Besides using him to get close to Kema, she had convinced him to compromising military secrets. She'd managed to find a loop hole big enough to squeeze a sizable amount of cash from his dead-end minimum wage job.

"Lou-Lou."

Roy's voice shattered the cemented blocks at her feet and she kept trucking. Finally she located her car. After slipping behind the wheel she mashed the push-start button, causing her baby to purr.

"Lou-Lou."

"Yes, I'm here. I've got another proposition," she said, grabbing a stick of gum from the armrest. "Need more of that medicine for the doctor."

"He called?" Roy sounded surprised.

"Yep, just got off the horn with him. We're scheduled to meet."

"When?"

"Tonight."

"You a bad bitch."

She smiled. "Hold up, that's my other line."

She clicked over, still cheesing. Before she could say anything Ace's voice came through a bit annoyed.

"Damn, can't a brother get a goodbye; see you later, a note on the nightstand, perhaps a couple of dollars to pay for my services?"

"Didn't know I was renting the dick."

"Didn't know you would leave me hugging my pillow."

"Didn't wanna wake you."

"Well, next time wake me."

She grinned. "Next time?"

Heat kicked in, warming her fingers and toes. She caught a glimpse of herself in the rearview. A huge frizz ball sat at the top of her head. Ace liked to do it in the shower, and humidity was not her friend.

"Are you superstitious?"

He chuckled, "A little, why?"

"A black cat crossed me while coming out your building. The damn thing hissed and pointed its paw," she said nervously,

"That's bad luck right?"

"I've been trying to catch that stray for months," he said bitterly.

"*Why*... never mind...Can I call you back?"

"Wow, so it's like that now?"

"I got my cousin on the other line," she said in a hurry.

"You sure you don't wanna be my date for the wedding?"

"I'm sure, besides it's too late of a notice. I have nothing nice to wear; my hair is chopped and... *never mind*... get some rest."

"Cool. Hit me later."

She clicked back over.

"Roy."

"I was just about to hang up. Don't leave me holding for that chump."

She screamed.

"What happened?"

For a few seconds he heard nothing but static. He called her name several times but she never answered. Suddenly, her voice came through heavy. She was panting, and breathing harder than ever. "Damn cat jumped on the hood. It hissed at me."

"*Yo*, for real, stop fucking around. You play too much."

She flipped the high beams on, activated the wipers. *Where'd it go?*

"Call me back when you get over your fear of cats."

"*Wait.* Don't hang up."

Her head whipped in all directions. *Where'd it go?* She gripped the wheel, inhaled. "I'm working on something big."

"How big?"

"Pretty big. It pays handsomely."

"This cat Ace involved?"

Oh God, don't mention the word cat. She swallowed. "He's our new golden boy."

Her eyes glanced upward towards her rearview mirror. That tiny blue *On-Star* button was an open mic, a sure fire way of telling the law exactly *who, what, where, and how.* Tiny speakers had the potential to capture incriminating evidence. Back in the day, police had to manually set up bugs to tap into crooked conversations. Now, all they had to do was tap into *On-Star.*

"Too much damn technology for my comfort. Meet me at our spot in two hours."

"Where are you headed now?"

"Back to the hotel. I need to wash the cooch, and press my hair back into shape."

"Too much info. I'll see you soon."

***

They pulled up at the same time, parking several cars away from each other. Lou-Lou hopped out first, smoothing her tress, and popping the collar to her waist length biker jacket. Roy leaned against his ride, watching her closely. Each step she made was slow and sensual.

"You're walking funny."

"You would be too if you had the kind of night I had."

"I'm going to pretend you didn't just say that to me."

Like a true gentleman he opened the door, but halted her stride when he noticed a crowd of rambunctious teens heading their way. The skinny leg, tight shirt wearing, Geek Squad pushed and shoved each other into the parking lot. Once Roy realized their behavior was all in fun, he allowed her to enter.

"Whose idea was it to meet here again?" she asked.

"It was your bright idea."

The Waffle House on Tara Boulevard, corner of Upper Riverdale Road was packed. Every stool, booth and table occupied. Lou-Lou scanned the joint and immediately wanted to leave.

"Let's go someplace else."

"Naw, we already here."

Roy spotted a table in the back. He went to snatch it up before someone else did. They both ordered coffee that remained untouched. Dark roast aroma sat between them.

"The doctor got some friends he'd like to share his skittles with. Need some more of that Ya-yo too."

Roy nodded. "Consider it done."

"So, you ran into some money last night?"

He glanced up at her, then down at his phone. It was buzzing.

"Came off like a fat rat."

"By yourself?"

"With whom I do my business with is *my* business. Besides, I called you first."

"Stop the games. You brought Kema along."

He gave her a quizzical look. "What if I did?"

"How much you know about her?"

He looked at her suspiciously. "Know enough, why?"

"She got brothers or sisters," she quizzed.

"She's got a brother, why?"

She studied his face, watched his lips, his eyes, his brows for any sudden signs of fabrication. "You ever met him?"

"What the fuck for?"

"I don't know, just asking if you've met him."

"Don't see any reason to meet him. She ain't my Queen. Meeting members of the family is another level. She knows her place."

She sensed he was telling the truth. "Good to hear you ain't made her wifey."

He quickly thought of wifey. He needed to call her, say that he was still alive. She worried about him. He left her for weeks and was so damn inconsiderate with checking in. "What's up with this dude Ace you keep yapping about?"

She studied his face again. His eyes, nose, lips, all remained still. She whispered the words slowly, "Military Burners."

Roy's eyes lit up like a Christmas tree. "How'd you get your hands on something like that?"

"Ace works dispatch on base. He's in contact with drivers."

"What kind we talking?"

"*AR15's*, real deadly shit." She winked.

Roy got excited. "How many?"

"Small shipment. Five cases. Twelve of them thangz per case. Ace got the route and time."

"Whoa, slow down. You talking about moving some big heat," he whispered.

She shoved her coffee aside, scooted her chair further in, looping her arm into his. Her head touched his shoulder. She looked up into his eyes. "Just sixty of them thangz. I wanna hit the big rig but we ain't got that kind of man power. We hit this small shipment, and tag five cases. All we need is one. Maybe two buyers," she paused, looked around, checked her surroundings. Her eyes were on two officers of the law that just strolled in.

"You follow me?" she asked.

Roy peeked over his shoulder. "I follow."

"We sell fifty-five of them thangz, keeping five for our stash."

"Why five?"

"Working on some new money, might need that big heat to solidify the deal."

"A proactive crooked mind. Love it."

She smiled, feeling like a real business woman. "If we sell at three grand a pop, that's a hunnit and sixty five-thou we stand to profit."

"Why just three grand, I say we up the price, charge a convenience fee. Let's shoot for four a pop, closing out at... two hunnit and twenty-thou. That's a hunnit and ten for you, and a hunnit and ten for me."

"Not exactly see, we gotta hit Ace for linking everything together."

"True dat. How much you talking?"

"A third."

"Fuck outta here, a third?"

"*Shush.*"

Roy peeked back over his shoulder, and noticed one of the officers staring hard. He wrapped his arm around her shoulder, kissed her forehead.

"He's the brain behind this. Let's be fair," she said.

"Cutting him a third hardly seems worth the trouble."

"He's asking for a third, final offer. Besides, if all goes well who knows what else he has up his sleeve. He's hungry. We could use that kind of appetite on our team."

"What about the buyers? We need to have them on deck to transact immediately. I'll be damn if I'm sitting on some military burners."

She lifted her head from his shoulder, patted his forehead playfully. "That's your job."

He smirked. "Why am I not surprised?"

The boys in blue left the restaurant, holding their waffle and steak meals covered in Styrofoam and plastic.

"You're still connected with your peoples in Dade County?" she asked.

"No doubt."

"Hit them up; see who's got that type of bread."

"Consider it done."

"We just need one more buyer, just in case," she said.

He snapped his fingers. "Got this white boy who hates niggas, but we cool. He one of them confederate flag wearing, bald head dudes with a million and one tattoos. He got that kind of paper."

Her brow arched. "And you know him how?"

"Let's just say we did a little business down in Baton Rouge."

"Fuck that. I'm not selling to the Aryan Nation. They hate blacks. We hate them."

He stretched, yarned. "Don't be so closed minded."

"I have boundaries."

"Green is green. This is business."

"They buying from us, to turn it around and use it on us."

"And? We buy black and use it on black every day."

"That's different. What I look like giving some sick white boy some heat?"

"What you look like giving some sick black boy some heat? We all bleed the same color. And that green, that spends the same."

She sat back and pouted. He was right. Violence was still violence. And business was still business. Who was she to turn down money because the color of someone's skin? Fair or not, her goal was to sell, and sell quickly.

"Look, I'll holla at my cousin, my Baton Rouge connect, and one other person as a backup precaution."

"Cool."

Her cell vibrated. She quickly read the text. Her fingers swiftly glided across the keypad and replied. She dropped a ten on the table and stood. Roy followed her out into the parking lot, quiet as a mouse. His mind wrapped around the thought of moving military issued burners.

"You mentioned something about a big rig full of them thangz."

"As you know I'm always up to make more ends but..." she shook her head vigorously. "It's a suicide mission if you ask me. Let's stick to the smaller shipment."

"You sure, because I can get my fam from Dade to drive up. My people can be here in the *mizzorning*."

"Trust me, less is more."

Her phone vibrated again. She checked the text. "The doctor is waiting for that package."

Roy scoped out his surroundings before popping the trunk. She scooped the duffle bag, and slung it over her left shoulder.

"You want me to follow you, make sure all is well?"

She snickered. "No, all will be well. You make some calls, come up with two solid buyers. I'm looking to make moves in the next twenty four."

"Why so soon?"

"I've gotta get back to New York. I promised Kosha I'll be there."

CHAPTER 20

T he window to the Maserati came down. To her surprise he wasn't alone. Sun bathed blonde with ruby red lips rode shotgun.

I got a feeln'... ooooh-oooh-oooh

The doctor and his wanna be *Fergie*, obviously already high, on a *Black-Eyed-Peas* tip. "This is Bunny. She's looking to have a little fun."

"What kind of fun?" Lou-Lou asked.

"Ecstasy, and blow," Bunny said flinging her long mane over her boney shoulder, then whipping it into total disarray, only to finger comb it back into prospective.

Damn this bitch is high!

Dr. Milton drummed his fingers against the steering wheel, pumped his fist in the air, singing like he was *Will-IAM* the man.

I got a feeln'... ooooh-oooh-oooh.

More fist pumping, head knocking, hair whipping action continued. Lou-Lou grabbed her phone, hit record. *Candid camera bitches!*

He grabbed her head, they kissed. Tongue action for a little over a minute before Lou-Lou blew her horn. Their performance became old and downright nauseating. She had better things to do. Time was money.

"Where you wanna do this?" Lou-Lou asked sharply.

Dr. Milton took a lungful of air. "Follow me."

She stayed two cars behind, kept her distance. Bunny's head disappeared into his lap, and stayed there the whole ride into midtown. When they pulled into the Westin, Bunny's head reappeared like magic. She felt a tinge of jealousy developing on the inside. Not too long ago, she was in that same position. The doctor had professed his love, but now he had beach Barbie polishing his knob. She wondered whose BJ was better. She wondered if the white girl tea bagged him the way she did.

She has nothing on me.

Once inside the suite, they transacted. She gave him the product, he paid her the cash. Thirsty for a hit, Bunny headed straight for the wet bar and snorted her way to a higher place. *Heaven.*

"Whoa. Chill. Don't kill yah self on my watch," Dr. Milton said, laughing hysterically. He thought his voice sounded funny. Tripping off that blow had his vocals doing strange things.

After a couple of more lines, and a half a pill later, white Girls Gone Wild unfolded. Bunny stripped down to her bare bottom, careening in her stilettos. Twirling like a ballerina, dipping down low like a stripper, bringing it back to the top, whipping her hair like a rock star. Index finger and pinky pointed towards the ceiling. Devil's horns banging, fingers strumming her imaginary guitar. Her performance deserved a ten.

Lou-Lou nudged the doctor. "She's talented."

"You should see her do the booty pop. And she does amazing things with the beer bottle. Performs magic with a cucumber. Let me not forget to mention she's a professional NBA cheerleader. Well ex, considering she no longer works the court."

"Professional NBA Cheerleader?"

"Six years with the Lakers, until she got busted on her third DUI. She lost her contract."

"You don't say."

He snorted. Chuckled. "Care for a drink?"

"Sure."

He fixed them both a *Belvedere*, straight up. Lou-Lou sipped slow, watching the fake Pamela Anderson; *ex* Lakers' girl adjust her tits. She wondered who her surgeon was because he'd done an awesome job.

Dr. Milton cupped Lou-Lou's ass, running his eager hand up the back of her shirt. Bunny noticed their closeness. Caramel honey had stolen her man's attention. She went into a split; bare coochie slapped the marble floor. When that didn't work, Bunny bent over, touched her toes, spread her lean cuts apart and bounced. Her efforts went unnoticed.

"Tour?"

Lou-Lou hesitated for a fraction of a second, she wanted to say no, but that *Belvedere* entered her blood stream on contact.

"Sure, why not."

Luxury surrounded her. Everything was upgraded. The view was magnificent. It was moments like that, which made her wish that Bradley was still on top. She had the opportunity to see Atlanta from the sixty-ninth floor of the second tallest hotel skyscraper in the Western Hemisphere. *Damn, life is good.*

"This is one big beautiful suite."

"You're welcomed to stay," Dr. Milton said.

"No thanks. Got some business to tend to," Lou-Lou said keeping a close eye on the *Devil Wears Prada*.

"Honey, come do a line," Bunny called out.

His attention obviously wrapped around Lou-Lou. She felt her bra loosen. The girls were free from the elastic restraints. Leisurely roamed hands crawled towards her erect nipple. "Stay for a little fun. I'll make it worth your while," he said, practically begging.

"Maybe another time."

"*Honey,* you really should check out this awesome-panoramic-view," Bunny insisted.

He leaned in, kissed her earlobe. "I'll pay for it. Just name your price."

Lou-Lou giggled. "Stop it."

"I'm serious. What will it cost me?"

"Honey... come see the city lights."

He held his hand up, silencing Bunny's nagging voice.

"That's wifey?" Lou-Lou asked, just as equally annoyed with Bunny's attention seeking.

"Please. She's just enjoyment," Dr. Milton assured, "Look, if you want, I can send her home in a cab." He winked.

She blushed, leaned in and grabbed between his legs. "Another time, promise."

"How about tonight? Bring lots of blow, and pills. Bring enough to feed a crowd of about twenty."

Cha-Ching. My Nigga!

"Name the location."

"Right here sweet heart. Party jumps off about eleven-*ish*."

She smiled. "Eleven-*ish* it is." She squeezed him harder, feeling him ready to bust. Bunny shot an evil glare her way, she in returned winked. It was all business, never personal.

Lou-Lou left, and returned as promised. This time she came prepared to feed a small village. Dr. Milton's circle of friends had money to blow. She was beyond thrilled for the exclusive hook-up. Flap's work was moving at a steady flow, but the level of excitement had plummeted to an all time low. The fun factor on the fun-o-meter had taken a nose dive with each fake hug, and air smooch. *I hate fake people.*

As Lou-Lou baby sat a glass of wine, she couldn't help but listen in on some of the conversations around her. Plastic surgery, Money Market reports, Demographics, Obama, the Dow Jones, *yada yada yada. Boring!*

She circled the room, and ended back at the bar where she initially started. Two gentlemen stood whispering. They were dressed to the nines in their expensive Brooks Brother's suits, and pricey hard bottom shoes. Their eyes never left each others. She figured whatever they were discussing had to be worth eavesdropping on.

"He's reputable." The man with the silver streaked goatee said. The other guy, with the weird *Owen Wilson* nose tilted his head. A few long strands came across the center of his shiny bald spot. "I don't know. I've been going to the same guy for months now."

"And you're still struggling." Silver beard patted his friend on the shoulder.

"Losing your wife suddenly had to be traumatizing. He'll help you find your peace. He will help you discover your Zen."

Penis nose said, "Two hundred an hour is steep, especially in today's economy."

Two hundred an hour for a shrink? I'm in the wrong business. She thought.

The short Mexican man tending the bar asked to refresh her drink. She downed the last of her Chardonnay and pointed towards the bottle of Belvedere. If she would survive the next hour or so, she needed to get blitz.

Pale face, heavyset woman, draped in expensive fabric offered a smile. Her teeth were perfect, her lips and nose, looked original. Lou-Lou smiled back.

"You're a new face."

Dah. I'm the only sistah in the room Einstein. "Yes. How do you do?"

"Very well. Thank you."

The lady ordered an Appletini, heavy on the Stoli. "My husband drags me to these events. I hate coming, but it beats sitting at home watching Reality TV."

"Which one is yours?"

The lady pointed her chubby index finger. "The tall thin one by the buffet table, stuffing his face. I swear I don't know where he stores it."

On you perhaps, Lou-Lou wanted to say, but just offered another smile. They were complete opposites, but they made the perfect number *ten* while standing side by side.

Lou-Lou stepped out into the open air, not considering the winter chill. A small crowd of four stood huddled, passing a joint, whispered amongst themselves. As she made an attempt to engage, they tightened their circle.

Doctor Milton insisted that she stayed a while; mingled, perhaps extended her services to a few big wigs, but now she wasn't so sure. His crowd just wasn't as receptive as he'd promised. She'd already been paid, and there was more than enough blow and pills to keep everyone *highly* entertained. Feeling out of her element, she shot back her poison. *Fuck this I'm out!*

"I had a dream last night."

Lou-Lou stopped, leaned against the balcony railing. *Okay, maybe I've stumbled upon something worth listening to.*

"About what?" someone asked.

"About me dying a horrible death. Somebody raped me. Beat me. Threw me in a ditch to rot away. Maggots discovered me. My body chewed away by vermin, and maggots," dirty blond, freckled face, hippy like wardrobe confessed in a ghastly voice.

Lou-Lou could only imagine how much those rags ran her. *Vintage my ass!*

"Rose, that's horrible," White boy rocking the *Fedora* and pinstripe suit said, wiping his nose every few seconds.

Definitely blow.

Lou-Lou struck a match. Fired up a tightly rolled *J*, pulled twice before outing it. She blew smoke from her painted lips. *Damn, you've got my attention now.*

Bunny stepped onto the balcony, joining the *"in"* crowd. Dr. Milton followed closely with both hands at her waist. "Was that the end of the dream?" Bunny asked, backing her bony ass up against him, and winking in Lou-Lou's direction.

"No."

"What happened next?" A woman dressed in an off the shoulder Chanel number, rocking mink earmuffs eagerly wanted to know.

"The person who did this to me returned. He returned with gasoline. Lit my remains, charred what was left of me."

"Talk about adding insult to injury," The man sporting the *Fedora* hat exclaimed, wiping residue from his pencil thin nose.

"Who would bother? I mean who would fucking bother dumping a body, obviously leaving the crime scene for days, returning only to douse the body with gasoline? It just doesn't make sense," a Brad Pitt look alike said angrily, spilling his drink.

"It makes lots of sense Adam. The assailant went back to cover his tracks. He needed to burn away his DNA. Burn away the blood left beneath the finger nails that scratched his neck while he penetrated against her will. Burn away the tiny pubic hairs left behind as he fucked her pelvic to pelvic. Burn away the saliva left on her body while he so viciously raped and murdered." A black man puffing a stinky cigar interceded.

Everyone grew silent.

That's why these crackers are quick to blame your black ass for everything. Stupid! Lou-Lou fought back her laughter while dumb ass O.J. Simpson told on himself.

The *Fedora* Hat, "Fuck Charlie, you seem to know much about committed the perfect murder. Are you telling us something buddy?"

Everyone snickered.

"I watch Forensic Files. CSI. The Last 48 religiously," said Charlie.

All the white people gasped. Lou-Lou couldn't help it any longer. She burst out into an old negro, slap your knee, *I'm about to tear this place up* laughter. Everyone, including the tight ass-brother joined in.

"When they discovered me..." Rose continued.

"Who discovered you?" A man with a heavy Irish accent asked, puffing on a square, nursing a corner of Scotch. He swiveled his drink, sipped.

"A drifter on his way to New Orleans discovered me."

Lou-Lou re-lit her joint, and pulled strongly at it. A haze of smoke clouded her face, blew away. She looked up, saw Dr. Milton grinning. Lips puckered, air smooches thrown her way. Devil Wears Prada jabbed her finger into his chest.

Ah shit, here we go.

Just when Lou-Lou thought she would have to break Bunny's bony ass in two, Dr. Milton smoothed things over. He whispered into her ear, kissed her chin, rubbed his hands down her back, and stopped at her size zero waist. Bunny nestled her brainless head against his chest, and smiled victoriously.

Lou-Lou shook her head in pity, turning her attention back towards the narrator for the evening.

"It felt so real. Just horrible I tell yah," Rose said, damn near in tears. She began to shake uncontrollably. She looked off, past the crowd, out into the city lights. A single tear slid down her face.

The crowd gasped.

"Detectives combed the scene for clues, took pictures, and gathered what was left for evidence. My body was so badly decomposed. My murder remained unsolved."

"So the bastard got away?" Bunny asked.

"My murderer never saw a day in court. Never felt iron against the wrist. Never once felt the coldness of a cell. Murder unsolved. Some dream huh?"

The man rocking the Fedora, pinstriped suit, flexed a Cuban from his mouth applauded first. Laughter and applause echoed throughout the sixty ninth floor of the Westin. Lou-Lou watched in amazement. *Bravo!*

"Tell us another one," Dr. Milton insisted, peeling Bunny away from his chest. He headed inside to mingle with a few guest. She watched him chit-chat, shake hands, and air kiss a set of long legged twins. He pulled up a stool next to the old man with the silver goatee, and began conversation.

"That night was like no other. The sultry metropolis had me feeling erotic." The mysterious Rose started up again. Just as Lou-Lou was accepted into their circle she received a text. *"Bedroom"* Her eyes darted across the open space, landed at the bar. The old man with the goatee sat by himself. The doctor disappeared.

"The humidity took my breath away as we made sweet love in the hot tub. Noises from beyond the bushes stopped his thrusting. His penis, still inside me, his eyes roaming the dark. There was movement beyond the shrubs."

Ooh's and awes' escaped the huddled group of listeners. Lou-Lou eased away from the crowd, head low, remaining unseen, trotting across marble towards a set of french doors. Inside, he stood with his back turned, facing the city of Atlanta. Big lights illuminated against his skin. She stepped in, shut the door. Sudden privacy had her wanting to free her inhibitions.

"That lady with the tall tales, was she hired help?" Lou-Lou asked.

"What do you mean?"

"Crowd control, entertainment, the hired magician."

He laughed. "No, Rose is a good friend of mine. She's a bit demented. Rich as fuck. She owns a chain of upscale massage parlors, and runs a successful physic hotline. Would you believe people still buy into that crap? Five dollars for the first minute, ninety nine cents each additional minute to see into the future. Amazing."

"Demented or not, she sure knows how to keep folks attention."

"Are you kidding me? They love her. She should consider a career in murder mystery novels. Her imagination is out of this world."

"She really should. I would totally buy."

He turned and looked back at her. "I've been watching you." She twirled around, showing off her mini skirt and beaded open back top. He glanced at her tatted back. *So sophisticatedly urban.*

"Do you like what you see?"

"Love what I see, but I noticed something about you."

She eased closer to him, kissed his lips hard.

"You don't indulge," he mumbled while sucking her tongue.

She stepped away, kissed his chin. "I don't know what you mean."

"You don't ride the white horse like the rest of us. Aside from a little weed, and the occasional cocktail, you don't use."

She gazed into his piercing blue eyes. "It's not my thing."

"Then what is your thing?"

She slipped him more tongue. "Finding more ways to make money."

"Looks like you made a killing tonight."

"All thanks to you."

"You got something set aside for me?"

"Of course. Can't forget the man of the hour." She stepped out of her *Jimmy Choo* heels, made her way towards the bed.

He followed. "Tell me, what gets you off?"

She hiked up her mini, swiveled her hips. "You really wanna know?"

He pushed her down onto the bed. "I really wanna know."

Her beaded top slipped off, and flew across the room. Her skirt landed the same. No panties. No bra. No restrictions. She grabbed him into her clutches, snatching the buttons from his shirt apart, rubbing her fingers against his chest. She kissed him hard, and then kicked him away with the flat of her foot.

"The one thing that gets me off is when a man..." She opened the palm of her hand, revealing a variety pack of all the doctor's favorites. The pouch was laced with an assortment of skittles, marijuana, cocaine, and oxycod. Her legs spread wide as an eagle. The doctor was all smiles.

She sprinkled a line of powder between her vaginal lips. Coke trail ended at her navel. He dipped his tongue inside her wetness, savoring the drug, tasting her addiction, experiencing a high like no other. She moaned, back arched, head thrown into her spine.

His tongue, curling and flicking away at her clitoris. She moaned softly as he played between her folds. Her body stiffened. Knees locked. The big one made her squirm. Orgasmic bliss interrupted by a tap on the door. Neither of them moved. His head stayed buried inside her honey walls. She moaned loudly, running her fingers through his hair. The tap at the door turned into a knock. Determination stood on the other side. *Go away!*

"Coke and Pills at the bar!" she yelled, locking her legs around his neck, forcing him further into her web. The door swung open. The party was in full swing. Music blaring, white people dancing and jerking like epileptic patients.

"Hey man, sorry I'm late. My cabby made a wrong turn on Peachtree street *NE*, instead of *NW*. Too many damn *Peachtrees* for one damn city if you ask me."

Light filtered through the dimly lit room. The doctor lifted his head. Cocaine residue outlined his mustache. His head was spinning. Tongue and nose was numb.

"Fuck man, can't you see I'm busy," Dr. Milton spat.

"What the fuck is *she* doing here?" The voice boomed!

Lou-Lou snapped out of her trance, opened her eyes. Mortified by his presence.

"What the fuck Bradley?" Dr. Milton said, hopping up, feeling froggy.

Bradley pointed at Lou-Lou. *"You bitch."*

"What the hell is going on?" Dr. Milton was furious.

Both men looked at Lou-Lou as she slid off the bed, and went to retrieve her skirt.

Bradley's watery eyes scanned her perfect body, stopping at her breasts. Her implanted bosom he missed. It was his Black Card that paid for those babies. He stepped into the room, almost slamming the door off the hinge. He adjusted the lighting, blinding them with the high beams from the ceiling.

"You slut bitch," Bradley spat.

"Hey man that's not necessary."

Bradley glared at Dr. Milton, and then directed his attention back to Lou-Lou.

"You ruin my life, now you're sleeping with my brother."

Her mouth dropped to the floor. Embarrassment covered her face. *"I... I didn't know."*

"What the hell is going on?" Dr. Milton demanded to know.

Bradley grabbed him by the neck, shoved him against the wall.

"Don't act like you don't recognize her." Bradley's hurtful eyes beamed in anger.

"Whoa... chill out Bro... what the fuck is going on?"

"We didn't know," she bellowed.

"Bryan I swear to God I will snap your neck in half."

"Dude... I swear to God I didn't know."

At that point Dr. Milton didn't know much of anything. His brother's anger was a for sure thing. The pain in his eyes was certain. And the grip that wrapped his neck was without a shadow of a doubt a guaranteed promise.

"Don't hurt him. We didn't know," she co-signed. "Let him go Bradley."

He pointed an agitated finger in her direction. "Shut the fuck up!"

Bradley slammed his brother into the wall again. The back of his head bounced against the mounted digital thermostat.

"C'mon Bro...for fuck sakes... I didn't know."

"You did know. How could you have not known man?"

She covered her mouth as Bradley cried real tears. She touched his arm, he loosened his grip. Dr. Milton fell to the floor, struggling for air. It wasn't until then did she notice the resemblance. She could tell Bradley was older.

"I promise we didn't know," she said, holding both hands to her chest.

Bradley's piercing blue eyes bore into her like a rusty drill. Hot tears slipped from his cheeks. She slipped her arms into her top, grabbed her skirt, shoes, and headed for the door. It was time to blow that joint. She needed some fresh air, needed to get the hell away from Bradley all together.

Bradley called out for her. His voice coated in hatred.

She stopped.

Fingers tips slipped from the doorknob.

"Bring your black ass here."

"Hey man, chill," Dr. Milton defended.

"Shut the fuck up Bryan."

Just keep going Lou. He has a legitimate reason to act this way. Just keep walking. Her fingers gripped the knob.

"I said bring your black ass here, *now.*"

She made an about face, and dug into her purse.

"We can be cool, or things can turn ugly," she said, not yet revealing what lined her designer purse. Bradley was quickly reminded of her rage.

Dr. Milton struggled to his feet. "Look, everybody relax."

Bradley collapsed onto the bed, looking defeated. *"Come here Lou-Lou."*

She didn't budge. Hand still inside her purse, hip poked out, ready for war.

"Please," Bradley begged.

She stepped in front of him, but kept a nice distance. Dr. Milton grabbed his shirt, covered his bare chest. "Maybe I should leave you two to talk."

"No. You stay right here," Bradley demanded.

"Bro, I've got guests waiting, besides you two need to come to terms with..." his hands moved in a wayward motion. "...you know."

"You're staying, and that's final." Bradley growled.

Silence engulfed them all.

Motionless bodies.

Faint breathing.

Bradley noticed the variety pack on the bed. He grabbed it, went straight for the coke. They watched as he did a line. A more relaxed Bradley leaned back against the mattress, unzipped his slacks.

"Ah, c'mon bro, didn't need to see that." Dr. Milton turned his back to sniff some blow off the nightstand.

She knew what he wanted. In essence, she wanted the same, but not with her client in the room. *His brother.*

"Lil Bro, you don't mind sharing do you?" Bradley asked out of common courtesy, with an underlining hint of sarcasm. Dr. Milton eased onto the mattress. His eyes ablaze in lust. "If you don't mind, I don't mind." They both stared at her, awaiting her decision.

Just do it and get it over with, she thought dropping her purse to the floor. She could have easily denied the three way love affair, but something deep down in her gut wanted it, needed it. There was a knock at the door. Everyone froze. The knob jiggled but it was locked.

"It's me, Bunny. Everyone is asking for you baby."

Dr. Milton's face screwed. "Okay. Give me a moment. I'm speaking with my brother."

"Okay. Don't be too long. The party is jumping."

There she lay, sandwiched between two brothers. Brothers who shared a commonality of sexual desire. Bradley, her ex-fiancé wanted her strictly for himself, but was obviously trying to prove a point. Dr. Milton, her client was willing to share. In essence, she owed them both.

If Bradley didn't get what he wanted, he would ruin all ties between her and a set of deep pockets. She had to figure out a way to please them both. Dr. Milton was her connect, her source of income. Bradley was obviously still broke. The trail of cash landed in Dr. Milton's lap. She strapped the condom on and straddled the *best* choice. She bounced her way towards possible millions, taking him higher than any drug known to mankind.

Two minutes later the doctor cried out a shriek of ecstasy. After a few deep breaths she rolled off and hopped onto Bradley's already rock hard covered penis. He smacked her ass. "I'm not my brother. Take your time." Her movements were slow, sensual, and meaningful. They got into a familiar groove. Moans and groans heighten with each touch.

"I miss you," he said.

"I miss you too," she said.

They kissed like two individuals in love.

Dr. Milton inched towards the door.

"Where you going man?" Bradley asked smirking, still in sync, never losing his rhythm.

"*Dude...* you got this area covered."

"You sure Bryan... she's enough woman for the both of us."

She peeked over her shoulder, staying the course, riding him slow and sensual.

"*Dude*... wax that ass. I'm going to party with my peeps."

The door slammed shut. Just the two of them grinding and moaning, squeezing and pleasing. She couldn't recall a time when Bradley was that good. She cupped his scrotum, rolling his dice softly between her fingers.

"Oh baby. That feels so damn good."

She smiled knowingly.

A Letter from the Author

Dear Reader,

So, you're probably screaming out loud, gripping your book, or in today's technically advanced world, your electronic device. After long consideration, I've decided to split *Just One More* into two books. I thought it would be best to give you time to digest, refill your glass, or perhaps reenact the last scene. Just kidding ~ unless you're into that kind of thing. I'm not judging (SMILE). Thank You for reading my work. Your purchase is greatly appreciated.

***Just One More 2* is just a click away. Get it Today!!!**

Best Wishes,

Author LaQuarn Michaels
www.LAQUARNMICHAELS.com

About the Author

LaQuarn Michaels is a freelance writer, poet, and author of *The Last One*, and *Just One More*. She was born and raised in Jamaica Queens, New York. Ms. Michaels now resides in Atlanta, Georgia with her husband and children. You can expect more blazing stories from this author.